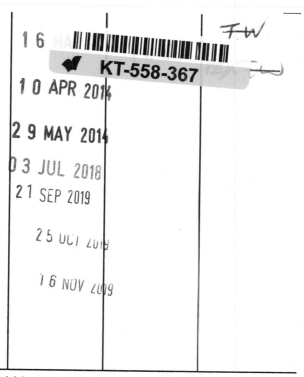
Books should be returned or renewed by the last date above. Renew by phone **08458 247 200** or online *www.kent.gov.uk/libs*

Libraries & Archives

DEATH'S DOOR

DEATH'S DOOR

Jim Kelly

CRÈME de la CRIME

This first world edition published 2012
in Great Britain and the USA by
Crème de la Crime, an imprint of
SEVERN HOUSE PUBLISHERS LTD of
9–15 High Street, Sutton, Surrey, England, SM1 1DF.
Trade paperback edition first published
in Great Britain and the USA 2012.

British Library Cataloguing in Publication Data

Kelly, Jim, 1957-
  Death's door.
  1. Shaw, Peter (Fictitious character)--Fiction.
  2. Valentine, George (Fictitious character)--Fiction.
  3. Police--England--Norfolk--Fiction. 4. Detective and
  mystery stories.
  I. Title
  823.9´2-dc23

ISBN-13: 978-1-78029-519-0 (cased)
ISBN-13: 978-1-78029-524-4 (trade paper)

All Severn House titles are printed on acid-free paper.

Severn House Publishers support The Forest Stewardship Council [FSC],
the leading international forest certification organisation. All our titles that
are printed on Greenpeace-approved FSC-certified paper carry the FSC logo.

MIX
Paper from
responsible sources
FSC
www.fsc.org   FSC® C018575

Typeset by Palimpsest Book Production Ltd.,
Falkirk, Stirlingshire, Scotland.
Printed and bound in Great Britain by
MPG Books Ltd., Bodmin, Cornwall.

To Judith
For knowing, always, the right answer.

ACKNOWLEDGEMENTS

I'd like to thank my new publishers – Severn House – for their belief in *Death's Door.* My publisher, Kate Lyall Grant, and Sara Porter, editor, have both been professional and truly welcoming. Our team of volunteer copy-readers have done a sterling job led by the eagle-eyed Jenny Burgoyne – with thanks also to Rowan Haysom. My wife, Midge Gillies, not only read the manuscript but provided the spark of inspiration which created the plot. My agent, Faith Evans, has shown loyalty, verve and skill during interesting times. And special thanks to Rosa, for reminding me that books are fun.

ONE

Friday

The dead woman's face was white, as bloodless as china. Only the veins, blue beneath the skin, provided any colour, a perfect match for the duvet under which she lay. She looked blankly out of the window of the bungalow's main bedroom, and DI Peter Shaw thought that was the saddest detail: that she died contemplating a field of sunflowers, rather than with her eyes turned to the wall. It implied, it seemed, so much: that she'd been able to make a decision, even in the last few seconds of her life, to take with her that gold and black shimmering image of mid-afternoon summer heat. *She wouldn't have suffered.* That's what they'd tell the relatives, at least today, while they waited for the coroner to finish the tests on the body, tests on the pills beside the bed, tests on the glass of water. *She wouldn't have suffered.* It was a form of words, a term of art which created a comforting image: the human body tucked up, snug, warm and at peace, which is why they wouldn't let the relatives *see* the body, at least not yet. The reality of death was always shockingly unambiguous: the victim's hand was not like any living hand, the fingers flexed up like the legs on a dead spider. And the bone structure of the woman's face was just that, *bone structure*, as if the skull was already beginning to emerge from the skin. But the deadest thing of all was her left eye, the one he could clearly see, turned to the window, catching the light like a cold mirror.

Shaw stood on the threshold of the room, reluctant to break the spell which seemed to hold everything still, like a scene inside a glass paperweight. His DS, George Valentine, had got him on the mobile at home. Shaw had a half-day off, and he'd been out on the stoop facing the sea, treating the wood for the coming winter sea-spray. A fatality, said Valentine: No. 5, The Circle, Creake, five miles inland from Wells-next-the-Sea. It was a reluctant call – that was plain. Valentine had made the situation perfectly clear. Forensics at the scene had requested CID attend. Valentine had driven out from Lynn in his battered Mazda, delighted to be separated from a month's worth of case reports and the temptations of the public bar of the Artichoke. He'd found a lonely circle of post-war bungalows, a woman dead in bed, evidence at the scene pointing to the clear conclusion that she'd taken her own life, although there was no note.

But the head of CSI – Tom Hadden – was not satisfied. Hadden was ex-Home Office, studious, punctilious and, in Valentine's experience, a pain in the arse. Could DI Shaw attend? Valentine didn't like being second-guessed. He didn't like being out-ranked. His call to Shaw had been perfunctory, and he was currently sat outside the dead woman's house in the Mazda, smoking his way through a packet of Silk Cut.

Shaw had met Hadden at the front gate. The CSI team had finished in the bedroom so Shaw was welcome to go in, but nowhere else for now – especially not the bathroom. Shaw had asked Hadden to keep his particular reservations about this lonely death to himself, because he wanted to see the deathbed with fresh, objective eyes.

He took his first step over the threshold. Young, fit, an athlete to anyone who saw him running on the morning sands, Shaw was able to control his body precisely. So he took the next step over the scene-of-crime tape slowly, lowering his left foot by the inch on to the bedroom carpet. The rest of his body followed, smoothly transferring his weight, like a martial arts enthusiast practising in the park.

Eventually he stood, his feet set wide to match his shoulders, listening. He could hear a clock ticking by the bed and had to suppress the illusion that it had only begun to work – to measure the time he was in – in recognition of that first moonwalk step. Despite the fact that he could see the victim's body, at least the head and naked shoulders above the edge of the duvet, the room was, nevertheless, entirely *inanimate,* because she had become simply another object in it. The shadow on the pillow, cast by the woman's head, was as solid, as permanent and as passive as the shadow which stretched from the bed to the wall, encompassing a pair of stylish black slippers and a magazine: *Hello!,* open at a picture of a celebrity wedding, so that the perfect dentistry of the bride smiled up at the dead spider hand, thrown over the edge of the bed.

Shaw felt the heat even here, the heat of the dead hour between two and three. All the windows were shut; only the front door stood open, where the community police constable stood guard. The air in the room was still, a cube of stale, spent air which seemed to offer its own resistance to movement as Shaw approached the bed. He'd been offered a face mask by CSI but he'd turned it down, so that when he breathed – even through his mouth – he caught the sweet smell that didn't come from the bowl of fruit on the table in the hall.

He was good at registering scents and aromas, getting better with each passing year, as if the world was growing more pungent with the passage of time. It was one of the unexpected compensations of the loss of sight in his left eye just four years earlier in an accident. His other senses seemed to be rallying round. So the sweet smell was of pine sap, perhaps – furniture polish, or the woods behind the house? But there was something else, something aromatic and earthy that eluded classification. Later, he'd chide himself for not dwelling on that one detail.

Shaw took another step forward, his heartbeat picking up, as it always did in the presence of death. He tried to separate this physical reaction from his ability to think, because this was the moment when he should be the cool observer. His father, Chief Detective Inspector Jack Shaw, had always told him that any decent copper should carry a perfect picture in his head of the scene of crime: digital quality, flat screen, Dolby sound, and that throughout the investigation it should be at hand, as retrievable as a family face on a snapshot in the wallet. And that was easier than Shaw had thought it would be because of the excitement he always felt – there was no other word for the electricity in his body, in the room. That was the greatest irony: that as this woman had died, becoming an object, she'd given to everything in the room a kind of vitality, as if each thing acquired a brief, fleeting brightness and clarity.

Everything was important. Everything was relevant. The room rang with tension, like a freshly struck bell. Objects: a chair loaded with clothes, a dress – antique print, a leather belt a hand-span wide and a pair of espadrilles. A dressing table in MDF with a mirror which reflected the only picture in the room: a garish image of the quayside at Wells-next-the-Sea in oils. On the dressing table a computer – an old iMac, a printer on the floor. Two identical bedside tables – on one a glass of water. And a packet of pills – Nurofen, the top open so that he could see the shucked plastic from which the pills had been pressed. But if this was a simple case of suicide then he wouldn't be here. Tom Hadden was possibly one of the sharpest CSI experts in the country. *He'd* seen something in this room. If this was just another statistic – a lonely death in a rural bungalow – then the SOC light and reflective umbrella wouldn't be stood in the corner. There wouldn't be fingerprint powder on the bedside table and the glass. So there must be doubt. Something was wrong; something in this room.

Shaw walked to the bedside table closest to the window – cheap, utility furniture, like the rest of the house. Three books: a Jilly Cooper novel, a biography of Kate Moss and one of those romances which always have the couple on the front, a Gothic house behind. The duvet looked right. It didn't always look right. They'd once found a body dumped in a bed, then a corner of the cover tucked in, as if you could do that from *inside* a bed. Or the hair. It was disconcerting, but oddly comforting, that most killers couldn't resist rearranging their victims; just a few hairs, perhaps, drawn away from the face, or splayed on the pillow. But this woman's hair was twisted slightly, back around her neck and over one shoulder, as if she'd got into bed to face the wall, then turned over before she died to look out of the window, to see the wave-like motion of the breeze over that field of sunflowers.

He stood back, looking at the whole bed, which gave him two impressions: first, that the duvet had indeed been tugged upwards, and that the hand had left a scrunched mark in the material, suggesting that it had been done with some force. And second, from this angle, he could see the woman's left foot, and could see that beneath it was a tear in the sheet, through which was thrust the heel. So that was an image that didn't fit: one hand gripping the duvet, the leg kicking out. If she'd taken sleeping pills, painkillers, she'd have slipped off into a coma then died in her sleep. This looked like a more violent reaction to whatever she'd swallowed. Or, just a violent reaction.

He walked around the bed to the head and knelt down. Up close he thought something else was wrong – the glass of water?

It was nearly empty and the sides were patterned with concentric rings where each summer's day had evaporated a millimetre of liquid, as if it always sat there, for emergencies, but never got refilled. And the level of water was only a hair's breadth below the last ring. So she hadn't taken the pills then gulped the water. And now that he could see inside the packet of pills he could see that some were left, perhaps most of them. So that wasn't right either.

He looked at her face, edging his own to within six inches of the victim's. There wasn't a personal space to intrude upon any more, because with death that sense of a projected barrier is destroyed, thought Shaw, or dwindles, with each moment that passes after life has gone. So getting close, really close, didn't make his skin creep. And besides, this was his passion, his area of expertise: the human face. He was one of only three detectives in the country qualified as a forensic artist: he could build a human face in 2D on paper, from the bones outwards, laying the muscles out, the tendons, then the skin. He could take this face, any face, and run it backwards a lifetime to show you what it had been like; or forwards twenty years, to what it would become. He'd been taught to read a face like the opening paragraph of a book.

What did this one tell him? Age: mid or early thirties, the features combining two polar opposites in showing the first signs of wrinkles and an almost childlike openness, the lack of make-up suggesting innocence. The teeth were visible, the lips curled back in an ugly jagged line. The colour of the eyes was fading but had, perhaps, been a vivid green. Shaw had studied forensic art as part of a general degree in fine art so he often tried to classify faces, dead or alive, by painter. And if he had to put this woman's face on canvas he would have hung that canvas in the room reserved for the Pre-Raphaelites: Millais, perhaps, with the fine jawline, the almost unnaturally symmetrical features, but above all a look of almost innate tragedy, as if she'd been caught in some legend from which there was no escape. That was the one thing that irritated him about the Pre-Raphaelites: they always tried to tell you a story, to weigh down the vision with a narrative. He didn't know what story this woman would have told if she'd lived, but he knew she had one.

Shaw inched his head back to the point where he could see

her whole face. Beautiful in life, there was no doubt. But beauty, he thought, is the composite of the features held together by the life within, and that had gone now: death reduced every face to a photofit.

What was odd, he thought, was that this woman's sexual aura – the fact that she *was* a woman – had outlived her life. How much more striking had that sexuality been just a few hours earlier? Was she naked beneath the duvet? There was nothing to stop him pulling back the edge of the duvet, if he wanted to pull back the edge. He didn't need to – the pathologist would examine the body in situ; nor did he want to – but he understood, for a brief moment, why someone would: a strange emotion, not longing or lust, but a kind of thrilling curiosity. The stronger urge, than pulling back the edge, was to pull it up and over the face. But that wasn't his job either. It wasn't even his job to close the eyes, although it would have been a decent thing to do.

He knelt on one knee and forced himself to look into her eyes. He thought that this woman hadn't died in sadness, or desperation, or release. The only human emotion Shaw could confidently attach to her was fear. The sclera, the whites of the eye, were visible, completely circling the iris. So fear, perhaps, of death, but her eyes turned for that lingering last look at life.

He stood and noticed for the first time a single pine needle on the floor, and looking back towards the door saw two others, together. A lungful of air confirmed his first analysis: pine, natural pine. Through the window he could see the edge of the woods beyond the sunflowers, a dark curtain of shadow offering a cool haven from the heat of the day.

Outside he heard a noise, a dull percussion, and he thought it must be a shotgun. In the garden Tom Hadden was taking pictures of the house. He saw Shaw standing beyond his own reflection in the bedroom window and walked towards him. The white SOC suit Hadden was wearing emphasized his colouring: red hair fading to strawberry blond with age, freckles and almost colourless eyes – an insipid green.

They met at the window, one inside, one outside. On the window ledge was a series of miniature pottery houses. Up close Shaw could see the lesion on Hadden's forehead. The CSI man had already had one small cancer removed, but the blemish had returned. And it was because he was focusing on the wound that he didn't see what was *between* them on the glass.

Hadden's eyes narrowed. Shaw saw it now, and the shock of recognition made his heart freeze for just one beat. This was the dangerous moment, and he recognized it as such: the moment when the thrill of other people's deaths began to outshine the everyday joys of being alive.

It was a kiss on the windowpane: quite clear, the patterned upper lip meeting the lower in a perfect bow. The rest of the window was spotless – inside and out, freshly cleaned. 'It's on the outside,' said Hadden, and Shaw heard his voice as if from far away.

TWO

D S George Valentine sat on a bench in the middle of the green at the centre of The Circle. The dead woman's house was silent in the heat. It was difficult to avoid the word *lifeless*. The village of Creake, two hundred yards distant, was a cluster of thatch, Norfolk stone and woodwork painted that precise shade of blue beloved of the Chelsea-on-Sea weekend-cottage set. A round Norfolk church tower was just visible between the acorn-brown foliage of a great oak tree. Somewhere in the far distance he could hear tennis balls being hit in rhythmic succession.

There was nothing Chelsea-on-Sea about The Circle. West Ham-on-Sea, perhaps. A deflated football lay on the parched, kicked earth of the 'green', while a union flag hung from the open bedroom of No. 2. A few cars were parked in the cul-de-sac – but none of them were new except the two CSI vehicles, and none of them were four-by-fours. The green, kicked dry and grassless, was dotted with unwanted possessions: a bicycle without a saddle, a water pistol, and a dog's plastic bone.

Valentine yawned, the effort making his jaw crack. He leant back and his neck clicked in sympathy. The green, he'd noticed, wasn't just empty ground. A two-storey medieval ruin stood to one side: roofless, with narrow arrow-slit windows, a massive chimney stack, and some elegant herringbone stonework over an arched doorway. A small area outside the walls was enclosed by a rusted set of railings which ended with a 'kissing-gate' just opposite the Norman doorway. Valentine had seen an English Heritage information board, but not what it said. The most remarkable feature of the ruin was the cedar tree which had grown up within it, maybe thirty-five foot high, spreading its dark green-layered branches out over the curtain walls. The Circle and the modern access road had clearly been constructed to avoid encroaching on this ancient monument. It was an odd place, but it didn't excite the DS's curiosity, because he wasn't a curious man.

He checked his watch, a Rolex he'd bought at Lynn's Saturday market for a fiver. The gold lettering of the word Rolex had faded with suspicious speed. He'd watched Shaw walk into the dead woman's house twenty-one minutes ago. Fed up with waiting in the Mazda, he'd dragged himself to the bench. Imagination wasn't Valentine's strong point but he was pretty much astonished his DI could spend that long deciding he was looking at a case of suicide.

Valentine had been in the room. He'd spotted the glass and the pills, and he knew, like the CSIs, that she hadn't died of an overdose of just three Nurofen. But unlike CSI he couldn't be bothered to cover his bony plain-clothed arse just because a few of the details didn't fit. She'd died of something, and she'd died by her own hand. Valentine guessed she'd done it in the bathroom – a handful of painkillers – then gone to bed. He'd been a copper for thirty years and that was the detail that still unsettled him – the way people go to bed to die, as if being comfy helps. The only thing missing was a letter. But George Valentine had an insight into quietly desperate lives, and he understood that all *that* probably meant was that she had no one to write to. All of which meant they were wasting their time.

Shaw appeared from the side alley of No. 5, walking down the path, past the gate off its hinges and out on to the makeshift football pitch. His step was light, almost weightless, thought Valentine, as if he might begin to tread air, rising into the Norfolk sky. Shaw always wore a white shirt, crisp, open-necked, and Valentine suspected him of the worst vice of all – that he ironed it himself. In the flat, late-afternoon sun the shirt just seemed to drink in the light. Shaw was six foot one, slim, with blond hair and a beach tan. Up close the brand image was slightly under-mined by the eyes: one was blue, that kind of washed-out blue that's almost not a colour at all, like falling water, and the other was blind, a moon-eye, white, floating. His face, which his DS considered now with a kind of half-hearted disappointment, was wide with high cheekbones. Outgoing was what Shaw's face was. George Valentine had always been aware that his face was ingoing: pinched, narrow, his small black eyes set deep, his narrow hatchet-like head appearing too heavy for his neck, so that it hung forward like a vulture's. This was George Valentine's self-image, but it was only one of the reasons he didn't have a spring in his step.

Shaw turned, filled his chest with warm air and stared at the dead woman's house. 'Tom's right – something's not right,' he said.

Valentine didn't move a muscle.

'She's put her foot through the sheet; she's clutched at the duvet. And the eyes . . .' Shaw looked to the horizon as the distant tractor engine whined. Beside it, over the brow of the hill, stood a wind turbine eighty foot high, Shaw guessed, turning now so slowly you had to stop and watch it to see the movement at all. Batches of turbines had begun to appear on Norfolk's north-facing hills, catching the Polar winds. 'She hasn't fallen asleep, she's struggled violently,' he said. 'The pills and glass are wrong . . .'

'She died alone,' said Valentine, his furred-up voice hardening. His narrow, two-dimensional head seemed to flip from right side to left side with nothing in between. Shaw always thought that if he had to put Valentine's head on canvas it would be a Picasso – all those bony, angular, asymmetrical lines, like a skull constructed from parts of a wrecked car.

'Really, George. Why alone?'

'Windows are all locked. Uniform had to force the door.'

'Have you come across the notion of a key, George?'

Valentine's eyes went blank.

'What *do* we know?' asked Shaw. He had a light voice, as weightless as his step, surprisingly tuneful, suggesting an ability to hit a note first time.

Valentine had a notebook open on the bench beside him, taking up the space where Shaw might have sat. He didn't need to check it, but he certainly wasn't going to move it. 'Marianne Osbourne. Thirty-four. Mother-of-one. Husband is Joe, owns a locksmiths in Wells – family business. Daughter's Tilly, aged seventeen, still at school.

'Last person to see her mum alive that I can find was one of the neighbours – bloke with racing pigeons . . .' Valentine nodded at No. 2. Down the side alley they could see the pigeonhole shed. 'That was at eight this morning – at the front gate, shouting at the daughter. Apparently that was standard. The kid stormed off down the lane to the village.'

Valentine felt a bead of sweat running down his back. He took a double lungful of air into shredded lungs, lifting his shoulders with the effort. He'd never been a talker, and he knew Shaw hated prattle, so he always kept it short – which was just as well, because with *his* lungs long sentences were getting harder to finish. 'Kid from No. 3, Lewis, found the body. He's seven. All the kids seem to run wild. He's home alone, playing in the street, and he falls over and cuts his leg. So he goes to No. 6, a Mrs Robinson, a friend of the family. But she's not there. She's usually at home but she's got a part-time job up at Well's Lido, so the kid tried next door.' He looked around The Circle, a pause which disguised a deep breath. 'No answer at the front door. Dead woman works on the internet flogging stuff according to one of the other neighbours: cosmetics, toiletries. There's a website and a company, which is in her maiden name by the way – Pritchard. She also works part-time down in Wells, at Kelly's, as a beautician.'

Kelly's was the town's funeral directors. Shaw tried to imagine that face, dripping with Pre-Raphaelite tragedy, bent over the dead, applying make-up. It was a striking thought, because she hadn't bothered with it herself.

'So the kid wanders round the back to see if anyone's in the garden,' said Valentine. 'Then sees the victim in bed.'

'And that's another thing that's wrong . . .' said Shaw. 'You'd pull the curtains, wouldn't you? You'd take the pills, go to bed . . . you don't leave the curtains open.'

Valentine shrugged. 'The kid may be only seven, like I said, but even he knows what a stiff looks like. Eyes open, that colour. He goes and finds someone. They ring us.'

Shaw detected a cynical, casual tone in his DS's voice, the

source of which was no mystery. DS Valentine had been up in front of a promotion panel the previous week. He'd expected to get back the rank of DI, the rank he'd lost more than fifteen years earlier after being accused of fabricating evidence in a murder inquiry. That stain had now been removed, thanks largely to Valentine's doggedness in uncovering the truth. So he'd gone into the promotions panel expecting it to be a formality. He was so sure he'd be walking out a DI he'd had a couple of pints at the Artichoke as a pre-celebration celebration. The panel was a nightmare: no one likes being taken for granted, especially by a fifty-two-year-old DS slouched in the interview chair emitting the aroma of warm beer. Twenty years ago belligerent self-belief might have got him his DI badge back. Not any more.

'Where's the daughter? Husband?' asked Shaw, wishing silently that Valentine would leave his raincoat at home. They were in the middle of the hottest summer for a decade but the DS still wore the grimy gaberdine like a comfort blanket. Its only saving grace was the cluster of charity stickers on both lapels, evidence the DS couldn't pass a street collection without putting a coin in the tin. At home Shaw had a family snapshot of George Valentine and his father leaving the Old Bailey in 1988 after a high-profile murder trail. DI Valentine, as he then was, had that same raincoat over one arm. The fact that Valentine had known Shaw's father so well added a bitter taste to their relationship. It was an immutable fact of life that George Valentine knew his father better than Shaw ever would.

'Hubby's been told; he's not a well man apparently, asthmatic, and he took it badly,' said Valentine. 'Had some kind of attack. He's under sedation at the old cottage hospital in Wells. Not very coherent but the uniform who spoke to him said the wife's got a history of depression – a couple of failed attempts with aspirin over the last five years. One bash with a kitchen knife, but only superficial. He did say the daughter should have been home with her mum 'coz she flunked her exams and they want her to resit. She's doing media studies – God help us. Wants to be a campaigning journalist. Right the world's wrongs. But she's seventeen, so you know, she does what she likes and apparently she reckons she doesn't need to revise again. She's probably right. These days all you've got to do is turn up.'

Valentine thrust his hands into his raincoat pockets and flapped the material against his narrow thighs. He didn't really believe what he'd just said about exams, but a lot of the time he couldn't stop himself sounding like someone else. 'Kid could be anywhere, anywhere 'cept inside that house with her mum,' he said. 'Victim Liaison's getting a woman PC out to look round town; apparently Tilly is no stranger to the amusement arcade by the harbour, or The Ship for that matter. They do underage, always have, in the back room round the pool table.'

Shaw nodded, stress making his shoulders bunch. All of which was local knowledge to Valentine, because after they'd busted him down to DS they'd sent him out to the backwater that was the North Norfolk coast. Wells-next-the-Sea, and the villages around it, had been George Valentine's manor.

Shaw looked at his watch. They needed to find the girl and wait for the pathologist's report, then they'd know if there was anything suspicious about the death. But for the moment they didn't really have time for this because they had a press conference at 4 p.m., down at Wells. The West Norfolk Constabulary had secured a £400,000 grant from the Home Office to use the latest forensic techniques to examine cold cases on its files: they'd reviewed eight then chosen one – a murder from 1994. The reopening of the case was guaranteed to get wide media coverage because it was based on using the latest DNA tracing techniques. West Norfolk's new chief constable wanted a splash to mark the reopening of the file, to show that even sleepy backwoodsmen could match the country's finest, and he wanted his whizz-kid DI Peter Shaw to front it up. They'd got half of Fleet Street up for the day and it was Shaw's job to put on a good show.

Which was why Shaw didn't need this distraction. He hadn't said it, just thought it, but he felt a surge of guilt, matching the word *distraction* with an image of the dead woman in her bed. Lena, his wife, had often warned him to watch out for the day that his natural scepticism rotted into cynicism. He always said it would never happen. He forced himself to conjure up an image of the dead woman's room. 'There was a kiss on the window. Outside,' said Shaw.

Valentine disguised his surprise by shaking out a fresh Silk Cut. He'd missed that, and the error brought back a familiar feeling that sometimes the world moved too quickly for him, and that it didn't matter how hard he tried he'd never quite make the

pace. But while the first blast of nicotine made his vision hazy
and the smoke made his lungs buzz, the exhilaration was bliss.
His brain made a series of connections in less time than it took
to exhale.

'My money's on the daughter for the goodbye kiss,' he said.
'Big argument with Mum. She storms out. Perhaps that pushes
Mum over the edge. Everyone's life's a mess from the inside.
She takes the pills in the bathroom then goes to bed to die.
Daughter comes back to say sorry, she's got a key, lets herself
in. Finds her mum. Perhaps *she* opened the curtains to let in the
light. Then she runs off into the woods – that's when she plants
the kiss on the glass.' Valentine looked around, noticing that the
heat was making the image of the distant hill buckle.

Shaw thought about the pine needles on the carpet in the
bedroom, which he hadn't mentioned to Valentine. Maybe that's
where she *came* from, out of the woods, creeping back home.
He thought about his own daughter and felt a surge of anxiety,
and the pit of his stomach felt empty.

'Alright George – the daughter's the priority. If she did see
her mum she could do something stupid. So let's find her. Tell
Wells we're concerned that she might harm herself. Let's find
her quick.'

THREE

The narrow hedge-lined lane flashed past in a double blur.
Shaw had bought the Porsche 633 second-hand because
of the narrow A-bar – the stanchion between the windscreen
and the side window – which allowed wider vision to anyone
with only one working eye. It was all part of living with the
disability, developing skills, avoiding excuses. He'd lost his sight
in a freak accident on the beach three years earlier, a canister of
chemical waste washed up on the tide line, a kid playing with a
stick, stirring the Day-Glo green goo seeping out of the rusted
metal, then waving it in Shaw's face. He didn't want an artificial
eye: he didn't want to fool anyone, least of all himself, which
was a decision which held a hidden, secret danger – one that he'd

never shared with Lena. Keeping the blind eye meant that there
was a risk the good eye would begin to deteriorate in sympathy
– a not uncommon reaction which led most people to have
damaged eyes removed. It meant that Shaw was vigilant for the
slightest indication his remaining sight might be failing.

They slowed, approaching a police checkpoint as they
climbed a hill half a mile beyond the village green. The line
of cars ahead was being directed into a side street. As they
crept forward they caught sight of a row of cottages, one of
them charred, the windows black rectangles, smoke still drifting
from the beams of the roof. Two fire tenders stood on the
cobbles, a single hose playing a mist over the facade of flint
and brick. A West Norfolk gas van and support vehicle were
parked in the street.

At the roadblock a uniformed officer approached, saluting
Shaw. 'B road's closed ahead, sir – gas explosion in the house,
and it's ruptured the gas main under the road.'

Shaw recalled the dull percussion he'd mistaken for a gunshot
when he'd been standing in Marianne Osbourne's bedroom.
'Anyone hurt?' he asked.

The officer nodded. 'Haven't found the body yet but the old
bloke who lived in the house is missing – floor's ripped out,
might never find him.'

Shaw checked his watch. 'Can we sneak past . . .'

The PC shepherded the Porsche up on the pavement and round
the cracked road surface, which was slightly buckled, as if
disturbed by a giant mole. Just beyond was another row of
cottages, all with broken windows, two women on one of the
doorsteps, clutching elbows.

'Hell of a bang,' said Valentine. 'Poor bastard's probably still
in orbit.'

The Porsche effortlessly scaled a straight incline to the final
brow of Docking Hill and the open high grassland which hugged
the coast. To the right a security fence ran beside the road,
mowed meadow on the far side, and in the distance three giant
wind turbines, turning slowly, one of which had been visible
from The Circle. Along the perimeter fence, by the gates, a
crowd of demonstrators stood, spilling into the road, slowing
the traffic to a crawl. Beyond, on the open downland, was a
small group of tents. Shaw had passed the spot several times

that summer and noted what a disparate group they were: belligerent pensioners, middle-aged bird watchers with their binoculars
and Alpine walking sticks, teenagers out of school and college
for the summer, a few more seasoned campaigners, and the odd
'usual suspect' he recognized from the magistrates courts in
Lynn, plus a couple of activists from the local animal rights
movement.

What did unite them were the placards they held – each one
off a production line, each one carrying the same slogan:

Save Our Unspoilt Landscape.
SOUL

Valentine had the passenger window down as they inched past.
'Nutters,' he said. He was still annoyed Shaw had pulled rank
and insisted they go in the Porsche. He'd have preferred twenty
minutes on his own.

Shaw had to stop as several demonstrators stepped into the road
and one leaned in the open passenger side window, offering a leaflet.
He had a kind of *Brideshead Revisited* mop of hair, a T-shirt marked
ANARCHY INTERNATIONAL, and a birthmark on his left cheek.
Valentine noted an understated, expensive watch on his tanned wrist,
the kind that shows the phases of the moon, and a 'bum bag' wallet
on the belt of his black jeans, which were slung below his hips.
He wasn't as young as he'd like people to think. Up close Valentine
guessed thirty, maybe more.

'Thanks for your support,' he said, trying to make eye
contact.

Shaw looked him quickly in the face, noting the birthmark – a
naevus flammeus, or port-wine stain. He'd studied facial disfig-
urements as part of his forensic art studies. This type was treatable
using lasers, but rarely with a hundred per cent success. The
worst long-term effect was emotional. But in this case the young
man seemed to have suffered no damage to self-esteem or
confidence.

'There's plans for two hundred of these things along the
Norfolk hills – and more than five hundred at sea. There's a
petition – the details are on the leaflet . . .' He tossed two on to
Valentine's lap.

As Shaw edged the Porsche forward the young man kept pace

with the car. He'd already sensed Valentine was hostile so he was talking to Shaw. 'This kind of thing happens because of apathy. I mean, look at it . . .' He pointed at the nearest turbine.

Shaw did; he thought they were beautiful. Elegant, Aeolian, immensely unhurried. They always made him think of the plastic windmills he'd stuck in the sand as a child.

'And the bird strike's horrific. Geese alone – thousands of them cut to pieces. They won't release the figures but you can see the dead ones out at sea, after an offshore wind. Plus the noise . . . Not now. But in winter it's, like, constant.'

'Beats a nuclear power station,' said Valentine, pressing the button so the window went up.

The crowd cleared, ushered out of the road by some bored-looking security guards. Shaw accelerated away but he beeped three times and the little crowd cheered, because he admired anyone who could be bothered to demonstrate about anything.

Half a mile further and they saw the sea, revealed like a backdrop on stage, as if the marine blue was a vertical painted board. The wide arc of the horizon was unbroken, stretching east to west along the north-facing sands. Out almost on the edge of vision they could see another wind farm, thirty, forty turbines, off the unseen Lincolnshire coast. In the mid-distance a school of yachts was bunched in a tight U-turn around a distant buoy.

A mile from Wells they slowed to join a queue of holiday traffic. Valentine dropped his window, letting the breeze cool the sweat on his scalp. On his lap was the file on the inquiry they'd selected to reopen and were about to reveal to the press. While there was a decent chance they'd find the killer, even after an interval of seventeen years, he knew the real reason they were here, why they'd be on this case for the next few weeks, pretty much full-time. West Norfolk's new Chief Constable, Brendan O'Hare, the former No. 2 from the Royal Ulster Constabulary, was a high-flyer amongst high-flyers. He hadn't taken the job on to be forgotten. He wanted the world to know the West Norfolk was there, fighting crime on the front line with the latest scientific techniques. That morning he'd had the press over to the West Norfolk's HQ, St James', for interviews – his aims, methods, targets. This afternoon the press got their sweeties to take home – a nice juicy cold case to write up under embargo for Monday's papers. A fat little maggot of a story just right for the so-called 'silly season' when the news dried up from Westminster, the Law Courts, even the City. This was all about publicity, and netting O'Hare his next chief constable's ribbon, preferably a big metropolitan appointment: Manchester maybe, or Bristol. Then he'd be poised for the final run-in, the big push for the only job he really wanted: Commissioner of the Metropolitan Police, with a gleaming office looking out of New Scotland Yard at the London Eye and Big Ben. Then, arise Sir Brendan.

Which is where Shaw came in. Valentine glanced in the rear-view mirror at the DS's face. Young, good-looking, sharp. The face of modern policing, the face O'Hare wanted to present to the media. Because putting yourself right up front was dangerous. If anything went wrong, it was Peter Shaw who'd take the flak. Valentine didn't often look in mirrors to see his own face. In fact, sometimes he couldn't recall it – not in detail. But he was pretty certain it wasn't the face of modern policing.

The quayside at Wells-next-the-Sea was crowded with small boats. The press were already aboard *Osprey*, a modern sixty-seater, which spent most of its time running parties out to Blakeney Point to see seals. Today it was rigged out to keep journalists happy, with an icebox full of bottled beer. Shaw parked in a reserved police bay by the harbour master's office and retrieved a box file from the boot containing information packs including a CD with pictures, a map and cuttings from 1994 – the year the cold case broke. All the journalists had to do was sit back, drink a cold beer and listen to the story. Then they could tap it out on their laptops as they took the train back to London. Like water, Shaw thought, most journalists took the path of least resistance.

Walking the gangplank to *Osprey* he thought he'd judged the event perfectly: he hadn't just netted the familiar faces from the local weeklies, the evening paper in Lynn, and the *Eastern Daily Press* in Norwich, he'd also snared three nationals and the regional man for the Press Association, who'd put it out to the rest of Fleet Street and the big regional dailies. As long as nothing broke through on to the news agenda for the UK over the weekend he thought they had every chance of getting a page lead in half a dozen nationals.

Shaw nodded to the skipper and the Merlin inboard engine coughed into life.

Osprey swung away from the stone quay, leaving behind a line of children and parents on the quayside crabbing – plastic see-through buckets dotted between them, full of skittering silhouettes. Behind them the little car park was crammed full, heat radiating from metal bonnets making a mirage of the shop fronts, the council attendant's caravan office adorned with a large sign which read: CAR PARK FULL.

Shaw settled with the sea view, his back to the town, drinking his beer, and talked to the woman from the *Guardian*: dangerously thin, with long, bare legs, a short grey skirt and a white collarless shirt. Her name was Nikki – Nikki Tailor. She squinted at him through narrow, horizontal glasses which were electric pink. Her hair was short and expensively cut, but she fiddled with it, brushing it back from her forehead whenever she spoke. Seated, she wrapped one leg round the other so that her ankles were entwined.

She stubbed a biro on her notebook, mildly smug that she'd worked out that if the West Norfolk was reopening a cold case after nearly seventeen years – as the press invite they'd all got stated – then the science they'd used to open it up was almost certainly DNA analysis. She was right, wasn't she?

Shaw gave her a surfer's smile. He was aware of the effect he could have on some women. Her own smile broadened, a flush of colour rising on her narrow, elegant neck, and her legs crossed and uncrossed, locking again at the ankles. 'Ten minutes you'll know everything,' he said.

She scratched some shorthand and readjusted the pink glasses, then dropped her notebook. 'It's John, isn't it?' she asked, when she'd retrieved it from the deck. 'DI John Shaw.'

'Peter,' said Shaw. He thought this woman radiated a kind of perpetual low-level anxiety. 'And we're off the record, as I think your letter of invitation made clear.' She nodded. 'The information pack, which I'll give you later, contains a statement from us – feel free to use that.' He smiled, but she didn't smile back because she'd got the point. All the quotes on the record would come from the chief constable. The last thing Shaw needed was to discover he'd stolen the boss's limelight. Shaw's time to take centre stage would only come if the inquiry turned into an expensive fiasco.

Osprey threaded its way through moored yachts. The boat had a canvas sun-cover but the sparkling seawater reflected light up, dappling the shadowy interior.

They'd been at sea for ten minutes and the quayside was almost out of sight, although they could still hear a one-armed bandit shuffling in the amusement arcade, the sound bouncing over the mirrored water of the long harbour. To the right the marshes stretched out of sight, deep channels of chocolate mud wandering through the reeds. To the left ran the sea wall, holidaymakers on the top walking out to the beach rather than taking a ride on the miniature railway which ran, unseen, on the far side. The smell of fish and chips lingered. But the air was cooler out here and the soundtrack was fluid – the screw turning, the water slapping the fibreglass hull and, just audible, the thud of waves falling on an unseen beach.

Shaw stood on one of the bench seats which circled the deck, his hand gripping one of the poles which held up the awning. Valentine noted with irritation the DI's stance: his weight down one leg, the shoulders relaxed, the face devoid of any trace of stress. It was one of the many facets of DI Peter Shaw that got under his skin – the effortless ability to be at ease.

'Ladies, gentlemen,' said Shaw, the voice lighter than you'd expect. 'Thanks for coming. I have to remind you at this point that in accepting this invitation from the West Norfolk today your editors signed the embargo notice, so nothing can appear in print until after one a.m. Monday – and we take that to mean that nothing will appear until your Monday print editions. Websites can carry the same information, but only from one a.m. The information is being released only to print media – radio and TV will get the press release by email on the Monday morning at nine a.m.'

Shaw watched as the reporters exchanged smug looks of contentment. It was what they called in the trade a '*beat*' – not quite a scoop, because they were all being given the story, but they were going to be firmly one step ahead of TV and radio. He paused as the man from the *Daily Mail* rummaged in the cool box for a bottle. He had clearly decided, thought Shaw, this was a day off. He was in a pair of moleskin shorts with a shiny brass buckle, and a Polo shirt: baby blue, with a Lacoste brand label of the little crocodile. He'd once been able to fit into these clothes. Shaw guessed he was sixty, perhaps older. His skin was

shiny, without surface tension. His name was Forbes – the first
name Shaw had already forgotten.

'So,' continued Shaw, 'just so that you can get your bearings . . .'
He pointed back to Wells. 'The town's to the south of us; we're
just leaving the harbour, marshes to the east, reclaimed land
behind the sea wall to the west. Over there – coming into view
beyond the Lifeboat House – is the beach.' They could see a line
of beach huts in seaside colours, a wide expanse of sand, room
enough for several thousand holidaymakers. Even now that they'd
picked up the sea breeze, you could hear the sound of a summer
beach: the whisper of a crowd punctuated with children screaming,
a dog barking, the flutter of kites. On the steep sandbank beside
the channel a cluster of seals basked in the sun, roped off from
a small crowd of inquisitive holidaymakers by a flimsy fence of
tape and sticks.

As *Osprey* slipped past the Lifeboat House Shaw trained his
binoculars on the window in the mess room, on the second floor.
Two figures in RNLI work overalls were at the glass, looking
back at him. He waved once and both responded. Shaw had been
on the lifeboat at Old Hunstanton, along the coast, for nearly ten
years, having joined the RNLI while at university in Southampton.
But he'd done shifts at Wells, which was one of the few full-time
stations left on the coast, so he knew his way around. The doors
of the main boathouse were open, revealing the blue and amber,
sleek-hulled boat within.

'And there,' he said, raising his voice over the sudden cawing
of seagulls, 'is our destination,' he added, pointing out to sea.
The marshes turned inland here, to the east, to follow the coast.
At the far point, about a mile offshore, was a low island, crowned
with dunes, marram grass and cowed pines. 'East Hills,' said
Shaw. 'That's the scene of the crime – it'll take us twenty minutes
to get to the jetty. So do help yourself to a drink, and we've got
some food too . . .' Shaw nodded to Valentine, who heaved a
picnic basket up on to the engine cowling in the middle of the
deck. The journalists descended like the gulls – all except Forbes,
from the *Daily Mail*, who insinuated himself into a seat next to
Valentine and tried to listen to his conversation with the man
from the local paper.

Shaw studied the distant island. He had come here many
times with his father as a child on the little ferry boat that ran

out from the quay. Like most of the locals they'd avoided the trip in the high summer because the boat was crowded out with tourists and the ticket prices were steep. They'd gone at the weekend, spring and autumn. Despite the inconvenience – there was no drinking water, no shop, no nothing – it was one of the few places he'd ever seen his father relax. Even as a child he'd understood why, standing, holding his father's hand, watching the ferry depart. Six hours before it came back. Six hours when the island was theirs. But even back then East Hills had a racy reputation – a kind of insular lover's lane, with couples disappearing quickly off into the grassy dunes and pine trees as soon as the boat left. Shaw had stumbled on one pair, up in the pines, and the memory still brought the blood to his cheeks. He'd have been ten, maybe a year older, so the tangled naked limbs had made some kind of illicit, thrilling sense. But he didn't know what to say – just a mumbled apology before running back to his parents. He'd sat, guiltily, feeling like a Peeping Tom who'd been caught out. He'd seen the couple, loose limbed, emerge from the dunes when the boat had come back, sounding a claxon as it bobbed off the floating landing stage, and they'd laughed at him – openly, and he'd felt that sickening adolescent certainty that he was never going to be admitted to the adult world.

But East Hills, like all his childhood haunts, looked smaller now. About six hundred yards long, a narrow ribbon of high dunes cut off from the coast by a deep channel and a persistent and lethal rip tide. Shaw noted the stone pines, the navigation buoy off the point, the pillbox: at an angle now, subsiding into the sand on the distant point. And the small wooden floating dock, beyond which the crowd on the beach was thickest.

He heard a question being asked and realized it was being asked of him. It was the man from *The Daily Telegraph*: a three-piece suit in a green country cloth. He'd be fifty-five, maybe sixty, radiating a kind, avuncular personality. But Shaw perceived something else beneath the unthreatening exterior. Accents quite that perfect were almost always manufactured. And when he'd got a hip flask out of his leather briefcase Shaw had seen a sheaf of cuttings on the West Norfolk force and its new chief constable, annotated in a neat, pencil, copperplate. So he'd done his homework.

The question he posed was a simple one: why the three-day embargo until Monday? It was a good question – sharp, business-like, despite the attempt to bumble his way through it. He tried to recall the reporter's name from the briefing sheet he'd sent Valentine. Smyth – that was it, and now he wondered if the 'y' was an affectation.

Shaw sipped his iced beer. 'That's a good question – and the answer's coming, I promise.'

Smyth smiled, nodding, but there was nothing jovial about his eyes, which were slate grey.

Osprey's engine changed its note, the speed dropping, edging into East Hills past swimmers – most of them, despite the summer heat, in wetsuits, bobbing like tadpoles. The sea breeze had picked up once they'd got beyond the sand bar at the mouth of the channel and the breakers drummed on the sands, so that Shaw almost didn't hear his text alert on the mobile. It was from Inspector Jack Craxton at Wells Police Station.

NO SIGN OF DAUGHTER. Shaw looked at Valentine, who'd got the same text.

'Trouble, Inspector?' asked Smyth from *The Daily Telegraph*, on Shaw's shoulder.

'Routine,' said Shaw.

Osprey dropped anchor fifty yards off the beach. In the late afternoon sun about sixty people lay on the white sands. The ferry ran just two trips a day: out and back. The last time Shaw had been in Wells with Fran, his daughter, in the early summer last year, he'd checked out the price: twelve pounds. So you got social exclusion as well as spatial. Plus the lack of facilities kept kids and families to a minimum. A woman stood, topless, and waded into the sea, shoulders back.

With the exclusivity of East Hills came one other major benefit on a north-facing coast: the south-facing beach, which attracted serious sun-seekers, dedicated heliophiles. One man stood close to the landing stage, towelling a flat stomach, one foot on a cold box, drinking from a plastic bottle covered in icy condensation.

Shaw leant on the little capstan house where the skipper of *Osprey* was now theatrically filling a pipe. 'OK, everything I'm gonna say is in the briefing pack, as I said. So sit back, enjoy the sun and I'll tell you a story.' He opened a bottle of fizzy

water as the sea slapped the hull of *Osprey*. 'In 1994 there were
seventy-five people on this beach one Saturday afternoon in
August,' said Shaw. 'We know it was seventy-five by the way
because the boat which ferried them out sold tickets. Still does.
One of those tickets went to a young Australian called Shane
White; he was twenty, travelling in Europe. He'd picked up a
summer job as a lifeguard, employed by the local council. Back
home – that's a small place up the coast from Sydney called
Barrie Bay – Shane had been the school swimming champion,
and he had all the certificates you needed: life saving, endurance,
first aid. It was his job to make sure no one got into trouble out
here on East Hills. On the boat he'd have briefed all the tourists,
the message clear: it's a good beach to lie on, you can even have
a paddle and a dip, but don't try to swim out, especially back to
land, because the currents are treacherous and when the tide's
running you'd need to be Mark Spitz to have any chance of
making it alive. It doesn't look it, but it's nearly two thousand
yards to safety. A country mile.'

Several of the reporters squinted into the distance.

'At about four twenty p.m. that afternoon – the return boat
was due at four thirty p.m. – Shane White's body was found
floating in the water just over there . . .' Shaw pointed along the
beach towards the open sea. 'He'd been stabbed in the midriff
and had lost a lot of blood. The wound was a slash, about eight
inches long, delivered by a blade at least five inches long. The
woman who found him got help and he was dragged ashore. He
died about ten minutes later. The boat which arrived to take
everyone off the sands had a radio, and so assistance was called.
The RNLI launched and came across the channel. A police launch
came out too. Officers took everyone off the beach and back to
police headquarters at Lynn – St James' – to take statements.
Shane was a good-looking lad . . .'

Shaw nodded to Valentine but he was already on his feet
handing out the press briefing packs. The first print in a set of
photographs was of the victim. The local paper had done a
story that summer when he'd helped save a horse and rider
who'd got caught out on the sandbanks beyond Holkham. Shane
had swum out while the lifeboat launched. He'd gone to comfort
the rider – a ten-year-old girl who'd got separated from a riding
school outing. Shane looked like a lifeguard: two-tone dyed

blond hair, muscled, in red and gold shorts marked WDC –
Wells District Council. His face was as forgettable as most
handsome faces – too symmetrical to be really interesting, like
the computer-balanced features of some comic strip hero. The
ten-year-old looked mortified and clutched White's hand
without enthusiasm while he held the wrecked bridle of her
horse.

'From the statements we were able to piece together Shane's
last few hours alive on East Hills,' said Shaw. 'He'd chatted up
a few of the girls on the beach. Subsequent interviews revealed
he did that a lot, and didn't always stop with the chat-up line.
At the funeral, which was held at Hunstanton, there were half a
dozen heartbroken teenage girls in the congregation. All of them
thought they were Shane's one and only. Anyway, when he wasn't
sorting out the local talent he sat up on the dunes, near the ridge
with a pair of binoculars, keeping an eye on the swimmers.' Shaw
glanced at the beach and they all saw a lifeguard sat on a high
chair below a single red and yellow flag. 'About an hour before
Shane's body was found he swam out and dragged a kid back
to shore on an inflatable dolphin. There hadn't been any real
danger – the winds were very light – but it was the right thing
to do. The kid's father apologized and offered Shane a beer,
which he declined. The next thing we know about Shane is he's
floating in the water leaking blood.

'By 6.45 p.m. that evening we had evacuated East Hills. Each
person on the beach – all potential suspects – were asked to
take with them everything they had brought over from the
mainland: towels, picnic baskets, kites, the lot. We took seventy-
four people off the beach. Shane's body went later after the
pathologist had finished an examination at the scene. The
preliminary cause of death – confirmed at autopsy – was
drowning. He'd lost nearly three pints of blood due to the
puncture wound. There was also a wound to his eye, possibly
caused by a fist, but not a knife. Once we had his corpse off
the sands, and his stuff, the beach should have been empty. It
looked empty. We let the sniffer dogs loose and they found a
spot up in the dunes where there was fresh blood in the sand,
and buried in the sand they found something else – again,
there's a picture in your pack.' A threadbare towel, blue and
white stripes, bloodstained, in a polythene evidence bag. 'None

of the seventy-four people left alive on East Hills would admit to recognizing this towel,' said Shaw.

'And they all had their own towels?' asked Smyth, from *The Daily Telegraph*. Again, sharp, businesslike.

'Yes. Everyone – but then some had two. Lots of people take spare towels. So that's no mystery.'

They all looked along the beach. Shaw was right; the nearest couple were lying on two wide coloured towels but they had others drying from a parasol stuck in the sand.

'We examined the towel thoroughly but it yielded nothing but bloodstains – a match for the victim. There were several layers of footprints at the spot – too many to be of use. But given the progress being made in forensic science at the time, especially in DNA analysis, it was thought wise to keep the towel in a secure environment in the long term . . .'

'What kind of *secure* environment?' asked the man from the *Daily Mail*.

Shaw's temper, never that far from the surface, flashed briefly. 'A secure one.' That was the problem with his temper: it came and went so quickly hardly anyone noticed. He swigged some water, letting the lack of control recede, then pressed on. 'Fresh tests, undertaken in the last six weeks at The Ark, West Norfolk's own forensic laboratory, using the £400,000 Home Office grant the chief constable has, I think, told you all about, and later under contract at the Forensic Supply Laboratory, have revealed several skin cells on the towel from which a DNA profile has been drawn. It is not the victim's DNA profile. We can assume, I think – an assumption we're confident a court would accept – that the person whose cells are on the towel shed the cells as they cleaned the victim's blood from their own skin. The DNA sample – Sample X – is that of a man. It has no direct match on the National DNA Database. We believe, with some confidence, that Sample X belongs to the killer of Shane White.'

Shaw ducked as a seagull flew under the awning.

'Of the seventy-four original suspects eight have died. We have invited the remaining sixty-six to St James' tomorrow. The majority will be travelling some distance – most of the boatload that day were here on holiday. Thirty of those sixty-six are men, and they will be asked to give a voluntary DNA sample – cheek cells by swab. Then, they will join the thirty-six

women in being invited to read their original statements given
in 1994. If they wish they can amend those statements. Each
will be re-interviewed. Of the eight who died between 1994
and today five were men and their DNA has been determined
with the cooperation of family members. All the samples will
be analysed and compared to our scene-of-crime sample –
Sample X. All seventy-four original witnesses are accounted
for; all those alive have agreed to attend.' Shaw smiled at Smyth,
the man from *The Daily Telegraph.* 'Hence the embargo. We
want to get all the potential suspects into St James' and out
again before the publicity kicks in.'

Smyth coughed, and Shaw could see a glint of real excitement
in the soft eyes. The reporter undid a button on the green cloth
waistcoat. 'So, Inspector. Let me think this through, if I may.
The chances are – given that seventy-five people went out on the
boat and seventy-four came back plus our victim's corpse – that
when you complete these tests you will know the identity of the
killer. You will have a DNA link to the towel, a blood group link
to the victim, and the original statements of the seventy-four that
they didn't recognize the towel. Right?'

Shaw inclined his head in recognition of the summary.

'And the lifeguard's towel?'

Shaw glanced at Valentine, because it was a good question
and he didn't know the answer.

'Recovered on the day,' said the DS. 'From up by the dunes.
Along with water, biscuits, suntan lotion, a book . . .' Valentine
closed his eyes. '*Airport*, by Arthur Hailey. And his camera.
Nikon – with a telephoto lens.'

Shaw had to remind himself that George Valentine had been
on more murder inquiries than he'd had skinny dips. Behind the
cynical, antagonistic exterior there lurked a first-class brain, even
if he didn't always know how to use it.

Osprey's passengers were silent. Every one of the journalists
was wide awake and paying attention. They knew a good story
when they had one. And this was a good story, even if it was
embargoed until after the weekend. But that was fine – they'd all
worked that out, because by then there was no way the police would
have announced the results of the screening. So the story stood:
the police would have their killer's DNA, the public wouldn't know
which one of the thirty-five male suspects was in the frame. Perfect.

'How, exactly, do you know the skin cells were not Shane White's?' asked Smyth.

'We took a sample from White's brother, care of Sydney CID and Interpol.'

Shaw swigged fizzy water. 'Which brings us to motive,' he said, moving quickly to regain the initiative. 'And that camera that DS Valentine has just helpfully mentioned. When we developed the film in the camera we found some disturbing images. Shane White took pictures of couples in what we like to refer to as compromising positions.'

Forbes started rifling through his briefing pack.

'None of which are in your press pack,' said Shaw.

Some of the reporters booed.

'Mostly they were taken in the woods and sand dunes along the coast, a few on East Hills. When you think about it he was well placed. He spent his time looking through binoculars. He'd spot a couple slipping off somewhere private. Then he'd follow, get his snaps. The real question is what did he do next? We considered the possibility at the time that he may have tried to blackmail some of the people he photographed.'

Forbes' eyes widened. Violence, death, and now sex. 'Did you put any names to the pictures?' he asked.

'A few, but as far as we could see at the time none of the people pictured were among the seventy-four survivors that day on East Hills, or indeed, related to them in any way. As I said, the vast majority of the trippers were on holiday. Not locals.'

'Other rolls of film?' asked Smyth.

'We turned over his digs and found a makeshift dark room and developing gear. CID in Australia confirmed he'd done a photography course at school. But there were no photographs like the ones in his camera, or negatives. The answer may be in a detail – White's neighbours insisted Shane had been burgled a week or so before his death. Door broken in, bit of a mess. He told the neighbour he'd report it. He didn't. So maybe that was the killer's first stop. He stole the pictures. Then decided to seek a more permanent solution, deliver a warning, in person. Scare him off.'

'Burglary suggests premeditation,' said Smyth.

'To some degree,' conceded Shaw. 'But it's always dangerous

to think that one premeditated act leads to another. Life's not like that, or death.'

Smyth scowled, unhappy at the public lecture.

'If the killer's alive he'll just run . . .' cut in Nikki Taylor. 'Surely?' She looked at her colleagues for support, but they were all looking at Shaw. 'He's not going to walk into a police station . . .'

'The Home Office funding is £400,000 – not four million,' said Shaw. 'We can't watch them all. But if they run – well, that kind of answers our question. All the surviving witnesses were given the invitation to attend at St James' in person. All were asked to stay in the country until the results are processed, so we collected passports. We understand from the FSL that processing will take approximately forty-eight hours, although, clearly, if they get a match in the first batch they'll let us know. But you're right. We are prepared for a no-show tomorrow. In fact, I think it's odds-on. So we'll be ready.'

'And you'll let us know, of course, if that happens?' Smyth again, closing his notebook, smiling to himself.

'That's an operational matter,' said Shaw, thinking on his feet. 'But I can't see why not.'

It wasn't an answer and the reporter knew it. Smyth carefully unscrewed the top of a small hip flask and drank.

'Questions,' said Shaw. For the next ten minutes he fielded their queries, while Valentine texted DI Craxton, telling him they'd be back up at The Circle in an hour. He didn't have the exact statistics in his head but he knew that the chances of finding a missing seventeen-year-old six hours after they've gone missing are a lot shorter than after one hour. If there was still no news then the dismal prospect of another self-inflicted death became ever more likely.

The tourist ferry boat turned away from East Hills, packed – literally – to the gunwales. 'OK. Let's head home too,' said Shaw. 'Unless anyone's desperate for a dip.'

The skipper of *Osprey* hauled the anchor and they drifted offshore into deep water before the engines fired into life. As the boat turned Shaw didn't move his head, so that the motion of the boat gave him an exhilarating tour of the northern horizon.

Once they were moving forward Shaw noticed that Valentine was stood alone, a bottle of beer in one hand, a set of briefing notes in the other. It was a rare sight, but he had a smile on his face, the genuine article. Shaw was reminded of a black and white snap his father used to keep on the sideboard at home: a Christmas party at St James', DCI Jack Shaw clinking glasses with a young detective with a career in front of him – DI George Valentine.

Valentine came and sat beside him. The journalists were huddled at the other end of the deck, comparing notes, double-checking. Valentine had received a list of the seventy-four people taken off East Hills that hot August evening – a list the press did not have. He scanned down it, then pressed a grubby thumb on one of the names in the 'P's. Shaw read the name twice, then took the file to make sure he'd read it right. *Marianne Pritchard.* Shaw saw the victim's face again, white against the pale pillow, looking out at the swaying sunflowers: Marianne Osbourne, née Pritchard, on her deathbed.

FOUR

The sun was setting on The Circle, shadows reaching out from the houses across the parched green, the cedar tree which grew in the midst of the ruins collecting the dusk. Most of the semi-detached bungalows had windows and doors open, trying to capture the night breeze, hoping to let the heat of the day drain out into the dark. The deep blue evening sky was dotted with a single star. Shaw could have spotted the dead woman's house even if he hadn't known it: the houses of the dead always looked like that as night fell. The lights blazed: every window lit, and a security light to the side and a SOC lamp out the back, so stark it gilded the distant pine trees on the edge of the wood. It was as if the people left behind needed to keep the darkness away that first night, as if death was going to hang around, looking for fresh pickings. Shaw and Valentine stood outside No. 5.

'Hubby at home?' asked Shaw.

'Yup. He's a bit shaky, but he's OK. Asthma; like I said, stress makes it worse. Worried about the kid, Tilly, so that can't help.

He wanted to join in the search but we said no. Otherwise the scene's secure,' George said.

'And there's no mistake?' asked Shaw.

'Nope. Marianne Osbourne, née Pritchard, is on our list of the seventy-four people evacuated from East Hills on the day of Shane White's murder.' Valentine had got through to the desk at St James' and double-checked: a DS from Wells had called at No. 5, The Circle, Creake, a week ago with the letter requesting Marianne Osbourne attend St James' police headquarters, Lynn, to be re-interviewed in connection with the murder inquiry of 1994.

Valentine wasn't sure what the consequences were of the dead woman's name being on that list, but he knew what to do. He'd contacted DC Paul Twine on the line at the Metropolitan Police Training College at Hendon, North London. Twine was graduate-entry, smart and well organized, and part of Shaw's team. He was due back in Lynn overnight. Valentine told him to go straight to force headquarters at St James' and organize a mobile incident room to be on the green at The Circle, Creake, by seven the next morning. First job: repeat the door-to-door enquiries, checking for any links with the East Hills murder.

Together, alone, on the grassless green, Shaw and Valentine double-checked they'd covered every base before interviewing Marianne Osbourne's husband. Each stood on the rim of a six-foot wide imaginary circle, facing each other, but not making eye contact, talking into the warm night air. Valentine's spot of Marianne Osbourne's maiden name on the mass screening list had been inspired. Without it they'd have faced the acute embarrassment of discovering the link at St James' when she failed to show up. They'd have wasted twenty-four hours, maybe more. So Shaw owed his DS a commendation. He took a deep breath, but it didn't come. 'So,' he said instead, 'what happened?'

'In 'ninety-four?' Valentine had got the duty officer in Records to read out Marianne Osbourne's statement on the phone, taken at St James' on the evening of the East Hills murder. He gave Shaw a smart summary: she was sixteen years old, out of school that year, a trainee hairdresser/beautician with a part-time job selling cosmetics door-to-door. On the statement she'd put the word 'model' in the box reserved for occupation. She'd planned to go out to East Hills with a friend on her day off but the friend

hadn't turned up at the quay, so Marianne went alone. She'd
been before – again, with the friend. She had a book with her,
and she'd only just got into it so she read mostly – on her back,
because the previous week she'd been on her front. She didn't
notice the lifeguard. She went for a swim early on – about
eleven, before the sun was hottest. After that she'd sunbathed
until she heard the boat coming back to pick them up. When she
looked out to sea she saw the red slick of blood and the floating
body, and someone else had screamed at the same moment.

Valentine jiggled something in his trouser pocket. 'Stevie
James, in Records, said you've only got to see her picture to
know the story. Absolute corker, says Stevie, even in a standard
black and white police mugshot. Said he'd put his mortgage on
her being eighteen. Twine's first job is to track down the missing
girlfriend, 'coz that doesn't sound right.'

Shaw nodded, watching crows clatter round the ruins, recalling
Marianne Osbourne's cold, pale face.

'So what'd you reckon?' asked Shaw, again. 'What happened
on East Hills?'

Valentine nodded several times, as if agreeing with himself
before he'd spoken. 'I reckon she might have gone out on her
own but she wasn't planning on staying on her own. Sixteen –
and only *just* sixteen – she's been Miss Jail Bait in a bikini for
a couple of years. I think she met someone. Someone she'd met
before. They went off in the long grass and our lad with the
candid camera got a shot. Then chummy – that's the bloke poking
Marianne – spots him, pulls a knife, wants the film. Why? Maybe
he was married. After that we can all join the dots up . . .'

Shaw clasped both hands on top of his head, bracing the
muscles in his neck and back. 'Yeah. Maybe. Maybe not.' That
was one of the most annoying things about George Valentine.
He could imagine a crime, then set out to find the evidence which
went with it. And ignore the evidence that didn't go with it.

'Why go to the beach armed with a knife?' asked Shaw.

Valentine watched an arrowhead of geese heading towards the
coast.

Shaw rocked back and forth on the balls of his feet. 'Unless
. . . Maybe this isn't the first time. What if Shane White already
had his pictures, but this time he wanted the money? Don't
forget the burglary at his flat. That suggests he'd demanded

his money, and that someone knew he had the pictures. So the
killer takes the knife to help make the point that White's not
getting his money. Then, like you said, George, we can all do
the dots.'

They heard heavy footsteps: cork shoes striding down the path
from the dead woman's house. Dr Justina Kazimierz, the force's
resident pathologist, her white SOC suit fluorescent in the dusk.
She'd been on the force nearly a decade after moving to the UK
from Poland. She had a reputation for brusqueness bordering on
outright rudeness, not helped by the occasional lack of fluency
in English.

'Peter,' she said, handing Shaw a small forensic evidence bag.
Inside was what looked like an aniseed ball. Slightly larger,
perhaps. It was broken open like a tiny egg, weathered – the
rubber having perished so that it was marked with a patina of
cracks, like the surface of Mars.

'Is this what killed her?'

'I think so – the body has only just gone. Tomorrow – ask me
tomorrow, for sure. But I guess yes. Lodged in her back teeth
– here.' She pushed her own lip up to reveal the upper left-side
molars.

'One?'

'Enough, Peter. From the smell there is no doubt.' She took
the bag, unzipped the seal, and held it up to Shaw's nose.
Almonds. The detail he should have lingered over when he first
stepped into Marianne Osbourne's room.

'Cyanide,' she said, without any note of distaste. 'Tom said
the tap in the bathroom was dribbling, so I think this woman
took one, then she runs to the bed. The poison works fast.'

Valentine stood, lighting a cigarette, trying to relax, sensing
one of those rare moments when a crime becomes distinctive,
unclassifiable. It was one of the moments that made his life worth
living.

'I still don't understand,' said Shaw.

'A suicide pill,' she said. 'I've seen such a thing before – a
military museum, Crakow. The rubberized exterior is to protect,
so it cannot be accident to break it open. They were hidden –
sewn into a sock, a lapel.' She thought about what to say next,
struggling with the subtleties of the language. 'A comfort for
these men, that death was at hand.'

'Fatal?'

'Without doubt.'

'Age?'

She held it up to the street light. 'Twenty years, more – maybe much more. But this is not my job – Tom, maybe.' She gave Valentine the bag. 'Someone will know.'

Shaw rang the CID suite at St James' and got hold of one of his team – DC Fiona Campbell. Her father was a DCI at Norwich, so she was a copper from a copper's family, just like Shaw. She'd been with him for two years and she was smart, efficient and steeped in the traditions of streetwise policing. Shaw told her to spend an hour tracking down military/intelligence suicide capsules: where could you buy one? He suspected they'd end up looking at the former Soviet block so he advised a quick preparatory call to Interpol, and the MoD in Whitehall to see what the position was with the British Military. Home Office too, MI6 and MI5.

Then they stood in silence, together, until the church in the village struck the hour, a slight echo coming back off the hills.

'She killed herself, Peter,' said Valentine. 'Just 'coz it's simple doesn't mean it isn't the truth.'

'Why?' asked Shaw.

Valentine rearranged his feet. 'The letter we sent her made it clear we'd interview everyone, DNA test all the men. So she thinks we'll get to the killer – she *knows* we'll get to the killer. Maybe she thinks he'll drop her in it. She's an accomplice.' He rubbed the back of his neck where the muscles ached. 'She knows she'll be facing questions. Not just a statement this time. She lied first time round. This time she'd have to tell the truth. An ordeal. We know she's depressed – she's attempted suicide twice, for all we know loads of times – perhaps this was the trigger. This time it's not a cry for help. It's goodbye.'

Shaw didn't look convinced. 'So she pops into the bathroom and opens the cabinet to find that handy cyanide pill she'd set aside for such occasions?' He wondered what Lena would make of this conversation with its cold edge of cynicism, the emotional distance. 'I don't think she was alone when she died,' added Shaw. 'I think the killer was with her. We get a DNA match from the mass screening and we've got a good case, but it's not watertight, is it, George? A good defence lawyer might get under our

skin, suggest to the jury that we'd contaminated the sample. At
that point Marianne's evidence would have been crucial. She'd
be the key witness.'

Shaw forced himself to lock eyes with his DS. 'So the killer's
worried. He talks to Marianne. Coaches her. But she can't go
through with it. She's haunted by the truth. She's a pretty fragile
human being. She'd tried to kill herself before, like you said.
Painkillers, blunt kitchen knives. This time there's someone there
to offer her an easier way. Death in seconds. And that suits the
killer just fine, because we can't put a dead woman on the stand.
It's a painful, excruciating death. But maybe he didn't mention
that.'

FIVE

J ackie Lau was on the doorstep of Marianne Osbourne's house:
four foot nine of pretty belligerent detective constable, in a
new leather driving jacket and wrap-around reflective glasses.
Lau was ethnic Chinese, ran fast rallycross cars for a hobby –
largely, it was said, to get closer to the men who liked speed as
much as she did. The other thing she was interested in was being
the force's first female plain-clothed DI. There wasn't much she'd
let get in her way. Being on Shaw's team was a good place to
start.

She took off the glasses. Her face was broad, faceted, like
beaten metal. 'Sir. Dead woman's husband is in the front room.
He's on the whisky – but not bad. Daughter's still missing. He's
worried, desperate, really. She's never been missing this long
before. I've checked her room. Usual teenage stuff, plus some
politics: Far Left, Greenpeace, Save the Whale. Packet of
condoms in the bedside cupboard but Dad says she hasn't got a
boyfriend. No . . .' She stopped herself. 'He says she's *never* had
a boyfriend.'

Shaw wondered if he'd know as much as Joe Osbourne about
his own daughter when she was a teenager. He and Fran were
close now, there was a real bond, but would it survive the
turbulence of adolescence? If he ever got to make the father's

speech on her wedding day would he, too, be talking about a stranger?

'She's resitting exams, right?' he asked, trying to focus, aware he was dangerously tired. But he wanted the detail, and wanted to know if DC Lau had asked.

Her face tightened, the skin like a drum. 'A-levels – media studies, French and music. School says she was on course for straight As – fluffed it. Maybe nerves. She plays guitar.' She looked Shaw straight in his good eye. 'Classical Spanish. Her Dad plays too.'

'Classical?'

'Nope. Acoustic.'

They shared a smile, even here, on death's doorstep.

'He's older than the wife,' Lau added quickly. 'Thirty-five. She was a year younger. He's sole owner of the business in Wells – key cutting, locksmith, that kind of thing. Father's business before him. Gets about on an old motorbike – BSA Bantam. I get the impression there's not much money about. The door-to-doors haven't altered the estimated time of death. That still has to be between nine a.m. – when hubby left for work – and one forty-five p.m. when the kid saw her through the bedroom window and raised the alarm.'

A blare of static came from a police radio in one of the parked squad cars.

'One other thing,' said Lau, catching Valentine's eye, indicating that this was new. She checked her notebook, but Shaw guessed it was a theatrical gesture, designed to make them both wait for the detail. 'I got control to run Osbourne's name through the files online. Two years ago he was picked up in the red light district in Lynn trading slaps with one of the hookers. Punch up over the price, apparently. Just push and shove, really, so the PC on the beat took a note of the names – no action, but cautions all round.'

Shaw thought about that Pre-Raphaelite face, the mask of tragedy, and the body he hadn't seen below the duvet.

'Well done,' said Shaw. But he was an honest enough copper to realize the information would now fatally colour his judgement when he met Joe Osbourne. It might have been best to find out afterwards. He wasn't there to judge; he was there to enforce the law. All this told them was that if Joe Osbourne tried to tell them he had a perfect marriage they'd know he wasn't telling the whole truth. Nothing more. His father's maxim was a good one, even if it took a definite control of willpower to put into practice: *never judge a marriage from the outside.* After all, who would ever know what hatred, or love, had existed between Joe and Marianne Osbourne.

Osbourne was in the front room, bent forward in a wooden chair, elbows on the narrow arms, his head cradled in his hands. Lanky, slight, muscled; Shaw got the impression his body was folded into the chair, ready to spring out. For a man sat motionless in a seat he radiated a remarkable physicality, a latent energy. But he was also a living embodiment of the difference between fit and well. His skin was oddly lined, as if the wrinkles of his face had fallen in the wrong places, and his complexion matched the fat on dead meat. His eyes – a light grey – were lively enough, but the whites were bloodshot. Shaw had no doubt he could move like a thirty-year-old, but he looked a generation older.

Behind him against the wall stood two acoustic guitars, one battered, one almost new.

'Mr Osbourne?' said Shaw, sitting opposite, waiting for the head to come up. 'We're sorry for your loss, sir,' he added, immediately regretting how little emotion he'd put in the sentence.

He coughed, ploughed on: 'Your daughter, Mr Osbourne. We can't find her. We're concerned. One of the neighbours said she had an argument with your wife this morning. Was that common?' Shaw checked a note. 'She'd be seventeen, I think?'

Osbourne's eyes were grey and flooded, an echo of the North Sea in winter. 'They clashed,' he said. 'She didn't understand Tilly.' He gave a small shrug, which Shaw guessed hid the unspoken addition. 'And neither do I.' Osbourne looked round the room as if searching for more words. 'They weren't close.'

It was such an extraordinary thing to say about a mother and child that Shaw sat back, and he noticed Valentine, standing, edged back as well, as if they'd both decided to give him the time to carry on.

Osbourne began to cry, but the tears fell only from his left eye. 'She wants a life of her own,' he said. 'To escape.' He

coughed once, which triggered a series, until he retrieved an
inhaler from his pocket and took three breaths.

Shaw felt what he'd first felt standing by Marianne Osbourne's
bed: a sadness that seemed to permeate the house, seeping into
each of the rooms, as if fingers of misery ran through the home,
like strands of dry rot. He took an empty glass from Osbourne's
hand, placed it on the table, and locked eyes with him.

'Any ideas where she might be, sir?'

He shook his head.

'It's possible she saw your wife's body on the bed through
the window,' said Shaw. 'A kiss was left on the glass. It may be
hers. So you see, we really do need to find her quickly in case
she hurts herself or does something stupid . . .'

'Oh, God,' said Osbourne. He let his hands open and clench
and Shaw saw he'd been holding a snapshot. The picture was of
the two of them on a beach, Marianne in a bikini, him in trunks
– trendy Speedos – his legs painfully thin, his taut frame strung
with muscle and tendon. They looked like kids. They were kids.
Shaw took the snapshot, flipped it over and read: *Cromer. July
1994.*

'We'd asked Marianne to come to the police station tomorrow
to be re-interviewed about the murder on East Hills in August
1994. Do you think that might have had something to do with
her death, Mr Osbourne?' asked Shaw.

'She never swam after East Hills,' said Osbourne. The voice
was light, matching the slender hands. Shaw imagined the fingers
manipulating the cogs of a lock. 'I was working that day, the
day of the murder; otherwise I'd have been there too,' he said.

'Your father's shop – the locksmith's?'

'She went with a girlfriend,' he said. Shaw and Valentine
exchanged a glance, noting that Marianne had kept the precise
truth from her husband: that she'd gone to East Hills alone,
or at least without the friend she'd agreed to meet. Sometimes
they had this ability, Shaw and Valentine, to know they were
thinking the same thing. Did Marianne's omission mean they
were right? That she'd gone out to East Hills to meet a secret
lover?

'It really shook her up,' said Osbourne. 'Seeing the body – I
suppose they all were. She'd have nightmares sometimes – always
the same. She'd be swimming out and she'd get entangled in the

body, in the arms and legs and she'd run out, covered in blood.' He covered his mouth. 'It was the blood – the sight of it. She wasn't squeamish. But he bled to death. And she said you wouldn't believe it – the amount of blood in the water, like a cloud, all along the beach. Like there were hundreds dead, or dying. She said one of the men on the beach said his father had been in Normandy for D-Day – on the beaches – and that the sea was red there too, for miles. It was like the colour was in her head, for ever.'

He coughed again, trying to limit it to one, but failing, so that he needed a second dose from the inhaler.

'She never said anything else about that day? Perhaps she met another friend out on the beach by chance? Did she have lots of friends?'

'She was popular,' said Osbourne, his voice flat, atonal.

'You were going out by then . . .'

'That's right.'

'So no other men?'

'We were an item,' said Osbourne, wiping tears from his face with the back of his hand, but there'd been a hint of bitterness in his voice.

Shaw decided then that they'd come back and interview him when he wasn't still in shock.

Osbourne looked around the room, and Shaw sensed a kind of tedious hatred for what he saw. 'It's why we're here, in this house, in this *fucking* house,' said Osbourne. He spat the word out, as if his wife's death gave him a sudden freedom.

'Why?' prompted Valentine.

'After East Hills she couldn't live by the sea. She couldn't wait to get out of Wells. Ruth – that's her sister – lives next door, has done since she was married, so when this one came on the market we pitched in. I'd have stayed . . .' He shrugged, as if he'd been happy to give up the sea. 'But prices were soft so we got it.'

'They must be close – the sisters?' asked Valentine, thinking it was a kind of nightmare for him, the thought of relatives next door.

'Ruth's always been there for Marianne,' he said. 'And Tilly.' Shaw considered the testimonial. In his experience people who were 'always there' for others got their satisfaction in life from not being somewhere else.

Osbourne was up out of the chair, the spring uncoiled. He walked quickly to the makeshift bookcase and took a bottle out of a gap between two encyclopaedias, refilling his glass, his hands shaking rhythmically but slowly.

'For the record, sir,' said Valentine. 'Today you were at the shop again, all day?'

He turned back to them. 'Yes. I closed for lunch, but I was out the back in the workshop.'

'And your wife worked at home?'

Osbourne nodded, but his jaw was straightening. 'No. She was due in at Kelly's – the funeral directors down in Wells. It's a part-time job but we need the money. She got up, had a bath, got dressed. Then, after Tilly went, she got back into bed. Said she couldn't – not today. You know . . . she suffered.' He drank, then added: 'Low mood,' making it clear he knew it was a euphemism.

He let the words hang there. 'So I made the call for her – told 'em she was ill. That's where I left her . . . in bed, about nine.'

Shaw watched Osbourne sip the whisky. Each mouthful was substantial and he didn't gag. Shaw got the impression he was in it for the long run, and that he'd been down the road before.

Osbourne filled his narrow chest with air, squaring the fragile shoulders. 'How did she do it?' he asked. 'This time.' He sat, rocking slightly in his chair, and Shaw thought how tiring it would be to live with his bristling energy, the lack of peace.

'We're pretty certain that she swallowed poison, a cyanide capsule. A suicide pill. Have you any idea where she could have got such a thing?'

'I don't understand.' But he did, Shaw could see, it was just that he didn't have an answer.

'And we believe that she may not have been alone when she died,' added Shaw. 'Have you any idea who might have been with her, Mr Osbourne?'

'Not alone?' Osbourne stood, as if he'd suddenly found the strength to be upright. He put the whisky glass down with exaggerated care. It was as if he hadn't heard the question. 'Can I see her – Marianne? I should.' His voice was rising, taking on a note of panic. 'I want to see her.' His head, which was small and compact, seemed to tremble at a very high frequency.

Before Shaw could answer they heard voices in the front garden – women's voices – and then the door opened and slammed and they heard heavy footsteps in the hall, and a teenage girl appeared in the doorway. Her face was already disfigured by shock – the mouth hung open, the micro-muscles beneath the skin malfunctioning, so that her face seemed to shimmer and distort. But even in distress Shaw could see the resemblance to the dead woman: the colouring, although the hair was dyed a more striking red, and the fine bone structure, which seemed to stretch translucent skin.

She walked to Osbourne, who'd slumped back into his seat, and knelt down so that they could hold on to each other. Osbourne slipped from the chair to his knees and Tilly took his weight, letting his head sink to her shoulder.

A woman stood at the doorway. Shaw could see the resemblance to the dead woman in her too, in the colouring – the auburn hair, the green eyes. This had to be Ruth, Marianne Osbourne's next-door sister. But she was also a striking opposite to her sibling: fleshy and rounded, the skin tanned from the wind and sun, so that she had no hint of tragic paleness. Shaw recalled that she worked at the Lido at Wells, and he could imagine her, executing an efficient breaststroke, effortlessly covering length after length, her head clear of the water. She looked at Shaw. 'I told her,' she said, 'that Marianne's gone.'

They heard Joe Osbourne thank her, his mouth buried in the nape of his daughter's neck. Osbourne, sitting back now on his haunches, was sobbing, his hands fluttering in front of his face like a pair of bird's wings. He kept saying, 'Thank God', and touching his daughter on her head, as if giving her a blessing.

Shaw and Valentine went out into the hallway. By the front door, thrown down, was a placard with a wooden stump.

Save Our Unspoilt Landscape.
SOUL

Ruth followed them out. Up close Shaw could see her skin was unnaturally clean and slightly rucked, like corrugated paper. 'I don't think she can face any questions tonight,' she said. 'But she did say they argued this morning because she didn't want to revise for the resits. She wanted to go with her mates – that's

what she said. In fact, she wanted to go up to Docking Hill, to
the wind farm demo. But she didn't tell Marianne that, or Joe.'

Shaw thought how odd it was that no one in the family ever
shortened the victim's name to something less formal, less cool.
Marie, perhaps. And he wondered if Tilly had been there, up by
the wind farm gates, when he and Valentine had driven through
on the way down to the coast.

'She's been up there all day,' added Ruth, answering a question Shaw hadn't asked. 'Till four. Then she went to the
boyfriend's down in Wells and they went for a drink on the front
– The Harbour Lights. Marianne wouldn't have approved of that
either.' Ruth looked down the short corridor to the bedroom,
where the door was open but still blocked with the yellow and
black tape. 'It's an awful shock,' she said. 'But the worst thing
is she's going to think it's her fault.'

SIX

S haw parked the Porsche by the lifeboat station at Old
Hunstanton. It was past nine but a necklace of beach fires
still sparkled along the dunes. He shrugged himself into his
rucksack and began to run north along the high-water mark. Out
at sea the spot where the sun had set was marked by a flash of
green-yellow light, and silhouetted in it were the wind farms off
the Lincolnshire coast. As he picked up speed he passed the new
lifeboat station, built to house the inshore hovercraft. He'd been
the pilot for nearly four years and the radio call-out pager was
strapped to his belt, but the summer had been quiet and they
hadn't had a single shout in July. Tonight the sea was a sheet of
mercury, untroubled by any wave.

The halfway point to his house was marked by a single stone
pine, the branches buckled by the wind, thrown back as if in
shock at the sight of the sea. He stopped, climbing the low dunes,
to breathe in the view. He filled his lungs with the air that he
always imagined had arrived direct from the distant Pole – a
3,000-mile fetch uninterrupted by any landfall. He unpacked the
parcel of air he'd drawn into his lungs: salt, ozone and a trace of

the exposed seaweed on the cockle beds. But with the wind following the shore there were other elements – a hint of a chemical barbecue tray, the strangely inert aroma of sand itself and a citrus edge from the lone pine.

He could see his wife and daughter long before they saw him, in chairs set out in front of the Beach Café. Lena had bought the old shop, derelict, four years earlier, a job lot with a small cottage to the rear and an old boathouse beside it, now transformed into *Surf!*, selling anything from beach windmills at seventy-nine pence to a sand-yacht at £3,999. Wetsuits had got them through the first year because the surfing revolution had transformed the British beach into a stretch of sand dotted with human seals. And while surfing and the North Sea were not natural companions the north-west-facing beach at Hunstanton did catch a decent swell if the wind was right. Next year they planned to open the café in the evenings, thanks to a newly acquired alcohol licence. Supplies for the cafe and shop were currently ferried along the sand in an old Land Rover that Lena drove. But they'd need a new 4x4 van to run daily deliveries if they opened late, using the wet, hard sand below the waterline when they could. They'd made the most of this last summer of perfect sunsets because next year Lena might be struggling to serve iced Chardonnay, or bottled Adnams, to thirsty trippers.

His wife stood, black skin showing off the white bikini. Five foot three inches tall, a full figure, but the skin taut and lustrous, especially at the close of a sunny summer. She'd just been in the sea and as she shook her hair Fran screamed, jumping away, the old dog their daughter loved barking at the sudden movement.

Lena brought him a glass of wine, standing close with a hand pressed against his stomach, insinuated through the gap between the buttons on his shirt. Her face was made up of curves, not slight subtle lines but bold, strong facets, so that sometimes he thought of an African mask, the curves around the eyes defining the face. She had a slight cast in her right eye, an odd match for Shaw's blindness in the left.

They watched Fran taking a Chinese lantern on a string out on the sand. She lit the candle within and it rose, just beyond her reach, and in the windless air drifted at walking pace to the north. She followed it, trying to coax it round, so that she could bring it back to show them. Shaw noted that she walked as he did, as if she might at any step float free of the earth, her elbows slightly out from her narrow body. It was one of many physical similarities: the fair hair, the wide cheekbones, the almost colourless pale blue eyes. One of the mild complications of having an only child was that discussions about which side of the family she took after were loaded. It wasn't as if the fact that she looked like Shaw – the light brown-sugar skin aside – would one day be outweighed by another sibling's likeness to Lena. Thankfully Fran's psychological make-up was entirely in her mother's mould: forthright, outgoing, matter-of-fact – with just the same added ingredient: an ability to step back and watch the world go by.

He sipped his wine, his hand on the back of Lena's neck. This was the moment he had to fight the urge to talk about work, because Lena had left the city, left Brixton and an urban life, to get away from the kind of lives people had to lead there. She didn't believe in trying to create a paradise, Shaw understood that, but she didn't want any glimpses of hell either. In the winter they'd be lucky to sell a pot of tea, let alone a beach yacht, so there was nothing easy about it. On a wet Tuesday in February, under a grey sky, it could be soul-destroying, watching the sea through rain-streaked glass. It was going to be a struggle, but she was prepared for that. She didn't think life owed her anything. But the lives that Shaw saw in his work were not everyday lives; they were a cross-section of the damaged, the cruel, the victimized. It was his job to deal with that, said Lena, not bring it all home.

When they'd met she'd been a lawyer for the Campaign for Racial Equality, picking through the London housing benefit system, trying to help families get a home. She'd always thought that if she immersed herself in that world, a world of poverty, crime and abuse, she'd be untainted by it – be able to just walk away at the end of a day's work. By the time she met Shaw – on his first placement from the Met College at Hendon – she'd realized she was wrong. The sceptical, logical, forensic mind she'd trained so well was being coloured with cynicism. She always recalled something a judge had said in chambers. 'To the jaundiced eye, Miss Braithwaite, everything is yellow.' And that's how her world looked: tainted. So they'd planned this: to live away from the city, outside Shaw's urban manor, and for Fran to have a childhood. Their daughter could do with her life what she wanted, but first they'd give her this: a wide sky and a beach.

Shaw looked out to sea, nothing in front of him and the world behind him. Lena pulled on a pair of Boden-style shorts. Shaw recognized the patterned material because *Surf!* sold the range. 'Good day?' he asked.

She thought about that. Lena's attitude to the business was fiercely practical. This wasn't a hobby, it was what she did, and it made her independent.

'£1,400 in the shop. I had Jon and Carole in the café and they took £550. Most of that was ice cream and coffee. A good day – up there in the top ten for turnover. Profits? Decent.' Lena sat on the stoop steps, stretched her legs out and curled her toes into the sand, cold now the sun was gone. 'You?' she asked, a ritual invitation to talk about his day. Just the basics. If she wanted more, she'd ask again. There was no point Shaw *hiding* his life from his family.

Shaw told her about the death of Marianne Osbourne. The dynamic tension in their relationship sprang from his decision as to when to *stop* telling her about it. Shaw believed in the police, he thought they made people's lives better. And he knew that Lena thought the same way. So most nights he told her what he'd done at work. Then they moved on. He outlined the case in two hundred words then stood, preparing to set out and join Fran at the edge of the motionless sea.

'So this woman, Marianne, was on the beach at East Hills? Alone?' said Lena. The moon was up now and she tilted her face to it as if it was the sun, so that the light gave her face an architectural quality.

'Yeah.' Shaw thought about that, sitting beside her. 'Well, she said she hadn't planned to be alone. Her friend just hadn't turned up at the quay. And she may have met someone out there. But she said she was alone. I got George to read through her statement – the one she made at St James' the day they took them off the island. She was sixteen, out of school, doing a course at the college, selling cosmetics door-to-door.'

'Takes guts,' said Lena, 'at sixteen. Think back, how you'd feel, having to walk up strangers' paths and just knock. That *is* a cold call.'

Shaw stopped, realizing that he hadn't thought about Marianne

Osbourne as a businesswoman: capable, competent, just like Lena, perhaps. His wife was right: it did take guts, a maturity as well, to work alone. Had a dream sustained her, as it did Lena?

His wife was shaking her head. 'I'd have gone to the main beach – given the island a miss.' She examined her toes, easily reaching to touch them. 'Mind you, maybe there was someone she fancied on the boat? That would be perfect – she'd be alone, but she had a reason she was alone, 'coz her friend had let her down. Good opening line . . .'

'In the statement she said she got there early,' said Shaw. 'Got herself a ticket because she didn't want to miss out. It was a perfect day. She didn't want to waste it if the friend didn't turn up, and there was a crowd there already. And she liked East Hills more than the other beaches. She had a picnic, the lot. Anyway, she went. Says she sunbathed at the south end of the beach till lunch – had a swim just before – then read her book.' Shaw slipped a notebook out of his pocket. 'George says they took an inventory when they evacuated the island of what everyone had. This is Marianne's . . .' He handed her the notebook with the list. Towel. Bag. Bottle of made-up orange squash. Sandwich box – Tupperware, empty. One apple. Shell of a boiled egg in greaseproof paper. A yogurt carton – empty. One spoon. Radio. Paperback. Suntan oil. Lipstick. Vanity mirror. Eyeliner. Tissues. *Daily Express. TV Times.* Purse: eight pounds fifty-six pence in cash. Membership card for West Anglia College Students' Union. *What's On* leaflet for The Empire, King's Lynn. ATM debit card – NatWest. Membership Card: Docking Lido.

Clothes: shorts, pants, T-shirt, bra, sandals.

'What's missing?' asked Shaw, not knowing if anything *was* missing.

Out on the sands Fran had corralled the Chinese lantern and was walking it back towards the house. The thought crossed Shaw's mind that she was growing up an only child, and what would that do to her? They didn't want another child; they felt comfortable, close-knit and intimate. But was it fair? Lena had siblings – two brothers, a sister. Being part of that family, embedded in it, was important. Why deny Fran that life?

'You said she went swimming?' she asked. 'So where's her costume?'

Shaw checked back: no costume. She'd come well prepared

for the day – so she had one. A mistake on the list? Was it rolled
in the towel and they didn't unfurl it? Maybe.

'Did they talk to the friend – the one that was supposed to go
with her?' Lena turned towards him, suddenly sure of herself.
'Because that's what's odd, isn't it? She's brought her own food,
like, one yogurt. Her own sandwiches. One boiled egg. But she
said she always went with the friend – the girlfriend. You wouldn't
do that – you'd share. Like, this time I do the sweet stuff, you
do the sarnies. That kind of thing. Food's part of the fun, not
fuel.' Pleased with herself, she turned back to look at the sea.

'Alright, why would you leave the kiss on a window?' asked
Shaw. He'd painted that image for her already – the image he
couldn't forget, the two lips forming a perfect bow.

Lena stiffened, knowing they were close to crossing the line,
that they were going deeper into his world and he wanted her to
follow.

'It's for her. A goodbye,' said Lena, thinking it through.

'A lover?' asked Shaw. He studied her face.

'A lover,' she said, pulling a jumper on, letting her foot touch
his in the sand.

'Because?'

'It's for him, isn't it? Because she's dead. It helps him avoid
the guilt.' She stood, shivering slightly now the day's heat was
flooding out of the sand into the cloudless night. She took his
hand, pulling him to his feet.

'So she was dead already, and he's outside the window, and
he knows she's dead, so he puts the last kiss on the glass?'

She took his face in her hands. 'Yes. Now that's it. Enough.
Let's eat.'

While the pasta cooked Shaw took a tennis ball and bounced
it off the sidewall of the shop. Each night he did this 200 times
– often more. Continuous practice developed innate skills which
helped him to catch a moving object with 2D vision. As so often
with the human brain it could develop astounding talents when
faced with the challenge of operating normally despite disability.
One trick he was working on was to move his head rhythmically
side-to-side just a few inches – much in the way that a pigeon
would – so that his one eye got two views of the moving ball,
the brain putting them together as it would with two eyes, to
create a 3D picture. He did it 300 times, dropping the ball twice,

then went to his office and booted up the iMac. He used Skype to contact The Ark – the West Norfolk's forensic lab. The screen flicked into life. Dr Kazimierz loomed then disappeared, and Shaw heard a chair being dragged into place. Shaw stood and closed the door. When he got back to the screen he could see the empty lab. The roof of the old chapel was original – carved beams, and the thin lancet windows were green stained glass. On the far wall was a single carved angel, its hands over its eyes, as if in grief.

Kazimierz came back into view, both hands held up, one – gloved – smeared with blood. 'Peter,' she said. She looked beyond him, recognizing the cottage office. Since her husband had died the previous year the pathologist lived alone in a cottage further along the beach. They'd become friends, but no one at work would ever have guessed.

'Anything?' he asked.

She touched her forehead and Shaw thought for a moment she was going to cross herself. He'd seen her once, on the steps of the Catholic church in the centre of Lynn – a converted carpet warehouse. She'd stood for a second, bracing herself for the world.

'I double-check the victim's throat and mouth. We have a scenario – yes. She takes the cyanide pill, holds it in her mouth, goes to the bed, then she bites down. The poison stops her swallowing entirely, but enough fluid is in her throat for the toxin to seep into the bloodstream.'

She leant out of the picture and reappeared with a skull – plastic, with movable joints for the jaw and upper neck. 'Here . . .' she said, pointing at the bony peg which joined the jaw to the skull. 'There is a micro-fracture. I lift the skin and some of the muscle. On the other side there is no match. But broken capillaries here . . .' She touched her own chin, fleshy, heavy-set. Shaw recalled the dead woman's finer features, the narrow, elegant jawline, fragile even in death.

'She broke her jaw then . . .' said Shaw, 'biting down?'

'Not possible,' said the pathologist, leaning back, a hand and coffee cup appearing from the left of the screen, the glove gone. She looked up into the rafters above her head. 'Just possible,' she conceded. 'But one in a million chance. No. I think she put the capsule between her teeth, then someone do this . . .' She put down the cup and slung one arm round her own neck.

'A half Nelson,' said Shaw.

'Yes. Then the other hand presses the top of the cranium down as the grip tightens. That is when the jaw breaks. The pressure is very much . . . sustained. Maybe a strong man, maybe a strong woman. I could do this . . .' She meant physically, not morally. 'There are no signs she struggled. So I think she agreed in this, but only as a passive person. The word I don't have . . .'

'Acquiesced?' suggested Shaw.

'Thank you. Certainly up to the point when this other person applies this pressure. After that she has no choice. You understand this, Peter?'

Shaw thought that this was what Justina Kazimierz did well: the picture she'd painted was authoritative, clear and final; it was what made her a first-class prosecution witness. He heard Fran's dog barking out in the corridor, the paws scrabbling at the door.

'And these things . . .' He struggled for the right word. 'The capsules. They keep. They don't perish?'

'Tom is looking at this. Certainly they perish, but as long as the internal seal is intact then they still can be used. Constant temperature, out of sunlight, that would help. Fiona emailed me – you are already begun on this? She have the same question. I gave her the same answer. I need to get on,' she said. The screen blanked.

Shaw heard the door open behind him and suddenly Fran was on his lap.

SEVEN

Saturday

Twenty-two semicircular York stone steps led up to the main doors of the West Norfolk Constabulary's headquarters, St James' Street, King's Lynn. St James' had once been an imposing Victorian edifice, built at the junction of two of the town's main streets, a bold statement of order amidst chaos. It had been cruelly used by the advent of the motor car, which had left it isolated, beleaguered on a traffic island. The inner ring road swept by on one side, enveloped in a perpetual blue cloud of carbon dioxide, while the street that led into the town centre had been unable to save itself from a long and seedy decline: kebab shops jostled with a brace of burger bars and one of Lynn's roughest pubs – The Angel, the regulars of which saw the proximity of the police HQ as an incitement to riot. The sun was up and already high enough to penetrate the cool shadows in the old streets. Across the thoroughfare stood Greyfriar's Tower, a remnant of the abbey which had once stood on the edge of the medieval town. A ruin, restored, it stood at a giddy angle, Lynn's very own leaning tower.

Shaw savoured the moment of sudden silence as he pushed his way through the revolving doors and into the hush of the main reception area – a high ornate hall with busts of long-dead civic dignitaries in niches beneath a painted dome.

It was 8.15 a.m. A large white sign stood in the middle of the floor marked with an arrow, pointing left, and the words, EAST HILLS INQUIRY. Shaw walked lightly down a marble corridor. There were two doors at the end: one led into a spiral staircase, down into the old basement of the building and the cells; the other – marked with a second East Hills sign – into a courtyard, already splashed with sunlight, bouncing off freshly polished squad cars. Shaw noted that the chief constable's limousine was in its reserved space.

On the far side of the car park stood The Ark, the West Norfolk's forensic lab and in-house mortuary, converted from a nineteenth-century Nonconformist chapel. The original church's nickname came from its resemblance to Noah's floating quarters – the box-like deckhouse of the Biblical boat. The only hints that it had been given a new role for the twenty-first century were an aluminium flu, a bristling communications aerial and a set of three new garage ports, currently housing two of the CSI mobile units and a hearse.

The East Hills mass screening had required the addition of three standard Portacabin blocks: one for re-interviews and for all those called to reread their original statements, one for the DNA swab tests, and one for witnesses not amongst those evacuated from East Hills on the day of the murder – the original CID team, the RNLI crew who turned out to help, the harbour master, the local uniformed officers who'd secured and searched East Hills. Each of these would also be asked to reread their original statements. Shaw might have a reputation as a whizz-kid but it was mostly built on being thorough. He had a talent for organization but a genius for not letting it get in the way of inspired detection.

One of the West Norfolk's mobile canteens was also set up to provide tea and coffee, completing a temporary East Hills 'village'.

Shaw bounced on his toes as he walked, feeling good. He'd swum that morning as the sun rose, the sea still deep summer warm, his hands rising and falling over his head as he let a rhythmic backstroke take him out to sea. Then he'd run to the Porsche – his measured mile, and clocked six minutes eighteen seconds, a new record. He could still feel his blood coursing, and the burst of endorphins had cleared his mind. It had taken nearly a month to organize the East Hills mass screening, a constant low-level stress that had been difficult to accommodate with his everyday caseload. Now the day was here he felt the thrill of liberation and the freedom which comes from reaching the point of no return. By Monday they'd have their DNA results – and the name of the man who had killed Shane White and had probably helped Marianne Osbourne take her own life with a cyanide pill. A large A-board stood before The Ark with an arrow pointing towards its Gothic double doors.

EAST HILLS INQUIRY
ALL VISITORS PLEASE SIGN IN AT RECEPTION

Inside, Valentine was talking to two women at a desk set in the vestibule of the chapel – a room panelled in mahogany, a simple board listing the ministers from the first incumbent in 1823. Shaw's DS was perched on the table edge, his face relaxed, in mid-anecdote – some Byzantine story about a DNA sample that got mixed up with some dog food that Shaw had heard him tell before at one of the CID's ritual parties at the Red House – the St James' boozer-of-choice. Shaw had noticed that Valentine seemed to be able to relax in female company. Surrounded by men he always maintained a mildly irritable exterior. Shaw's father had once told him that the tragedy of George Valentine's life was losing his wife in a car crash. Shaw had tried, but never succeeded, in trying to imagine what she'd been like. It didn't help that as a child he *had* met her – probably many times. He just couldn't remember her. In truth, he couldn't remember George Valentine either, not in those early years. But then perhaps he'd been a different person.

Shaw introduced himself to the women. The one he didn't know in a smart blue Customs & Excise uniform introduced herself as Christine Pimm. Shaw might not know her face but he knew all about her – Tom Hadden had sent over her file when they were setting up the mass screening. Christine was twenty-six and worked at Stansted Airport, checking passports. She had three GCSEs, a certificate in advanced hair care and an IQ of 122. Pretty quickly it had become clear she had a genius for her job. In April 2007 she'd recognized a terrorist posing as an academic en route to an international conference at Cambridge University. He was listed as the US's sixth most wanted target – the Jack of Spades in the pack. She'd routinely memorized his face from a circular she'd seen a month before he'd stood in front of her, checking his mobile phone. He'd had minor cosmetic surgery, no beard, a pair of heavy black-rimmed glasses and false teeth. But she'd still recognized him.

Shaw shook her hand, realizing that she was one of the few people in the world who shared his own obsession with the human face. The difference was that he'd had to learn his skills while hers appeared innate. She was here for a very simple reason: if the killer really was amongst the men called to the mass screening then there was one high-risk option he could take to evade capture: he could send someone else to give the DNA sample. Christine Pimm's job was simple: check documents, match faces to documents and be a hundred per cent sure they had the right person on the day.

The other woman was Tom Hadden's deputy as head of CSI, Dr Elizabeth Price, dressed in a crisp white SOC suit. Dr Price was sixty and would never get the top job, due to a burning lack of ambition and an unhealthy zeal for her real passion in life – teaching promising young pianists how to play Bach. Shaw liked her: she was efficient, cheerful – joyful, even. She was living proof the job didn't inevitably lead to a cynical world view.

'So how does this work?' he asked, accepting a coffee from Dr Price's thermos flask. She'd brought a little stack of six plastic coffee cups – a typically thoughtful gesture. Shaw had left the on-the-day detail of the DNA sampling to the CSI unit, so he wanted to know what was happening. Hadden had been involved in a similar operation to catch a golf course rapist in Hertfordshire in the nineties. On that occasion they'd taken nearly 12,000 DNA samples before catching the culprit, but catch the culprit they had.

'Well, it's pretty simple,' said Dr Price. 'As you know each of the seventy-four holidaymakers taken off East Hills in 1994 – those still alive – was visited by the police and invited to attend. Early slots went to locals – those in East Anglia. Most are travelling from London, East Midlands, a family from Scotland. They can all claim for travel expenses. The women are re-interviewed and invited to make new statements if they wish. The men start with Christine here, who makes sure they are who they say they are. We take a DNA sample. All thirty-five male DNA samples – that's thirty from today, plus the five taken from close relatives of those who have died – will be taken by courier to the FSL laboratories in Birmingham after lunch, first batch, then late tonight, final batch. A twin set of matching samples will be kept at St James'. If a case comes to court it will be these samples, the ones we don't send to the FSL, which will be tested again and will underpin any conviction. The FSL should complete the whole mass screening in under forty-eight hours – they run a 365-day 24/7 operation. All samples will be checked against the East Hills sample – Sample X, which is already on the National DNA Database and has never triggered a match, so we know our killer hasn't given a sample before.'

It was a clear and confident summary, thought Shaw, but he knew that if they did get someone into court the first thing any defence lawyer would attack would be the DNA evidence. 'Matching' DNA samples involved scientists making judgements on probabilities. It only took a moment of doubt in the witness box to destroy a case. If they did identify their killer through the mass screening they'd still have to provide evidence of opportunity, not to mention motive, but at least they'd have a name, which would give them a fighting chance of getting the rest, and securing a conviction.

Shaw sipped coffee as Dr Price explained the rest of the procedure. After they'd got the DNA samples the men would be invited to join the women for interview, to reread their original statements and give new ones if they wished. Giving them this option was a barely disguised trap. If one of the suspects did alter their statement – perhaps to include the possibility that they'd talked to the victim – then it was, probably, an attempt to undermine any potential DNA link. They would later no doubt argue that their DNA had innocently come in contact with the victim's own skin, or the towel. But by changing the statement they would be alerting the police and inviting the closest of scrutiny. Shaw had juggled the pros and cons in his own mind and come to a clear decision: if he was the killer he'd rewrite his statement, blur the DNA link, and hope the police had no other evidence.

Shaw checked his watch. The first batch of six suspects – due at eight – were already being processed. Three men were giving DNA samples, three women rereading their original statements. Dr Price said they'd had one call on the emergency line they'd set up for the mass screening: an elderly woman now living in Norwich said she couldn't make it due to an acute attack of shingles. She was housebound on doctor's orders so they'd despatched a team with her original statement. Otherwise everything was running like clockwork. If they had a 'no-show' they had instructions to alert one of Shaw's team immediately.

'You think that might happen?' asked Dr Price. She hugged herself, suddenly vulnerable to the excitement around her. He could see that what this woman had in part, which he lacked completely, was an ability to detach herself from what was going on around her. She was a professional, here to do her job, and that was all.

'Maybe,' said Shaw. He'd always thought failing to turn up was the least smart option open to the killer. But if someone panicked it was still a possibility, probably followed by an attempt to disappear. That was Valentine's favoured option. His view of the criminal mind always shaded towards the chaotic, the visceral – cock-up over conspiracy.

Out in the main yard Valentine got on the mobile to check on the inquiry's progress up at The Circle where the incident room was now in place outside Marianne Osbourne's house. Shaw checked out the Portacabins then went back into The Ark, pushing through the doors into the chapel itself. It was a building he liked – the space still redolent of prayer and clarity. His own religious beliefs were insubstantial. He felt a life spent in pursuit of divine insight was a life wasted. It had been a point of friction with Lena and her family, who had been brought up as Catholics and still kept the faith, however intermittently. Occasionally Lena had managed to suggest, subtly, that Shaw's inability to float free of the world of work was in some ways a symptom of his lack of faith. Shaw thought it was due to lack of time. But none of that meant he lacked any concept of the spirit. He loved churches and the feeling he got that they radiated a kind of compressed devotion. If he'd been alone now he'd have sat for a while and enjoyed that sense of place. Sun streamed through the original green glass of the narrow lancet windows, splashing the interior with an eerie underwater light. Shaw always imagined that if he wanted to he could just float into this space, swim through it, rising up to join the stone angel with its hands to its face.

The long nave had been cut in half crossways by a frosted-glass screen. A set of swing doors led into the force's pathology suite and mortuary – unseen. Shaw was aware that beyond would lie Marianne Osbourne's body, probably in the chilled vaults, but just possibly still on the aluminium mortuary table. At one of the desks on this side of the screen, where Tom Hadden's SOC unit had its office space, sat DC Jackie Lau. Her job was to monitor each witness as they passed through the process and manage any requests to change original statements.

'How's it going?' asked Shaw, his mobile signalling an incoming text.

Lau had left her leather jacket on a hook by the door and her reflective sunglasses were up in her short-cropped coal-black hair. 'That's my text, sir. Six through so far – one's just elected to modify his original statement. He gave me a verbal outline of the changes.'

Shaw felt his heartbeat pick up. 'Substance?'

She checked a notebook. 'Christopher Philip Roundhay. Lives in Burnham Market with his family – wife and two kids. A partner at a Lynn firm of chartered accountants. He says he was too embarrassed to tell the truth at the time and thought it didn't matter. He went out to East Hills with a friend – male. They both fancied White, the victim – chatted him up on the boat. Roundhay says that about an hour before the lifeguard's body was found the Aussie was up on the top of the dunes, so Roundhay walked up too, sat down and had a chat. He said he sat on the kid's towel, and it might be the one that was left on the beach, but he didn't think it was.'

'He said he sat on the towel?' checked Shaw, the excitement making his voice vibrate.

'Yup. Classic. Could be our man, sir.'

'What happened next?'

'Roundhay says he got his signals crossed, that White wasn't interested. In fact, the only thing he was interested in was the girls. So he left him to it. Later, he just panicked. He was living at home then, his parents didn't know he was gay – well, they hadn't talked about it. He says his Dad wouldn't have understood. Old-fashioned values – whatever that means. So he kept his head down.'

'OK. When's the other lad in – the one he went out with?'

'Died nearly ten years ago. Car accident on the Norwich bypass.'

'Check that,' said Shaw.

Lau suppressed a smile because that was one of Shaw's verbal tics. 'Check it.'

'Where's Roundhay now?'

'Portacabin B.'

'OK. Here's what we do,' he said. 'Get chummy's mobile off him. Make sure he doesn't leave until I say so. Double-check we've got his passport. We need to re-interview him. Can you get me some photos of Marianne Osbourne? There's a beach shot at the house. Paul could scan it over. I'll need it.' Shaw went out to reception and told Dr Price the news.

They discussed the logistics and the cost. If they rushed Roundhay's DNA sample through so that they got a result that day they'd be down £12,000. It was a lot of money. But if they got a match then they could put the rest of the samples on a non-urgent check, saving the best part of £100,000. So it looked like a no-brainer. *Except*, if they didn't get a match they'd have wasted £12,000 overnight. With the West Norfolk facing swingeing cuts in the latest round of the public spending freeze that was the last thing they could get away with. Price suggested a compromise: they'd put samples through as planned but ask for Roundhay's sample to be analysed first. That way they'd get a result tomorrow – Sunday afternoon at the latest. If they got no match they'd go ahead with the whole batch at the fast-track price. That would have to do.

Shaw went back into the nave of The Ark. Valentine was by the emergency exit – a door which led out into one of the back streets that fed into the Vancouver Shopping Centre.

'News?' asked Valentine.

Shaw pushed open the exit door roll bar and held it open for his DS. They'd come here before after autopsies to talk through the case in hand. There was something about the scruffy informality of it which suited them both. The street was hot, the tarmac sticky under foot. Shaw filled his lungs and detected the unmistakable aroma of the town: heated pavements and grit. He filled Valentine in on Roundhay's request to make a fresh statement.

'Bullseye,' said Valentine, spitting into the dust.

'So what happened?' asked Shaw, knowing that was George Valentine's forte.

Valentine shrugged, aware he was being led on to shifting ground. 'He fancies the lifeguard with the six-pack. Thinks he's on to something, chats him up, follows him into the water, maybe cops a handful of something he shouldn't. White belts him. Roundhay's got a knife. Stabs him, gets out of the water, lets him drift down the beach towards the landing. That's why he made a false statement. Now he thinks we've got his DNA on the towel – his towel, or a spare towel the two brought with them, or even White's spare towel. So he's made this up. It's clever.' He paused for effect. 'It's what you said would happen.'

Shaw wasn't convinced. 'Same question – where did the knife come from?'

'In his trunks with the hard-on.'

'We both need to talk to him,' said Shaw, tapping both feet. 'Together.'

Valentine held out the hand holding the cigarette, offering another version of events. 'Perhaps it *was* blackmail. Maybe White had got pictures of them before, these lads, in the long grass, so Roundhay takes a knife. He says he's got the money and they meet up in the dunes, all three of them, including Roundhay's chum. Someone pulls the knife, threatens White. There's a fight, White picks up the wound, then Roundhay drags him down into the water over beyond the trees, out of sight. Then the body drifts round.'

'And where does Marianne Osbourne fit into this scenario?' asked Shaw.

Valentine didn't answer; he was looking over Shaw's shoulder, and a look of genuine horror was spreading over the DS's narrow features. 'You're on parade,' he said, ditching the cigarette.

Shaw turned to see the chief constable walking up the back street towards them.

'Peter,' he said, looking at Valentine. 'Give us a second, George.'

Dismissed, Valentine went back into The Ark.

Brendan O'Hare was in a suit. He was bony, medium height with very short hair, not quite a crop. Shaw knew that he ran marathons for fun. He was fifty-one and the second youngest chief constable in the UK. Briefly, on the way up the career ladder, he'd been a DI here in Lynn. Six months was all it took to tick another few boxes in the perfect CV and leave behind a reputation for clinical self-interest. A retiring DI had marked Shaw's card when the Home Office had made the announcement of his appointment as chief constable. 'Gold-plated bastard, our Brendan,' he'd said. 'Sell his grandmother? He'd put her on eBay for the best price.'

Despite his almost inhuman self-control O'Hare had one uncontrollable tic. Before speaking he'd duck one shoulder, just a half inch, the chin would come across like a boxer's jaw reflex, ducking an imaginary punch. It identified O'Hare for what he was: a street fighter in a suit.

'Someone said you'd be here,' he said. The jaw ducked. His accent still held a strong Northern Irish burr, which seemed to give everything he said a paramilitary edge. Shaw always thought that if he was cast adrift in an open boat with Brendan O'Hare, and a single bottle of fresh water, that there would be only one survivor. And it wouldn't be Peter Shaw. 'So, I got your overnight report on this woman at Creake. What do we think, and what do I need to know? I'm in Whitehall all day – Home Office. Spending cuts – again. I don't want any surprises, Peter. Monday East Hills hits the headlines. We don't need anything else in the way . . .'

They heard the ticking of an expensive engine and at the end of the street O'Hare's car crept into view – the black Daimler, a driver in grey. Shaw noted that the belt-tightening hadn't stretched to the chief constable's perks.

'I've got a minute,' said O'Hare. He hadn't looked at Shaw once. He didn't do eye contact unless it was a fleeting and accidental connection.

Shaw thought about what he was going to say, then said it, slowly. 'Two things. The woman found dead at Creake wasn't alone when she died.'

O'Hare eyes narrowed dangerously. As he'd made clear, he didn't like surprises, and that detail had not been in the overnight report.

'She died, as you know, by crunching a poison pill – a cyanide capsule – between her teeth. But there's clear evidence someone else helped her bite down on the pill. Her jaw had been broken. And . . .'

Shaw paused for effect and O'Hare couldn't stop the jaw reflex filling the gap. 'She was on our list of East Hill suspects.'

'Christ,' said O'Hare. 'That's all we fucking need.'

'So, either she wanted to die and someone helped her,' said Shaw. 'Or she didn't want to die but somebody wanted her dead, although there's absolutely no sign of force being used up to the very last moment – the bite.'

O'Hare gritted his teeth.

'Plus, one of the suspects today has changed his story. Male, name of Roundhay. Says he fancied the lifeguard, sat on his towel, chatted him up. We won't let him out of our sights until we have the DNA feedback. He went out to East Hills with another man – that's why he didn't tell the truth first time round. But the other man is dead, involved in an RTA a decade ago, but we'll check that out too. We'll get the DNA match in twenty-four hours – less.' Shaw couldn't resist the rider: 'No extra cost.'

'Right. But none of that is going to break before Monday, is it?'

'Sir, nothing substantial. I thought I'd give the local radio a tip on the cyanide and the woman at Creake. No link to East Hills, just the bare bones – lonely suicide, but where did she get the pill? That kind of thing, because someone might know – in fact, someone almost certainly knows. But otherwise we'll take a view on publicity after Monday,' added Shaw.

'Yes. *I* will,' said O'Hare. 'And then *I'll* decide when to call the next press conference, the press conference when we announce we've arrested the killer of Shane White. It's your job to bring me that name, Peter. Leave the publicity to me.' He turned to go, but then turned back. 'I was given to understand you were North Norfolk's brightest detective, Peter.' He stepped closer, eyes studying the point where Shaw's tie should have been. 'Maybe, one day, Britain's youngest chief constable.'

Shaw didn't say a word because he hadn't been asked a question. O'Hare seemed to take silence as insubordination. 'Don't fuck up. Don't even think about it.' He turned his back again and walked away, got in the back seat of the Daimler and opened a briefcase. Shaw had a sudden insight into O'Hare's character, because generally he was charming and considerate with his officers, particularly junior ones. But Shaw understood for the first time this bristling antagonism towards him – in private. It was because the chief constable saw DI Peter Shaw as a rival. On the whole, he thought, that was a very bad thing to be.

EIGHT

Chris Roundhay brushed thinning blond hair back from his forehead. He kept himself in good condition, thought Shaw: the tight white polo shirt showing off gym-conditioned chest muscles. His voice was a dull, flat monotone, *Blue Peter*-English, with a weak undercurrent of a Norfolk burr. He'd have been handsome but for an oversized jaw, which made the rest of his face look weak. The interview room was in the basement at St James', well away from the bustle of the Portacabins – windowless, airless, but cool.

George Valentine came back into the room with a tray of three teas and a plate of Nice biscuits: six, canteen-issue, arranged in a neat fan by the woman who he sometimes met out in the car park having a smoke, always still in her green hairnet. It occurred

to him as she'd arranged the biscuits on the plate that if he didn't
smoke he'd have no friends at all.

Chris Roundhay had already told them his story, and it had
been lucid and convincing. He was seventeen years old that day
in 1994. His birthday. His father, a builder, had bought him a
second-hand Suzuki motorbike – 175cc. His mother had got him
a new set of binoculars because he spent so much time out bird
watching. He'd gone to East Hills with a friend – eighteen-year-
old Marc Grieve. Grieve already had his own bike – a Triumph
Bonneville. They had been at school together. Roundhay was an
outsider, not many friends, and Marc was lonely – he'd been in
council care, then adopted, an unhappy child. As thick as thieves,
they'd recognized each other as loners. Marc was a trainee-driving
instructor at Holt that summer; Chris was with a firm of accountants in Lynn. The two of them had been to East Hills before.
They didn't talk on the ferry and went to separate spots on the
beach. Then Chris would take his binoculars and go off into the
pines to spot waders on the far sands. He'd find Marc in a hollow,
where the north wind had carved out a valley in the sand. The
deserted dunes and marshes beyond the thin partition of pine
trees gave them the privacy they wanted. The privacy – said
Roundhay, meeting Shaw's good eye – that they had a right to
enjoy.

But that day, on the trip to the beach, Marc had broken their
routine, sitting beside him on the ferry, telling him that he was
thinking of moving to Norwich to join a driving school run by
a mutual friend. It became clear that this plan had in fact moved
well beyond the 'thinking about' stage. Roundhay had been upset
by the news. By the time they reached East Hills they were hardly
talking. Abandoning their usual routine they'd thrown down their
towels on the far end of the beach and Grieve had gone swimming while Roundhay had sunbathed, listening to the transistor
radio. Radio One. They ate lunch in silence – a brace of Cornish
pasties, Mars bars.

Roundhay said he knew Shane White by sight. He'd chatted
to the lifeguard once or twice. That day he'd wandered up the
beach to the edge of the dunes to strike up a conversation, prin-
cipally to inspire jealousy in Grieve. He'd told the young
Australian it was his birthday but he seemed not to hear. The
lifeguard had two large towels, Roundhay recalled. Valentine had

noted the detail and double-checked the original inventory, finding that they'd found only one towel with the Australian's other things after his death.

Roundhay said they'd talked about the surf on the distant beach across the tidal cut where they could see the summer holiday crowds. White had surfed at Bondi, and he told Roundhay an anecdote about a shark attack which he hadn't believed: a leg washed ashore, parents dragging children out of the white waves. During their conversation White had periodically used his binoculars to scan the beach, talking about the girls. After about ten minutes Roundhay had gone back to Grieve. They'd brought some cans of beer with them and they started to drink. The mood thawed. They swam, larking, then stretched out on their towels. Roundhay had fallen asleep. He'd been woken by the shouts and screams, when someone had found the Australian's floating body. Grieve had been in swimming again and he came out of the water, a thin trace of blood across his skin. They stood, trying to clean it away, Grieve retching.

'These girls he was looking at with the binoculars,' said Shaw, pushing the picture of Marianne Osbourne in her bikini across the table. 'Recognize her?'

'Yeah, maybe.' He frowned, as if something he'd feared would happen had happened.

'He took a special interest in her?' pressed Shaw.

Roundhay looked at each of them, perhaps trying to work out where the questions were leading. He reached inside his back trouser pocket and put a thin wallet on the table, expertly picking out a colour snapshot of a family on a beach – Greece, probably, white houses like sugar lumps on a green hillside beyond a sickle-beach. Two kids, with Roundhay, sat beside a woman in a bikini. She looked older than him, with slightly greying blonde hair, and laughter lines splayed from both eyes.

Shaw thought carefully about what he was going to say next. Early in his career he'd been tempted to cut deals, make promises he couldn't keep. It was almost always unnecessary. Roundhay sensed he was being drawn into the case, that he might end up giving evidence in court. He wanted anonymity, protection, but it was too late for that.

'I can't make any promises,' said Shaw, and he felt Valentine stiffen, leaning back, away from the interview tape. 'If you want a bit of advice instead, I'd recommend telling the truth. It's what you should have done that day in 'ninety-four. This girl . . .' He tapped the picture.

Roundhay readjusted the snapshot so that he could see it clearly.

'We're not interested in what you did,' said Shaw, his voice half an octave lighter. 'We're interested in what you saw.'

Roundhay just stared at the snapshot.

'Chris?' prompted Shaw.

Roundhay said he'd been sitting with White and the lifeguard had just completed a sweep of the beach with the binoculars. He'd put them down and nodded to the far north end of the beach where a girl was lying on a towel. She'd got up right then, adjusting the straps on her bikini top and the edge of the bikini bottoms where the sand had got under the material.

Roundhay said he remembered what White had said. 'Just watch.' Just the two words. So they did. White retrieved a valuables bag from a shallow hiding place in the sand underneath one of his sandals and found a watch. ''Bout now,' he said.

She went for a swim – just a dip in the waves breaking – and then came back and dried herself, still standing. Roundhay said she'd done it very elegantly, as if she enjoyed the touch of the soft material on her skin. Then she'd walked north, towards the point. And Roundhay remembered *how* she'd walked, one foot right in front of the other, the way people walk when they're being watched, like she was on a catwalk. There was an old boat on the beach – just the half-sunken rotten timbers of a dingy – and when she got to it she'd turned to walk up the beach, into the marram grass, and into the shadow of the pine trees.

White had stood, readjusting his swimming trunks, his hand thrust inside the thin material. He'd said it was time he took a walk and pulled on his lifeguard shorts and top, put one of the towels over his shoulder, and set off along the beach.

Roundhay went back to Grieve. Lying down on his stomach, letting his friend rub suntan oil into his back, he'd watched White stroll into the trees. He hadn't seen anyone else. The next time they'd seen White he'd been floating in the sea, in the pink seawater. And that was the truth.

'And he took one of the towels with him?' asked Valentine.

'Yeah.' But Roundhay couldn't meet their eyes, haunted

perhaps by the lies he'd told before. But was he telling the truth now? If he was then the scene he'd described fitted nicely into the scenario they'd constructed for the last day of Shane White's life. The lifeguard was blackmailing Marianne Osbourne; he'd followed her into the dunes to either take more pictures or collect his money, and there he'd met his killer, whose DNA would match the sample on the towel found buried in the dunes.

And if Roundhay was lying? Sitting in the empty interview room, after Roundhay had gone, they agreed it was possible. What if the lifeguard had been blackmailing Roundhay and Grieve, and what if it had been them that he'd followed into the dunes that day? In which case Roundhay's new statement was a calculated package of lies designed to allow him to wriggle out of the forensic evidence. He'd simply claim he'd left his skin cells on the towel when he'd sat on it to talk to White. No jury would convict on the DNA evidence alone.

Valentine felt Roundhay was their man. He'd organize a unit to stick with him till they had the mass screening results. Shaw wasn't convinced. He had no illusions that Roundhay was anything but an accomplished liar. But he suspected that was just the way he'd lived his life. There was something about the scene that Roundhay had painted for them that rang true: the beautiful, self-conscious, sixteen-year-old Marianne Osbourne, alone on the distant beach. And then that catwalk stroll into the pine trees, as if she'd been the bait, and the trap was set.

NINE

C hris Roundhay was the only one of the sixty-six surviving East Hills suspects to opt to change his statement. The last DNA swab was completed just before 3.30 p.m. The East Hills inquiry would be on hold for the weekend, especially as the chief constable's latest round of cost-saving cuts had specifically banned overtime expect in exceptional circumstances and only if personally sanctioned by his office. With O'Hare in London any decision to bankroll overtime would fall to Dep. Chief Constable Don Clarke, a man who'd got to the

top by avoiding mistakes, and avoiding mistakes by rarely making
any decisions at all. Shaw hadn't even considered an application
to keep the inquiry running at full steam.

Shaw and Valentine listened to the throaty roar of the courier's
BMW 1,500cc motorbike as it edged out into the traffic outside
St James' on its way to the forensic laboratory in Birmingham.

'Now we wait,' said Valentine, arching his back over, trying
to squeeze the stress out of his bones, thinking about a cool pint
in the Artichoke. Did it open at five? Then he realized he was
kidding himself. He knew the Artichoke was open at five.

Shaw checked his watch, which showed the time, and the tide.

'One more call, George, then we'll wrap it up. Separate cars.
The funeral parlour where Marianne Osbourne worked
– name?'

'Kelly's – out at Wells.'

'Right,' said Shaw, using the remote to unlock the Porsche.
'Let's find out what she was really like. Once we've got our
name from the lab on Monday we'll need to find a link to her.
So if she had a secret life, we need to know about it.'

Valentine didn't say a word, but he thought it was typical that
their last call was on Shaw's way home. But he made a decision
then that he'd hang around Wells once they'd checked out the
funeral parlour, maybe grab a pint by the quayside, fish and
chips, then look up a few old contacts. After all, it had been his
manor. Plus Shaw had asked him to leak a few details on Marianne
Osbourne's death to the BBC local radio station – he could do
that on the mobile from The Ship. Very pleasant – and all on
expenses to boot.

They made a convoy on the coast road, the Porsche at half
speed, the Mazda's engine heating up under the rusted bonnet.
The sea front at Wells was already Saturday-evening packed; the
funfair's piped-in music at full throttle, both the quayside pubs
spilling customers out on the greasy pavements. Cars looking for
parking spots edged bumper-to-bumper past the crowds. Shaw,
the Porsche's window down, thought that was the authentic tang
of the British seaside – chip fat and exhaust fumes.

The council car park sign was out – FULL – and probably
had been all day, so Shaw edged past and turned up one of the
old streets which led directly inland. The back lanes were a
medieval maze in miniature. He pulled a left, a left and then a

right, into a single carriageway, waiting beyond each turn for the Mazda to appear in his rear-view mirror. As he trundled the car past a row of small lock-up shops he noted Joe Osbourne's locksmiths, a grubby window display showing inscribed pewter tankards, keys and handles. The facia read simply:

KEYS CUT
while you wait
emergency lock-out service
0770 870 1938
Open Monday-Saturday 9.00am to 5.30pm.

Above, over the window, was an old-fashioned hand-painted sign that read:

G.T. & H Osbourne: locksmiths and gunsmiths

Valentine stopped outside the shop and took a note of the number. The shop was shut; a sign turned in the glass doorway gave no indication of when it might reopen. There was a single window above on the first floor, and one above that in the roof, but neither had curtains, and the lower one was obscured by what looked like the back of a cupboard.

The lane gave into a small courtyard. The one-storey building which dominated the space was a shop, with nothing in the large plate-glass windows but two arrangements of white lilies, under a black facia carrying the words:

Kelly & Sons
Funeral Directors and Monumental Masons

Shaw pulled himself easily out of the bucket seat and stood listening to the distant sound of the crowds on the quayside. Valentine parked the Mazda, the offside wing nudging the stonewall.

Inside, they both noticed the cooler air – unnaturally cool. Shaw searched for the sound of an air conditioning unit and discovered the persistent note almost immediately, the vibration making a vase of plastic flowers hum on the counter.

A man who came through a door had white hair framing a

middle-aged face, with an expression of half-hearted condolence already in place. Italian heritage, there was no doubt, the darkness of the features striking against pale olive skin. He hadn't been expecting business, not in the hot dead airless hours of a summer's Saturday, so he was knotting a black tie hurriedly in place.

Valentine put his warrant card in his face. Shaw said they were there about Marianne Osbourne. Had they heard? The man held both palms out sideways, and his eyes flooded, an eloquent if silent answer.

'Mr . . .?' asked Valentine.

'Assisi.' He set his head to one side but didn't offer a first name.

'She worked here?'

'Yes. Poor Marianne,' said Assisi.

'I'm sorry to disturb you,' said Shaw. 'We just needed to check a few facts. You must have known her well.'

Shaw watched as genuine emotions rippled over the man's face, dislodging the professional facade. Grief? No. But certainly sadness, and maybe even loss. Shaw wondered if that was going to be the standard reaction to the death of this woman, as if she was simply a beautiful object that people wouldn't see anymore.

'My wife is best . . .' Assisi flipped up part of the counter and indicated the way, through the door he'd come in by, down a corridor painted institutional pink. Assisi walked in front. 'Always unhappy, Marianne,' he said, over one shoulder.

'Did you take the call yesterday, Mr Assisi, to say she wouldn't be in?' asked Shaw.

Assisi paused with his hand on the next door. 'Yes,' he said, frowning, dark eyebrows drawn together. 'Joe – her husband. She is often not well. But that is the first time he phones . . .'

'Joe's never phoned before?'

'No. Always Marianne. But always too before we open, so a message, on the answerphone. My job is to listen – first thing.' He shrugged slightly, reluctant to articulate any criticism of the dead.

They followed Assisi through the doorway, down a second corridor of peeling lino, through an empty chapel of rest into a small room. Shaw guessed the public, the grieving, never got this far. It was utilitarian, almost industrial, with steel sinks and a tiled floor. The blare from the radio was so loud it was distorted.

There were two metal tables, and two coffins, but only one was occupied, by an elderly woman with unnaturally black hair.

Assisi introduced his wife Ella. She was sitting on a high stool beside the corpse. She was Italian too, but perhaps not first generation, because the genetic photofit, thought Shaw, was clouded with other influences.

'I'm not surprised,' she said, before Shaw could speak. 'It's Marianne, isn't it? We heard. Everyone's heard. But I am sorry,' she added, as if that might be in doubt. 'And poor Tilly . . .' She shook her head, then smiled at Valentine as if she knew him. 'Suicide, of course,' she said.

'We're just tying up loose ends,' said Shaw, avoiding an answer. 'A few questions. A minute of your time.'

She thought about that, her long fingers fidgeting with her hair, and then said she'd have to keep working because the funeral was first thing Monday and they had another one coming in, and that they'd been relying on Marianne.

Her husband looked at his polished black shoes, then fled.

'You'd known Marianne long?' prompted Shaw.

'School – secondary school here in Wells. Met first day.' As she talked she worked, selecting cosmetics from a box and applying them to the skin of the deceased. 'You collect friends that first day, don't you? One you think's funny, one you think's loyal. Marianne was beautiful, so we collected her too. We were in a crowd but, you know, never really close, the two of us. Our lives just got mixed up together. Like bits of washing in a drier.' She was happy with that image, examining the cosmetic red on her fingertips, studying the face of the dead woman who lay before her.

Never close. Shaw noted the echo of Joe Osbourne's description of the relationship between his wife and their daughter.

'Was she close to anyone, other than family?' he asked. 'She doesn't seem to be that kind of person. Private?' he asked, pleased he'd avoided the gaping cliche: *kept herself to herself.*

'I'm not sure she was even close to Joe,' she said. Her chin came up, defying the convention that she shouldn't speak ill of the dead, and unable to stop herself adding more: 'All the years she's worked here you know they never met for lunch – I mean, how far is it? A hundred yards – less?' She shook her head, working some powder into a paste in the palm of her hand. Shaw thought about Joe Osbourne, arguing with a prostitute on Lynn docks after dark. 'She liked men,' she said, and Shaw realized she wasn't being coy. It was just a fact, as if she liked them in the same way that you can like sliced bread. 'And she saw all women as rivals,' added Assisi. 'God knows why.' She drew back some greying hair from her forehead and tucked it under a hair band. 'She was in a league of her own. No competition.'

'There were lots of men?' asked Shaw, leaving the time frame deliberately unspecified, fascinated at how this conversation had suddenly drilled down into the private life of Marianne Osbourne.

Assisi began to work the pale red cosmetics into the skin of the dead woman, working out from the centre of one cheek. 'I don't think so – not now, not for years. She suffered from depression – we understood that. It made her a cold person. Also, I don't think she had the energy for other people. She liked to be admired, but even that seemed . . .' She searched for the word: 'Passive. Like she thought she was an oil painting, which I suppose she was. A vase. Something brittle.' Shaw caught it then in the woman's voice – not just the emotional distance, but a little electric charge of hatred.

Valentine coughed, realizing some kind of chemical was getting down his throat, into his eyes.

Shaw noted that despite the mundane surroundings the presence of the corpse was making his heart beat race. He licked dry lips. 'You'll remember the East Hills killing – the Australian lifeguard. You know Marianne was out on the island that day?'

She leant back from working on the dead woman's face. 'Of course – is that why she did it? We'd heard you were calling people back in – we've got friends on the lifeboat. She wasn't good at dealing with stress. Always pretty close to the edge.'

'I just wondered if she'd ever mentioned it to you. She went out there alone, to East Hills, but we wondered if she'd met someone.'

Assisi laughed, reaching to a shelf for a bottle of mineral water. 'She was *never* alone. Ever.'

'Any names?' asked Valentine, producing his notebook.

She arranged a white linen square below the chin of the corpse and began to apply a foundation, smoothing away wrinkles, adding a lifelike blush to the marbled skin.

'We'd left school by then – both of us. Like I said, we weren't close. Just about any bloke she knew was after her, so that's quite a list.'

Valentine stashed the notebook. 'But there was Joe Osbourne – they were going out that summer, right?'

'There was Joe,' she said.

Shaw got the very strong impression she did know names. 'Mrs Assisi, we need your help. Would it be easier to talk down at St James'?'

Assisi stood and turned off the radio. The dying echo of the last note seemed to circle the cold room.

'There's one thing you have to understand about Marianne,' she said. 'What she wanted, back then, the only thing she wanted, was to have what her big sister Ruth had.'

'Where was Ruth that summer?' asked Shaw.

'Back home. She'd been away to university. But she had a boyfriend in Wells – Aidan Robinson, her husband now.'

'You're telling us Marianne and Aidan were lovers?' asked Shaw.

She nodded – a tight, jerky movement of the chin. 'Early that summer, spring even,' she said, avoiding the direct confirmation. 'When Ruth came back from the university vacation to work at the Lido she didn't know what had gone on. I don't think she's ever known. It would kill her to know.'

'And Joe, did he know? Did he turn a blind eye?' asked Shaw.

'Joe was star-struck,' she said. 'He never guessed what she was like – not until it was too late. I don't think Marianne would have bothered with Joe at all but she got pregnant the next year, 'ninety-five. I think she thought about getting rid of the child; we had a friend who'd had an abortion up at Lynn. I know she asked her about it. But in the end she had Tilly. Know what? Know why she had that child?'

There was something in this woman's eyes that made the cold room colder.

'Because it was something she could have that Ruth didn't have – a child. And then it got better, because it turned out big sister couldn't have kids at all. And it's the one thing Ruth's always wanted.'

Shaw felt oppressed by this image of Marianne Osbourne. As they edged closer to understanding the woman her beauty seemed ever thinner, almost transparent, so that they could see something else beneath, something not exactly ugly, just something darker.

'She was unhappy, Marianne, wasn't she?' asked Shaw. 'What do you think she was unhappy about?'

'Her life. She had dreams – to be a model, to be admired. She thought her face was her fortune. It wasn't.' She'd tried to keep that note of bitterness out of her voice but failed. 'Then Tilly arrived, and that pretty much ended the dream. She hadn't thought that bit through. Women never do. She's not going to be all over Page Three of the tabloids, is she, with a kid at home.'

Valentine rearranged his feet, feeling inexplicably giddy.

'*She* never complains – Ruth. There's nothing Ruth wouldn't do for you. Then there's Marianne next door, with that child. And Joe – smashing bloke. And she walks round like life owed her something.'

Mrs Assisi began to brush the dead woman's hair. 'This is what she really hated. Working here. She used to sneak in and out as if anyone was bothered what she did. Brought a packed lunch so she didn't have to go out and be seen.' She stood, took a step back, to look at her work: 'Mind you, she was good at it.' She began to cry. It was so unexpected Valentine wondered if it was staged. 'It's just the thought,' she said, looking at the corpse lying in its coffin, 'that she'll be here, won't she? One day soon, when you've finished, when the coroner's finished. And then I'll have to do this, for her.'

TEN

They drove up to The Circle beside the field of sunflowers, the heads closing, unruffled by any wind. The incident room stood on the green like a gypsy caravan – next to the St James' mobile canteen, an awning stretched out over a few plastic chairs, a hatch open, light spilling out, one of the St James' canteen staff handing out tea in plastic cups to some of the door-to-door team. *CSI Miami* it wasn't – and Shaw was briefly thankful that they'd kept the lid on publicity. The last thing the new chief constable wanted was his big media national paper splash overshadowed by a picture of his ace detectives clustered around what appeared to be a lay-by greasy spoon.

Inside the caravan unit there was a single interview room, a toilet and an office: three cramped desks, three computers online, with the West Norfolk's logo as screen saver. The temperature had to be eighty degrees Fahrenheit, despite lengthening evening shadows. DC Paul Twine was at one of the desks, in shirtsleeves, a desktop fan almost in his face. Twine was in expensive casuals: Fat Face jeans, open-necked shirt from Next, leather shoes with a light tan, buffed not polished. Twine might be graduate fast-track entry, but he was smart enough to know he was twenty years short of the kind of street nous you needed to be a first-class copper. His strong suit was complex organization, management multitasking. Shaw was aware of his weak suit: that he was desperate to be good at things he wasn't good at.

As Shaw jumped aboard the unit rocked on its springs. 'This isn't perfect, is it Paul? A tin box in August. We need to do something . . .'

DC Fiona Campbell was at one of the other desks, talking into a pair of headphones. She finished the call and stood up – all six foot of her, her neck slightly bent to avoid a collision with the tin roof. 'I've sent details on the cyanide capsule to the Home Office, MoD, Department of Health and Interpol,' she said. 'We might get something. Tom's analysed the rubber casing and reckons we're looking at pre-1960. Maybe even older. And probably not British. You go online you can buy this stuff . . . Mostly former Soviet block – Poland, Belorussia, Baltic states. 1940s – early fifties. As I say – all Soviet manufactured. It's an interesting market.'

'Paul, let's talk outside,' said Shaw. 'We need a decent incident room – not an oven on wheels.' They stood in the shadow of the canteen awning watching two uniformed PCs re-interviewing the elderly man who kept pigeons at No. 2.

Twine gave Shaw a sheet of paper – the top copy, off a wad of twenty or more. 'This is the first return off the door-to-door. We're going back to take statements, but this is a decent summary.'

Shaw took the paper but didn't look at it. 'We've done the obvious?'

'None of the East Hills witnesses lives on The Circle,' said Twine, 'other than our victim. None of them are related to anyone who lives on The Circle, except the victim's husband, sister and daughter. None of them were interviewed in the original investigation.'

Shaw caught Valentine's eye. Leaving the funeral parlour they'd discussed the news that the dead woman's brother-in-law, Aidan Robinson, had been a secret lover back in 1994. If he wasn't on the list of evacuees he could hardly be their killer. But that didn't mean he and Marianne hadn't been blackmailed by Shane White. They needed to talk to Aidan Robinson – and quickly.

'And we've run all the neighbours through the system,' said Twine. 'In fact, all the residents of The Circle. Nothing screams out. Old bloke at No. 4 was done for assault in 1976 – domestic dispute.'

'Prison?' asked Valentine.

Twine speed-read a sheaf of A4 in his hand. 'No. Six months suspended. I've got someone looking out the case notes.' He rearranged the papers. 'Woman at No. 3 was done for reckless driving in 2001. £1,000 fine plus a ban. And the victim's daughter, Teresa, aka Tilly. She was arrested last year in London on the anti-war march.'

'Charged?' asked Shaw, trying to recall the news bulletin pictures of the crowds clashing in Trafalgar Square.

'No. Processed at Bethnal Green, released under caution. No further action. I can get the papers up from the Met?'

'Right little Rosa Luxembourg our Tilly,' said Shaw, shaking his head. But the details were hardly relevant. That was another piece of advice he'd taken to heart from his father: that one of the tricks with a big inquiry was to limit its extent, to take rational decisions, and to resist the temptation to follow every avenue. In the end too many investigations suffocated under their own weight.

'OK, Paul, good work. We're pretty much stymied now until we get the DNA results – that's going to be Monday. There's not a lot we can do for now, and there's no money for overtime, and certainly none for double time on Sunday. But I've got funding for one duty officer, so I'd like you to man the incident room just in case. That suit you?'

'Sure.'

'Any thoughts?'

Twine took a lungful of air and thought about what to say. It was a skill Valentine admired in others because he pretty much said what he thought without hesitation.

'Well, given the blank on the door-to-door its odds on whoever was with Osbourne when she died came in via the woods,' said Twine. 'Tom found some pine needles on the bedroom floor too; it's all in the initial forensics report which is up on the secure website. Each of The Circle's gardens has got a back gate. The woods lead off up into the hills then down to some old estate – there's a tumbledown wall once you get to the boundary. We've had a search team do the first hundred yard apron. There's plenty of paths. Too dry for prints. So if someone came to see the victim from the woods, and left by the woods, they'd just disappear. If you want to take a good look up there Marianne Osbourne's brother-in-law – at No. 6 – is your man.'

'Aidan Robinson?' asked Shaw.

'Yeah. He played here as a kid; he's always lived in the house. Grew up here. Knows every inch of the place – reckons himself as a bit of a countryman. He's at home with the sister now looking after Tilly. Plus, he says he saw someone, someone suspicious, out the back about a fortnight ago. 'Bout noon. He works on a poultry farm up the road but comes home for lunch. Not much of a description: medium height, build. Maybe fair. Says he watched him for ten minutes standing on the edge of the woods, looking down on the houses.'

'Right,' said Shaw. 'First, we need an incident room we can breathe in.'

He led the way fifty yards over the green to the English Heritage ruin. The information board announced:

WARRENER'S LODGE

This twelfth century building is now unique in Britain – the only surviving example of a warrener's lodge. The Romans brought rabbits to England, but it was not until the Normans' organized artificial warrens that they were farmed. This lodge was home to an official appointed by the Cluniac Monastery at Thetford; the first recorded holder of the office was Roger de Lacy in 1176. He would have spent time here, but more probably appointed under-warreners to oversee his livestock. The warrener dug tunnels, often lined with brick or stone, for

the rabbits, fed them in winter, and provided cover in snow by
cutting timber and gorse. Rabbits were valued for their sweet
flesh, especially in winter, and their fur. The lodge has arrow-
slit windows and high walls because bands of poachers, espe-
cially in times of famine, would 'walk the night', often attacking
warreners and their officials in a desperate attempt to feed
themselves and their families. Some estates kept warreners into
the 1950s. But the popularity of rabbit as food fell, largely due
to their enforced inclusion in diets during the war, and the
terrible scourge of myxomatosis, a disease introduced to reduce
rabbit populations. Originally the lodge would have stood on
a wide downland, dominating the landscape and providing
visual confirmation that this was the lord's property.

A metal sign hung on the kissing-gate, saying, simply: ENTRY
FREE.

Shaw went in, through the overgrown plot and then under the
arch, and Valentine and Twine followed. They stood together,
looking up at tiny patches of purple-blue sky, seen through the
branches of the cedar. Twine stopped at the door, examining the
intricate stone-carved lintel. The air was deliciously cool, the heat
kept back by the three-foot-wide stone walls and the multiple
layered roofs provided by the cedar. It was a stone larder.

Shaw walked to what was left of a staircase and climbed three
steps to touch a metal grill which barred the way up. He turned
on the step and surveyed the interior of the lodge. The grass had
been recently cut so the space was neat, contained, in deep
shadow. 'This'll do us,' he said. 'Paul, ring St James' – we just
need to run the mobile unit to the gate, then a cable in for the
computers and the kettle. We can't work in that sauna. Drag
the desks and chairs in. OK, let's jump to it.'

DC Campbell appeared at the Norman archway. 'Sir. Tom's
up at the house – he's ready to let the team go. Wants a word
first – just routine. Nothing spectacular.' She thought about that,
anxious to make clear that she hadn't made the judgement. 'His
words,' she added.

'I'm on my way,' said Shaw. 'And Fiona, can you pop into
the sister's house? I need to speak to the husband, Aidan
Robinson.' Shaw checked his watch. 'I'll be with him in half an
hour. Fix it, please.'

Shaw checked dispositions with Twine: the team could knock off, back on site at six thirty Monday. In the meantime everyone was on call. Shaw would get any news from the lab via Tom Hadden. They'd have Chris Roundhay's result first, probably within twenty-four hours. If it was positive then they'd have to call everyone into St James' for a briefing; pick up Roundhay, get him charged – maybe a holding count, not murder. But Shaw said he thought that was a long shot. He thought Roundhay had told the truth. If the result on Roundhay was negative they'd wait for the full mass screening report, which would probably land Monday morning. Any earlier Shaw would contact Twine, then they'd work out the next move.

Valentine watched his superior officer walk away towards the victim's house. Apparently, Valentine had been dismissed too – just another part of the team. He had a grudging admiration for Shaw's abilities as a copper, but he thought now, and not for the first time, that a quick booster module in man management wouldn't be a total waste of time. He was as keen to know what Tom Hadden had to say as Shaw was, and as the unit's lynchpin DS it would have been pretty efficient for him to be included in the briefing. Besides, he was reluctant to face the rest of the weekend alone. He enjoyed his own company, but only by choice.

Shaw found Hadden in Marianne Osbourne's bedroom. With the body gone the room had lost its tension. It was like a room in a museum, thought Shaw. English interiors: 1970–2000. Again Shaw was struck by the innate sadness of the house, especially this room. Perhaps, he thought, it was the view that did it: the distant sunflowers, their faces closed now, the pine woods, dark and still. All that beauty, and freedom, outside, but the windows painted shut. 'Are all the windows stuck shut?' he asked, fighting the urge to walk over and force the frame.

'Yeah. She had hay fever, allergies. Husband says that's how she dealt with it. Wouldn't have worked, but there you are. We're all creatures of habit.' Hadden had fled London and a career at the Home Office to escape a messy failed marriage. He had a capacity to forgive the faults of others.

'Did she have a desk anywhere?' asked Shaw. Hadden was on his knees, lifting fibres from the carpet.

'Dressing table doubled-up. We're running through the

computer memory now down at The Ark. Fiona's given us some keyword targets to track on the cyanide but there's nothing yet. And we've done the obvious,' he added.

'And?' asked Shaw, letting his eye roll quickly over the empty bed, stripped down to the mattress.

'Nothing yet. We've collected emails off the East Hills survivors as they came through the Ark – work, home, the lot. No matches with anything on her hard drive or in her email account. Most of the traffic is with a mail-order cosmetics company in Lincoln.'

'Fingerprints?'

Hadden sat back on his haunches. He closed his eyes – a tic – which indicated he was thinking carefully about the reply. 'Family mostly – a few we can't identify but we're still on to the daughter's friends. She's next door by the way with the aunt – dad went to work this morning, slept all afternoon.'

'*Work?*'

'That's how it takes some people, Peter. He'll probably carry on for a month, a year, even two. Then one day he'll wake up and he won't know how to tie his laces up. Then he'll find himself sitting on the beach, but he won't remember how he got there. Then he'll fall to pieces. Doesn't mean he's a hard bastard, or that he didn't love her.'

It was quite a speech, the longest he'd ever heard from Tom Hadden.

Shaw thought about the locked-up locksmiths shop in Wells. When they'd driven past it didn't look like the dust had been disturbed for a week, let alone a few hours. If he hadn't gone to work, where had he gone?

'On the kiss, by the way,' said Hadden. 'I couldn't get any material out of the moisture left on the glass. So no chance of a DNA profile. But, for what it's worth, I'd say we're looking at a man's lips. Adult. Height – if he didn't bend down, or stand on tiptoe – somewhere between five nine and six foot.'

They walked back out into the evening air, Hadden carrying a cardboard box of files and papers. He put it down on the low front wall. 'This was on the floor behind the dressing table.' The CSI man pulled out a manila A4 folder marked: EXAMS. Inside were random certificates: GCSEs, a diploma awarded by Avon for a course on cosmetic science, registration forms for her work at the funeral parlour, an application form – untouched – for a residential course on skin care. Shaw put the file back and picked out another marked CV. With the documents and newspaper cuttings was a plastic see-through holder with a DVD inside marked SHOOTS.

'Show time,' said Shaw.

Twine already had a desk in the Warrener's Lodge, a laptop working on battery. The rest of the team had gone – all except Valentine, who was inputting the team's mobile numbers to his own phone. Shaw gave Twine the DVD to fire up, while he flicked through the newspaper cuttings in Osbourne's CV. Most were local – a couple from advertising free sheets with adverts ringed in lipstick. One was for kitchen units and he recognized Marianne Osbourne poised expertly, one hand caressing a fake-marble work surface. There was one shot from a national newspaper – *The Mirror*, 1995, just six months after the East Hills killing: Marianne Osbourne, in a bikini, lying down, propped up on one elbow, a miniature chocolate car in her hand, held towards the camera. The story said one of the big Japanese car makers had got Cadbury's to make replicas of their forthcoming four-by-four to send out to garages as a publicity stunt.

The caption read: 'Two new models: curvy Marianne Pritchard, eighteen, test drives the tastiest new car on the road.'

'Lied about her age,' said Shaw, passing the cutting to Twine.

The DVD flickered into life on the laptop showing the feature-less white contours of a photographer's studio.

'Alright sweetheart,' said a voice off-camera.

Valentine stood, his backbone creaking, and came over to the screen to stand beside Shaw.

Marianne Osbourne walked into the shot, turned, and looked back at the camera. Shaw guessed the stills camera was set next to the video. Her face was extraordinarily blank. Her arms were held awkwardly, her bare feet slightly pigeon-toed, and she looked – maybe – eighteen. Still holding the camera's eye she slipped the bikini top off, revealing small breasts, but no variation in her lightly tanned skin.

'No, no, kid.' A laugh, slightly furred by age or nicotine. 'Keep your kit on.'

As she fumbled with the strap they heard the voice, but a whisper this time: 'Jesus.'

The photographer came into shot – middle-aged, pepper-and-salt hair, avuncular. He arranged Marianne lying down, in the pose Shaw had seen in *The Mirror*. Then he produced a box of the chocolate cars and set them in a line, beginning at her foot, up the narrow leg, over the very slight bulge of the hip, then up an arm to end at the shoulder, which she tucked under her chin.

Alone in the shot, Marianne spoke for the first time. 'Tell me.'

'Tell you what, darling?'

'When you're taking a shot.'

The blank face stared into the lens.

'Alright, here we go.' They heard the whirr of a camera taking multiple shots.

Marianne's face was transformed. The chin dropped, the eyes looked up, the body tightened slightly so that the skin seemed to attain a sudden surface tension. Then the smile, a hint at first in the eyes, then breaking the lips apart to reveal the small, white, perfect teeth.

'There ya go,' said the voice, genuine now, excited.

And then the smile opened, like an orchid in time-lapse photography: a full hundred-watt transmission of what looked like joy.

The photographer came into shot, on his knees, his upper body swinging from left to right as he took his pictures. He got close, and Marianne didn't register the intrusion into her personal space, just kept the smile tracking the lens. He gave her one of the chocolate cars and she opened her mouth, holding the fragile carapace of the model between her teeth, giggling, then crunching down so that a crumb or two of chocolate fell on her chin and she had to use a finger to push them back between her lips.

The photographer leant back on his haunches, still on his knees, laughing too.

'Right – some black and whites next. Alright?'

He'd turned away before she answered, clipping a lens cap over his camera, otherwise he would have seen the smile leave her face, falling away like a mask.

ELEVEN

'Right here?' asked Shaw, standing in the deep, cool shadow of the edge of the pinewood above The Circle. The field of sunflowers was in gloom, the heads closed now for the night. Below them they could see lights in the Warrener's Lodge, and spilling from the mobile incident room. Evening noises rose up gently – a radio, a chip pan, a swing creaking. In the Robinsons' back garden – next to Marianne's – chickens gossiped, unsettled. The run took up most of the space between the house and the open ground that led to the woods – all, in fact, except for a large woodpile.

Aidan Robinson stood beside him in the shadows, looking down on his house. Even in the half-light it was impossible to ignore his huge hands which hung at his sides, like weapons.

'Yes. Right here, or close. I was down by the back door so he was a way off, but yes. It looked like he was looking at us, but now, now I think, it could have been the back of Joe's he was watching – their bedroom.'

Shaw could just see the bedroom window behind which Marianne Osbourne had died, a flash of silver, reflecting a ribbon of red sky. Aidan Robinson had seen the stranger, a rare sight on The Circle, on the Wednesday afternoon at about twelve fifteen – it had to be then, because he'd been doing a long shift at the poultry farm and he always took lunch at noon and it was only five minutes away by car. 'I need the break,' he said. 'I'm inside all day.' There was something understated about that description which made it sound, to Shaw, like hell. The noise, the heat, the *smell*. And no glimpse of the sky.

Shaw walked to the precise spot Robinson had indicated and looked down. He was trying to draw out the moment because he wanted the witness to relive what he'd seen, just in case there was a detail buried in his memory. All they had was a crude outline: a man, possibly fair hair, stood still, then retreating into the wood after two or three minutes. Really? Shaw had pressed him on that point. Did he mean he'd stood still for two or three minutes? Because that's a very rare thing – to be still. But Aidan Robinson was sure, and even in the few moments he'd been talking to him Shaw could see that this man knew more than enough about stillness. He wondered if he'd learnt the skill: fly-fishing, perhaps, or poaching in the woods, or standing watching the sky with a shotgun broken over his arm. He didn't think it was a quality you'd pick up in a battery farm.

'So, just a figure?' asked Shaw.

The technique required to bring a memory alive had been a key skill Shaw had learnt as part of his forensic art studies, because getting witnesses to remember faces was a subtle, even fragile, thing. Memory recall was not a linear, absolute, process but rather piecemeal, flashes illuminating lost fragments which could be retrieved, then reassembled.

'A man,' said Robinson, stepping out of the shadows so that the last of the day's light lit his face. 'Sturdy.' He shook his head, looking about, embarrassed. 'That's it. Sorry.'

'That's OK,' said Shaw. And it was, because Robinson had already added to the picture he'd given with the word 'sturdy'. If Shaw took it gently he might recall more.

Robinson shifted from his right boot, to his left, and back again. As they'd climbed the hill Shaw had noticed the lameness in his right leg, the foot seemed to hang from the right ankle, as if broken. He was broad, an agricultural frame, heavy and powerful, so that it was easy to underestimate his height, which had to be six-one or two. When he walked the injured leg made his shoulders rock from side to side, like a human pendulum. His face was wind-tanned; his hair brown without a trace of grey, but it was the eyes which held a surprise – a shade of grey that suggested silver, unnaturally light.

'And you were down there?' asked Shaw.

They both glanced at the Robinsons' back garden a hundred foot below them. Up by the kitchen door, beyond the chicken run, they could see Ruth, sat at a picnic table with Tilly. They had their arms around each other and in front of them a candle flickered in a glass cylinder, growing brighter as the day died around them.

'Yeah. And he was up here. That's what was odd. I just watched, thinking he'd move on.'

'Do you think he saw you?'

'Doubt it. Like I said, I was down by the back door. Ruth brings a paper home if she's up at the lido in the morning and it was stifling indoors, so I got the kitchen chair out, but right on the hardstanding, in the shadows.'

'Definitely a man?' repeated Shaw.

'Sure,' said Robinson, but he didn't sound it.

'Fair?'

Those oddly colourless eyes focused on the mid-distance. 'Like I said, maybe.'

The heat of the day was flooding out into the sky but there was no wind here, in the lee of the hill. Shaw didn't like the sound of the 'maybe' – suddenly they were going backwards, losing the memory.

'Did Ruth see him?'

'Yeah. I told her, and she glanced up the hill. But she was busy in the kitchen so she saw less than I did.'

Shaw changed tack. 'And then he took a path?'

Robinson nodded, but seemed reluctant to enter the woods. He looked down at his wife, comforting his niece. 'They've always been good together,' he said. As they watched, Ruth Robinson lit a second candle lantern, embracing Tilly. She drew a cork from a bottle and they heard the pop a second later.

'Where's Joe?' asked Shaw, not to get an answer, but to make the point that he wasn't there, below, with his daughter.

'Asleep on our couch. We'll wake him later, for food. He needs to eat. He doesn't want to go home.'

Shaw wondered what Aidan Robinson had done with his memory of the summer of 1994. The time he'd spent with Marianne Osbourne as her secret lover. Perhaps he'd locked that image away, so that he could get on with the rest of his life. How else could he have lived here – a single course of bricks between his own bed and Marianne's? How had he lived with that memory, lying next to her sister Ruth?

Robinson didn't say another word until he'd led Shaw deep into the woods, perhaps a quarter of a mile, up towards the crest of the hill. He hadn't asked to go this far and so Shaw wondered if Robinson was buying time. Despite the gathering dusk Shaw didn't rush, negotiating the half-light as well as his single eye would allow. One of the unexpected repercussions of losing his eye had been the loss of light due to the 'shadow' cast by the

nose on the one remaining eye – as if a screen hung to his right.
And not just light. One eye left him with ten to fifteen per cent
less peripheral vision. So he took his time, one hand raised
constantly to ward off any stray branches on his sighted side.
Losing his good eye in another freak accident would be a disaster
which would pretty clearly end his career. He'd had to sit a series
of medical boards to stay on active duty, even now, after the first
accident.

They made their way over the brow of the hill and then reached
the tumbledown wall DC Twine had mentioned – the edge of
the large estate which ran south from Creake. It was the kind of
wall nobody could afford to build any more: four bricks deep,
fired locally, with a stone coping. But it had not been repaired
for years, and at regular intervals had been breached. Beyond it
the trees opened out into a clearing, at the centre of which stood
a tree without bark, blanched, but scarred down one side with a
black charcoal seam. It was leafless, architectural; a fossil tree.
Around the tree were a series of stumps.

'You think he came here?' asked Shaw.

Robinson sat on one of the stumps. Then he put his hands
together and, using his left, pulled the index finger on the right,
producing a crack of cartilage: a sickening noise, and a habit
Shaw loathed. And with Robinson it conjured up an image: the
same hands, pulling a neck straight on a chicken at the poultry
farm.

'Little choice.' His voice was gentle, like most of his movements. Gentle giant was a cliché but, thought Shaw, that didn't
mean it couldn't be true. 'You'd end up here whatever – the paths
all take you down to the old house.' He rolled a cigarette with
one hand and pointed north. 'That way you'd be able to walk
for about 300 yards, but then you'd hit the security fence at
Docking Hill – the wind farm?'

Shaw nodded, unfolding an OS map, trying to orientate it to
unseen compass points.

Robinson lit the cigarette he'd fashioned, squinting as it flared.
He didn't say anything more and was clearly unembarrassed by
silence. Lifting his right leg he adjusted the angle of the damaged
foot and then set it back on the ground. The silver-grey eyes
seemed to help suck what light was left out of the air. 'I don't
come up here – not anymore,' he said, and there was a sudden

note of bitterness in his voice. 'Not for years. But you get poachers
– we hear the guns at night. And kids from the village.' Robinson
pointed into the edge of the trees where a rope swing hung.

Shaw looked around, thinking of his own childhood, played
out in a block of flats in North London. 'Great place to play.'

'I came up here with dad and granddad. We always had guns
– we'd take rabbit, a few pheasant, set traps. Even then there
were outsiders – professional poachers. They'd come for the
venison on Old Hall. These days you'd get fifty quid for a carcass
– if you can drag 600lb out of the woods without being seen.
They come over from the Midlands – a white van – bag a few
and then go. High velocity rifles – night sights. Old days it was
all traps. That's how I did this . . .' He jerked up his trouser leg
to reveal the calf, lacerated by an old circular wound, triangular
teeth scars cut deep into the muscle. Shaw winced at the thought
of the trap shutting, the bone shattering, the energy in the springs
enough to bring down a stag.

'Here?' Shaw asked, almost in a whisper.

'Blickling – the big wood.' Shaw knew the spot, acres of estate
around a fine Jacobean house. 'We went everywhere, me and
dad that was – granddad was dead. Gun went off when the trap
sprang – I nearly blew dad's head off.' He laughed, but his eyes
didn't join in.

'When was that?'

'November 'ninety-three.' Shaw looked at Robinson; the grey
eyes seemed colder, like ice on the river. So the accident had
happened while Ruth was away at university for her first year, and
before East Hills and the year of his affair with Marianne. Shaw
thought that for him, and for Marianne, the year had been a fulcrum:
one of those points in your life when the number of possible futures
suddenly narrows, as if the path ahead has been chosen.

'Look,' said Shaw, deciding that there would be no better time
to talk about the past. 'This is painful – and it's private. But I
want to ask you about your relationship with Marianne, the year
after the accident –1994.'

Robinson's backwoods colour drained from his face. He half
stood, but had to sit again, and Shaw guessed that his knees had
given way because he almost fell back.

'What do you mean?' he asked, trying to sound aggressive,
aggrieved, but the words came out in a whisper. And those

penetrating eyes didn't meet Shaw's but scanned the edge of the woods, as if the primeval urge to escape threatened to overwhelm his self-control.

'I understand this is something you don't want to talk about,' said Shaw. 'And it's certainly something the police don't wish to make public unless it is absolutely necessary. But I do need to know about Marianne that summer: who she was with, who she was seeing. She saw you?'

The light in the clearing was failing fast, and Shaw knew that soon the moment would come when his good eye shifted to night vision, giving up the effort of seeing the world in colour, and switching to black and white. In the gloom he watched Robinson struggling with the consequences of telling the truth – or, possibly, with the benefits of a lie.

'I think there were plenty of us,' he said. Was that how he'd dealt with it over the years? That he was one of many? A random indiscretion, not a betrayal.

'Ruth came down after the accident,' he said. 'I was up at the Queen Vic – they tried to reattach the tendons in the ankle. Then I had physio – three times a day, every day. I wasn't . . .' He struggled to find the word that would take him forward: 'Recovering. I knew it was over. I'd had this dream, to be like granddad – a countryman. Dad had worked on the land too, farming. But granddad was the real thing. This was his land, just as much as if he'd owned it. He knew every leaf, every rabbit hole. I thought maybe I'd work for one of the big estates or run a small holding, take some game.'

He lifted his leg, repositioned the foot, and set it back on the leaf litter. 'Ruth said I needed to rethink my life. Find another goal. She was a bit distant – different too. We spent Christmas together but she'd sort of changed, I suppose, and I didn't think she'd come back again – not for me anyway. I thought it was over.'

He locked eyes and Shaw decided that this was another excuse: that he'd been sure she would dump him, so he had a right to play the field.

'Ruth's Dad knew this farmer who'd gone into chicken farming. So I went there. I sit down most of the day at one machine or another. Government's got quotas for people like me so the firm gets help with the wages. I've been there nearly twenty years.'

He shook his head as if his life had been sand, falling through his thick fingers.

'Marianne came to see me at home one Friday night,' he said. 'May – end of May. She said she'd had a letter from Ruth, that she loved being a student, that she'd like to teach, maybe stay up north. She was upset, she said, because it meant she wouldn't see much of her anymore. Didn't mention me.

'We went for a drink down at Wells. Then she said she wanted to swim – she was a bit drunk, a bit out of her head. There was a moon so we walked along the sea wall out to the beach. I couldn't swim – never could swim – and after the accident it was impossible. I'm a dead weight. But I'd go in the water with Ruth – Marianne knew that. I'd go out as far as I could. The tide was in, filling the pool.'

Shaw knew the spot, at that precise time, under moonlight. The tide washes in round an island of dunes and forms a lagoon. Just five feet deep, sheltered, a giant mirror of unruffled silver.

'We dumped our clothes in the trees and ran in. When I looked around she wasn't in the water, she was back on the shoreline, naked, just waiting. So I went back.'

He lit another cigarette and suddenly Shaw knew it was almost dark, the flare of red and orange shockingly bright.

'She was sorry for me,' he said.

'How long did it go on?'

'Until early summer. Just a few weeks, really. Then Ruth came back. Nothing had changed – it was my Ruth. She wanted to be with me, here. She said she'd teach in Wells, maybe Lynn. We could live here on The Circle, the house I've always lived in. Start a family. We got married in 'ninety-five. Mum was still with us then but she died in 'ninety-eight so we had the place to ourselves. Six months later Marianne and Joe hitched up and Ruth said why don't they come out here? The house next door was up for sale and it was too good a chance to miss. Marianne and I never talked about what had happened. It was like it hadn't happened.' He thought about that. 'Hadn't happened to us.' He stood, a dark figure now. 'Ruth doesn't know, or Joe. It would kill Ruth.' There was an edge of belligerence in Robinson's voice, so it almost sounded like a threat.

'I can see that,' said Shaw. He felt like a priest in confession. 'There's no reason they should know – ever. I'm interested in who killed Shane White on East Hills. I'm sure Marianne met someone on the island that day. Do you know who it was? Maybe White? He'd been taking pictures of lovers that summer, along the coast. Had he taken a picture of you and Marianne?'

'No way. We met here, in the woods,' he said. 'Never again on the beach. Everyone knew us on the beach.' And again, the left hand pulled the index finger on the right, this time followed by the right hand pulling the left – a double, plastic click.

'So you didn't ask someone to help Marianne out that day, provide a bit of muscle, bit of support, frighten the Aussie off?'

'No way.'

A cloud of rooks swung in the air, then dropped into the trees.

'How far's the fence to the wind farm?' asked Shaw.

By way of answer Robinson set out to the edge of the clearing, then down a path, still clear and visible despite the dusk. The fence, when they reached it, was nearly eight foot high, steel and wire, with an angled top ridged with razor wire. There was a gate, in iron and mesh, with a keypad padlock.

'Tilly's one of the demonstrators, up by the gates?' asked Shaw, rattling the padlock.

Robinson thought about an answer. 'Right. She told us. She does press releases, that kind of thing, because it's something she believes in. She didn't tell Joe or Marianne. There's been scuffles, stuff thrown, and Tilly's got a temper. She thought they'd worry.'

Shaw thought about the demo in London. Clearly, Tilly too had a secret life.

'But she is serious about the issue – me too,' said Robinson. 'People think it's gonna be a few big turbines but it isn't like that. To meet the targets they'll need hundreds. All through these hills. Granddad's hills.'

They turned back, retracing their steps, the path only just visible now, a pale, sinuous, line ahead. 'I've been up to the demo,' said Robinson, stopping, massaging the lame leg. 'I can hold a placard with the best of 'em. And they're right. It's all big business – out for a buck. This one's owned by Yanks. Fencing cuts off the footpath but the council doesn't seem to mind. Ask me they've been given a backhander. I'm proud of Tilly for standing up to 'em.'

They took a fresh path downhill. Shaw found that he had to

slow his pace as they descended, and that he could hear the slight rustle of Robinson's lame foot dragging in the loose forest litter behind him. Just as they left the cool shadow of the trees Shaw stopped abruptly. He'd chosen the spot deliberately so that Robinson would have to come close, because the path here was edged with thorns. He tried to pin him down by looking in his eyes. 'Do you think Joe could have helped Marianne kill herself?' It was one of the scenarios which had been worrying him. That the killer of Shane White wasn't at Marianne Osbourne's deathbed. That Joe had taken pity on her, and helped her end it all before she faced the ordeal of the being cross-examined about the East Hills murder.

He'd prepared the question and waited patiently for the answer. In the garden below they heard laughter and saw that Ruth and Tilly were now surrounded by candlelight. And Joe was there, beside his daughter, oddly diminished, as if he was a younger child, a little brother, perhaps.

'I think he wanted to,' said Robinson. He took a breath. 'I think he found it tough, seeing her suffer like she did.' He looked Shaw in his blind eye. 'They loved each other once,' he said, elegantly implying that they hadn't by the time she'd died. 'But no. I don't think he could have helped her.'

'Someone did,' said Shaw.

Robinson's jaw set: 'When they do it with horses – put them down for their own good – they say they *destroy* them,' said Robinson. 'It's a good word because it makes you realize that's what they're doing – that something beautiful is gone for ever.'

They heard a barn owl hoot, and then, astonishingly, it was there, gliding over the grass, luminescent.

'I've remembered something,' said Robinson. He took half a dozen steps out into the open grassland. 'The man – the one I saw here? It's been in my head that I did recognize him – not him, but a . . .' He searched for the word: 'A type.' Again, the shift from right foot to left and back again, nodding to himself in self-encouragement. 'I thought, at the time, there's something *military* about him. And when he did move it was unhurried, powerful too – a stride. I didn't say anything because it sounded daft. But there had to be something else. His hair was short, but not like trendy short, and not a skinhead like the squaddies. Officers' hair.' He laughed. 'But the thing I can see now is he was wearing one of those jumpers: green wool, with leather shoulder patches. They always wear them – it's a sort of off-duty uniform. So maybe army?' He looked down at The Circle. 'It's not much,' he added, but Shaw was already texting Twine on his mobile.

TWELVE

Valentine left the Mazda on double yellow lines on the quayside at Wells, a West Norfolk Police pass propped up behind the steering wheel. The bar of The Ship was empty, all the customers out on the quayside or in the whitewashed backyard, enjoying the coolness of the night now the sun had set. He got himself a pint from a silent barman and shoved the change in a RNLI charity box, helping himself to a sticker which he put on his lapel. Then he walked out on to the quayside, a spring tide almost level with the stone blocks of the wharf. High water brought a strange mood over the town, as if the sea was brimming up and might spill over the edge of the land, filling the narrow streets. Valentine sat on the wharf with his back to a low wall, watching the lights come on in the yachts out in the harbour. It was hypnotic, the way the dusk was thickening, as if the air itself was getting heavier. His eyelids drooped.

Waking from sleep a minute later, or a nanosecond, it seemed darker. He was surprised, and always was, by the sudden vibrancy of the colours – like those on the cover of a jigsaw box. The town's only amusement arcade blazed out into the night: reds, oranges and yellows. The floating pub on the quayside was festooned with white bulbs, the pale purple sky beyond crisscrossed by contrails. In his ten long years of exile out here on the coast this had been his salvation: the evening light, a feeling of peace and a brief glimpse of a life seen in proportion.

The rest of his time in Wells had been a kind of perfect torture. He'd hated the pettiness of small town life, the profound feeling that he'd been banished to the edge of the real world, and that back at St James' coppers with half his ability were dutifully sitting their DI exams. He'd hated walking into a pub and knowing everyone, and knowing they knew him just as well. And he'd walked into plenty of pubs.

He checked his mobile, rereading a text Shaw had sent DC Twine, with a copy forwarded to him FYI. The dead woman's brother-in-law, Aidan Robinson, had recalled a detail about the stranger he'd seen behind Marianne Osbourne's house ten days before she died. A useful snippet; the man he'd seen might have a military connection, as he thought he was wearing a green combat jumper with leather shoulder pads. Twine was to liaise with the Red Caps at Boddington Camp, an army transport depot along the coast near Sherringham, and see if they had anyone reported AWOL or acting suspiciously – such as a last-minute unscheduled demand for leave. Then Twine needed to check the mass screening records and see if any of the men at East Hills on the day of the murder were in the military, or ex-military, or Territorial Army. Priority. So that was Paul Twine's Sunday sorted. Valentine knew why Shaw wanted quick results. If the mystery man was military it gave them a possible source for the cyanide capsule. And something else: an expertise in the art of killing.

Valentine took an inch off his pint and didn't jump when someone touched him on the shoulder: a woman, leaning over the low wall, already very close, in white fish-and-chip shop overalls, a scrunched up hairnet in one hand.

'Georgie,' she said. 'Long time.' She laughed once, a single note, like one of the birds calling on the marshes.

It had been. Three years. The day he'd left Wells to go back to force headquarters at Lynn. The little staff canteen at the local nick had been packed, which was something he'd never understood. He'd been unhappy at Wells – despite what he felt today, he'd been beached, like one of the rotting boats in the marsh creeks. But he'd been popular, and he couldn't even now guess why.

He put his pint down and then realized he didn't know what to do with his hand. She'd stepped easily over the wall but had turned away, sensing the awkwardness of the moment. Straightening his back against the concrete he didn't get up, knowing the stoop he'd developed made him look older than he was.

'Jan,' he said. 'God,' he added, shaking his head.

She was late-forties, early fifties, slim, with short hair which he remembered as dark but was now blonde. She was one of those people whose hair always seems to fall right: the fringe carelessly jagged, but framing the pronounced arc of dark eyebrows. Despite the shapeless overalls he could see her narrow waist, biro marks on the white breast of her top where she'd missed the pocket. She adjusted the length of a trouser leg by pulling at the material at the knee, and then sat down.

'I'm sorry . . .' he said, holding out the hand now, palm down, by way of apology.

She shook her head quickly so that he wouldn't go on. She'd been married to DS Peter Clay, Valentine's partner at Wells for most of his years in the town. Clay had been born in Wells, the son of a boatyard owner who'd gone bankrupt in the fifties. DS Clay had died the year before. Bowel cancer? Maybe. They'd sent flowers from Lynn but he hadn't signed the card.

'We're OK,' she said, and Valentine struggled to remember the details. Two daughters, he thought, grown up and married. 'I do this afternoons and early evenings,' she said, tugging at the white chef's overall. 'Sit it out at the museum in the mornings at the front desk. Pin money, but it all helps. And there's a pension from the job.'

The Job. To insiders, always The Job.

Valentine knew the little museum, up an alley off the High Street, half a dozen rooms crammed with smugglers' memorabilia, old photos and a gallery full of naval paintings including one, in pride of place, of Nelson up at Burnham Thorpe, a painted ship behind him, upon a painted ocean.

She nodded at his pint, took no answer for yes, and went into The Ship. He followed, hauling himself up when she was gone, then watched a silent TV in the bar as she ordered, a televised press conference from Norwich about a missing child. But he wasn't concentrating. He was thinking about the first time he'd met Jan. He'd got a flat in town above a charity shop and he was looking for a cleaner – someone to do some washing too, iron a few shirts. His partner Pete Clay said his wife would do it. Ten quid a week, every Tuesday. He'd never met her – she had a key – then he'd gone home one morning because he'd left a case file by the telly. She'd been there, ironing by the radio. That was a summer's day too, and she'd been in shorts and a T-shirt. It was the first time he'd thought to himself how much she must know about him – being in his space, reading detail into the discarded books, the empty bottles, the Christmas cards taking up too little space on the mantelpiece.

'I could have got that,' he said, taking the fresh pint.

The barman waved away the crumpled fiver she'd put on the bar top. Back outside they sat together on the top of the wall, like children, kicking their heels.

Valentine recalled that DS Clay had been teetotal, just one of the reasons they'd never been an effective partnership. At least Shaw would take a Guinness: rarely more than one, but it was the one that counted, because you can't trust anyone who doesn't drink, because they can't trust *themselves.* Valentine was honest enough to admit that was what all alcoholics said, although he didn't think of himself as an alcoholic. A toper, at worse.

'Break?' he asked.

'Twenty minutes. It's like World War Three in the bathroom in there. Enough to put you off fish and chips for life.' She sipped at her cider steadily, like it was doing her some good. Her foot tapped to an imaginary beat.

A tourist boat was unloading at the quayside. Her name was *Christine* and according to the chalkboard she'd been out to Blakeney Point to see seals and then on to Morston. Twelve pounds for the round trip, five pounds for kids. Little yellow tickets littered the deck as the passengers got out.

Jan looked at Valentine's profile – the hatchet, facing out to sea. 'Pete said they cleared your name, that they'd have to give you the rank back.'

He turned to look at her. 'That's what I thought.'

'Still on the cornflakes diet?' she asked, looking out to sea.

She'd have seen the evidence in the flat. A catering-sized box of Kellogg's, milk delivered to the door on the street, and nothing else in the fridge.

'Six white shirts,' she said.

Christine's engine burst into life, the skipper getting ready to take her out and moor her to one of the buoys.

'Nice little earner,' said Valentine, nodding at the boat.

'Needs to be. Day after August Bank Holiday this place is deserted. Got to make it while you can . . .'

One of the many things which had infuriated him about living in Wells was that, like any small seaside town, there was a kind of low-level conspiracy against visitors. The locals formed an invisible network dedicated to extracting every last pound from anyone who stepped out of a car, got off a bus, or trekked in along the coastal path. Short of charging admission they made sure every day-tripper paid their way. There was an almost religious feel to this collective attitude to strangers to which he'd always been immune. He was always an outsider, he felt, wherever he lived.

'The boat that goes out to East Hills?' he asked.

She looked down at her feet, her head hung, as if suddenly disappointed.

'We're on the case again,' he admitted.

'I know.' She hugged herself. 'Charmers' boat, along there . . .' She nodded east to an empty berth. An A-board was up, not in chalk, but sign-written . . .

VISIT SUNSHINE ISLAND
Outward bound: 10.45
Return: 5.30
Tickets: £15 adults. £7.50 children.
Remember: there are no facilities on the island. So travel prepared!

'Always has been Charmers' boat.' She thought for a second. 'The *Arandora Star*. The only thing that's changed is the name of the island. After the murder, the publicity, they dropped East Hills. Looked a bit sick last year, mind you, Sunshine Island – we had a monsoon in August.'

'Same boat?' he asked.

'No, new. Couple of years now. That's the old one . . .' She pointed across the channel to the marsh where a wide inshore clinker-built boat lay half sunk in the mud. It had a single stand-up cabin for the skipper and a central engine cowling, the twin flaps broken off to reveal a rusted fuel tank.

Valentine tried to imagine it chugging into the beach at East Hills that afternoon in 1994. A slick of arterial blood still mixing with the salty water.

'New one's smart. Sonar. Radio. Automatic life rafts,' said Jan. 'Rumour is they're on to the Wildlife Trust to get permission for a floating dock. Then they could tie up, flog the trippers drinks off the boat. Double the takings.'

'Skipper?'

'They change. Move around.'

It was a thought. Valentine tried to recall all the statements he'd read from the suspects the police had lifted off the beach that afternoon in 1994. Had they got one off the skipper of the boat? Did it matter?

She put down the half of cider. 'Right. Final treat.' There was an ice-cream van parked by the water's edge. 'You?' He shook his head, draining the pint, thinking he might have a third. He watched her queue for the ice cream until she took a cornet, a ninety-nine, and again, he noticed, no money changed hands.

'Anyone pay for anything in this town?' he asked when she got back.

'They get free chips – it's the seaside black market. Swings and roundabouts.' Over behind the quayside amusement arcade they could see a small Ferris wheel turning.

'East Hills?' she asked, crunching into the wafer cone. 'You know Pete was on that – they all were.'

Valentine rocked his head, feeling one of his neck bones grate. It was before his time – three years before he'd been sent to Wells – but even then the case was still open. Every year they'd get pressure from St James' to re-interview, kick the tyres, make sure there wasn't something they'd missed.

'Mass screening's over,' said Valentine. He filled his lungs, suddenly short of breath, but with one long, controlled intake he managed to disguise the usual heave of the chest. 'We've counted them all in, and we've counted them all out. Come Monday we should have a name.' They watched a teenager being escorted off the floating pub by a man with grey hair tied in a pigtail. 'What *did* Pete think?' he asked.

'Not much. He wasn't exactly driven, was he, Georgie? Just another case; besides, St James' were all over it like a horse blanket, so none of the locals had much chance anyway. He knew the kid, the Aussie.' She remembered something, opening both hands out, fingers extended. 'I know what he did say. The kid had saved some girl out on the sands that summer, out with her pony. Pete went down to the lifeboat house to take custody of the child while they got someone from the riding school to contact the parents. The pony swam for it but the Aussie kid cut its bridle free, case it got caught up. So he had a knife, didn't he? Pete looked back at the inventory from his flat and what he had out

on the beach the day he died. No knife. No sign of a knife. So
perhaps he pulled it first? He told your mob – St James'. She
narrowed her eyes, watching a varnished yacht motoring down
the channel. Then, not looking, she reached out her hand and
touched Valentine's shoulder. 'See you again,' she said, pushing
down on the bone to lever herself up. She straightened her back.
Valentine watched her go, engulfed by the crowd that was queuing
now for a fish supper. He stood, picked up a yellow boat ticket
from the ground, and decided against the third pint.

THIRTEEN

Sunday

Shaw took his coffee and went out on the stoop of the café.
Inside, Lena was making sandwiches, setting out cakes and
fruit, matching chairs to tables. It was a moment which
always annoyed him: the cottage wasn't really big enough for a
kitchen of its own so they'd decided they'd eat, as a family, in
the café. So it was his home, Fran's too, but breakfasts were
always consumed on a conveyor belt. Then the moment would be
gone, which was a shame, because it was one of the moments he
liked best: a cup of coffee, the day ahead, the sound of the sea
through the open windows. Even on a Sunday he had to make
way for the paying customers. Later they'd wonder if this little
peak of stress and anxiety had sparked what was to follow.

'Are you really going into work?' asked Lena, her head at the
window, her hands in blue gloves. 'Look at it.' she added, glancing
at the horizon, where a single fair-weather cumulus was sailing
by like a sky galleon.

'I have to. Tom phoned – he thinks he's getting the mass
screening results early.' He wanted to explain but she'd gone.
The lab in Birmingham had been in touch, a job had fallen
through so they'd been able to put all their resources on the DNA
checks. They were just running double-checks before emailing
coded results.

He'd have swum if the sea had been in but it was low tide,

dead water, and all he could see was sand, with blue bands of trapped water, running parallel with the coast, right out towards the horizon. If he walked a mile he might get into five feet of water. This was the reason Old Hunstanton had a hovercraft as well as an inshore lifeboat: so that it could operate in this strange landscape of nearly-land, threaded with nearly-sea. It wasn't his favourite time on the beach. The view was bleak, bleaker for the sun and the sky which both needed the sea to provide a reflection.

To break his darkening mood he walked out, still holding the small china espresso cup, to the edge of the first lagoon. Technically, he knew, this was a 'lead' of water – an open stretch, but pronounced as a dog's lead, not the metal. Navigating the North Norfolk coast was all about knowing how these leads joined up or, more to the point, didn't. What was a real surprise to many sailors was just how undulating this landscape could be. Down in the water you could be several feet below the nearest sand bar and unable to see beyond it, to the next lead. In its own way it was a maze.

He stood at the crest of the nearest sand bar and, using his good eye, tried to locate his three regular landmarks – to the south, about two miles, the small stump of the lighthouse on the cliffs at Hunstanton. Then the Boston Stump, the 270-foot-high parish church in the Lincolnshire town on the far side of The Wash, a landmark so unmissable Winston Churchill wanted it blown up during the war to stop German bomber pilots using it to navigate their way to London. And finally, the single break-water at Holme to the north, the only unshifting feature on the exposed outward curve of the coast, as it turned to face the open North Sea. This routine – configuring his own position from these three points – was a ritual that helped. It made him feel rooted, as if he had some innate, onboard GPS.

He turned to look back at the café. Fran was sat on the stoop, morose, unhappy to face the rest of the weekend with her parents both working. She held something on her lap and Shaw guessed it was a DS, her favourite game, SinCity, loaded up. It was Shaw's favourite too – a complex 3D fantasy in which you were able to build a city and watch it grow, spreading a latticework of streets and highways across an imaginary landscape. He wondered, for the first time, whether she'd have been happier growing up in a real city. Summers were fine because she had the beach and a steady stream of visiting friends, but the winters were lonelier and, perhaps for a child, dispiriting. And he wondered, but had never shared the anxiety with Lena, if they were robbing her of the magic of the sea by giving it to her every day of her life.

Looking once more to the horizon he tried to glimpse open water. But in the mid-distance he saw instead two black specks: seals, undoubtedly, lounging on a sandbar summit where the sun had already dried out the damp colour to leave it a poster paint yellow.

The image flickered. Shaw's heartbeat jumped, an injection of adrenaline making his blood race. He closed his eyes, trying to think of nothing. The sensation in his right, damaged eyeball was like one of those tics you can get above or below the eye when a fibrillating micro-muscle signals how tired you really are. But he wasn't tired. He'd slept well. He opened his good eye and focused on the two seals, but the image flickered again, and this time there was a pain in the good eye – right through it, as if the ball had been lanced with a needle. Both eyes closed, he knelt on the sand, placed the cup carefully down, and willed his heartbeat to slow. It took a minute, and even then he knew it hadn't returned to normal. He stood, distressed to feel the muscles holding his left knee straight were unsteady too, so that the kneecap shook.

Looking south he found the lighthouse tower. The image was clear. But when he traced the distant horizon for the Boston Stump the image blurred; two horizons suddenly separating, then meshing. Stress was pumping water into the eye which made the image mist completely, so he closed both eyes again.

He waited, feeling his heart thud, the sound of blood in his ears. Without the visual world he felt adrift, the distant sound of waves falling adding to a feeling of disorientation. What next? Wait, then open his eyes and get back to the cafe. Was this what he'd see for ever? The thought made him sick. Even if his vision cleared he'd have to see the eye specialist. Perhaps they'd have to take the blind eye out because that might help. Or operate on the good eye. He could see the word 'blind' on a page, diagrams of the eyeball above and below. The world for Shaw was intensely visual; the loss of it would change him for ever. And then, sickeningly, he remembered what he'd tried to forget over these last few days and weeks – the rapid and almost preternatural heightening of his powers of smell and hearing.

His body had *known*, even before his brain; it had begun to prepare for blindness, honing other senses to take the place of the pictures by which he navigated his way through life. He couldn't stop himself then, trying to still the panic by opening his eyes. The fluttering stopped and the image sharpened: one of the seals was trying to get in the water, like a sleeping bag on the move, while the other rolled away. But the eyeball still felt wrong, as if he'd suddenly become hyper-aware of its movements, synapses opening up in his brain to monitor its position in real time. A footstep behind him sucked at the sand and he turned to find Lena just a few feet away, with a fresh cup of espresso.

'Peace offering,' she said, then froze. 'Peter, you're crying.' She kept walking towards him and put her free hand round his neck, gripping the base of his skull, sliding her fingers through the close-cropped hair. 'Peter, what is it? Peter, look at me.' And they were the words he'd always remember from that moment. 'Look at me.'

FOURTEEN

Tom Hadden had a flat in the Baltic Tower, a ten-storey converted grain mill in the centre of Lynn, overlooking the Boal Quay and the old cranes, the centrepiece of a miniature waterside Manhattan. Around it clustered the smaller medieval lookout towers the merchants of the town had built to keep a watch on The Cut as their ships came home, testament to the town's three centuries as one of the great ports of Europe. The Baltic Tower was the highest, a misplaced Victorian statement of confidence in Lynn's prospects as a port in the age of the railway.

Double-glazed windows looked out west, over the river to the flatlands along the shore of The Wash. Hadden had a door open

on to a small wrought-iron balcony which gave a view north
towards the sea. Shaw stood with a cup of tea, Earl Grey, with
a twist of lemon, and an ice cube shaped like the letter H.

Concentrating on the cup, Shaw tried to forget about his eye.
He studiously avoided the panoramic view, any strain on his
vision. The pain had gone; his close-up vision was clear and in
an odd way each minute that passed without a return of the flickering images made his spirit rise: perhaps it had been a one-off,
a momentary response to stress or overworking the single lens.
Talking to Lena had helped. She'd found the name of the specialist
who'd treated him at Lynn after his accident and checked he was
still practising at the Queen Elizabeth Hospital. Switchboard had
routed her to an answerphone and she'd left a request for an urgent
appointment. Then she'd bathed the eye in warm water and
massaged Shaw's neck and scalp. She said his muscles had been
hard with tension and that he'd never been good at knowing when
he was overworking. Shaw had phoned ahead to postpone his
meeting with Hadden until mid-afternoon, then rested, his eyes
closed, pretending to sunbathe while Fran played nurse – bringing
food, reading snippets out of the papers. Then he'd let her go,
free to run to the beach huts near the town where a school friend
would be out with her family; a school friend with her own DS,
so that they could link them up and play building cities together.

Three hours later, behind the wheel of the Porsche, he felt
restored. He'd left Lena in tears, standing by the car as he drove
off, adamant he should take a few days off; rest, give himself a
chance; certain, above all, that he shouldn't drive the car. But
he'd set her anxieties aside, aware that the most immediate way
he could make himself feel better was to go to work. The fear
of imminent disaster which had overtaken him on the beach had
receded. He saw it now as irrational, born perhaps of some
subconscious anxiety about total blindness.

The North Norfolk coast had flashed by in streaks of blue and
green. He'd been in a good mood, on an artificial high, so he'd
jogged up the ten flights of stairs to Hadden's door. The CSI
man got the bad news over with indecent haste. 'Peter, sorry. No
match on Roundhay.' He stood aside from the door. 'Overnight
email, but I thought I'd wait until I saw you.'

Bad news, certainly, Shaw had agreed. But not unexpected.
And it told them something: that Roundhay's version of what

he'd seen that day was almost certainly true. That Marianne Osbourne had walked off into the dunes, followed by Shane White. Now the rest of the mass screening results should place the missing jigsaw piece on the table: the name of the man she'd gone into the long grass to meet. Roundhay was in the clear. He'd lied back in 1994, but there was no evidence he'd lied again.

Hadden said there'd been some sort of problem at the lab because they'd phoned him to say they were double-checking the double-checked results. The final email should drop at any moment. Now the little balcony was in the afternoon shade he said he'd get his laptop and they could wait in the fresh air.

The open laptop was silent for twenty minutes. So they talked about kids, swapping tales of rights of passage. Then the iMac pinged. Hadden opened the email inbox and brought up the earlier message from the Forensic Supply Laboratory containing the Roundhay result. Shaw tried to speed-read the text but it was mostly maths – a complex statistical analysis. And there were no names, just coded letters, corresponding to a sheet Hadden had beside the laptop.

Hadden covered his mouth with the back of his fingers. 'As I said – no match. You know the science here?'

Shaw nodded. They'd done DNA matching at the Met Police College at Hendon.

Hadden opened the new email from the FSL. It was about 3,000 words – complex analysis again. Shaw stopped staring at the screen, leant back in the seat, and let his shoulders relax, forced them to relax, his eyes closed, waiting to hear the name of their killer.

'Right,' said Hadden. 'Good job you're sitting down.' He went back into the flat and came back with a bottle of wine, a white Burgundy, the glass blushed with condensation. Hadden had the corkscrew in and the cork out in one fluid movement.

Shaw left the glass untouched. 'What's wrong?' he said.

'Clean sweep,' said Hadden, taking an inch of wine out of the glass. 'No match – they finished the whole batch overnight. Given the result they ran it all again this morning. All thirty-five male samples, both from the living and relatives of the dead. No match.' Hadden closed his eyes. 'From a scientific point of view. From a forensic point of view, I would say that was a disaster. That's a technical term we boffins use, but you get the drift.'

Shaw pushed the wine glass away by the stem. Hadden's eyes were still closed, so that Shaw was able to study the freckles clustering on his forehead where the lesion of the skin cancer op still showed. 'The towel was buried on the beach,' said Shaw, trying to cling to logic, to any structure that might explain the inexplicable. 'The bloodstain is White's. The skin cells gave us Sample X. The boat took seventy-five people to the island. We brought back seventy-four alive – thirty-five of them men. We've taken samples from all thirty-five – thirty in the mass screening, five from relatives of those who'd died since 1994. There was a police unit on the island overnight, and the whole place was subject to both a fingertip search and a thorough examination by two dog units. The killer has to be in our sample.' He tried to keep any note of antagonism out of his voice, any trace of a witch-hunt, but the 'we' was enough to put the forensic scientist firmly on the spot.

'What are we missing?' asked Shaw.

Hadden opened his eyes but avoided Shaw's face.

'There's only one answer,' said Shaw. 'Sample X was on the towel when it was taken out on the boat.'

Hadden formed his hand into a fist and tapped it on the table. 'No, Peter.' His voice had returned to its usual whisper. 'The science is clear and persuasive. The DNA sample – Sample X – was co-mingled with the victim's blood cells on the towel. That's not a term I've picked out of the air. It's a term I'd use in the dock, in court, giving expert evidence. It means the two trace samples of blood and skin were deposited on the towel *simultaneously*. It is not possible – in the real world – for that to happen in any other way. If you asked me to re-create that double sample in the lab at The Ark I couldn't do it. No way.' He held both his hands out as if warming them at an open fire. 'OK?'

They'd had this discussion before, when Shaw and Valentine had chosen the East Hills case to reopen. He'd talked it through with Hadden, testing his hypothesis, searching for a loophole in the logic. In the real world there wasn't one. It *was* airtight.

'But is it watertight?' asked Shaw. 'It's a country mile out to East Hills but the rip-tide is so bad you have to swim twice that to be sure you don't get sucked out to sea. Can it be done? Sure. We only discounted the possibility entirely because of the

numbers: seventy-five out to East Hills, seventy-four back plus
the victim. It adds up. But it doesn't add up anymore. So maybe
someone swam out then swam back.'

Hadden refilled his wine glass. 'You're right, we did go
through this. You'd have to be an expert swimmer to do it one
way, but there and back again? Without being spotted? You've
got to come ashore, you've got to swim back. White was actually still alive when his body was dragged in. The killer had
only just struck. Within minutes you had a police launch out,
the lifeboat – we checked all this. Witnesses were looking out
to sea, scanning the water. The harbour master came out as well,
and he was specifically asked to stand off in the channel while
the island was secured. Plus, the lifeboat called out the inshore
crew and they went round East Hills, checking to see if someone
was in the water. So if we've got some latter-day Captain Webb
on our hands he'd have had to swim out to sea, straight out. We
always said it was *theoretically* possible, Peter. But it's a one
in a million chance.' Hadden's eyes were closed; he pressed his
lips to his fist.

Shaw recalled a beach barbecue they'd held at the cafe that
spring. He'd invited Tom Hadden and he'd spent the evening
drinking white wine and gathering driftwood for the fire. At
sundown Shaw had suggested a swim. A group of them – thirty
strong – had charged into the breaking surf. But Hadden had stayed
ashore, explaining he wasn't a strong swimmer and had never been
an enthusiast for the sea. So that two-way marathon swim might
look like an Olympic feat to him, but to Shaw it looked very
different. He could have done it. Head down, sideways breaths,
and a long series of languid dolphin body strokes. Difficult –
dangerous even, but not impossible.

'What other options have I got?' Shaw closed his palms
together as if in prayer.

'The mass screening's not foolproof,' said Hadden. 'I'll check
back through the DNA matches.' He tapped the laptop. 'I've no
doubts about the samples we took from the suspects still alive.
But those we had to do from the families of the dead – just
maybe. I'll see if there's any long shots.'

'So, what are we saying? That our killer might be one of the
five men who died between 1994 and now, and that the DNA
sample we took from their kids, or their mothers or whatever,

didn't give us an accurate reading across to theirs? Because with them we weren't looking for a direct match – we were looking for a family match – right?'

'We were careful but you never know. One family secret can screw up any amount of science. We try to stick to maternal lines: it's pretty difficult to get the identity of someone's mother wrong. But it's not always possible to stick with mothers. So if we went for a paternal line there's a danger – clearly. Exhumation's the only foolproof method. And we didn't go down that line because of the cost, which is pretty eye-watering.'

Hadden began to tap out some emails. Shaw retrieved his wine and stood at the edge of the balcony, letting the breeze cool his skin. Was there an upside to bad news? It did mean they could now consider suspects for the killing of Shane White who were *not* amongst those they'd taken off the island. So who was the obvious suspect now?

'Joe Osbourne,' said Shaw, out loud, but Hadden didn't respond, focusing instead on the statistics on-screen. Joe thought he was Marianne Osbourne's sweetheart back in 1994 but she was playing the field. That was a motive – the most common and most lethal motive of all: jealousy. What if Marianne was wandering off into the dunes to meet White? Maybe it wasn't blackmail; maybe it was just sex. Plus Joe had an alibi no one alive could support or disprove. Had he really been in his father's workshop that afternoon? And when they'd reopened the case and called Marianne in to double-check her statement it had been her husband who'd been the last person to see her alive. And it was Joe who'd phoned in to the funeral parlour to say she wouldn't make work that day before taking his BSA Bantam down into Wells to open up his shop. What if Marianne had been dead before he left the house?

Shaw phoned Twine at the incident room at The Circle, Creake, and filled him in on the results of the lab tests. The young DC was all for interviewing Joe Osbourne that day. But Shaw counselled caution: by the morning they'd have some idea if their mass screening results were copper-bottomed, and the rest of the team would be in place. And their suspect wasn't going anywhere. He told Twine to check on Osbourne: nothing heavy, but tell him Shaw and Valentine had some loose ends to tie up and they'd be at the house first thing. And for elimination purposes they'd like to take a DNA sample. 'Play it softly, Paul,' said Shaw. 'Just routine.'

Shaw felt better, energized. But his memory threw up a sound, not an image this time. The chief constable's grey Daimler, the engine ticking. It had been unpleasant giving Brendan O'Hare *good* news. Telling him the North Norfolk Constabulary had wasted £400,000 on an abortive mass screening was most definitely *bad* news.

Shaw's mobile trilled and he checked a text from Valentine. OVERTIME. I'VE FOUND THE BOATMAN. WELLS RNLI – 4.

When Valentine had mentioned trying to track down the ferryman who'd taken the *Arandora Star* out to East Hills on the day of the murder it had seemed like an academic loose end. Now, suddenly, it seemed like a very good idea. Any idea looked like a good idea. The ferryman had been one of the first on the scene when White's body was found. Inexplicably he'd not been asked to make a full formal statement back in '94 – just a cursory one page outline. That mistake had been compounded by Shaw's own error: leaving him out of the request to attend at St James' with the other witnesses.

Shaw went back into the flat and worked through the case files on Hadden's desk until he found a snapshot of Joe Osbourne. He put it in his wallet, patted it once, and left without a word.

FIFTEEN

The lifeboat house at Wells stood a mile from the town, out where the channel met the sea, on a bluff of sand. Beyond it the beach opened up, miles of it, running west and dotted with a Sunday crowd, families clustered round tents and windbreaks. Most of the beach huts on the apron of the pinewoods were just in shadow – many open, deckchairs clustered by the wooden steps, which led up into each. The tide had turned, the water draining into Wells' harbour like sand in an egg-timer, covering a patchwork of sandbars which had been drying in late afternoon heat. Dogs ran in great circles, lapping up the space. A few kites flew, catching the breeze which always sprang up with the turn of the tide, their plastic tails crackling like firewood.

Shaw tapped on the hot roof of the Mazda, startling Valentine, who was listening to the local news. The car was parked by the lifeboat house, with a view north over the sea. The DS got out, as stiff as one of the deckchairs along the sand.

'You didn't need to come – I can do this,' said Valentine. 'The text was just for info.' He flexed a hand, trying to get the circulation back. 'Radio's picked up the appeal on the cyanide capsule,' he said. 'The papers will run it tomorrow. BBC website too.' They listened as the local commercial radio news broadcast the item. Anyone who knew anything about a supply of cyanide capsules, possibly wartime, should contact police at Lynn. Any such information would be treated in confidence and could assist police in ongoing enquiries.

'Good work,' said Shaw. He took a deep breath: 'I've just been with Tom – mass screening results are through.' He caught Valentine's eyes – dark, but catching the light. 'No matches. Not one.'

'What?' It was the closest Valentine would get to a shout. 'You're kidding.' Sweat prickled his skin, making him shiver.

'No, I'm not.' Shaw looked away, allowing a flare of anger to subside. 'He'll kick the tyres on the results, but I think we may have run out of luck.'

Valentine looked into the mid-distance, letting the sea air seep out of his lungs. They'd considered the possibility of failure, but only in an academic sense, as the last possible option. He'd spotted the 'we' in Shaw's sentence, although he seriously doubted that the DI's career would take as big a tumble as his. He was eight years from retirement, and he'd failed to get past a promotion panel three times in the last eighteen months. This wasn't a bad result for DS George Valentine: it was a disastrous one.

'Roundhay?' he asked, a flicker of hope making him pause, a match struck, a fresh Silk Cut in his lips.

'First up. No match. Not close. Our next best shot has to be Joe Osbourne. He fits the bill: jealous boyfriend. Then an unhappy marriage. Tussle with a hooker.'

'It was a bit of push and shove. And why'd he kill White?'

'Maybe Marianne was one of White's many conquests. Maybe she was being blackmailed and he did the noble thing – turned up to put the frighteners on White. *And* he could have helped Marianne Osbourne take that pill before setting out to work. I've fixed us up with an interview first thing tomorrow at the house. Station later if we get anywhere.'

'Back to square one,' said Valentine. 'That's where we've got.' He didn't want to sound bitter, or accusatory, but he failed on both counts. They'd already talked to Joe Osbourne. What did Shaw think they'd get at the second attempt – a confession?

Shaw walked down a slope to the sand and looked at his boots. 'If he is our East Hills killer then he has to be a swimmer, there and back again. So we need to check that out. It's all very well posing on the beach. Could Osbourne swim the distance? We always knew that was a loophole. That's my fault. I got seduced by the numbers. Seventy-five out, seventy-four back.'

Valentine looked out to sea over the marshes. At high tide East Hills was a sliver of sand. The pine trees that marked its spine seemed to be set on the horizon itself – impossibly distant. He'd no more try to swim to it as walk to it. He couldn't resist pointing out the obvious: 'He's an asthmatic. When we told him his wife was dead he passed out. You serious about this?'

Shaw didn't answer.

Valentine rubbed his hand over his jaw, the sound of skin rubbing on the five o'clock shadow like sandpaper. He still found it hard to believe they'd struck out on the DNA tests. 'There's no chance we fucked up the mass screening?' It wasn't a question, more a lament.

'We'll think it through later but Tom reckons there's only one possible way out. Maybe there's a mistake in the DNA profiles of the five men we took off East Hills who are dead. One of the samples could be duff – maybe someone thought they'd keep a family secret. Or there's a family secret that's a secret even to the family. But it's got to be a long shot.'

'Any longer than Joe Osbourne turning into Mark Spitz?' asked Valentine.

A sudden wave broke on the edge of the sand and looking up they saw one of the small fishing boats motoring out along The Cut. 'Anyway, all that can wait for tomorrow,' said Shaw. 'Osbourne's at home and Paul's keeping tabs. Meanwhile, let's do what we should have done seventeen years ago and interview the ferryman.'

Valentine handed Shaw a file, inside of which was a one-page statement. Shaw looked at the close-lettered type and the heat of the day seemed to suck any vitality he had left out through his feet and into the sand. He didn't really have the energy to read it.

'Summary?'

'His name's Philip Coyle. Known as 'Tug'. I think I met him once – someone nicked some gear out of his boat and I must have interviewed him. He's got a small inshore fishing business here at Wells – mainly shellfish, flogging scallops and stuff to the posh pubs for the tourists to eat. He's on the RNLI crew. Grandfather before him. I checked with the coxswain for personal details: he lives alone in Lynn. Married about fifteen years ago, divorced since. One child, a boy, lives with the mother.'

Valentine cracked the single page of A4 so that it was rigid. 'Back in 'ninety-four he took the boat out to East Hills, dropped off the seventy-five ticket holders, carried on to Morston where he picked up twenty-eight to go out to Blakeney and see the seals. He ran them back, then came back to East Hills. He gave a statement here at Wells – we didn't take him back to St James' with the rest. And we didn't call him on Saturday for a review. A loophole. So we haven't got his DNA sample either.'

They'd just opened the main doors of the boathouse and the first group of visitors was up on the observation platform, looking down into the cockpit of the *Mary Louise*. Paintwork gleamed in blue, red and gold. The smell was military: polished wood, brass; the air dustless, laced with engine oil and beeswax.

'Tug' Coyle was in the small tractor at the prow, used to tow the lifeboat down the ramp for launches, checking oil levels in the engine. He jumped down, more nimble than his thirty-six years should have allowed, but heavy nonetheless, carrying muscle and big bones, with most of his power in his shoulders, short neck and arms. Shaw was immediately reminded of a crab.

He smiled at them both, shook hands with fleshy fingers, and nodded twice at Shaw, the green eyes signalling recognition. '*Hunstanton Flyer*?' he asked, the voice heavy with a Norfolk burr. The Flyer was the name of the RNLI's hovercraft.

'Toy compared to this,' said Shaw. The prow of the *Mary Louise* towered over them.

'How can I help?' asked Coyle, stooping easily to close the metal butterfly wings of a toolbox.

Valentine's eye had been caught by one of the photographic portraits framed on the wall. This image was in pride of place, in a heavy wooden frame with gilt carving and behind a thick layer of glass. The citation under the picture read:

Archibald 'Tug' Coyle MBE
Coxwain 1938–52
RNLI Gold Medal

He tapped the edge of the picture.

'Sure,' said Coyle, nodding. 'Grandfather. Not that he had much to do with us – Dad was the black sheep of the family and Tug was a funny old bugger. But I got the name, and the boat, so I shouldn't complain.'

Shaw knew of Tug Coyle, a legend on the coast but many years before his time. One of those iconic lifeboatmen who always, in retrospect, seem too good to be true. He noted that the grandson hadn't just got the nickname and the boat – he noted the genetic inheritance too, the 'lifelong look', the one facet of the face that would hold the family likeness. In this case it was the bone structure of the skull, the way the eye sockets were set firmly apart, the bridge of the nose notably wide.

'This about East Hills?' Tug said.

'You were running the *Arandora Star* that day,' said Shaw. 'I just wanted to run through your statement – just to be clear. It would help us a lot.'

'Yeah,' said Coyle, glancing back to the lifeboat. 'Look, I thought it might help – we could go out, to the island?' He smiled again, hands together, and Shaw thought he'd planned it like this so that they'd be out in his elements, the sea and air, not here, landlocked. 'Shift's done and I need to check the pots. Couple of the Burnham restaurants are screaming for fresh stuff. Crab, scallop. That OK? And I could do with catching the tide.' Coyle's manner was charming, smooth, and Shaw imagined he'd honed those skills flogging his shellfish to the Chelsea-on-Sea fishmongers and pubs along the coast. But the gentrification of the coast hadn't all been good news, because while it provided Coyle with a living, he clearly couldn't afford to live locally anymore. Having to drive back into the seedy suburbs of Lynn to a flat at the end of a long shift would make a bitter man of anyone. He wondered how much of Coyle's cheery nature was manufactured – the shell on the crab.

'The pots are on the Nor Bank, then we can swing back to East Hills.'

Coyle led them to an eighteen-foot clinker-built fishing boat moored at the foot of a short wooden wharf beside the lifeboat slipway. It was called *Ellie-May,* and registered at Wells.

They cut out to sea, Coyle expertly judging the angle of impact between the small boat and the modest swell. Half a mile out he cut the *Ellie-May*'s speed, expertly picking up a series of buoys and lifting the pots, putting crab and two lobsters into white plastic buckets, scallops into trays. Valentine found the plastic clicking of claws unnerving, turning his stomach, where he'd recently deposited a full English breakfast roll and a pint of tea.

Their arrival at East Hills was watched by a curious Sunday crowd on the beach. The scent of burning skin and suntan oil hung heavy in the air. Many of the faces, Shaw noted, were vaguely belligerent, as if they saw the *Ellie-May* as an intruder in a private paradise. Coyle snagged a wooden pile on the jetty with a rope and cut the engine, putting his feet up, and leaning his back on the tiller.

Shaw wondered why they hadn't got out of the boat. Was he trying to make a subliminal point; that he never got out of the boat, because he was always the ferryman? It was a way of separating himself from the crime. 'Just for the record,' said Shaw, 'can you talk us through that day from your point of view – the day of the murder? We're just making sure that everything fits together. Routine.'

Coyle had the story pat: it matched the original brief statement. A full boat that day, but for a few seats. Tickets sold: seventy-five. Had they ever packed them in over the limit? asked Valentine. Never. They'd swapped a look at that, Shaw and Valentine, because both of them knew that none of the boats along the coast ever turned away the odd extra customer. So that was a little white lie. An indication, perhaps, that they weren't guaranteed the unvarnished truth.

Coyle said he'd got out to East Hills at a few minutes past eleven, dropped everyone, then sailed along the coast to Morston to run out a charter to Blakeney Point to see the seals. He'd landed them back, then returned to East Hills to run everyone back at 5.30 p.m. As he edged the boat towards the floating dock that day he'd heard a woman screaming. She was at the water's edge, her arms out rigid, her skin patterned with blood. She kept screaming, pointing into the water. Coyle had stood at the tiller, looking into the blue clear sea until he'd drifted into the blood-clouded waves. Then he'd seen the victim, face down, in trunks, tanned skin and straggly dyed hair.

They knew the rest.

Valentine thought about the little black market that kept seaside places like Wells alive: an economy built on favours, not cash. For the first time he had an idea, and he was angry with himself for not having it sooner. 'Ever give a free ride to anyone – friends, family? You wouldn't bother with tickets for them, would you?'

'Everyone got a ticket,' he said. 'I start taking people for nothing I'd have a full boat in a week and nothing in the cash box. It's fine running a barter system if you own the business. It wasn't my boat. Not my place to give a free ride.' He spat in the sea.

Shaw looked to Valentine, indicating that his DS should press on, because that was a line of inquiry he'd missed: the idea that they'd taken seventy-six out, and the killer had only to swim one way. And it *was* possible because the boat that day was largely full of visitors. It wasn't as if anyone would have spotted a missing passenger.

'Must be tricky, though,' said Valentine. 'You get a free pint on the quayside, a round of ice creams on the house when you've got the kids in tow, then they turn up in your boat. Like I said,' Valentine added, when Coyle didn't answer. 'Tricky.'

'Not really,' said Coyle. 'I sell shellfish to people who run businesses with a million-pound turnover. They'd cut your throat for another one per cent on the profits. What am I saying – a tenth of a per cent. You think I'm the sucker who gives it away to family and friends?'

Shaw retrieved his wallet and took out the snapshot of Joe Osbourne. 'So no chance he was on board for the trip out?'

'Joe? I think I'd remember,' said Coyle, laughing at Valentine.

'You know him?' asked Shaw.

'Sure. I've got family up at Creake. Next door, in fact. Aidan Robinson's my cousin. He's the old man's other grandson. The favourite grandson – the son of the favourite daughter. Old Tug went to live with them after grandma died. So they were close.'

'Right,' said Shaw, re-computing his view of Aidan Robinson.

'Aidan would have inherited the boat if he hadn't had that accident – he's pretty much a dead weight in water and he never could swim. Mind you, that doesn't stop 'em – plenty of the older generation never bothered to learn. They concentrated on not falling in.' He laughed, showing small childlike teeth. 'But you need to be good on your feet in these small boats. Aidan's a liability.'

Shaw climbed up on to the floating dock, a fluid movement without any apparent effort. The family link to The Circle was intriguing. But did it really lead anywhere? He'd soon learnt that once you left the urban sprawl of Lynn the North Norfolk coast was a complex matrix of family and community; a hidden pattern, just below the surface.

Then he realized Coyle hadn't answered his question.

'So, for the record. You didn't give Joe a lift that day. A free trip?'

'Nope. I know the family now; back then, they were just locals to me.'

'So when you dropped everyone here that day, before you left for Morston, there was no time to stick around, have a break?' he asked.

Coyle shook his head.

'Return trip?'

Coyle licked his small bowed lips, putting both hands behind his neck in an exaggerated show of ease.

Valentine tried to recall the statements he'd read from the East Hills witnesses. He thought one, maybe two, had mentioned seeing the boat offshore. He drew savagely on his Silk Cut, aware he'd missed that, failed to think it through.

'I guess I had a few minutes to play with. I usually do because you can't be late. Kids, families, they need to be back, and people get anxious. So I was on the dot at five thirty here, at the jetty. Never late. To be that punctual I have to leave some time.'

'How much time?' asked Shaw, his voice sharper.

Coyle swallowed hard. 'Twenty minutes. Less.' Shaw thought he was going to leave it at that, but he went on: 'I don't come in. If you hit the dock they all get on board – well, some of 'em. Then they have to wait around. So I stay out, have a fag.'

'Where?' asked Shaw.

Coyle indicated the northern point. 'Nor Bank, where we dropped the pots, just round the point. I'm out of sight mostly, so no one gets excited. Perfect.' But the smile was curdling on Coyle's face. He knew as well as Shaw and Valentine that he'd painted them a picture. The *Arandora Star*, just offshore, for the last twenty minutes of Shane White's life, hidden to the north.

'See anyone in the sea that day, out beyond the point, swimming maybe?' continued Shaw. 'Anyone swim out to the boat?'

'Nope. Like I said, it's a break, about the only one I get. I usually close me eyes. I didn't see a thing that day.'

'And you didn't bring anyone else in – from Morston maybe? Let them swim ashore?' asked Valentine.

'No way. I can't let anyone swim off the boat; we're not covered on the insurance. So no, I didn't. Never.' Coyle unlaced his boots but didn't get out of the boat. Shaw was again struck by the power in his upper body, the broad carapace of shoulder and back. He knelt and dipped a hand in the sea, feeling the warmth, the slightly viscous saltiness.

'We're going to be five minutes, Mr Coyle – you OK with that?' He didn't wait for an answer but walked away, along the floating decking which led on to the beach. When he got past the high-water mark he turned to see Valentine following.

They made their way up to the grass on the edge of the pinewood, past a ten-year-old doing cartwheels. Valentine felt uncomfortable in his suit and noted that most of the people on the beach were watching them.

'He's sweating like a pig,' he said, looking back to the boat where Coyle had pulled a blue fisherman's hat down over his eyes.

'It's hot,' said Shaw. 'But you're right. Something's not right. But is it anything to do with the murder? It doesn't really add up, does it, any way you play it. If the killer swam out to the boat where did he hide? If the killer swam ashore, where did he go when we evacuated the island?'

'I've seen the original boat – it's down in the mud by the quay-side,' said Valentine. 'There's nowhere you could hide anyone, no chance.'

'Feels like a dead end to me,' said Shaw. 'However you play it.'

They looked back at the boat.

'Dead ends are all we've got,' said Valentine, with a hint of self-pity. 'I'll get Paul to run a check on Coyle, see if there's anything we should know.'

Shaw led the way further up into the marram grass, following a path, until they reached the high sandy ridge which ran along East Hills like a dinosaur's backbone.

From the modest summit he could see the distant blue line of the coast. 'If the mass screening results are right then there's no way round it, George. The killer swam. What does that tell us?'

'That he was desperate, because it's miles. And even if you can swim that far it's dangerous – the rip-tide, the marshes.' Valentine tried to focus on the small outline of the distant lifeboat house. 'Maybe he never got there.'

Shaw had not thought of the possibility that their killer had died that day too, along with his victim. 'So that's our nightmare scenario,' he said. 'He tried to swim but never made it. The body drifted out, or into the marshes. It's rare, but it happens. Couple of years back we went out to a yacht off Scolt Head: a kid had fallen overboard. Never found the body.'

'I'll check missing persons. It's an idea,' admitted Valentine.

'What if we ask a more useful question: why did the killer *decide* to take that chance? Why didn't he just sit tight after the murder?'

Valentine turned back. It was a good question. 'He's covered in blood. There's all the forensics – clothes, nails, skin. He doesn't want to answer questions. Take your pick,' said Valentine.

A lone hawk hung over them, catching the updraft from the dunes.

'Really? This was 1994. How many cases had been through the courts with a prosecution based on DNA? Two? Less? He could clean any blood off in the sea. Bury any bloodstained clothes, trunks, whatever. It was low tide – he could have buried stuff out on the sand and it would have been underwater by the time we got here. Go deep enough it'll never come up – what, four feet? Easy in wet sand. The knife – again, bury it in the sand. The reason the bloodstained towel turned up is that someone panicked – just put it a few inches down. So why did they panic? Why did the killer swim for it?'

'If it was panic there doesn't have to be a reason. That's what panic is.'

Shaw stepped closer. 'Know what I think?' he asked. 'I think the killer was wounded. We've always thought it was a coward's lunge, the single unexpected blow. But maybe it wasn't like that. Maybe it started with an argument. We know there was blood up in the dunes and footprints, loads of them. What if they fought over the knife? What if the killer was cut too?'

'Blood in the dunes was White's,' said Valentine.

'No. The blood we *tested* that was found in the dunes was White's. I'm not saying this was a life-threatening injury, just enough that we'd see it – so on the face maybe, or the hands. He has to get away because the wound says he was in a fight. It says he was there. It says he was the killer. It's a *fresh* wound.'

Valentine could see that was common sense and that holding on to common sense was one of the most difficult things a detective had to do in the middle of a murder inquiry. 'I'll check round the A&Es – they may have records but it's seventeen years ago. Paper records'll be in the landfill by now. Without a patient's name it's a nightmare . . .'

'You can try Joe Osbourne's name for a starter,' said Shaw.

Valentine straightened his back, trying to look willing. 'When does O'Hare get the mass screening results?'

'Tomorrow. First thing.'

'Great. Monday mornings. I love 'em. What do you think he'll do?'

'Cover his arse,' said Shaw. 'Cut us adrift. The real question, George, is what do we do? And the answer is we start again. And we start with Joe Osbourne.'

Coyle didn't speak on the return trip, not until they'd tied up the dinghy and walked back up to the lifeboat house. Valentine asked if he'd mind giving a fresh formal statement down at St James'. Coyle must have expected the request because he didn't miss a beat: no problem, happy to help. They watched him drive away, crammed into a two-door Fiat with a badly rusted bonnet. Even this late in the day there was enough heat for the air to buckle, so that by the time he was half a mile away the car was lost in a blue mirage.

SIXTEEN

Shaw was always surprised by the flowery swim cap: blue, with white and pink primroses. He watched it as she swam towards him through the breakers with a lazy breaststroke, each rhythmic action ducking the head. When she was twenty foot away she was in her depth so she stood, pale shoulders exposed to the evening sun. Dr Justina Kazimierz, St James' resident pathologist, was smiling. 'I find you here,' she said. 'Always.'

Shaw let his body sway as the swell passed by, breaking on the shore side, sweeping across the sands. The tide was coming in, compacting the summer Sunday crowd into an ever-narrower stretch of dry sand. It was a very British scene: families getting closer, renegotiating personal spaces, apologizing for accidental encroachments, games of football turning into water polo.

'Drink?' he asked. They'd just shut the café after an afternoon of almost chaotic business. A queue had snaked out on the stoop and along the high-water mark for hours. They were there for ice creams mainly, or the tea trays Lena had bought in the winter: a red plastic tea pot, red milk jug, cups and saucers, and a plate for biscuits, saffron cake extra. Five quid. A deposit on the tray of five quid. Gold mine.

Shaw had got home, changed and dashed out to catch the sun for a swim, leaving Lena with two of the part-time staff loading up the double dishwasher in the utility room. Fran was amongst the waves with Shaw, which is why he was standing in his depth, watching her feet disappear shorewards on the back of a belly-board.

'A drink – yes,' she said, pulling off her hat. Her face was intensely pale, a middle European pallor, slightly plump. In a year she appeared to have recovered from the death of her partner, although she did hold part of herself so privately they would never know how she felt to be alone. They'd met Dawid, her husband, just once – a quiet man, intensely thoughtful behind dark grey eyes. Her eyes were brown, and the single feature of her face which always reminded Shaw that perhaps she'd been beautiful once. Shaw imagined her as a child pictured in a stiff Polish family tableau: the adults seated, the child held to the side of the father by a hand on the shoulder.

She adjusted the strap on her one-piece swimsuit – the blue a perfect match for the hat. 'Tom told me – the screening results,' she said. 'Not Roundhay then, or any of them. I'm sorry. A mess?'

Shaw sank in the water so that his body floated, his knees up. Weightless, he always felt oddly elated, as if he'd achieved some kind of freedom. 'Pretty much. It's not official. Paperwork drops tomorrow. So that's something to look forward to. Then we start again. Least we know the names of seventy-four people who didn't do it.'

They shared a brave smile.

'Rerun the screening?' she asked, filling the swimming cap with water.

'No way,' said Shaw. 'Out of the question. O'Hare's already bleating about the costs. The only reason we got DNA profiles from the five men who'd died since 1994 by using familial samples was to keep the cost down. He's watching his back, and I don't blame him. He's got to find ten million quid's worth of cuts this year on the budget. He's looking at every penny. Which is why he's going to be so pleased when he finds out the mass screening is a wipeout. So, rerunning is out of the question. But we'll double-check the samples we got from relatives. Maybe there's a blip, a mistake. If not we're looking at a swimming killer . . .' He put the palms of his hands on the surface of the water and slapped down, producing two small splashes.

Fran ran towards them from the beach, the board held sideways in the surf. Up at the café the OPEN flag was being lowered from its pole.

'How's business?' asked Justina, waving at Fran. Shaw thought how odd it was that he couldn't remember when they hadn't been friends with the pathologist. She'd been a distant, brittle character, but her husband's illness had brought the couple out to the coast for the final months of Dawid's life. She'd bought a house up behind the dunes and walked a dog on the beach. Since her husband's death she'd slotted into their lives as if she'd always been there. The perfect neighbour, because she never outstayed a welcome.

'Fantastic,' he said. 'People told us, along at Hunstanton, the fairground, the pier; they said one good day can make a summer and they're right. It's been good, but today . . . The world and his wife, and the kids. All spending. It's like the beach,' he turned his back on the swell, waving a hand along the coast, 'doesn't change for a year. Sand, sandbars, pools. Nothing changes. Then one night there's a storm and you wake up and it's a different beach. Trade's the same. We take a hundred quid a day for six weeks then £5,000 in one afternoon. Suddenly it's a different business.'

Looking up at the café Shaw saw Lena come out on to the stoop with a bottle of wine in a cooler. 'This time next year we'll be open for drinks too – wine and beer. Keep going on the good days. Catch the evening crowd.' Shaw put his feet down and turned shorewards but Justina held up her hand.

'One thing,' she said. The pathologist hated herself for doing it, for stopping him having the rest of the day that he'd been

looking forward to. But her job was her life, even more now that
Dawid was gone, and she was nothing if she wasn't a professional. So she didn't have a choice. 'I am not here by an accident,
not completely. I knew I would find you – Tom asked me to. I
think, yes, you should concentrate . . .' She often did this, sifting
through some mental thesaurus for the right word from a language
she'd never quiet mastered. 'Focus – yes, you should focus – on
the Osbourne case. The woman in the bed. You know this is
important. But I think perhaps it is the key.'

She looked into Shaw's good eye, sinking in the water, ducking
her head, then standing. 'There was a gas explosion in the village,
close to the house where she died?'

Shaw nodded, studying Justina's face, ignoring the long arc
of the beach behind her, the sea dotted with swimmers, inflatables,
surf and body boards. His good eye was sharp now, painless,
and the anguish he'd felt just that morning was now a cloud on
the horizon, distant, retreating. He thought of the black smudged
ruins of the house they'd past after leaving The Circle that first
morning, the road surface buckled by the blast.

'The explosion,' said the pathologist. 'Tom's team is still on
the site but they say the heart of it was in an upstairs bedroom.
They're helping the fire brigade unit now. The house is dangerous
– you cannot go now. Not today. The blast goes up through the
floor.' She held both hands up, elbows down, as she often did
in the autopsy room. 'The victim – an eighty-seven-year-old
man – was in bed at the time. His body did not survive. Just
pieces. Already they have two men who need help.' She searched
for the right word again, this time finding it first time.
'Harrowing?'

Shaw nodded. The sound of the beach, of children screaming
with fun, had receded.

'What there is of this man is on a table at The Ark.' It was a
starkly brutal sentence.

Shaw thought of the cold green light coming through the old
chapel windows: the aluminium autopsy tables set out below the
single stone angel, its hands covering its face.

'The physics I do not understand. But in such cases, often,
you are surprised what survives. The blast blew out the candle
which lit the gas, you see? Only a few seconds of heat, then
gone. So some things survive. A newspaper, perhaps. A picture

on a wall. Here, this time, this candle. No – a tea light. Set in a saucer.'

Shaw thought about that.

'Where?'

'By the bed.'

'Power supply?'

'The house next door is on the same circuit and when they go to bed the night before they have lights.'

'Perhaps he was afraid of the dark,' offered Shaw, but he didn't believe it.

She lifted a hand from the sea and held two fingers together, as if she was moving a chess piece.

'It was set on a small table. Still in the ruins.' She shook her head, amazed at how lucky they'd been. 'So, I look more carefully at what is left of this man,' she said. 'I have the skull – in part. Some fatty tissue. The torso – two pieces. The test results are very clear but I can not confirm before tomorrow.'

'Confirm what?' asked Shaw.

'Cyanide. Bloodstream – anterior chamber of the heart.'

Shaw saw the summer's day in the pathologist's eyes but it was only a reflection.

On the beach Lena was waving to them both. She stopped suddenly, dropped her arms, and Shaw knew she'd seen the stiffness in his body by the way she held her jaw up, like a challenge, as if she'd been excluded. She began to wade in, Fran running ahead up the beach to meet her.

Justina shook her short hair. 'I've just left Tom at the house – what is left of the house. Even he cannot go in yet. The neighbours talk. This man – Patch – he was well known in Wells. He took tickets, Peter, for the car park – the one by the quay? Where the ferry leaves for the island, I think? For East Hills. For twenty years, more, he did this.'

Justina filled her swimming cap with water.

Shaw heard Lena call his name. He turned, manufacturing a smile he knew would disappoint her.

SEVENTEEN

A tramp played a penny whistle in the doorway of a furniture showroom as George Valentine walked past; head down, so that the smoke from his cigarette seemed to caress his face like cool white hands. Night had fallen as he'd driven west along the coast, and by the time he'd dumped the Mazda outside his house in South Lynn the stars were clear despite the orange reflection of the street lights. He walked into town, strolling in the middle of the narrow medieval streets, well away from the shadowy shop fronts and alleyways. He walked the white dotted line, the roads empty of traffic, and had gone twenty yards past the tramp before he recognized the song: *Down Town* – Pet Clarke, 1963. It had been one of Julie's favourites, so he walked back and threw a pound coin into a dog's bowl. He often put money in begging bowls and charity cans, so he laughed to himself as he walked on, imagining a sticker the tramp might have given him for his donation: *Dosser Aid*.

The only thing moving in town was the neon sign on the tower of The Majestic cinema, which flickered electric blue. Valentine cut through the memorial gardens by the central library to the ruins of Greyfriar's Abbey, a few pillars of a nave and the leaning Greyfriar's Tower, a floodlit eccentricity which Valentine hadn't consciously noticed in thirty years. What did he notice? A single hypodermic syringe by a bench catching the light, a discarded mobile phone on the grass and some graffiti on a wall by the library which read simply JayGo. He had an eye for crime, but little else. And it was often at its sharpest when he was off duty, and after dark.

His mobile rang and he stopped to take the call. It was Shaw, the sound of the sea in the background, bad news in the foreground: the old man who'd died in the explosion in Creake on the day they'd found Marianne Osbourne in her deathbed had been murdered, probably with a cyanide pill. And there was another, circumstantial link to East Hills. The dead man had run the council car park by the quay for thirty years. He'd have been there that day as the *Arandora Star* had slipped its moorings with Marianne Osbourne on board. Valentine stopped dead on the pavement. He was outside a Polish migrant workers hostel. Two men playing cards on the step watched him without curiosity. 'Cyanide?' he said, looking at them until they looked away.

Shaw gave him what facts he had, then fixed to meet at the scene of the explosion at nine – they'd move on to interview Joe Osbourne afterwards.

As they talked a new thought emerged: perhaps, oddly, it was good news, not bad. They were looking for a fresh start, after all. Now they had a double killing, a *linked* double killing. All of a sudden the clean sweep on the mass screening wasn't the best story in town. If they'd wanted a smokescreen they couldn't have made a better one up.

Shaw was going to ring off but couldn't resist the idea that Valentine was working. 'You?'

'Back to basics. Your Dad always said . . .' Valentine bit his lip, because he'd always been careful never to use that line. 'Just making sure we've got everything we need on Osbourne before we do the interview. If I strike lucky, I'll shout.' Valentine cut the line. The sudden complexity of the inquiry made him feel weary, and his shoes scuffed the dry pavements as he headed south again, towards the towering medieval bulk of the London Gate.

Traffic here, along the main road, was intermittent, whereas during the day the cars and lorries were always bumper-to-bumper, spewing blue exhaust into the street. He cut down a side street to the Red House, the CID's favoured pub. There was no one in the little side bar with its beaten copper-topped tables and quarry-tiled floor. Door and windows stood open so that as he drank his pint he could hear the sounds of the town; a little traffic, dogs, and somewhere close in the old council flats the steady bass beat of a music system. He thought about Jan Clay, and the light on the water off the quayside at Wells, and the way she'd pressed down on his shoulder bone when she'd stood up.

He bent his head back, looking up, annoyed to discover he'd forgotten that the ceiling of the pub was decorated with a huge jigsaw depicting an Indian maze – the garden of a maharajah's palace, paths interlocking, incredibly complex, the 3D world reduced to a 2D design. A puzzle. A riddle. One of the things he liked about the pub was its unselfconscious eccentricity. But why put jigsaws on ceilings? The second pint settled his mind. He left quickly, calling goodbye to the unseen landlord serving in the other bar.

Crossing back over the London Road he plunged into a network of small terraced streets which ran down to the river. The town's red light district was a thriving community. Vice crackdowns in Peterborough and the East Midlands had encouraged increasing numbers of punters to drive down the A37 to satisfy their needs. For a year, eighteen months, St James' had left well alone. But pressure was building for a clear out. Prostitution was encouraging the drugs trade, and social services were struggling to deal with the knock-on effects of addiction and violence. A coordinated operation between four constabularies was planned for late September. But for now, on a late summer's night in Lynn, it was business as usual for the oldest profession.

He turned into Leopold Street, past the imposing facade of the old Central Methodist Church, and was relieved to see two girls halfway down the street outside The Abbey, a corner pub which held illegal dog fights in the yard at the back. Valentine's blakeys clattered on the pavement as he walked, counting the upstairs bedroom lights that were lit: eighteen out of twenty, not bad for 9 p.m. on an August evening. The windows were open and he caught the authentic soundtrack of a world where you could buy affection: a match striking, a bed creaking, and a woman pretending to laugh.

The girls on the street didn't move. The younger one asked for a cigarette and he gave her one of his Silk Cuts, prolonging the moment of his own anonymity, and unable to deny the slight thrill this gave him. She was a teenager, in a black plastic skirt and stockings, a blouse open to reveal a pale cleavage. Underage? Maybe. Valentine looked at her hands because he always found that crime seemed to leave its mark on the fingers. Hers were very clean, the nails painted neatly and unbitten. An innocent's hands. An innocent in fishnet stockings.

Her friend was in her thirties, expertly perched on four-inch heels, her handbag reinforced with heavy-duty clasps and a lock. She said she might as well have a smoke too, and took a Silk

Cut. The two girls lit up from the same lighter, eyes shut, looks of bliss, and Valentine knew what they were thinking – that this would be the best moment of the evening, because there was a genuine emotion here, in this small communion.

He held his warrant card out, eye-level, in front of the woman on heels. 'Fuck,' she said, rocking back, so that her shoulders fell against the brick wall. 'What?' she asked, screwing a heel down on the Silk Cut, and looking over Valentine's shoulder.

He'd memorized the note in records. A Thursday night. June 14, 1996, the corner of Tilden Street. A police caution issued to Joe Osbourne, of No. 5, The Circle, Creake.

'Relax,' he said. 'I'm looking for someone. Name's Goodchild, Naomi. She'd be in her late thirties by now, so maybe she doesn't work anymore. She's not in trouble. Just routine.'

They didn't look impressed, but Valentine spotted a covert glance. 'What's it worth?' asked the teenager, and Valentine spotted a Northern accent, suburban, middle class. Manchester, perhaps.

'It's worth me not walking back to the nick and looking at missing persons. Worth me not taking you back with me to help look. Worth me not locking you up while I look. That do yer?'

She swore in his face, but there was just an edge of anxiety to the bravado, so that her voice caught, although she tried to cover it with a cough.

Behind him Valentine heard footsteps and he turned to see three men, all in their forties, all in shirts, no jackets, coming down the street. Classic long-distance punters, he thought. They've come in one car and parked it on the good side of town. They'd have left their IDs, wallets, rings and phones in the boot. Then they'd set out to find girls, with one of them holding the cash, probably in a body belt. He wondered who they'd left at home, and what story they'd concocted. A pub-crawl, perhaps. They wore one shared, mutual, overconfident smile.

'Look,' said the girl in heels. 'We need a trick – OK? It's a quiet night. They see that warrant card, it's getting quieter.'

The men had stopped mid-street, waiting to see which of the girls walked off with Valentine.

'Naomi Goodchild's well past working,' said the older woman. 'But try the house next to the church, the one with the steel door.' She nodded over Valentine's shoulder, down the street, towards All Saints.

At the foot of the street Valentine paused and, looking back, saw the men and girls in a single ring, chatting, laughing. For the first time he recognized them as hunter and hunted. He thought about going back and taking the Manchester girl down to the station anyway, but he told himself he'd given his word, as if that mattered in her world, or his.

He was on the edge of an estate, built in the fifties, in egg-box brutal blocks. At the centre was an open space, the ancient graveyard of All Saints, and what was left of the medieval church itself, minus a tower which had tumbled in the seventeenth century. Beyond was another street of terraced red-bricks, two-up, two-downs. The first in the row didn't only have a steel door; it had steel windows too. The whole house sealed off from vandals. But there were three neat council black bins in the front garden and a wheelie-bin set out on the pavement.

The door gave at the pressure of his knock and swung in, revealing a hallway with a new blue carpet and a hundred-watt shadeless bulb. Maybe it was the stark light that made the woman standing under it look so old. Perhaps *old* wasn't right, thought Valentine, because age hinted, at least, at other things. Experience, wisdom, even peace. No. She looked like a young person worn out. Valentine held up his warrant card. 'Naomi Goodchild?'

'I can't help.'

'Haven't asked for help yet,' said Valentine, stepping in, but leaving the steel door open.

'Just saving you time,' she said.

'Security's good,' he said.

'House was derelict,' she said. 'Now it's full.'

'I wanted to know if you remembered anything about a man – a customer – called Joe Osbourne. Fourteen years ago you had an argument with him in the street about the price. Cautions all round.'

'You're in my way,' she said.

Valentine stood aside. As she squeezed past she paused and looked him in the face.

'I haven't seen Joe since,' she said. 'You're wasting your breath.'

But he wasn't, because if she'd remembered Joe Osbourne after all that time he hadn't been a fleeting client, a one-nighter. Which begged the question: what had he been?

'Joe was a regular?' he asked.

'Maybe.'

'Why remember Joe?'

'He said he loved me. He said it because he wanted to be loved. Not because he meant it. It happens.'

Valentine was astonished to see tears on her face, two of them, one under each eye, catching the orange street lights like a pair of cheap beads.

'Christ,' she said.

'But he still wanted sex?'

She glared at him, and for the first time he saw her eyes were blue, like the felt on a cheap pool table.

'He didn't want me to see other clients. And he couldn't pay for that. I was saving to get out, off the streets. You stay, you never leave.'

'But why the fight in the street?' asked Valentine.

She struggled with the answer, not because she didn't have it, but because, Valentine guessed, this was a part of her past she didn't want to relive for more complex reasons than shame or embarrassment.

'One night, that night, he couldn't take it – me seeing other customers – so he went for the next bloke up the stairs. Said he'd make sure I never got another customer. Those days we had muscle on the door, so they threw him out. But I knew he was out there because he always came into town on that motorbike of his, and I could see it opposite. So I went out, later, when there was no more business. I knew he'd be there. We had the argument – the one we always had – just louder. That's when the uniform booked us.'

'He had a wife,' said Valentine. 'She was a model, sort of. Beautiful.'

'He said he was lonely,' she said. 'He said he'd made a mess of his life. I should have got him thrown out earlier. But he said he'd kill himself if he couldn't see me. Or he'd kill someone so they'd put him away. It was just talk.'

Valentine tried to picture the scene that night, knowing he'd missed a detail. What was it that Shaw always said? That you had to *see* what had happened. He thought of Joe Osbourne, the slight frame, the tense, fragile bones.

'When you say he went for the next bloke up the stairs – what with? Fists?'

She looked through Valentine as if she could see the past. 'He had a knife. He always had a knife. Joe was strong – wiry. But he didn't like the streets, so he carried that, in his leather motorcycle boot.'

EIGHTEEN

At home, closing the front door against the night, Valentine listened to the familiar sound of the echo of the latch and the clatter of the flap as the cat went out into the yard. Every time he came home the cat left, despite the fact that he fed it, filled its bowl. His sister had brought it round one Christmas Day with a cash'n'carry-sized pack of food. It wasn't a total stranger, because it would creep in front of the gas fire when he was asleep on the sofa in winter. In summer he'd wake to find it sat on the window sill – outside – watching, as if Valentine was an intruder. The house felt like a timeshare, an arrangement which meant that when he did come home the place felt slightly less empty.

He took a handful of post into the kitchen and put the kettle on, trying to pretend that he wasn't going to go out again, stroll down to the Artichoke, and watch *Match of the Day 2*. An accident of generation meant that this always counted as a treat. He'd been brought up in the years when there was no live football on television, just the highlights of one, often boring, match. Not so much highlights as lowlights. Dour struggles acted out on muddy pitches in front of black and white crowds. To see all the games, in colour, in frenetic snap shot was still a thrill.

He got a single mug, put a tea bag in with some milk, and waited for the kettle to boil. The interview with Naomi Goodchild was still fresh in his mind so he briefly reviewed it – a technique he'd discovered early in his career as an efficient way of burning the detail into his memory. The image of the knife stowed in the motorcycle boot was a vivid one, and he knew it would be the first thing he'd see when he opened his eyes in the morning.

Then there was a single, loud knock on the door. There was

a specific quality to the knock, as if someone had lifted the metal knocker and let it fall with a twist of the wrist, to maximize the noise. The second knock got him on his feet and he was mildly embarrassed to find that his nerves were humming by the time he got to the front door, as if he was some nutter afraid of the outside world, some recluse unable to touch a doorknob. It was Lena Shaw, but it took him a few seconds to recognize her, and he was so confused he didn't hear what she'd said.

She smiled. Her face was animated by genuine interest, and she didn't break eye contact. She had a remarkable ability to remain calm which he'd always found intimidating. He realized, at the same moment, that he'd forgotten the fact of the colour of her skin, which when he'd first met her had been the first thing he'd noticed.

'Sorry,' he said, and they both laughed.

In the kitchen she took a seat and he realized he was still wearing his raincoat. She was in a trendy kind of top with zips. Her body radiated a physical presence because the curves of it were so pronounced, especially in the face, dominated by the wide, full mouth.

'Sorry,' she said, as it appeared to be her turn. 'You're going out – I won't be a second.' Again, the dazzling smile, a bit too big for the face, and the strangely attractive cast to the eye, so that she seemed to be looking past him, as if Shaw was about to come into sight. But a note of businesslike organization as well. She'd taken control of the meeting, even though this was his kitchen, in his house. The cat appeared at the window ledge and the two females eyed each other.

'It's Peter,' she said. 'He'd be mortified if he knew I was here. Of course, you can tell him if you want. I don't expect it's healthy to keep secrets. But I hope you won't.'

'Where does he think you are?' asked Valentine.

'Majestic, with friends. The last Harry Potter. Well, I hope it's the last. Then an Italian – very good, on King's Staithe? It's my monthly night out.'

He nodded.

'I'll see them there. I just wanted to let you know something.' She placed both hands on the table, as if to steady herself. 'That Peter's not well. His eye . . .'

'He's OK,' said Valentine, misunderstanding. 'He gets by fine

– better than fine. Better than me . . .' He pulled open the kitchen door and they went out into the yard. Unlike most of the street his yard was the original: no conservatory, no porch, just the outside loo, a coal shed. The cat sat on the wall, a perfect silhouette against a perfect night sky. Julie had always insisted he went outside to smoke, and it was a rule he liked to keep.

'I don't mean his blind eye, George. I mean his good eye.' She told him what had happened on the beach that morning.

'What can I do?' he asked, but it wasn't really a question, more a bald statement of helplessness.

'You know him better than anyone else – it's nearly four years. You're together almost every working day. Just watch. If he's in distress, if he can't go on, ring me.'

Valentine wondered how she'd got this picture of his relationship with DI Shaw and struggled to imagine what symptoms the DI might exhibit if he was in distress.

'You're his friend, George,' Lena said. 'I just didn't want to be the only person who knew. That's selfish of me. I'm sorry.'

'He doesn't talk much,' said Valentine.

Lena recalled the first time she'd gone home to the Shaw family home in Hunstanton – a minor Victorian villa at the back of the town; one of a pair, the other with a GUEST HOUSE sign in the large bay window. Shaw's father had been forced into retirement by that point, and it was the last year of his life. Shaw's mother had fussed over her daughter-in-law, but ex-DCI Jack Shaw had said half a dozen words, a reticence she'd wrongly ascribed to the colour of her skin. By the time she found herself sitting at his deathbed she'd realized that he was a man of few words and almost no exterior emotions. That last time, as she'd waited in the car outside while Shaw said what they all knew would be goodbye, she'd seen George Valentine walking up the street. He'd stopped at the front gate and looked at the house for nearly a minute before walking up the path and knocking on the door.

'I know he doesn't talk much,' she said. 'It runs in the family.'

Somewhere along the line of backyards they heard the cat cry out.

'Like father, like son,' she said.

NINETEEN

Monday

Valentine stood on a pile of bricks in the street looking up at the corner of the house in which Arthur Patch had lived and died in the split-second of a gas explosion. The pinnacle of scorched bricks supported the staircase, the white wood of each step charred at the edge. The chimney stack stood as well, but little else. To the corner stack was attached a piece of bedroom wall, the blue and gold striped wallpaper untouched by the blast which had blown the floorboards through the roof, and the roof into the sky.

Valentine heard the low rumble of Shaw's Porsche at the roadblock down on the main street. He'd called Shaw first thing to tell him what he'd discovered about Joe Osbourne's secret life on the streets. A one-off incident, or a glimpse of a pattern? Joe had motive – Marianne's sexual indiscretions – a flimsy alibi which no one alive could substantiate, so opportunity as well, and now a weapon. Shaw had been particularly struck by Valentine's description of the incident, because in his experience the number of people who get through life without using physical violence on someone else was astonishingly high. It was just that those who did tended to make a habit of it.

Shaw made his way up the street, led through the rubble and broken glass by a fireman; Valentine noted the epaulette on his shirt – an impeller, a laurel leaf, then two smaller impellors, making him an Assistant Chief Fire Officer. Top brass. Shaw introduced him as Bill Harding, mid-forties, brisk and military. He gave them a two-minute summary report. The gas explosion had occurred at precisely 2.31 p.m. on Friday. Arthur Patch, aged eighty-seven, was the sole occupant. The house was rented. His wife Marie had died six years earlier. Social services had organized food and medical visits until last summer when Patch had elected to look after himself. Neighbours had rallied round. There had been signs of mild senility, but nothing worse.

The fire brigade investigations unit had made a preliminary examination of the scene. They'd concluded that the oven in the kitchen had been the source of the gas, but that the seat of the fire had been in the bedroom above, which is why the force of the blast had destroyed the upper rooms, torn off the roof, but left the ground floor virtually untouched. A single tea light beside the bed had probably provided the lethal spark. Given the power supply was uninterrupted for the area at the time the presence of the lighted candle in mid-afternoon was suspicious.

Initially, they'd tried to put together an innocent explanation for Patch's death. He *was* a smoker, and may have used the candle to light up. There was no law against pensioners lying in bed smoking. But it wasn't likely, and the neighbours reported that Patch was often seen in the daytime, and always dressed. A more likely scenario was that Patch had gone to bed Thursday night, died from natural causes, and it had taken several hours for the lethal concentration of gas to build up in the roof space and reach the candle. But what they had of the corpse was clothed: shreds of shoe, a jumper. So that didn't fit. There had been enough questions to ask the pathologist to take a closer look. They knew the rest. Cyanide in the bloodstream.

'Exit fire brigade, enter CID,' said Harding. 'My problem's what happened when the smoke cleared.'

The explosion, he explained, had sent half a tonne of burning wood and masonry up into the sky. Bits of brick had come down nearly 200 yards away, but burning paper and wood sparks had drifted on the wind. At first they thought they'd got away with secondary fires even though the landscape was a tinderbox, waiting for a match. But last night they'd spotted flames about midnight, up on the crest of the hill. They had beaters out now trying to stop it spreading. There might be more embers just waiting to flare into life. And each fire created its own embers. If the wind picked up they'd have a real problem. 'Which is why I'm here,' said Harding, 'and not on the beach with the kids. But I'll leave Patch to you boys . . . I think cyanide pills are way out of my league.'

The street looked like something out of the Blitz. The rest of the houses were still evacuated. None had kept their windows, and the two on either side of Arthur Patch's houses would need rebuilding – the partition walls laced with cracks, a hole in one showing the corner of a bed, the linen white and crisp. The tarmac was strewn still with bricks and glass, a scene-of-crime tape keeping the inquisitive down by the corner.

Shaw stepped over the threshold, a wodge of daily newspapers under his arm. Taking them into the small front room he spread them out on the dining table, which was unmarked by the blast but covered in a thick film of brick dust. East Hills had made the front of *The Daily Telegraph*, *The Times*, *Daily Mail* and *The Independent*. The chief constable had got what he wanted in spades – which was good news, set to make the bad news even worse.

As he reread the headlines Shaw felt a slight pain in his damaged right eye. That morning, at eight precisely, he'd seen the eye specialist at the Queen Elizabeth. There was no sign of deterioration in his good eye, and no indications of disease in the blind one. But the blurred vision was clearly a worrying symptom. Any repetition would warrant consideration of enucleation – surgical removal of the blind eye. If he was really worried about a 'fake' glass eye they could fashion one to mimic the damaged one – a synthetic moon-eye. He'd given Shaw numbers to ring if the symptoms returned. With flexibility on his part they could have him in for the operation within forty-eight hours. There was no guarantee the procedure would arrest any decline in the good eye, but in eighty-five per cent of cases it did. As odds went, for Shaw, they were good enough. He looked up through the charred rafters of the house and saw the daytime moon: mountains, craters and seas, in sharp focus. Natural optimism, his default setting, reasserted itself, like a caffeine rush.

Valentine walked into the hall and then into the kitchen. The oven was still in place, held by the heavy cast iron of the range. The door had gone, the steel box of the oven itself distorted into a ragged hole. Shaw crouched down on his knees and looked inside. 'So, George. Off you go . . .' he said, his voice echoing slightly. 'Tell me what happened.'

Valentine wasn't particularly interested in playing games. 'Killer gets in – walks in, 'coz this kind of street no one locks their doors,' he said. 'He forces the pill down him – maybe cracks his jaw too. We'll never know because every bone he had is now cracked like an old teacup. Then the killer carries the body up to the bed – let's say that's Thursday night – sets the candle, then turns on the gas. It took all night and half the next day for the gas to build up in the loft, the ceiling space. My guess is that's a lot longer than he thought it would take. But he'd closed all the windows so it was gonna blow eventually. When it does it takes Arthur into space. Our good luck was that some of him came back down.'

Valentine thought about the picture he'd painted then shook his head. 'Only thing that doesn't work is the candle – it'd have to be eight foot tall to burn all night. So maybe the killer came in the night? But then, that doesn't work, 'coz the old bloke's in his daytime clothes. That morning, perhaps – the Friday. Same day Marianne Osbourne died?'

'That's better,' said Shaw. 'The key question is why – why did Arthur Patch have to die?'

They'd been advised not to climb the stairs but Shaw said he'd take a chance, edging up, the wood creaking. Valentine stood at the foot, dizzy with sympathetic vertigo. Ten steps up he could see into what was left of the back bedroom. Part of the floor was left; on it stood a small bedside table on which they'd found the saucer and all-night candle. Part of the headboard of the bed was left imbedded into the wall. There were stains there, on the dark wood, so Shaw looked away. The glimpse reminded him they were dealing with death, and as always that focused his mind, making the real world clearer.

'Why'd he die?' asked Shaw again, feeling the gritty dust on the banister.

'He saw something . . .' offered Valentine, opening a file he'd got biked out from the council offices in Wells. Arthur Patch's employment records: 1951–1994. His last day on the payroll was October 1 – two weeks after the East Hills murder. He'd been the senior car park attendant at the quayside for eighteen years. 'Imagine what he had in his head,' said Valentine. 'All the locals, plus their cars. 'Coz it's the only place to park on the quay, so it's not just tourists. Most of the town's got double-yellows, so even the residents have to use it. He'd know everyone, they'd know him. Dangerous man if you're a killer trying to cover your tracks.'

'So you're saying Patch died so he couldn't come forward and give us an ID, and that the same man helped Marianne Osbourne take her life to stop her telling the truth when she got into St

James'?' It made sense but Valentine didn't react, so Shaw tried another question. 'If that's what happened why didn't Patch die in 1994?'

Valentine didn't miss a beat. 'Because in 1994 everyone thought the killer was one of the seventy-four people taken off East Hills. Whatever Patch saw wasn't suspicious in itself, only in retrospect. The killer knew we'd draw a blank with the mass screening – that we'd widen the net. There'd be publicity. We'd want witnesses, fresh witnesses, who'd seen anything suspicious that day. That's when the killer feared Patch would come forward.'

Shaw was quietly impressed. It had taken him an hour in bed just before dawn to work that out. 'You remember Patch?' he asked.

'Maybe,' said Valentine. The nick at Wells had a car park at the back so he'd never had to park on the quay. But he remembered the little caravan. He thought Patch had worn a hat – something jaunty – not a Tam o' Shanter, a Trilby maybe. Then, one day, he was gone with his caravan, and the machines took his place, which no one could operate, so the council lost a fortune, and one day there was a new caravan, smart and modern, with an attendant.

'Neighbours?' asked Shaw. 'Anyone see anything?'

'They're all down the parish hall. Jackie's organizing. I've got some copies of Osbourne's picture down there, just in case.' They'd seen DC Lau's Megane parked by the village green, racing red with go-fast stripes and bafflers. Spoilers too.

They stepped out into the backyard. Like most cottages along the Norfolk hills it had a long, narrow garden plot, big enough for a family to grow its own vegetables. A smallholding really, to bolster breadline agricultural wages.

Patch was past gardening so it was rough lawn, cut around a line of fruit trees. Hawthorns choked the end of the plot. But a rough path led through, and when they were in the shadows they saw a small caravan, just a box on wheels, rust eating through a coat of white paint.

'Christ,' said Valentine. 'You'd have thought he had enough of the sodding thing. Nearly twenty years and he takes it home.'

'Not everyone hates their job,' said Shaw, making a point of not catching Valentine's eye. 'Council probably thought they were doing him a favour. Plus it made way for the new machines.' He tried the door and it gave effortlessly, part of the lock falling to the ground. Inside was a pull-down table, a fold-up picnic chair and an old paraffin heater. On a row of nails hung circular bands of tickets, the colours – pink, blue, and green – faded where they'd caught the sun. On a hook hung a Trilby. Shaw looked at his watch. 'O'Hare'll have the DNA results by now from Tom and the FSL.' He imagined the chief constable opening the lab report with crisp, dry fingers. 'I better get back – face up. Tell him about this too. Can you go back to The Circle? Let's put someone on Patch's friends – with East Hills in the news perhaps he said something. British Legion, neighbours, usual stuff. And see if we can get someone to help Fiona trace the source of these cyanide capsules. Priority. We'll see Osbourne but not just yet. Let him stew a bit longer. I want to check something first. If he's our man he's a swimmer. So I'll meet you at Wells Lido at ten. Ruth Robinson's on duty.'

TWENTY

The lido was just beyond a fifties housing estate on the edge of Wells. A white art deco wall threw a sinuous embrace around an oval pool, a blue dolphin emblem over the entrance. Climbing out of the Porsche Shaw heard the unmistakable sound of an outdoor swimming pool – the splashing, the mock screams, the tinny jangle of muzak over a public address system. And the smell, an instant Proustian rush as he walked towards the little ticket window – ozone and chlorine and damp towels.

Valentine was sat by the ticket booth on a bench, his angular frame crowded into a tiny area of shade. Shaw showed his warrant card to the woman behind the grille and said they'd like to see Ruth Robinson – Marianne Osbourne's next-door sister.

She was just finishing a lesson, so could they wait?

Valentine's mobile rang and he walked away into the car park where the metal chassis baked under a rippling mirage. Shaw took the vacated seat on the wooden bench, watching the summer clouds build over the unseen sea.

He tried to clear his mind of the interview he'd just had with Brendan O'Hare. The chief constable had summarized the paperwork on the East Hills mass screening and listened to Shaw's own analysis of the state of the inquiry.

It had taken O'Hare less than ten seconds to formulate a response. 'The papers will be asking us about East Hills by when, Peter? I haven't checked but I bet the press office has had calls already. We need to respond. The junior league approach would be to slip out a press release saying the mass screening had drawn a blank but that we were following up leads, etc., etc. . . . But this lot are Fleet Street, not the local rag. They'd crucify us – me. No, what we need to do is give them a story. That's your job, Peter. Let's say 3.30 p.m. here at St James', the Norfolk Suite, Thursday,' he said, flicking open a laptop and tapping in a diary entry.

'Any inquiries before that we can tell them to wait for the presser. Best-case scenario is that you have, by that time, found the killer, or uncovered some concrete evidence which will lead, inexorably, to his identity. Maybe this Joe Osbourne character you seem so struck with. If I was you, Peter, I'd get him in here. Plenty of pressure, see when he breaks. I take it we are still looking for a man, Peter? No change there?'

'Sir. Sample X is a man's DNA.'

'Goodo. If you find yourself discernibly short of giving the press a thumping good story I would suggest you concoct one. Anything you like. Perhaps we can glean a lead from the statements taken as part of this exhaustive – and expensive – inquiry? Make it good. The press will run with it, we'll knock it into the long grass and then we'll have to rely on the goldfish-like attention span of Fleet Street news desks. I want something in writing three hours before the presser to my secretary or my email.' O'Hare closed the laptop. 'Great timing, by the way, Peter. We're trying to cut ten million pounds out of the force budget without impacting on frontline services and you contrive to blow half a million quid on a dud DNA sweep. Well done.'

Shaw had thought about interjecting the correct figure, but let it go.

'Next month, if we don't have the killer in custody, I will put out an internal memo to say that the senior officer in charge of the East Hill's inquiry has requested a transfer,' said the chief constable. 'That's you, by the way, in case you hadn't noticed, because I certainly might have missed it. The internal memo will leak inexplicably to the press. George can pack his bags too. Wells' nick is up to compliment – but I'm sure we can get him back in somehow.' O'Hare glanced at his diary. 'You can both attend the presser on Thursday. In fact, I insist on it. Back row. I'll do the talking if there's something to say. If not, you're giving the presser and I'll be in Whitehall; otherwise known as the West Norfolk golf course.' He pushed his chair back on oiled castors and stood. 'I think you should consider your future. Maybe a transfer isn't for you. Your wife runs a business, I think, locally. Long-distance marriages do work, of course. Mine didn't – twice.' O'Hare smiled inappropriately and then touched the file on his blotter. 'I see that following your unfortunate accident you were required to attend annual medical checks and a thorough ophthalmic examination. Should you fail to satisfy the police committee of your ability to continue in the job, certainly at an operational level, we would be in a position to recommend a disability allowance and pension.'

O'Hare looked at him for the only time in their interview. 'You're a good copper, Peter. But even good coppers have to be lucky. Get lucky by Thursday, or you're out. One way or another.'

Shaw requested authorization to spend a further £7,000 on asking the lab to run a familial search through the national DNA database to see if there was a close match to Sample X, rather than a direct match. As long shots went it was pretty much intercontinental. The chances of the East Hills killer being randomly related to someone on the main database by family were slight. But could they afford not to do the obvious? It was the standard next step. If they got a close match at least they'd know where to start looking for the killer.

O'Hare turned him down flat; in fact, he'd make a point at the press conference that he'd refused a request to chuck good money after bad. The next time the West Norfolk paid for a DNA mass screening the officer in charge of the inquiry would do his home-work first, said the chief constable, talking to his blotter, and make sure they weren't frittering away taxpayers' hard-earned income.

Shaw had been wordlessly dismissed. The anger he'd felt at the humiliation was still with him.

The sound of a bell echoed round the lido to mark the hour.

Valentine reappeared, texting on his mobile. 'Lincoln CID,' he

said, waving the phone. 'They tracked down Julie Carstairs –
the girlfriend who stood Marianne Osbourne up on the day of
the East Hills murder. She says that was a little white lie. She
never intended to go out that day, and there'd been no agreement
to meet. Marianne came to see her – she lived in Wells – the
evening of the killing, after she'd given her statement to us at St
James'. She told Julie she'd lied because she was meeting a boy
out there and she didn't want her parents to know. Apparently
she'd been out with Marianne a couple of times to East Hills
because her Dad wanted her to have a chaperone. Julie was
eighteen. She admits she didn't exactly watch her every move
out there. So I think we can read between the lines. She says the
boys followed Marianne like gulls after a trawler. She's got no
idea who she was going to see that day. And Marianne didn't
say if she had met him. And no names.'

They heard light steps on the tiled floor. 'DI Shaw?' Ruth
Robinson was in a tracksuit and her skin was dry and flushed
despite the heat, so that he guessed that she'd just done some
lengths and showered. The subtle reflection of Marianne's
Pre-Raphaelite looks was stronger in daylight. Shaw actually shook
his head, trying to dislodge the image of Marianne on her deathbed.
Ruth had to be twice the weight of her sibling, possibly three
times. Despite that she had a strange buoyancy, as if she could
float in air as easily as she no doubt could in water. She held her
arms and hands away from her body as if they too were floating
free. Mass she had, he thought, but not weight. An attractive
woman, because she seemed to wear her size well. Happy, thought
Shaw, in her own skin.

The pool was crowded, inflatables clashing, children toppling
off airbeds, balls being lobbed into screeching clusters of school
friends. There was no shade except a single slash across the blue
water – the silhouette of the high diving board. A grass perimeter
was crowded too, this time with sunbathers, older teenagers,
young adults. A cluster of toddlers with armband floats were
being shepherded along the poolside and Robinson gently cleared
a way forward with the calm assurance of an adult confident in
the company of children.

Three sides of the pool were open, with the perimeter wall
providing a windbreak. The fourth side was changing rooms.
There was a single-storey café built into the perimeter wall – a

long glass window displaying a rack of ice-cream flavours. Robinson went in through a side door and emerged with a cafetière on a tray, three large cups, three glasses of water.

'I wanted to talk about Marianne,' said Shaw. 'But mostly about your brother-in-law, Joe.'

She didn't look at him, but at the children in the shallow end. It struck Shaw that this woman, childless, spent much of her life with kids. He wondered if she'd tried for children with her husband Aidan. Ruth smiled, cradling the coffee. Shaw was struck that someone so benign, the word was difficult to avoid – wholesome – could also hint at something else, something slightly darker, because there was a calculating facet to her stillness: a stillness so like her husband's. She looked up at the sky where a line of geese were heading out to the marshes.

'Joe,' she said. 'Why would you be interested in Joe?'

Shaw ignored the question. 'Your sister said, in her original statement back in 1994, that she'd planned to go out to East Hills that day with a friend, Julie Carstairs. But that, we now know, is a lie. Julie didn't know she was going out that day. Why would Marianne tell that lie?'

'I loved my sister very much, Inspector. But I don't think I ever understood her. I don't know why she told that lie. She told lots. I think she thought it was one of the privileges of beauty.' She held one hand down on the table top with the other as if it might float away. Her voice was very light, lighter than air, and musical.

'We think she met someone out on the island – a lover,' said Shaw. 'And we think there's a good chance she was being blackmailed by White – the lifeguard who was murdered. Or, possibly, White *was* her lover.'

Ruth's eyes were small and quick and they were on Shaw's now, or glancing, sideways, at Valentine. 'You don't think Marianne was the killer, surely . . .'

'No. But someone killed White. Which was good news for Marianne.' Shaw let the coffee slip down his throat, following it quickly with the tap water. 'Do you think Joe knew what was going on – that Marianne was playing the field?' Shaw noted that despite the calm exterior the colour had drained from the woman's face. He wondered if she really didn't know about her

husband and Marianne Osbourne. Could such secrets survive in
a small town?

'Marianne told him later about the others,' she said. 'Once
they were married, once Tilly was born. She was proud of it –
the lovers. I always thought that was a calculated cruelty because
she didn't have to tell him, did she? She made out that she wanted
total honesty. I think *that* was a lie.'

'But Joe might have known at the time?' pressed Shaw, aware
she hadn't answered his question.

'Yes. I think Marianne was torn – she wanted secret lovers,
but she wanted people to know. Well, most of all she wanted me
to know.'

'Why did she want you to know about her success with men?'
Shaw asked.

'Because it was a competition she could win. I was the clever
one. I was the better swimmer, although Marianne was good, very
good. But swimming was Mum's passion and so we were close.
That left Dad. She wanted his love, his affection, and she got it.
And somehow she turned that idea – that she could compete for
affection – into competing for sex. I was a bit bookish, shy. So
she told me in her letters about the boyfriends. Not everything,
but enough. She lied to Dad, said it was all just a kiss and a
cuddle. So I guess that's why she lied about that day, so he
wouldn't cause a fuss.'

'Swimming was a big part of Marianne's life?' said Shaw.

'Before East Hills – after that I don't think I ever saw her in
the water again.'

'Anyone ever swim out to East Hills?' He'd been saving
the question. Robinson's reaction was half-puzzlement,
half-understanding.

She looked out over the pool. 'It's been done. Childish, really.'
She tugged at the tracksuit collar. 'But when you're young you
never think you're going to die.'

'You've done it – swum out and back?'

'No. We'd go one way – back, usually. It's very difficult to
go there and back because of the tides. So we'd all go out on
the boat and whoever was up for it would leave their stuff for
us to bring back. I did it once; I'd have been sixteen. No lifeguard
back then so that made things easier. It's actually pretty scary.
We'd have a word with the boatman because they always check

the tickets, to make sure they're not leaving someone out there.'

Another lie, this time Tug Coyle's.

'What about the rip-tide?'

'Golden rule: never swim against the tide. You have to go with it. The trick is to swim out, away from the island towards the north-east, and then catch the current back towards the main beach at Wells. So maybe half a mile out, a bit more, then all the way in. Mile and a half to two miles in total. It's a challenge.'

'And Joe – he doesn't look like he could swim a length,' said Shaw, smiling, looking out over the water, proud of the way he'd constructed the interview in reverse, so that the crucial question came last.

'Joe was one of the best,' she said. 'Champion here – age of fourteen, fifteen. Long-distance freestyle. Sickly kid – really bad. Asthma and stuff. But that's how some people react, isn't it? They're kind of aggressively fit, to compensate. He's skinny, not much muscle, but it's stamina you need and guts. That's Joe. I think he did it a few times.'

TWENTY-ONE

Shaw had the whole team assembled beneath the cool shade of the cedar tree, the midday heat penetrating only in a scatter of sunspots on the beaten grass. A thick cable of PC wires, taped together, had been slung out through one of the stone arrow-slit windows of the Warrener's Lodge to the mobile incident room. The temperature back in the metal box was 110 Fahrenheit and still rising. Twine had two nests of desks set out in the shade, a Perspex information board covered in SOC shots from Osbourne's bedroom and Arthur Patch's house, plus a poster from the original East Hills inquiry showing Shane White's handsome, if forgettable, face.

Overhead, ash drifted from the woods above The Circle. Another fire had sprung up, sparked by the gas explosion, as the fire brigade had feared. It had been doused, but the woods were still thick with clouds of acrid fumes from the smouldering pine trees. The drifting embers had kindled at least one other blaze – over the hill, deeper in the woods, beyond the reach of the fire brigade's hoses. The council beaters had been sent in, the workmen in Day-Glo jackets picking up gear and clothing from an open lorry parked on the narrow lane which led up to The Circle from Creake village. Under the cedar tree, inside the thick walls of the medieval ruin, the air was breathable enough. But they could all taste it, despite the thick, dark coffee from the St James' mobile canteen: a bitter burnt essence of pine needles on the lips and tongue.

The team had been told the result of the East Hills mass screening, or rather, the lack of a result. They all knew the inquiry was in trouble. So Shaw had called them together to tell them that it was time to refocus. They had three days – just – to find the East Hills killer. Their prime suspect was now Joe Osbourne.

'We need to drill down on this guy,' said Shaw. 'I want to know everything about him and I want to put pressure on his alibi – sorry, *alibis* – until they crack. Where was he when Shane

White died? Where was he when his wife died? Where was he when Patch died?'

Drill down – it was one of Shaw's favourite phrases, and seemed to encapsulate his own particular brand of intellectual precision.

Shaw pinned a picture of Osbourne to the board. 'Joe has motive, he had opportunity, he had means, and we now know that two years after the killing it was his habit to always carry a knife. In 1994 he said he was in his father's locksmith's shop all day. He'd been out the back in the workshop. His father had manned the counter. His father is now dead. On the day his wife died he says he was in the same lock-up. No customers till nearly noon, and that was someone he didn't know looking for electric time locks which Osbourne doesn't sell. The earliest time we can place him in the workshop is at 3.15 p.m. when a uniformed officer from Wells told him his wife was dead. So, as an alibi it makes threadbare look like thick pile. Plus, we know he was capable of swimming back from East Hills. In fact, he might even have managed it both ways – or he could have got a free ride out on the ferry from Tug Coyle. Were they friends, maybe? Eventually they'd be family.'

Shaw searched the faces amongst the fragmented shadows of the cedar tree. 'George and I will interview Joe Osbourne now. Let's get down to Wells to the locksmiths. If Joe's our man then he wasn't at the shop that afternoon in 1994, and he wasn't there on the day his wife died sixteen years later, unless she was dead before he left for work. See what the other shop owners know in that street – what the routine is. Where does he go for lunch? Marianne doesn't sound to me like a dutiful sandwich-maker. And we're told they never met in the day, even though they worked less than a few streets apart. Get on to Swansea and find out what Joe's driven in the past as well – he was eighteen at the time of East Hills. Did he have a motorbike? A car? If Patch died because he knew something about that day then there's a good chance it was something to do with a vehicle. Let's find out what vehicle we're dealing with.'

Shaw put his hands together as if in prayer and touched the tip of each index finger to his lips. 'That's a thought: Ruth Robinson reckons that if you swam to the mainland from East Hills the only way to do it and live to tell the tale is to go out,

then come back with the tide to the main beach. It's late evening
on a hot August day so you can wander around a bit in your
trunks, but pretty soon you'll stand out.'

'Unless you had a vehicle ready, or you could make a call,
get help?' said Campbell. 'Or walk back into town, but then you
would stand out.'

'There's the big beach shop out there, behind the woods,'
offered Jackie Lau. 'If you had cash you could buy shorts, a
T-shirt, then get a bus, or call a cab, or walk. Key question: was
it planned?'

'OK, let's think all that through,' said Shaw. 'But it was
seventeen years ago. I'm more interested in kicking the tyres on
Osbourne's alibi for this Friday, the day his wife died and the
day Patch was murdered. If Osbourne is our killer then either he
stopped at The Row, at Patch's house, on the way down to Wells,
or came back to the village. Again, let's check out his transport
options. If he's on the British motorbike someone will have heard
it – you can hardly miss it.'

They left Twine to organize a DNA swab off Joe Osbourne
after their interview. Shaw wasn't even going to ask O'Hare to
OK the costs of that. This was still Shaw's inquiry, and he could
authorize expenditure under £5,000 without going up the line of
command.

Out on The Circle a marked police car was parked outside
No. 5. The porch of the house was crowded with bouquets and
wreaths, dominated by a single bunch of sunflowers. Shaw looked
at the card and saw they were from Kelly's, the undertakers,
Ella Assisi's signature scrawled across an embossed card. *Best
Wishes*.

Again, thought Shaw, a curious lack of love.

Inside the house, Joe Osbourne stood in the hallway. 'What's
this about?' he said.

His fair hair was unkempt and his hands, slender, almost
feminine, hung by his sides, smudged with oil.

'A few questions,' said Shaw. 'Routine. There's been some
developments.'

Osbourne looked into the front room, then towards the
bedroom, as if trapped in his own house.

'Not here,' he said. 'Please.' He looked at his feet; his shoulders
slumped.

Shaw waited. 'There's a workshop,' volunteered Osbourne. 'Down the garden, we can go there. I often go there.'

A picket fence just two feet high separated the back gardens of No. 5, and the Robinson's next door at No. 6, which was mostly chicken-run. The Osbournes' was dominated by the allotment vegetables and a patch of rough grass, leading to a wooden workshop – almost the width of the garden, with just a narrow alley left to a gate which led out to the pine woods.

One of the padlocks on the workshop was proving difficult to open and the frustration seemed to be too much for Osbourne. He dropped his hands, eyes closed, as if trying to hold himself together. He tried again, and the lock gave. Inside, the workshop was a surprise – more a study or a den. Books lined one wall; there was a leather battered armchair in one corner, a gas heater for a kettle, a digital radio, a desk with pencils neatly lined up beside a mug. There was a workbench too, and Osbourne took the wooden seat beside it. As he sat he slipped an inhaler out of his pocket and took two surreptitious breaths.

'What developments?' he asked.

Shaw told him about the explosion at Arthur Patch's house, the traces of cyanide in the old man's blood, his tenuous link to the East Hills murder. Then he told him that they now thought the East Hills killer might not be amongst the thirty-five men on the island that afternoon in 1994.

Did he know Patch? Did he ever use the little car park by the quayside?

Osbourne laughed. 'Everyone knew Arthur. Bit of a character. He was in that caravan, or sat outside it, every working day of his life. 'Course I knew him. Never needed to park though – always had the bike. We have deliveries but I know the wardens and they turn a blind eye for twenty minutes, so no, I never used the car park.'

'Mr Osbourne,' said Shaw. 'We've also discovered some new information about Marianne, about the day she was out on East Hills. I'm afraid she didn't tell the truth – not the whole truth – about that day.'

'I don't understand,' said Osbourne, one hand automatically tightening, then loosening a G-clamp on the edge of the bench, spinning the well-greased metal handle.

'Marianne said she was planning to go out to East Hills with a friend, Julie Carstairs. That Julie didn't turn up, so she went alone.'

'That's right.'

'No, it isn't,' said Shaw, and Osbourne seemed to flinch. 'Julie says Marianne may have done this to meet men, Mr Osbourne.' Shaw took a deep breath, because what he wanted to say was cruel, but he thought he should say it: 'Several *different* men that summer.'

'I don't believe that,' said Osbourne. He ran his still-oily hand through his hair, leaving a grey highlight. But the denial of the possibility he'd been cheated on was perfunctory, Shaw thought.

'I think you knew all about it,' said Shaw. 'And I think you'd decided to do something about it. I think you were on East Hills that day. How did you get to the island – did you swim, or did Tug Coyle pick you up at Morston? That would have given you an element of surprise. So you could just walk out of the sea. What did you do? Look for Marianne? Then, when you didn't find her, did you wander off into the dunes? She was there, wasn't she – with White. And that's when you killed him. But you picked up a wound – something bloody but superficial. So you had to swim for it.

Osbourne swallowed, the Adam's apple bobbing in his bony throat. His face seemed to ripple slightly, as if from a blow.

'I don't think you meant to kill him – did you, Joe? Just scare him.'

And then Shaw saw it more clearly. 'Did he have a knife too? Was that what you didn't expect? We know he had one and it's never been found. And you *always* had one.'

Osbourne's eyes widened, and Shaw thought that he was trying to work out what else they might know.

'I don't know what you're talking about. None of it – not a word.'

'Since your wife died you've been going into work I think – most days. That's what Aidan told us. But the shop's been shut. Where have you been Mr Osbourne?'

Osbourne seemed to focus on a point equidistant between them. 'I walk. In the dunes. It helps.'

From the woods they heard the sound of dogs barking. Osbourne stood, knocking the bench, and walked to the back door of the workshop, keeping his back to them. He opened the top half of a stable door and looked out at the edge of the woods. Smoke was drifting out from the green shadows. Somewhere up the hill, under the canopy of trees, they could hear shouts. He fumbled in his pocket and produced his inhaler, and they heard three rapid breaths.

The shouts in the woods seemed to be getting louder, insistent, and Shaw heard a single police whistle, but a distance away, over the hill, towards the Old Hall Estate.

'I'd like to take a DNA swab, Mr Osbourne,' said Shaw, breaking the silence.

'One of my detective constables will call a little later to take you down to St James'. We'd like a formal statement as well. And if you could stay in Creake – or Wells. If you need to leave the area, even for a few hours, I'd like you to inform DS Valentine here – he'll leave you a mobile number. Are you able to accept those restrictions, Mr Osbourne?'

He turned then, and Shaw could see he was shaking, his narrow shoulders unsteady. 'I was at the shop the day the Aussie died. In the back. Dad was busy; if he hadn't been I'd have gone with her. I'd have been there.'

Shaw logged the denial in his memory, but was unmoved by it.

Osbourne's eyes widened and he almost fell. 'And Marianne, and that old man. You think I did that too?'

'Did you?' asked Shaw.

'No,' said Osbourne, simply. 'Why would I do that?' He looked at his own hands. 'How could I do that?'

'Because Marianne was a witness to White's murder,' said Shaw. 'She lied to save you, as well as herself. But not this time – this time she couldn't face it. Did she ask you to help her end it, or did you suggest it? Had she just had enough of life . . .' Shaw looked back down the garden towards the house: 'Life here, with you. Or just you?'

It was cruel blow but effective. Osbourne raised both hands to this mouth.

'And Arthur Patch saw you that day in 1994, didn't he? Saw the wound. So when we drew a blank on the mass screening, as you knew we would, you were afraid we'd start looking for witnesses along the coast that day and in town, and that's when he'd step forward. So he had to die.'

A shout from the woods made them all turn to the still-open half stable door.

Emerging from the shadows was a man walking quickly towards them: Aidan Robinson, with a beater's brush, a pair of overalls grimy with ash, the left foot trailing badly. When he got to the door he saw Joe Osbourne's face and froze.

'What's wrong?' he asked. The silver-grey eyes were bloodshot from the smoke in the woods.

No one answered.

He looked at Shaw. 'I've been helping up in the woods, keeping the fires down. You need to come up – we've found someone.'

TWENTY-TWO

Dead air filled the woods, the midday heat cloying, the trees stifling the thin breeze from the distant sea. The path led through the clearing with the lightning tree and then deeper into the woods, where drifting smoke and steam threaded the tree trunks. The world was reduced to a fifty-yard circle, branches dripped water, the pine tops above lost in smoke, the colours washed out to leave just greys. By the path, nailed to a tree, was a single sign . . .

THE OLD HALL ESTATE
PRIVATE PROPERTY
TRESPASSERS WILL BE PROSECUTED

'Where we heading?' asked Shaw. 'And what are we going to find?'

Aidan Robinson turned. He pulled one of his fingers straight, making the joint crack. Shaw was struck again by the stillness of the man, as if time didn't run as fast for him as the world around him. 'Down the valley a bit, through the woods. Not far. I don't know what's there; one of the uniformed officers said he'd found remains – human remains – and wanted you up fast. They sent me because I know the woods.'

Valentine had caught up: 'Fresh remains?'

Robinson shrugged, then turned and led the way.

Shaw ploughed on, concentrating on the rough path, watching each boot fall before lifting the next, avoiding the tree roots which occasionally arched over the track. Shaw tried to concentrate on the route ahead but he was worried about Joe Osbourne: he'd left him with DC Twine at the incident room, waiting for a squad car to take him into St James'. The stress had brought on an asthma attack and they'd arranged for him to see a doctor when he got down to police headquarters.

They reached a gully where a stream had dug down through the sandstone rock. Ahead, through the trees, they could see Old Hall far below them – a Georgian ruin, like an abandoned doll's house, just the four walls left, and a thicket of chimney stacks. Just over the gully, on a stretch of bare hillside was what looked like a stone folly, a rotunda, graced with pillars, and a low dome. On the grass beside it lay something more modern that defied any easy identification – a concrete circle, its surface grooved with what looked like a pair of bronze rails. Shaw filed the image away and set off after Robinson.

The trees here were burnt, smouldering still. Ahead, for the first time, Shaw saw flames – a gout, quickly doused, so that the wood was full of the sound of sizzling steam. Around them now they could see beaters, working in short lines, and a hose crossed their path, leading from the stream up into the woods.

And then they smelt it: instantly, the three of them. Only Robinson kept walking, his limp less noticeable now they'd moved on to flatter ground. Shaw had it in his mouth, nose and lungs before he could retch. Cooked meat, like a hog roast. But sweeter, infinitely sweeter. He heard Valentine retch behind him but he didn't turn to stare. He just stopped in his tracks and told himself this was a detail he'd have to make sure he didn't take home.

Robinson came to a halt, looked back, then down at his feet, giving them time.

Shaw and Valentine paused, as if waiting for some hidden barrier to lift, and then they took the next step, together.

A young PC stood guard on the rough path. He held up a hand, searching their faces, relief flooding into his eyes when he recognized Shaw. 'Sir, over there . . .' He pointed to a small clearing. 'And there's loads of this around . . .' In his hand he held a damp wodge of folding money, burnt at the edges, or blackened through. 'It's just blowing around,' he added, as if *that* was the crime. 'Twenty-pound notes.'

Whatever lay at the centre of the clearing it was still alight. While there were no visual clues Shaw knew it instantly as a corpse: the smell was beyond argument, but it was the emotional resonance that was indisputable. Even in death it radiated a personal space – diminished, *diminishing*, but still present. Thick white fumes pumped out of it like a smoke bomb. A single flame flickered on a limb-like projection which stuck up like a wick. The whole body was about the size of a large animal – a sheep, perhaps – and angled, like a collection of disparate bones and in a skin bag. But the surface was charred, furrowed, like wood left in a cold fire. Shaw's eye skated over the surface, trying to find a face, a foot, a hand, something he could recognize that was human, but all he found was a single unambiguous shape: a semicircular curve – two curves, in iron, almost joined together.

'Tom's nearly here,' said Valentine, taking a step back, working on the mobile.

Shaw took another step closer, put a knee down, and felt the warmth still in the ashes. 'It's a trap, right?' he said. 'An animal trap.'

Robinson was behind him, over his left shoulder. 'Not one of the estate's,' he said.

'They lay traps?'

'Sure. Fox, badger, stoat. Keep the woods clear for the deer.' Shaw heard Robinson crunch something in his mouth. A mint. 'But nothing this size.' Hadn't Robinson said he didn't come into the woods anymore – not since he'd been a child?

'Can't we put *it* out . . .?' asked Shaw, angry, but with no one.

They called in a fireman who set a fine spray on the burning corpse, turning smoke to steam. Shaw tried to see the shape of the jaws of the trap, which had sprung, then closed round a limb – a leg, but the foot had seared away, leaving a blackened stump. In the ashes he saw a buckle – metal, like a rucksack brace.

They heard footsteps coming through the trees and the sudden ghostly shape of Tom Hadden in a white SOC suit. He'd come into the woods from Old Hall, up the valley, so he came at the charred body from the opposite side of the clearing. He looked at Shaw. 'You need to be this side, Peter. George.' He pulled up a face mask which was over his Adam's Apple so that it covered his mouth.

They circled the burning body. Valentine saw it first because Shaw heard his breathing quicken, rattling in his throat. And then he saw it too – a human head, untouched by the fire, the skin still white, even the lips still red. The white flesh of the neck simply ended in the white ash of the rest of the body. It was a thought which shocked him, but Shaw thought it was as if the head was a cigarette filter, the rest of the body spent ash in an ashtray.

'Christ,' said Shaw, looking up at the tree tops, hoping to see a splash of blue sky, but finding only the drifting smoke. He'd let his eye return to the face for a nanosecond, but it had been long enough to know he recognized the victim, or recognized the birthmark on the unblemished cheek.

'It's one of the demonstrators – from up by the wind farm. George?'

Flames suddenly flickered within the body, crackling, so that the smoke thickened. Valentine covered his mouth with a handkerchief and stepped closer.

'It's him,' he said.

'Human candle,' said Hadden. 'Once the temperature's high enough the body fat just goes on burning. The head's the last bit left – the rest has gone. I'd say the source of the heat was on his back – there . . .'

Shaw thought of the night-light left beside Arthur Patch's bed, burning until it ignited the gas in the house, blowing itself out. These flames had proved more tenacious.

Hadden leant forward, using a pair of forensic callipers to mark the spot where the vertebra of the back showed through the white ash. The bone was black on the surface, but flaking away from the white calcium beneath, like a firestone in a chimney, set behind the hearth to collect and radiate the heat. 'It's a slow process, could go on for days,' said Hadden. 'We're going to have to cover it, Peter, cut the oxygen supply, otherwise the head will burn. I'll need a fire blanket . . .' he said, looking back at a fireman on the edge of the clearing. Then the CSI man let his eye run over the bundle of flesh and bone. 'There,' he said, using the pincers to point. 'Looks like a torch to me.'

There was cylinder, reduced to the metal core, and what looked like a reflective disc.

So night time, thought Shaw. At Hendon they'd done work on

victims of fire. There was a common belief that human beings can *spontaneously combust* – burst into flames, only to be found later, a pile of ashes in a room untouched by fire. But the science was clear. There needed to be a flame first – an intense source of heat, then the flesh burnt slowly, body fat feeding the flame, until nothing was left. The forest fire had flashed past the trapped victim, whatever had been in the rucksack had ignited and provided an intense source of heat for several minutes, igniting the body fat. Then the long, slow burn had begun. Question was: was he dead by the time the flames arrived, or did the fire overcome him?

The head was chin up, looking at the treetops, so Shaw got to within a few inches of the face. He thought if he did this now, quickly, the image wouldn't end up in his nightmares. It was certainly the young man from the Docking Hill demo, the one who'd kept pace with the Porsche. Had it only been last Friday? They'd been driving down to Wells for the East Hills press conference. The young man with the strawberry birthmark had put his hand on the passenger side sill, and Shaw had noticed the smart, stylish watch which showed the movement of the moon, catching the sunlight. 'Should be a Rolex – separate windows for the sun and moon,' he said.

Hadden began to sift some of the ash at the edge of the smouldering torso.

Shaw thought about Tilly Osbourne, up on the high lane with the demonstrators on the day her mother died. And Aidan Robinson, her uncle, had been up to the demos too, showing solidarity in the cause. And there'd been the placard, discarded in the hallway of No. 5, The Circle . . .

Save Our Unspoilt Landscape.
SOUL

Hadden stood, a charred wristwatch held at arm's length with callipers. 'Sun and moon,' he said.

Shaw edged one last inch closer. The mouth of the victim was open, revealing good teeth, still white. Shaw thought he could smell toothpaste, but wondered if it was just an olfactory hallucination, prompted by the pristine dentistry. Either way he had managed to put aside the stench of cooking meat, so that beyond it he could detect pine needles, which reminded him of Marianne

Osbourne's deathbed. *Sweet* pine needles. And then there was the scent he should have detected that day by her body: a thin trace of almonds in the air. The prickling hairs on his neck made his spine arch. 'Cyanide,' he said.

TWENTY-THREE

Valentine had taken a room at The Ship at Wells-next-the-Sea for the night. He lay on the bed for an hour, in the dark, his head on a pile of four pillows, so that he could look out of the bay window towards the sea. A moonless night, the harbour was just red and green navigation lights, motionless between the dead black water of high tide. Downstairs he could hear life in the bar, a one-armed bandit shunting, the base note on the TV's sound system, but no voices: Monday night, the hour for serving tourists food long gone, so maybe a local or two, but otherwise the bar would be empty, over-lit. There'd be a late rush from the campsites, but mid-evening was the graveyard shift.

The image he was trying to dispel was of the smouldering corpse they'd found in the woods. If he could erase that, free his mind from the moment, he could face a drink; that was Plan A. There was a Plan B: he could have the drink first, and that would almost certainly work; it had in the past. But he'd had a call from Jan Clay, who said she'd found out something that might help the East Hills inquiry and could they meet? He looked at his watch: 8 p.m. at Buccaneers', a wine bar in the Dutch Barge on the quayside. For some odd reason it was important to Valentine that he turned up sober: cold sober. So he'd live with the image for an hour or two, pretending he was worrying away at the case: motives, suspects, evidence. But really he was just staring at that image, through the dark glass of the bay window.

He'd been on his feet for five hours since they'd found the corpse in the woods. They'd left the pathologist, Dr Kazimierz, at the scene. She'd been unable to find evidence of a cyanide capsule in the victim's mouth, but was pretty certain that was

how he died. The smell was distinctive and the man's throat
muscles were set in spasm, closing his windpipe – a classic sign,
post-mortem, of cyanide poisoning. Shaw and Valentine had
returned to The Circle to get a preliminary ID of the victim from
his fellow demonstrator, Tilly Osbourne. The young man with
the birthmark was called Paul Holtby. She didn't know much:
he was the regional organizer for *SOUL*, and she thought he lived
at Morston, along the coast. Single, committed, serious and efficient, Twine had got the local community copper at Morston
round to the house. His nearest living relative was an aunt at
the same address and she'd agreed to do a formal ID in the
morning. Holtby had a flat in an old barn behind the main house
on Morston quay. He'd last been seen by the aunt on Sunday
afternoon at about five when he'd let himself into the main house
to use the washing machine. Twine was running the name
through the national computer. They'd get the team out to the
demo at the wind farm in the morning, collect statements on
the spot, try and build a picture. First question: why was Holtby
in the woods at night? Second question: did he have any link
to the original East Hills killing?

Out on the black water of the harbour a light winked out in
a yacht cabin. Valentine slipped into an uneasy sleep. When he
next looked at the Rolex it was a few minutes before eight.
Buccaneers' was below the deck of the Dutch barge, a central
staircase dropping into what had been the main cabin. It was
empty except for a party of German hikers, a family off one
of the camp sites, the barman and Jan: she looked impossibly
young, in jeans and a silk shirt, the neat blond hair lying
perfectly. Valentine turned down a seat and ordered a pint – the
Buccaneer served its beer from a barrel on the bar, and watching
the barman took up another minute. Then they had to talk to
each other.

'We found a body in the woods,' said Valentine, lifting the
pint to his lips with a steady hand.

'The barman told me,' said Jan in a whisper. 'He's pretty much
Sky News round here. Not much left, right? And Joe Osbourne
– arrested, charged?' She shivered, but only in a make-believe
way. She'd been married to a policeman for nearly twenty years
so Valentine guessed she'd become inured to the intrusions of
death. She popped a nut between her lips and Valentine noticed

that she left a smear of colour on her fingertips which she expertly removed by running her fingertips over the bar towel.

Valentine talked her through as much of the detail as he could. He was beginning to enjoy himself, thinking that he always used to talk to Julie about his day. But when they'd finished the drink Jan held up a bunch of keys. 'Follow me,' she said.

They walked up the High Street, then into an alley lit by an old gaslight converted to electricity. A sign hung, as if outside an old inn, and on it was drawn a wrecked ship, men struggling ashore with barrels held aloft. The word MUSEUM was picked out in fake gold coins. She expertly unlocked the door, then reached inside and hit numbers into a security pad. 'I was going to show you tomorrow,' she said, flicking on lights to reveal a lobby, dominated by a single black and white reproduction of the quayside crowded with sailing ships. 'But we're closed Tuesdays, so I got the keys. I'm glad I did now. You need to see it.'

She led the way through a room full of glass cabinets cluttered with fossils. At the back, near a fire exit, was a small lecture theatre with a video screen set up in front of six empty plastic chairs. Beyond was one last room, and over the door a hand-painted sign which read:

THE INVASION COAST
North Norfolk on the front line: 1939–42

The room was crowded with display boxes, the walls covered in framed pictures and memorabilia. Shaw noted a large picture of a Lancaster bomber on a grass runway, a brick conning tower in the background. Another showed an artillery gun on the edge of a pine wood, set on what looked like bronze rails, the narrow muzzle pointing skywards.

'We do an info sheet for each room,' she said, unfolding a piece of A4. 'You can have it. All you need to know now is this . . .' She took a deep breath. 'In the first years of the Second World War the government set up this weird secret army. They called them AuxUnits, the dullest name they could think of. Later they got called *The Stay Behind Army*, but that was after the war. During the war almost no one knew they were there. The idea was simple: if there was an invasion these men would go to ground, then come out and cause mayhem behind the lines once the Germans had moved on towards London. They'd hide in what they called OB's – observation bases. Holes in the ground really, dugouts: but they were well trained, well armed. This is a list of the stuff they were given.'

There were two or three documents in a single glass case. Jan put a fingertip on the glass above the smallest. Valentine squinted, struggling to read the lines, amazed at how haphazard the letters were on manual typewriters, even on an official document.

'I'd like to claim I spotted this, but one of the curators heard your appeal on the radio. He thought you should know.'

LIST OF ARMS, AMMUNITIONS STORES and EQUIPMENT required for one Patrol, AuxUnits.

1. ARMS
7 Revolvers .38 American
2 Rifles .300
7 knives fighting
3 knobkerries
48 Grenades, 36 M. 4 secs.
3 Cases S. T. Grenades
2 Cases A.W. Bottles
1 Rifle .22 with silencer
1 Thompson Sub-machine Gun

2. EXPLOSIVES
4 AuxUnits (boxes containing explosives and concomitants)

3. AMMUNITION
40 rds .38 American
200 rds .300
1,000 rds .45 for S.M.G.
200 rds .22

4. The provision of one Elephant Shelter for construction work. The necessary equipment for furnishing the base i.e. one Tilley lamp, two Primus stoves, Elsan chemical closet.

5. EQUIPMENT
7 Holsters (Leather American)
7 Groundsheets

7 Blankets
7 Pair Rubber Boots
7 Water bottles, carriers and slings
1 set of equipment Thomson Sub-machine Gun
I pair of wire cutters
I Monocular and case
6 cyanide capsules

Valentine speed-read the lot and didn't see anything. 'Sorry?' She put her finger on the glass right above the last line. Valentine straightened his back and there was an audible crack from his vertebra. He blinked three times, and read it out loud . . . 'Six cyanide capsules. Jesus, Jan. You superstar.'

Jan Clay beamed.

Then Valentine's shoulders slumped. 'But this is seventy years ago. So what are we saying – that there's one of these dugouts – out there, and *still* there, and someone's got access to these pills?'

She was shaking her head before he'd finished. 'No. It's possible, but no. I'm not saying that. These things were closed down by the end of the war, most of them filled in. The gear was supposed to go back to Whitehall but, you know, there was a war on. What if someone squirreled some of the gear away? That I can imagine, can't you? A cigar box somewhere in an attic: one of the pistols, perhaps, some bullets and the pills.'

Valentine looked through the glass at the old document, its jumbled type and foxed corners making it seem like a message from another, lost, world. 'Maybe,' he said.

'There's more,' she said. 'I checked with one of the archivists at the county museum. A lot of the records were burned but we do know there were several of these units on the North Norfolk coast. Locations are sketchy – precise locations unknown. But there was a persistent rumour after the war that they'd set one up at Creake in 1939, and that the dugout was up near that ruin – the Warrener's Lodge. When English Heritage took it over in the eighties they even did a geophysical survey – didn't find much, just a shadow of the old warren underneath. But what if it was up in the woods, George?'

TWENTY-FOUR

Shaw settled into his pace, bare feet thudding into wet sand, his work clothes and boots stuffed into the rucksack on his back. The night sea breeze was heavy with ozone, and he dragged in lungfuls, but still he could smell what they'd found in the woods. The charred corpse, a human candle: the stench of it was like a second skin on him, and he was desperate to shed it. When he got to the house he'd swim, then let the sea breeze dry him off, so that all that would be left would be salt, a pure crust. He looked along the beach towards the cottage and shop, the *Surf!* flag floodlit, pointing inland, with its blue dolphin on a white wave. Standing on the sand in a splash of light from the café was a uniformed police officer – male, on a radio, in shirtsleeves. Shaw picked up his running pace, cutting up the beach slope, feeling the air rasp in his throat over the final one hundred meters.

'Problem?' he asked, coming easily to a halt, his chest heaving, but his breathing already picking up its regular rhythm. He pressed the stopwatch on his wrist to record his time.

The PC's eyes widened at the sight of the force's most high-profile DI – in shorts and a T-shirt marked *Run For Your Life*.

'My wife runs this place,' said Shaw, by way of explanation. Ms Lena Braithwaite was the name over the door. She'd kept her maiden name after they'd married – a mark of independence and, as an only child, a way of keeping her family name alive; a delight for her father.

'Shoplifters, sir – a gang, over from the Midlands, we think. Two or three shops in town too – quite a haul.'

Lena appeared from the cafe, stepping lightly down on to the sand but dragging her toes as she walked, as she always did when her mood was down. She walked to Shaw and kissed him lightly on the lips, resting her forehead against his. The PC studiously studied his notebook.

'How many kids, men, women – what we got?' asked Shaw, pulling off the sweaty T-shirt and draping it over his shoulder.

'Maybe a dozen of them – we think it's a white-van job.

Traffic are keeping an eye on the A47. All men, usual profile. Eighteen to twenty-five.'

Shaw's eyes narrowed and he tried to remember the PC's name. Any standard description of a gang of away-day thieves would have included their ethnicity. Perhaps the young constable had been intimidated by Lena's Barbadian skin.

The North Norfolk coast's only mass tourist market was the East Midlands – Leicester, Coventry, Rugby. If the forecast was right they'd get thousands for the day trip. With the ethnic mix came a heightening of tension along the beaches, but it rarely boiled over into anything more than some name calling and a push'n'shove in the pubs. The pickpocket and shoplifting gangs tended to be mainly white, unemployed, and liquored-up. It was hardly a problem at all further east – the mileage limited the day-trippers to the campsites and amusement arcades of Hunstanton.

Shaw took Lena's hand. 'Black, white, Asian?'

The PC's Adam's apple wobbled. 'White, mainly. Maybe one or two of Asian descent.'

'They got three wetsuits . . .' said Lena, stepping back, putting her feet shoulder-wide in the sand the way Shaw did. 'Just snipped off the security rings, which isn't very encouraging. They tried to force the case with the watches but it held. I was over in the cafe, an old woman was taken ill. I think they just took their chance.'

The PC closed his notebook. 'CCTV's a thought,' he said.

Shaw was close enough to see some of the light fade from Lena's eyes.

'All the shops they targeted are camera-free.' He counted them off on his fingers: 'Turner's Gift Shop, toy and model shop in the arcade, and Menzies. Worth thinking about.' He said he'd call back later in the week or earlier if they managed to spot the white van on its return trip. 'But you know,' he said, shrugging. 'It's a white van, on the M6. Sorry.'

Shaw helped Lena take an inventory of the shop. Fran came back from a day with friends in Wells and they told her what had happened. She ran to her room to check her things, even though Lena told her the thieves hadn't been in the house, and that she'd already checked every room.

Later, Shaw ran back to the lifeboat house at Old Hunstanton and the pub beyond – the Mariners' Arms – where he had a pint of Guinness while he waited for three lots of fish and chips, a weekend treat, midweek, to cheer them up. The bar was packed with tourists, the picnic tables outside too, the sky starlit.

He stood outside as well, to finish the pint. His mobile rang and he answered when he saw Valentine's number.

'I'm in Wells,' said his DS. Shaw heard seagulls on cue, and a distant thread of fairground organ music. 'Just a head's up. I don't know what to make of this but you need to know.' Valentine gave him an expert one hundred-word summary of everything he'd learned in the museum.

Shaw was silent. Then he checked just one detail: 'Six cyanide pills?'

'Six.'

They agreed to meet next morning, then drive to The Circle. 'What you reckon?' asked Valentine, unable to resist the question.

'I reckon we need to look for this dugout. It's not just the pills, is it? It's the fact that if it's there then maybe he uses it. Like I said – the killer comes and goes. And there's Aidan Robinson's military man, up on the edge of the woods. And Holtby died up there. Either way we can't ignore it even if it does sound a bit fanciful. We have to look. Force helicopter might be useful – does thermo-imaging work in summer?'

Shaw took silence for ignorance and cut the line.

He ran back along the beach, the adrenaline clearing his mind. Lena had set out the picnic blanket on the sand and Fran had collected driftwood for a fire, and twisted a newspaper retrieved from one of the litter bins into twenty knots of kindling. Shaw added some dried seaweed off the high-water mark and then lit it with a light from one of three oil lanterns Lena had set out. Shaw thought that this was one of the joys of their life: beach craft.

They watched the fire burn, transfixed; the sight as hypnotic as the waves coming in, breaking on the convex coast, embracing the shore. Shaw thought it was one of the peculiarities of this stretch of coast, where The Wash met the North Sea, that the land was always leading away behind you on either side. No headlands, or bays, or great sweeps of coast interrupted the seascape. It was as if they lived on the edge of the world. He caught Lena's eye – the one with the slight caste – and was astonished to realize, by some leap of telepathy, that in her own way she was thinking the same thing.

She kept her lips together but still smiled, then went back to using the blank white paper the fish and chips were wrapped in to add up some figures with the stubby pencil she kept in her shirt breast pocket.

'Damage?' asked Shaw, when she'd screwed up the paper and lobbed it into the fire. He broke a piece of white fish in batter off and held it lightly between his teeth, letting the air cool it. Fran had finished and was drawing something in the sand with a stick.

'Nearly four thousand, but it's all insured,' she said, smiling at her daughter.

Shaw knew the calculations were subtler than that. They'd lose their no-claims bonus and the premiums would go up next time. If they went for CCTV that would be £10,000, minimum. The other way forward was to employ enough staff every day of the summer to put someone in the shop, someone in the cafe, someone in the kitchen. Minimum of three; whereas now they scraped by with two, three for weekends and holidays. That would significantly raise their costs. But the real damage was psychological, he knew, and the real victim was Lena. She'd always been clear that life on the beach only looked like paradise when the sun was out. But now, even on one of the best days of the summer, they'd been bitten by the first snake.

They ate ice creams from the Walls freezer in the shop, then took the old dog down to the water's edge. Shaw put Fran to bed, reading a chapter of the latest Terry Pratchett. His daughter complained that there was still light in the sky, seeping in through the curtains, but he said it would be gone soon because the stars were out, and the best way to sleep was to watch the dark creep into the room, filling up the corners first. For the first time that year she asked him to close the bedroom window. She said there was a chill off the sea, but Shaw knew she was lying, because she turned her head away on the pillow.

He closed the door and stood in the long corridor which joined the cottage to the shop, wondering if he should sneak in later and open the window. Then his phone vibrated: a text from Paul Twine up at The Circle to say that Joe Osbourne had seen the

on-duty doctor at St James' and been admitted to the Queen
Victoria Hospital. Acute, ongoing, asthma attack. Irregular heartbeat also noted. Condition: stable.

Shaw let himself into the cafe and took one of the OS maps
from the display on the counter. Out on the picnic blanket he
spread it out, realizing too late he should have asked. But Lena
wasn't looking at the map, she was looking at him. 'How's the
eye?' she asked. 'Tell me.'

Shaw took his good health for granted and he realized how
quickly he'd discounted the attack of blurred vision as a one-off,
a never-to-be-repeated episode, just a glimpse of a future he was
fated to avoid. He'd always presumed his life would be graced
with good luck – a presumption the accident had done nothing
to undermine. 'Fine,' he said, a word Lena had come to hate,
because he used it so often and it meant so little. It was just a
way of saying you didn't want to talk, but avoiding a confront-
ation at the same time. Lena's eyes were brown, aqueous, and
Shaw found them often very difficult to read. 'No more pain . . .'
he said quickly. 'Well, not much. And the vision's fine
– sharp.'

He looked out to sea, focusing on a freighter on the horizon.
Eight to twelve miles, the port-side red light as sharp as a star.
Lena's eyes dropped to the map.

'Sorry – work,' he said. 'Couldn't resist.'

'I don't want CCTV,' she said. 'I want someone permanent
for the shop.'

There was an edge to her voice that Shaw had long ago learnt
not to ignore.

'Right. Let's do it,' he said.

She didn't smile, just turned her face to the sea. 'Now, tell me
about the map,' she said, watching a small fishing boat skirting
the coast, the sound of the diesel engine pumping in the night.
Normally she hated talking through his cases, but she knew it
was an important ritual, and it allowed her to draw the line
between work and home more effectively than if they never
shared Shaw's world. And tonight it felt like a welcome
diversion.

Shaw outlined his problem. They had three victims all related
to each other by cyanide: Marianne Osbourne, Arthur Patch and
now Paul Holtby. They knew that the first victim – Marianne

– had been on East Hills, and she'd died the day before the
mass screening at St James'. Common sense suggested all three
deaths were linked, not only to each other, but to the murder
of Shane White on East Hills. Marianne had almost certainly
died because she was a witness. Arthur Patch had probably died
for the same reason: he was on the quayside that day, had taken
money from the hand of every driver who'd used the car park.
He knew everyone local well – and they knew him. He was a
living CCTV camera.

'But Holtby doesn't seem to fit in at all,' said Shaw. 'He was
only twelve years old in 1994 – is he really going to be able to
make a positive ID nearly twenty years later? I suppose he might
have been on the beach at Wells that day. It's going to be tough
to find out where he was. But if he was at home he was miles
away . . .'

Shaw traced his finger along the coast to the village of Morston,
at the entrance to Blakeney Pit, perhaps three miles from East
Hills: a small group of Norfolk stone cottages with a pub on the
coast road, a lane winding down to a small harbour, a car park
and tea hut. In the summer it was busy, boats running people out
to see the seals at Blakeney Point. There was a small campsite,
usually packed with bird watchers.

Lena knelt in the sand and studied the map, then went and
unlocked the door to the shop, reappearing almost immediately
with another set of maps. She was in shorts too, and a skimpy
Surf! T-shirt which left her midriff bare. As she sat Shaw pulled
her close, so that he could feel how cool her skin was. Her body
was made up of curves, strong lines, so that he was always
overwhelmed by her physical presence. She was just five foot
two, but he'd have never described her as slight.

The map she'd unfolded showed the coast from Wells to
Morston but there was no detail on the land as in the OS version,
it was all at sea: currents, rocks, depths, buoys, fishing grounds,
wrecks, lights, lightships and sand banks.

'They've started producing these charts for the windsurfers
– the stunt kites, that crowd. They're really popular. And eighteen
quid a pop. These little circles are really clever . . .' She pointed
to a small device – there were dozens along the line of the coast
– which looked like a compass. 'You'll know all about these
but they're new for the smart crowd.'

'A wind rose,' said Shaw. He'd learnt to read them as part
of the navigation course he'd taken to get his pilot's licence for
the RNLI hovercraft. The idea was simple: each wind rose was
a little cartwheel, with the spokes different lengths. The longer
the spoke the more the wind usually blew from that
direction.

'This is what I remember . . .' Lena stabbed a finger on the
flow of arrows indicating the current at the mouth of Wells
Harbour: they were all pointing east, towards Blakeney Pit and
the little village of Morston. 'And the winds . . .' All along the
edge of the marshes the prevailing winds were from the south-
west, pushing north-east.

But Shaw was shaking his head: 'Ruth Robinson, the dead
woman's sister, is a big swimmer. She works up at the lido.
According to her if you wanted to swim from East Hills to the
mainland, and live to tell the tale, the way to do it is swim out
. . . out here,' he said, indicating a point a mile north-west. 'Then
you relax, pick up this current and swing back into the beach at
Wells.'

'I know, Peter. But what if you *don't* know the currents, don't
have the local knowledge, or you're not a good enough swimmer
to strike out away from land, away from safety? It's what we
tell all the kids in the surf classes. If you get into trouble don't
swim against the tide. You'll tire, you'll drown. If your killer just
struck out for the coast from East Hills the currents and the winds
would take him east, to Morston, or on into Blakeney Pit. You
might be in the water for hours, but you'd have a chance of
surviving. Swim against the current you'd be dead in minutes.
That's how people drown, Peter. They swim, get exhausted, panic,
swim faster, sink.'

Shaw thought of that – the little shell-like beach at Morston,
beyond the harbour; a twelve-year-old Paul Holtby on the sands,
and a man walking out of the sea; in shock probably, wounded,
desperate for help. What had happened next? What could have
happened that a small boy would have remembered it nearly
twenty years later?

TWENTY-FIVE

Tuesday

George Valentine liked the dawn because it brought with it the day, which meant the night would follow. He'd get a drink then look back on what he'd done, and feel better about his life. Consciously, he was able to face the fact he was wishing his life away, because it was at least his decision, and it was a decision that harmed no one else. He'd watched the sun at dawn as he'd driven into town along the smoking river, a cold red orange ball, climbing above the Campbell's Soup Tower. The colours of dawn were no better than he deserved: cold, businesslike and unemotional, untouched by the passage of the day.

He was sitting now in the atrium of the Chamber, an upmarket health club built on Lynn's waterside, created from the shell of one of the old Hanseatic warehouses, which had once held the best wine in Europe. Now it held a swimming pool, visible through a glass screen, and beyond that what? Valentine could only guess. He imagined saunas, exercise bicycles, squash courts, and lean bodies in crisp shorts and designer sportswear. If he'd been forced to design his own hell it would have been just like that, with fluffy towels.

He didn't want to be here. When he'd got back to his room at The Ship the night before he'd found a text message on his mobile. A summons from the chief constable which meant he'd have to get up at some ungodly hour and drive back into town. All he'd wanted to do was have a sleep-in and drive down to the beach and tell Shaw more about what Jan Clay had shown him in Wells Museum. Instead of which he was in the Chamber. 'Torture chamber,' he said, under his breath, which made him cough.

Twenty arm chairs filled the atrium and he'd taken one on the end, facing the double automatic doors to the changing rooms. He'd got himself a bottle of water from a machine in the corner, quietly stunned to find it cost him two pounds fifty for 500mls. The bottle was icy cold and promised that the contents had been extracted from a borehole in the Italian Alps. George was of a generation which equated British civilization with the distinction that you could drink the water out of the taps.

Brendan O'Hare, Britain's second-youngest chief constable, was suddenly there in front of him. Valentine hadn't recognized him out of uniform, or wrapped in a white towelling robe. What he could see of the chief constable was tanned and replete, the skin-tone perfect. He had a slim towel over one shoulder, the end of which he was using to rub his face. O'Hare sat opposite and almost immediately one of the staff, in a skimpy pair of shorts and a bust-hugging top, stooped to place a single china espresso cup on the table by his knee, with a glass of water. 'George,' he said, ignoring her. 'Thanks for coming – sorry about the time. But I thought, you know, it was best out of the office.'

He sipped the coffee and left some space for Valentine to say something. Valentine said nothing, and felt no need to, but he did think that if silence was O'Hare's tactic he was on a loser, because he could do that all day.

O'Hare despatched the coffee then crossed his legs so that Valentine looked away, uncomfortable with the sudden sight of bare legs, but pleased to note they were oddly hairless and pale.

'I understand there's been developments,' said O'Hare. 'Out at Creake – another body?'

Valentine was going to answer then but O'Hare had hit his stride.

'You any good at reading between the lines, George?'

'I try.' However hard he forced his voice towards neutral Valentine knew he was broadcasting antagonism, even belligerence.

'Great. Listen then – and consider.'

O'Hare looked over his shoulder and the girl who'd brought him coffee took the hint. They heard the rattle and hiss of the Italian coffee machine being fired up. 'I am not impressed with the leadership in this case. Especially at the top. I expect my DIs to deliver. I'm not talking out of shop – Shaw knows what I think. I doubt that this latest development makes the case any less . . .' he searched for the word, 'lucid. So, it may well be that traffic, or possibly Family Liaison, will be getting a DI transfer from the Serious Crime Unit. Which means I'll be looking for a new DI. I've examined your file; it's been an impressive couple of years. You'd clearly be in line if the vacancy arose. But you knew all that.'

It wasn't a question so Valentine didn't answer it. He felt himself sliding out of his depth. He imagined that O'Hare's career had been littered with moments like this: subtle, clandestine, political. Valentine felt like he was being abused, soiled even, which was ironic given he was sitting in the cleanest place he'd be in all day.

'The next time you're up in front of a panel is when? October? So we may have to accelerate that process, but you can leave that to me. In the meantime . . .' He rearranged his robe, re-belting it, getting ready to move on. 'I'm not happy – even in the short term –with one of my key DIs being disabled. I realize you do everything you can to shield Shaw from the consequences of his unfortunate accident but the fact is he's on the front line. If nothing else it hardly enhances the brand image of the West Norfolk, does it? I think the least we can do is assure the general public we have able-bodied detectives.'

Valentine was too shocked to speak. Later, he told himself that otherwise he would have done. 'So, any problems he has in the course of his duties due to his disability, I'd like you to keep a record. Report back. Needless to say you'd be doing him a favour. A disability pension under present arrangements is quite generous. And there's a safety issue. He's not been properly evaluated by our people in terms of driving. Swanning round in a Porsche hardly helps.'

'It's safer,' said Valentine. 'Narrow "A" bars.'

'Whatever,' said O'Hare, standing. 'It's your choice, George. We're having this conversation here because I wanted to keep everything in the family, as it were. Strictly off the record. But I thought you should have the full picture. This way is best for everyone.' He tried out a smile, then just turned and left.

Valentine sat alone for five minutes. He was cold, and felt just like he'd felt the first time he'd given blood, as if his life – or any capacity for independent action – had been siphoned from his body.

Out on the waterfront he walked down to the Boal Quay, where some of the fishing boats were in, and smoked, looking at the boxes of silver fish catching the sunlight. He felt the need to talk to someone. Usually this came upon him after dark, and he'd stroll along to All Saints and sit opposite Julie's gravestone. But the sun, up now, and already hot, made that impossible, although he had no idea why.

Instead, he thought of Jan Clay at Wells, looking out to sea, a hand shielding her eyes from the glare.

TWENTY-SIX

As Shaw drove, his good eye on the narrow coastal road, Valentine told him everything he'd managed to learn about the AuxUnits, the so-called *Stay Behind Army*, and the standard issue of six cyanide pills. Shaw had picked Valentine up outside St James' at eight fifteen, as arranged, but had got the distinct impression Valentine had been there some time. He'd been sitting on the semicircular stone steps, his shadow stretching down to the street, a little heap of spent Silk Cut between his feet.

'And we're saying these units actually existed, George – they're not just some Whitehall boffin's dream?' asked Shaw, pointing the Porsche east through the docks. Given the state of the inquiry: stalled while they waited for Joe Osbourne's DNA check, baffled by Paul Holtby's brutal murder, and with just two days to the chief constable's press conference, they'd agreed that they could hardly ignore the outside possibility they could track the dugout down.

'I called the MoD last night, told 'em to send us what they could on these units by email,' said Valentine. 'But yeah, they're for real. Well, they were for real. This coast was heavily fortified – you saw those bronze rails up in the woods above The Circle, by the folly? They're gun rails, and there's loads more. Coastal defence. They thought that if the Germans are coming, they'll come this way. Long, flat, desolate coast, with the road open to the capital. It was our Normandy, waiting to happen.'

Valentine's normal listless tone had gone and for the first time

Shaw thought that for his DS the Second World War wasn't just a distant memory. For his generation, and Shaw's father, it was a backdrop to their lives, because their parents had lived through it. Perhaps that was why he seemed more energized by the discovery than Shaw.

'And who, exactly, is it that says there was one of these units at Creake?' Shaw asked, trying to think straight, while the road took a vicious double-hairpin bend at Burnham Overy Staithe, sneaking past The Hero – a pub in Chelsea-set blue, with a signboard showing Nelson.

'Nobody – not officially,' admitted Valentine. 'It was popular wartime gossip. They had engineers up there but they were probably building the gun emplacement by the folly. They'd do that, because it makes sense.' He turned half in the seat to look at Shaw's profile: 'They'd put the dugout near something else military so they could cover their steps. There's no point a platoon of sappers turning up to build a *secret* underground base, is there?' He stopped, dragging air into his lungs, disguising the breath. 'This way, if anyone was seen approaching the spot people would think they were going to the gun, or the pillbox, or the lookout, or whatever it was they'd built *above* ground, nearby. The rumour was strong enough that when English Heritage took over at the Warrener's Lodge a few years ago they did do a survey as part of a maintenance programme. They found fuck all, except a shadow of a brick warren, most of it plugged with clay.'

'Names – do we know who's in these units?'

'Local volunteers and they all signed the Official Secrets Act – and they were paid. But the documentation was all-central, and all of it was destroyed in 'forty-six. A few people broke cover in the eighties and nineties – MoD bloke said they had some cuttings. But basically they kept quiet – it's like Bletchley Park. They took it seriously; a secret's a secret. They chose people who could keep a secret. So names are going to be tough.'

Shaw nodded, letting him talk on. He'd never heard Valentine say so much.

'But we know what the AuxUnits were like – the people who ran the network were commandos; they wanted people who knew the local terrain and who could survive on the run: gamekeepers, farmers, field workers. You had to be fit too – so that means they

looked at the emergency services. Most were reserved occupa-
tions, so there were young men about – police, fire brigade,
coastguard. And anyone who could use a gun, so they recruited
at shoots, hunts, clubs.'

'And every one of these units got six of these cyanide pills?'
asked Shaw.

'Yeah, MoD guy said that was standard practice for anyone
working behind enemy lines, which is where they would have
been if the invasion had rolled over them. Kind of insurance policy.
If you thought you were gonna get caught, and tortured, at least
there was a quick way out. That was in everyone's interests.'

They swung past the end of The Row, the terraced street on
which Arthur Patch had lived for nearly half a century. A thin
line of smoke rose from the ruin of the house, and the rest of
the street still looked empty. The Porsche climbed the steep hill
beyond the village until the Docking Hill wind farm filled the
horizon, the vanes of the three giant mills turning lazily. Shaw
put the Porsche up on the verge.

They could see the usual group of demonstrators by the gates,
where they'd set up a vigil – a circle of candles – for Paul Holtby.
Killing the engine Shaw heard a thin dirge on the air being sung
by the crowd. Catching sight of the candle flames he thought of
Holtby's skin-white face, smoke pumping out of the ash, and
Hadden's chilling description: *human candle.*

TWENTY-SEVEN

D C Lau walked towards the Porsche from the direction of the wind farm's gatehouse. Leather trousers, leather jacket, open to reveal a crisp white collarless shirt. Wraparound reflective sunglasses hid her eyes. Shaw thought the effect was designed to radiate brisk, sexless efficiency but the walk was strangely sinuous, almost a cat walk.

Shaw threw the door open and put a booted foot up on the dashboard.

Lau nodded a greeting, taking the time to squat down so that she could catch Valentine's eye as well. 'We've got statements,' she said, her voice free of any hint of her Chinese descent. 'But they're pretty much the awkward squad. Talk about blood out of a stone. They seem to think Holtby's been murdered by a worldwide conspiracy – US corporates bankrolling the wind farm. CIA, us. Paranoid stuff. We've spoken to Holtby's aunt at Morston. She's pretty sure he'd have been at Morston on the beach in 1994. You know, that's a guess given it was seventeen years ago. But odds on he was there. A big family, they didn't go anywhere else, just let the kids run wild.' She smiled. 'Sounds great.'

'Biog?' asked Shaw.

Lau painted the picture she'd put together of Holtby: local rich kid, absentee parents in the City, a degree from York University in history, student activism, then the eco-warrior circuit. Justina had emailed a preliminary autopsy report from The Ark. The scenario was provisional, but clear. The trap had brought Holtby down, a cyanide pill had been administered while he was alive – the casing was in his lower gullet – then the body had been abandoned to the approaching overnight fire. Something in the rucksack had accelerated the heat next to the body – so far they'd found chemical traces of phosphorous. 'Tom thinks it might be a flare – you know, like an Olympic torch or something,' she added, shrugging.

'OK,' said Shaw, kicking open the door. 'Suggests he was up

there after dark – or expecting to be up there after dark. Any idea why?'

Lau slipped on reflective sunglasses. 'They're all playing dumb on that, but I think they know. The Osbourne girl might talk. She said she wanted to see you, sir. Alone.'

Tilly Osbourne stood away from the group, by the security fence of the wind farm, watching the nearest turbine, the sixty-foot blades slicing through the air like the sharpest of knives. She had her fingers meshed through the wire, her face pressed against the latticework.

As Shaw approached on the tufted downland grass she turned her head. The tears were drying on her face, which was puffy, with the surface tension of a week-old party balloon. 'How's your Dad?' he asked.

'Ill. It's the stress. He doesn't really deal with emotions – not properly. But he's comfortable, the drugs are working, he'll be home soon.' It seemed to be the thought of home that made her eyes fill with tears, so that she looked away. 'It's a man thing, right? Not talking.'

She straightened her back and looked up into the sky, an oddly adult mannerism for a teenager. 'Once you get used to secrets – collecting them – it's addictive.'

Shaw wondered who she was talking about: her dead mother, her father, or herself?

She stared through the wire at one of the turbines marked by a six-foot-high letter B in black stencil on the silver, elegant, tower of steel.

'Paul's death. It's linked to Mum, isn't it?' she said. 'It has to be. But I don't understand why.'

'Why linked?'

She shrugged and almost smiled and Shaw caught the ghost of a resemblance to her mother, or at least to the woman he'd seen smiling for the photographer in the Fleet Street studio. 'I'm seventeen years old – I've lived here all my life, in the village. Once, when I was little, there was a car crash by the pub and someone died. But that's it – seventeen years, one death, an accident. Now three in a few days. Mum, Paul and that old bloke up on The Row. You don't think Mum's death was an accident, do you? I don't know why, but you think someone else was there. At the end. And there's still people on The Row – people in white suits. So something's going on.' She smiled. 'There's not much to do up here but talk. We do conspiracy theories by the dozen.'

She watched the blade turning. 'If I tell you what I know about Paul, will it help?'

'Of course.'

'It wasn't Dad – at the end, with Mum,' she said. 'I know that. We talked, last night, at the hospital.' She pressed her fingers on either side of the bridge of her nose. 'And it wasn't Dad out at East Hills. I'd know.'

'OK. If he's telling the truth we'll know soon because we're checking his DNA, so there's nothing to worry about.' Shaw waited a beat: 'Which means we still need to know who it was, Tilly. Who killed that lifeguard and who was with your Mum. Who brought her that pill, who helped her take it – and in the end *made* her take it.'

Shaw gave her a brief summary of the autopsy findings on her mother.

Shocked, she released her fist from the wire, like a plant opening in time-lapse photography, and showed him that in one of her palms she held a key. In the sunlight it was almost too bright, as if it was emitting energy, not reflecting it. Then she told him what they'd planned. 'It was so exciting,' she said, and the smile flared again.

A construction company had moved on to the Docking Hill site in April to build a canteen and a new office block by Turbine C. The work had required a replacement computer system, designed to monitor wind speeds and the inclination of each turbine blade. The workmen had been given access to each of the three giant turbines, the other on-site facilities, and the generating block. One of the labourers was young and had been to school with one of the female demonstrators. Sweethearts, briefly, they'd drifted apart.

The demonstrators had watched this young man each Friday, blowing his wages in the quayside pubs at Wells. One night, in June, they made sure he met the girl again. By the end of the night he was lying in a back alley, head foggy with a mixture of alcohol and prescription sedatives. In his pocket were his work keys. Three of the keys were marked A, B and C. None were missing, but if he'd looked hard he'd have seen traces of Blu-tack in the teeth of B.

The plan had stalled there. It was no good having the key to the turbine if they couldn't get into the compound. As soon as the *SOUL* campaign had begun a security firm had been hired to patrol the perimeter. The gates in the fence were individually computer locked – opened only by a sequence of numbers changed daily. The group favoured a mass demo by the gates, then trying to break through into the compound so that they could occupy Turbine B – get up to the gondola at the top, unfurl a banner, and see how long it took the security firm to get them out with a TV crew training its telescopic lens on their every move. They'd take up some flares as well, so they could be seen after dark. 'A light of protest,' said Tilly, smiling for the first time. 'That's what Paul said.'

That was the plan, and they'd set the date a month ago, and it had been timed for today. The chances of it working, however, were extremely slim. The compound was patrolled by dogs. The security firm was mob-handed most mornings. Pushing and shoving would turn into a brawl, the police would be called, and they'd all end up in cells at St James'. Nobody really thought they'd make it to the turbine, let alone the gondola aloft. 'Then Paul called me on Saturday. He'd heard about Mum, so he said he was sorry. But there'd been a change of plan and he wanted my help. Would I help?' She looked directly at Shaw. 'I said yes, because I thought it would give me something else to think about, and stop me brooding about Mum. And if I felt better, I could help Dad feel better too. I'm in charge of media for the group, for *SOUL*, contacting papers, radio. It's what I do at college. So it was up to me.'

Holtby had found a way into the compound. Overnight, on Sunday. Once he was in he'd get to the gondola at the top, and unfurl the banner at precisely eight o'clock the next morning. It was Tilly's job to make sure pictures got to the media. She should take some herself, some on video camera, but best of all wait and see if the plan had worked and then get one of the TV companies out as fast as she could before the security guards worked out how to get him down the turbine steps. If he could stay up all day he'd light a flare after dark. That would shine for miles, like a beacon. 'I thought he'd found someone on the inside,' she said. She looked through the wire again as the vanes on Turbine B began to turn. 'Then, yesterday, nothing. No sign of him, and he wasn't answering his mobile. We thought the guards had caught him, but there was no sign. Now we know where he was.'

'Tilly . . .' Shaw put a hand on her shoulder but she didn't take her eyes off the slowly turning turbine. 'We'll talk to the company, and the security firm. But you're right, I don't think Paul died because he was planning to embarrass an energy company that wants to build wind farms. I think he died because he knew something about East Hills. Just like your mother.'

Her lower lip fell, showing small white teeth. She shook her head, as if trying to brush away the idea.

'Did you ever talk to him about East Hills? Your mum had been asked to attend for the mass screening and interviews – you knew that. Did you mention that to Paul?'

She dabbed at her face as if she was crying, but her eyes were dry and wide, trying to remember. She shook her head. 'Dad said – about East Hills. That Mum was upset, that it brought back horrible memories. He'd told me about it before because some years she was bad – on the anniversary, like she couldn't forget it. And she never came to the beach – not ever.'

'Right, but did you talk to Paul about any of this?' Shaw noticed that despite the heat she'd started to shiver.

'No. No, I don't think so. A bit,' she contradicted herself. 'Yes. We spend hours up here like I said so we just talk – so yes, I did mention it. He said he remembered it.' She turned to Shaw, as if the memory was a letter and she'd just ripped it open. 'Yes, he did. He took dirty pictures, didn't he, the lifeguard? Paul said he remembered the gossip. He was only a kid.'

Shaw stepped closer and lowered his voice. 'Paul spent the summers out at Morston, Tilly. He may have seen the killer that day in 'ninety-four. Did he say he'd seen anything?'

Tilly's eyes were blank. 'No.'

Shaw said she'd have to make a statement but she could do it in private – back at the house in Creake. He would have gone then but she reached out a hand and touched his arm. Shaw was shocked by the gesture because they seemed such a cold family: not cold, *isolated* – each from the other, and all of them from the world.

'I know it doesn't seem like it,' she said, 'but we loved Mum.

She knew she was unfair – to me, to Dad. That she blamed us for the way her life had turned out. She said that. She just couldn't stop herself. When she spoke all the bitterness came out. The depression. So sometimes we'd just sit, holding each other and not say anything. They were the best times.'

She smiled, and Shaw responded with a mirror-image, because it was the first time anyone had said anything sympathetic about Marianne Osbourne, and the idea that she'd tried to love her family brought her alive for Shaw, far more than the flickering film of her Fleet Street photo shoot.

TWENTY-EIGHT

The village of Creake was drenched in summer holiday sunshine, the shadows crowding back into the woods which encircled the Norfolk-stone cottages. Shaw swung the Porsche past a line of terraced houses and slowed to negotiate the tricky T-junction by the church with its circular tower in flint, and a graveyard spilling over a low wall. The local pub – The Ostrich – was set back, a long medieval range painted white, with black beams and window casements in eggshell blue. Ahead of them they watched a squad car carrying Tilly Osbourne, going up to The Circle to give her statement at the incident room.

Valentine let his eyes slide over the scene outside the pub – half a dozen picnic tables crowded with families, and a garden to the side, packed with lunchtime tourists. He thought, just for a moment, of suggesting an early lunch, brunch, a late coffee break, whatever. But he knew Shaw better than that. Lunch would be c/o the St James' mobile canteen on the green up at The Circle: a cheese salad, fizzy water.

The brief high Valentine had enjoyed the night before, a result of Jan's company, and their clandestine visit to the museum, had dissipated. A day of routine enquiries loomed. They'd be down to Morston to check out Holtby's flat, or back to The Ark for his autopsy, or conducting endless local interviews in a no-doubt doomed attempt to find the location of the elusive wartime dugout and its lethal cyanide pills. Valentine experienced a fleeting moment of despair, realizing how much of his life he spent wishing he was somewhere else. And his early morning interview with the chief constable overshadowed the day, like a bad dream. In contrast, another image didn't help – DCI Jack Shaw, Peter's father, walking across a bar with a pint in each hand, sunlight catching the beer in the glasses.

Shaw stopped the car, pulling over sharply into a lane beside a Londis supermarket. 'Come on, George. I'll buy you a drink.' He'd been planning to visit the incident room, brief the team, but his head wasn't clear. There was a pattern here now – putting aside the original murder of 1994 they had three deaths, a single motive, a rationale. They had a prime suspect – Joe Osbourne – and they had his DNA sample at the lab. Tilly's belief that her father was innocent sounded to Shaw like wishful thinking. She'd lost her mother – what else did she have to believe in? He wanted to pause, take stock; make sure they were on firm ground before taking the next step.

Valentine hauled himself out of the Porsche, telling himself not to feel good about this; that Shaw was probably planning a dressing down for his DS, and didn't want to do it up at the incident room.

The bar of The Ostrich was full of dining tables, crowded with plates of scallops, fish in beer batter, and oysters. Shaw bought Valentine a pint of Norfolk Wherry and a fizzy water for himself, with ice and lemon. Then he led the way down a whitewashed corridor and out into the garden.

Shaw made a quick call to St James' and got through to the control room. The force's own helicopter was on holiday traffic watch until noon, then back on at five. They could have it for two hours and the thermal-imaging gear was on board. Summer leaf cover markedly reduced the chances of getting a clear image, but it didn't make it impossible. The Serious Crime Unit would have to make an internal payment to Road Traffic for use of the helicopter – nearly £4,000. So they had a deal.

They watched a peacock strutting its stuff in the beer garden. Shaw had bought nuts and he put three of them out on the table top, spilling the rest in a pile so that they could both pick at them. 'Three witnesses to East Hills: Marianne Osbourne, Arthur Patch and Paul Holtby.'

Valentine took a nut from the pile.

'Patch died first, probably,' said Shaw. 'Then Osbourne, then Holtby.' He filled Valentine in on what he'd learnt from Lena's map of the tides and winds of the North Norfolk coast. So it made sense, especially if their killer was either an inexperienced swimmer, or had panicked, or more likely still, was struggling with a wound.

Valentine took two inches off his pint. He could recognize this moment now, the point in the day which seemed to act as a fulcrum, so that the afternoon would feel better than the morning, the evening better than the afternoon. It wasn't all to do with the alcohol, although he was well enough insulated against self-pity to know that it helped.

'The problem,' said Shaw, 'is that we appear to be dealing with a singular killer.' He'd chosen the word well and it pleased them both, he could tell. 'Singular. He – let's say he for now, because Sample X is a man, so it's a decent assumption. *He* operates in a purely pragmatic way. It's almost ruthless, but somehow even more bloodless than that.

'First is Patch. That's completely cold-blooded. But for the bizarre chance of the candle surviving in the bedroom we'd have put that down to a gas explosion. Justina – alerted to the possibility of murder – did the tests. Otherwise we'd have presumed the cause of death as all too plain, given he was reduced to a few pieces of random bone and flesh. Spotting that it was murder was a one in a thousand chance. Then, before the explosion at Patch's house, there's Marianne. My guess is this was an assisted suicide, if you like, maybe more than that. But he just walks away from it, except for that kiss on the glass. That's the only scintilla of emotion. If, and only if, it's the killer's kiss. He doesn't try to make it look any more like suicide than it is; he doesn't move more pills by the bed, or rearrange the body, or contrive a note. Nothing. He knows we'll find the cyanide in her system, and he just walks away. And then Holtby, up in the woods, two nights later. The killer lures him into the woods, is my guess, by promising him he can get him through the perimeter wire. He falls into the trap – literally. The cyanide is administered. The killer walks away again – and he's lucky again, but not quite lucky enough. The fire destroys our crime scene, but not all of the body.'

Valentine flapped his raincoat with his hands in the pockets.

'The killer could've just followed Holtby into the woods – he doesn't have to be privy to the plan.'

They drank in silence.

'The key here, George,' said Shaw, finally, 'is that he doesn't really care if we find the cyanide. The priority is the kill – each time. A professional.'

'A soldier,' said Valentine. 'Maybe the bloke Robinson saw above the house on the edge of the woods. It fits. But there's nothing from the army. Nobody's gone AWOL. None of the East Hills suspects was military – not even TA.' Valentine finished his pint and went for refills. He bought Shaw a half of Guinness.

'I spoke to Tom first thing,' said Shaw. 'The forensics aren't going to help us at any of the three SOCs. We've been all over the Osbournes' bungalow – nothing. Patch's house is burnt-out. We found Holtby in a pile of ash. It's not hopeful, is it? Plus the fact we don't have a single witness sighting for any of the three killings. Arthur Patch's neighbours saw and heard nothing. Nobody on The Circle appears to have seen anyone approaching No. 5 on the day Marianne died. And no one was seen around the woods Sunday night. 'Perhaps that's it,' he added, suddenly, irrationally, elated. 'We're looking for someone who can come and go without being seen.' He added that to the idea of the professional killer and thought it helped – an outline appearing, like a silhouette on a distant horizon. He looked up to the woods on the hill. 'So perhaps there is something up in the woods, one of these dugouts.'

Shaw was concentrating on Valentine's face – the way his eyes had come alive, despite the deep-set sockets which were often in shadow. So he didn't see the figure approaching and didn't take any notice until he took a seat at their table. It was the man from *The Daily Telegraph*, name of Smyth, Shaw recalled. He was in the suit, still, in country green cloth, with upstairs-down-stairs glasses and that carefully cultivated air of intellectual distraction.

'Lionel Smyth,' he told them. '*The Daily Telegraph*.' Smiling, he fumbled in the narrow pocket on his waistcoat and produced an embossed card. 'We meet again.'

'What's *The Daily Telegraph*'s interest in rural Norfolk pubs?' asked Shaw, trying to think fast and talk slow. If Smyth was here, in Creake, he knew something. The question was how much.

The reporter's face was benevolence itself. The kind, slightly rheumy eyes studied Shaw's face. He wasn't in a hurry to answer, so he took a seat and Shaw guessed he was calculating how much of the truth to tell. 'A few days holiday,' he said. But Shaw could see his iPhone on the table, beside a notebook, and that morning's copies of most of the national newspapers.

'Busman's holiday?'

'Well, maybe.' He sniffed the air. 'Body in the woods – that's what the locals tell me. And that gas explosion down in the village. That's terrible. You survive a world war and then get blown out of your bed one morning for no rhyme or reason.' He shook his head. 'Then there's the woman from up at that hamlet . . . The Circle? Suicide. And then you lot putting out a media alert on cyanide pills. Very exotic.'

Shaw tried not to react.

'Real question is – how does any of all that link up with East Hills.'

Shaw and Valentine locked eyes.

'Refills?' asked Smyth, and even Valentine said no. Smyth shrugged, setting his own glass aside. 'Because by now you must have the results of East Hills – the DNA screening. So you should have your killer. Instead of which, you're here, in the garden of The Ostrich.'

'There's a press conference Thursday – notice is going out later. You doing a story?' asked Shaw.

Smyth produced what looked like a hip flask from his inside pocket, flipped open a silver cap and extracted a cigar. 'I wasn't. It's *The Daily Telegraph* – not the *National Enquirer*. I need confirmation – facts. A statement. A story. So the ball's in your court.'

Shaw thought it was a nicely judged retreat. But he didn't believe a word of it. All Smyth had to do was formally ask for confirmation of what he already knew – that there'd been three deaths in this small village in as many days. Shaw could hardly deny what had happened.

Smyth lit the cigar, replacing the silver cap on the fumidor.

Valentine shifted on the bench, thinking how much pleasure it would give him to frogmarch the reporter to the car, slap on a charge – wasting police time, anything, just so they could leave him in a cell at St James' for half an hour, wipe that fake upper-class smirk off his fat face.

'OK,' said Shaw. 'I can give you what we've got. But first – anything you can tell me? You must have picked up plenty of local colour – that's what they call it, right?'

'Sure. But like I say – it's all gossip. This isn't the only pub in the village,' he said. Valentine pictured The Royal Oak, a fifties roadhouse, on the edge of a former council estate down past the church. 'The Oak's where all the real locals drink 'coz the prices here are pretty much Mayfair standard. And the food – Christ. How hard is it to catch a scallop? Anyway, The Circle's got a reputation – quite an interesting one, given the strange case of the cyanide pill. Locals reckon the woman – the suicide – was some kind of pervert. Beautiful, lonely, never went out, but did business on the computer. Adds up see, to the rural mind. Husband's odd too – I heard he pays for his sex down in Lynn. So, happy families all round. Daughter spends all her time up with the weirdos at the wind farm. Was she being knocked off by the bloke they found in the woods? Stands to reason. There's a tented village up there so clearly it's sex again, because there's nothing like six weeks under canvas to get the hormones raging. Locals reckon they run round naked at full moon.'

Smyth laughed to himself, then blew a smoke ring. 'So that's it – the fruits of two days on expenses. Anything you can tell me, I could do with it.'

'One new fact,' said Shaw. 'Marianne Osbourne, the woman who died in her bed up at The Circle, was one of the people we took off East Hills in 1994.' Shaw sipped his Guinness, calcu-lating. 'And she took a pill. A cyanide pill. Military-issue. We're trying to trace the source.'

Smyth just sat there, unblinking. 'Right,' he said, eventually, stretching out the syllables. 'And the old bloke in the gas explosion?'

'We can't rule out a link. He worked for the council back in 'ninety-four – the car park at Wells, right by where the ferry leaves.'

Smyth pursed his lips, as if producing a soundless whistle. 'And the body up in the woods?'

'Too early to say anything, but clearly we're concerned given
how close the three deaths are. What? Half a mile apart. Hell of
a coincidence. Give me your mobile number. Anything develops
I'll let you know if I can.'

'An arrest?'

'Maybe,' said Shaw. 'We're hopeful.'

This time Valentine offered refills and they all said yes. At the
bar he admitted, if only to himself, that Peter Shaw was a good
operator under pressure. Valentine guessed he'd given the reporter
the East Hills link to wrong-foot the chief constable. Could
O'Hare really remove Shaw and Valentine from the inquiry if
there was a triple killer at large? This wasn't an academic cold
case anymore. And all of a sudden that £400,000 mass screening
bill didn't look quite so important up against the fact they had
a murderer on the loose. It was a high-risk strategy. But it might
work. And the cleverest thing of all was that the reporter had not
been given the most important bit of news: that the mass screening
had scored a total blank. Cradling three drinks effortlessly in his
bony hands Valentine turned from the bar, squeezing through the
holiday 'scrum' and back out into the garden.

Smyth was already on his mobile, arranging with Shaw to
double-check dates, times and names. He cut the line, pushing
away his pint. 'We'll talk,' he said, standing, then walked away
without looking back.

'Smarmy bastard,' offered Valentine when he was out of
earshot, looking at the abandoned pint.

'You're not wrong,' said Shaw. 'But clever. He didn't ask about
the DNA results. Maybe he knows. That's all we need.'

Valentine's mobile registered an incoming text. An old
colleague at Well's nick, saying they had something on the Patch
case for him: FOR YOUR EYES ONLY. First Jan Clay comes
up with the link to the museum, now one of his old mates wanted
to help. Maybe his years at Wells weren't all wasted. He showed
Shaw the screen message.

Shaw stood, told him to finish his drink, and he'd see him at
six, down in Wells, outside The Ship. He was going east in the
Porsche to Morston: he wanted to see the spot where the young
Holtby had once stood, stand there too and imagine a figure
wading out of the water that summer's evening, and a young boy
watching from the sand. Then he'd get on the phone and see if

they could get Osbourne's DNA result out of the lab by nightfall.

When Shaw reached the Porsche he could feel the heat radiating from the paintwork. Glancing north, towards the coast, he was startled to see the first storm clouds of the summer, a great billowing mass of cumulus, each one with a heart so black it hinted at purple. On the breeze, thrillingly, he scented rain.

TWENTY-NINE

The storm was still at sea as Shaw drove the coast road. Clouds churned over sunlit water. Thunder and lightning crackled together, the sound so immediate it appeared to be inside his head. The coast road was busy with holidaymakers quitting the beaches, heading back to cottages or the amusements at Wells. He turned off at the village of Morston, waiting several minutes for a break in the bumper-to-bumper traffic. A lane led past a line of stone houses and a small caravan site down to Morston Quay. Getting out of the car on the grass beside the wooden dock Shaw could see grey parallelograms of falling rain on the horizon, like solid ladders between sea and cloud. The wide expanse of water trapped in Blakeney Pit – the tidal waters between the coast and the long shingle spit of Blakeney Point – churned with energy, creating thousands of small pyramid-shaped waves, slapping randomly at the boats tied along the quay.

Morston House was the last in the village, set on its own at the far end of the quay, with just the marshes beyond. Two storey, with playful naval detail in the bay-windows and balcony, it commanded the landscape before it, and Shaw was not surprised to find a small blue plaque on the stone gatepost:

Harbour House
Official residence of Morston's Excise Office
1823–1941

In the window by the front door was a poster for the Labour Party candidate in the forthcoming district council elections and a *SOUL* placard, just like the one Tilly Osbourne had brought home the day her mother died. Shaw pulled a manual brass doorbell and stood back. The exterior woodwork of the house was bleached white, like whalebone, and unvarnished. There were no net curtains at all, but it was impossible to look in because the immaculately clean glass reflected the choppy water and the chaotic sky.

Jeanette Holtby, Paul Holtby's aunt, answered the door and took Shaw through to the kitchen. The house had wooden parquet floors and high ceilings. Despite the summer the rooms were cool, a lot of the furniture stylish but threadbare. In the wide hall there was a grandmother clock, but there was no sound of it working. Ms Holtby was a small, sinewy woman in a darned skirt and a man's linen shirt, and cork deck-shoes. Making Shaw tea, mashing a bag in the mug, she added milk from a plastic half-pint carton.

'I'm sorry about Paul. You must have been close.' He'd meant it as a statement but he could see her considering it as a question. She said it was oppressive inside, would he mind talking outside, at least until the storm broke? There was a deck beyond the kitchen, looking out over the marshes to the north. Thunder rumbled in steady beats, but the sky directly above was blue by contrast.

'A policewoman called,' she said, looking out to sea. 'I told her . . .' She didn't finish the sentence, letting the cool air lift her short, workaday hair.

'Yes,' said Shaw. 'I just wanted to see for myself.' He looked out beyond the reeds to a narrow shell beach.

She gave Shaw a potted family history. Paul's parents had split up and she'd offered to take the boy in the summer holidays. It had become a ritual, one of the fixed points in his life. The house was full of cousins in the summer. She'd left his room in the barn untouched so he'd returned after university. His mother sent him money, the room was rent-free and he cooked his own food.

'And you remember the East Hills murder in 1994 – a lifeguard, stabbed out on the island?' asked Shaw.

She turned towards him then and for the first time Shaw could see she'd spotted his blind eye. 'Of course – an Australian? And there was something in the paper on Monday. The *Guardian*.' She glanced back at the kitchen door. The newspapers had been spread over a plane deal table.

'Well, we think – just think – that the killer may have swum ashore from East Hills. If he did, then he might have come ashore here. And we thought there was a chance that Paul saw him. Or saw something. The killer may have been injured, you see. Bloodied.'

She shook her head. 'There'd have been no blood, would there?' she said. 'What would it take to swim – forty minutes, an hour? That time the salt would have cleaned a wound – unless it was bad, really bad.' Shaw thought she'd have made a good copper.

'And that's why he died – because he saw this man?' she said, a note of disbelief in her voice. Another long pause. 'It would be good to have a reason,' she said at last. 'Because as a random act of violence it's pretty appalling isn't it? So *disproportionate*.'

'Were you born here?' asked Shaw, thinking the only way he'd find out anything now, after all these years was by chance, by giving her time to talk. Accessing someone's memory wasn't like putting a key in a lock, it was like getting a cat to come to your hand.

'Good God, no.' She talked about her life while Shaw watched the storm clouds darken. A degree in law, a career in the City, getting out before the stress killed her.

Finished, she looked out to sea with a smile on her dry lips. 'I met Paul just a few days ago, up at the wind farm protest,' said Shaw. 'He tried to give us a leaflet through the car window.'

'Well he was nothing like that, not really . . .' she said. 'That was an act, a performance. I mean that, precisely. Psychologically it was actually a performance, as if he'd fooled himself into thinking the real world was a stage. Inside, privately, he was fantastically self-conscious – the birthmark, I suppose, but maybe there was something else, something more rooted. Or uprooted.' The laugh again.

'He played on the beach – alone?'

'Well, not quite. The house was always lively in summer. Family, friends. But books were the thing for Paul. Later, politics and books. But back then, just books. Science fiction – that got him started. Clarke, Dick, Huxley. Then the classics – Austen, Dickens, Tolstoy, Conrad, Faulkner, anything he could pick up.

We talked about books and politics. Thank God we had that.'

Which was odd, thought Shaw, because he hadn't seen a book in the house, let alone a bookcase.

'But he wasn't a book worm – not a little nerd,' she said. 'He loved all this – the sea, the beach. So he'd have gone down with the rest – over there? Do you see? There's a slip of sand at low tide. The seals come in too and they used to swim with them. But Paul just used to sit; make himself a chair out of the sand. I did see him swim but it was pretty rare. Usually he was wrapped up – clothes, books, just wrapped up.'

Shaw felt the first rain drop on his head. It felt as big as a marble, and icy.

He didn't even have to ask to see his room. Behind the house was the barn, half brick, the loft converted to a bedsit with shower and loo. One wall was a scrapbook of political activism – an old poster from the Grunwick dispute, the Miners' Strike of '82, a black and white print of Castro. The bed was unmade, like a human nest, the sheets swirled. In the corner was a mechanical poster printer and a fresh pile of *SOUL* placards.

Ms Holtby flipped the window open from the bottom so that it lifted up, like the shutter on a counter, and at that moment the first lightning struck down to the marshes – forking like a synapse. The light lit the room as if it was a flashgun, and Shaw saw again what wasn't there.

'There's no books . . .'

'There'll be a few,' she said, flipping back the duvet. Two books: a study on green power and a biography of Ghandi.

Shaw recognized the cellophane binding, the Dewey Decimal code number on the spine. 'Library books?'

'Always. Paul grew up in a single parent household, Inspector. No money for books. And I've always been a big fan of libraries – the public services. We take them for granted, don't we? With the cuts and everything we won't have any left in ten years. Odd, isn't it, people always think civilization goes forward. But it can go backwards too.' She looked at the bed, as if seeing it for the first time. 'Libraries were an escape for both of us. So we went every week to stock up.'

Electricity crackled in the damp air over the quayside. When he turned to look at her she'd covered her mouth with both hands. 'I'm so sorry.'

'It's OK,' he said. 'A Saturday?'

'Yes. I always drove into Wells, for the week's shopping. Usually after lunch – no, always after lunch. Then the library. We'd be back by six because we'd stop on the way and get fish and chips for everyone. Saturday treat. So he wasn't there that day – he couldn't have been. How stupid of me.'

The rain fell at last: a curtain of almost solid liquid, drumming on the hard earth, the scent of fresh water for once overcoming the tangy salt of the sea. Shaw said he'd keep in touch if there were any developments, then ran to the car, soaked before he got to the door, so he gave up, and just stood in it, his mouth open, looking up at the falling drops.

THIRTY

George Valentine didn't take a seat. He stood at the duty desk in Wells-next-the-Sea police station, profoundly unhappy to be back. He'd spent ten years of his working life in this building; he'd hated each room, and the view from every window. In summer he'd watched the thin white wisp of cloud crossing the hills as the steam railway took tourists up to the shrine at Walsingham. It was a sight that had always added to a feeling of dislocation, as if his life had taken a branch line too. He'd been up to Walsingham himself once – way back – before Julie had died, before he'd been busted back to DS, before he'd been shipped out from St James' to the sticks. By chance they'd chosen a holy day for the visit, and they'd wandered the streets of the town, watching the pilgrims, then crowded into one of the pubs for lunch. Then, on the edge of the old abbey ruins, they'd found one of the churches, the congregation bursting out, following a procession down to the shrine. So the smoke always made him angry too, for what he'd lost.

'George?'

He turned to find the station sergeant, Ken Blackmoor. He had the decency to flip up the counter flap and come round. He gave Valentine a file.

'Thanks for coming – you need to see this. Frankly, you should have seen it last week. I understand if you want to make a formal complaint. But I thought I'd try to save us all the trouble . . .' He had the decency to look away.

The file cover had a typed note pinned at the top right hand corner which read:

ARTHUR JOHN PATCH
Case No. 4662
IO. DC Rowlands.

'Problem is Don Rowlands was on leave and no one picked up the link.' Sgt Blackmoor looked out the plate-glass door, which gave a view into town, so that they could just see shoppers spilling off the narrow pavements into the road. 'So that's a fuck-up,' he added. Above them thunder rolled, and the lights in the station seemed brighter in the gloom. 'It won't be the last.'

'Tell me,' said Valentine.

Blackmoor filled his lungs, squared his shoulders. Valentine recalled that in his ten years at the nick he'd often seen Blackmoor take flak directed at his juniors. 'Patch was burgled – end of last year. Nasty, actually. Two youngsters in the house, didn't bother to sneak in, just turned up, cleaned him out of some silver, bit of cash. Both in balaclavas. What do the yanks call it – house invasion? Then knocked him over when he cut up a bit rough. Broke his hip.'

Blackmoor was in his mid-fifties, but Shaw remembered that he played badminton, and kept fit. He bent down easily and picked up an ice-lolly wrapper off the fake wooden floor. 'And?' prompted Valentine.

'And, Rowlands had organized an ID parade here at the station for this Friday morning. Clearly not much point now.'

Valentine joined up the dots. 'What kind of ID parade – specific suspect, or usual suspects?'

'Specific. Kid called Tyler. Never been in trouble before – no record. But he'd been trying to flog a piece of silver round the backstreets of Lynn – one of those platters. It was Patch's. Tyler said he found it in a bag on waste ground behind the station. Plus he fitted the description of the kid who'd knocked Patch down.'

'How was Rowlands going to get an ID given the balaclavas?'

'The old bloke had guts. Either that or he was stupid. He spat in one of the kid's faces, so the kid knocked him down, probably thought he was out cold. But Patch was on his back, looking up, and he saw him take the hood off. Got a good look. He said he wouldn't forget the face, and that it wasn't one of the local kids from Creake.'

Valentine flipped the file open. He'd get Twine to run the name through the computer, make sure there was no direct link with East Hills. But what link could there be? He hadn't been born in 1994.

'How'd we think he and his mate got out to Creake?'

'Scooter. Neighbours heard the whine. Tyler's got wheels. A provisional licence, so he shouldn't have been carrying a pillion, but you know, sounds like he isn't exactly a law-abiding citizen.'

He thanked Blackmoor, took the file, and pushed through the door with his shoulder. Outside the rain had started to fall. Drops like paperweights bounced off hot pavements. Valentine shrugged himself into his raincoat, stashed the file into an inside pocket, and began to walk down towards the sea. Water ran an inch deep towards the harbour. Two children in swimsuits were stamping in puddles. He could feel Arthur Patch's file cutting into his bony shoulder.

Is that why the old man had died? To stop him identifying his callous, teenage, burglar? Senseless crimes happened all the time, he thought. They could happen here, in the sticks, just as naturally as in the back streets of Lynn. Which would leave their nicely honed little theory pretty much in tatters, because it meant Arthur Patch hadn't died because he could have identified the killer of Marianne Osbourne. But then there was the cyanide capsule: that one small spherical link between the deaths of Osbourne, Patch and Holtby. So there *was* a link with East Hills. There had to be.

THIRTY-ONE

The town smelt fresh for the first time since the heatwave had begun. The gutters ran with the rain, filling the air with the sound of falling water, despite the stretched-blue sky. The storm had blown through but gusts of wind still rocked the yachts, their masts clacking. Shaw was outside The Ship with just the road and the quay between him and the harbour. A crowd had briefly obscured the view after someone spotted a seal, taking shelter from the choppy waves in the Channel. But now the waterside was deserted. There was no table, so Shaw dragged a seat out of the pub and used the window ledge for his half pint of Guinness. He thought, for the first time, that one of the reasons he didn't drink much alcohol – certainly not as much as his fellow detectives – was that it meant you had to spend so much time indoors. If pubs were roofless he might have had a different life.

Squinting into the distance he realized he could just see the pines on East Hills across the marsh. The rain had cleaned the air, filtering out the dust, so that the far distance was clear, appearing to telescope the view, bringing the horizon closer. Shaw let his eye traverse it: pin sharp and no pain. He sipped his Guinness and closed both eyes, so that he only heard George Valentine's arrival. The way his DS' breath rattled in his throat was distictive, and he produced a peculiar whistle when blowing cigarette smoke out through narrow, dry lips. Shaw heard his footsteps pass and then, a minute later, the DS returned, dragging his own metal seat, the legs screeching on the pavement. Shaw opened his eyes.

'First of the day,' said Valentine.

They heard the church up in the town chime the half hour. The DS hadn't touched his pint, which he held on his knee at a slightly dizzy angle so that the head threatened to spill over the rim. He told Shaw about his visit to Wells' nick and the ID parade planned for Friday.

'And that's a motive for murder?' asked Shaw. 'You think this kid blew up an entire house to avoid a burglary charge?'

'We can't ignore it, Peter. And we're not talking burglary.

We're talking GBH here – in the course of a burglary. First time up in court – OK, but I reckon he's going down, and it isn't going to be six months is it? More like three to five years. That's a motive. And are we really saying this is a coincidence? Really?'

'Why do we only just know this?' said Shaw, angry because he could guess the answer.

'Poor communications – Wells slipped up. They're sorry.'

'If it makes you feel any better,' said Shaw, 'which it shouldn't, the same – or something like it – goes for Holtby, only this is definite: he didn't die because he was a witness to the East Hills murder. His aunt told us he was on the beach that day at Morston. He was actually in Holt library every Saturday afternoon. Right little bookworm. He didn't get back until late evening, and then the whole family had a fish supper. So unless the killer joined them for large cod and chips I can't see we've got this right at all – can you, George?'

'What about Osbourne: the DNA match?'

'Another twelve to twenty-four.'

A police motorcyclist and pillion edged to a stop by their chairs and Tom Hadden took off a helmet, stowed it in the carrier, slapped the rider on the back. The BMW 5,000cc was gone in a thin cloud of lead and sulphur.

'Classy,' said Shaw.

Hadden pointed at their glasses. Valentine drained his dregs, Shaw put a hand over his Guinness. The CSI man came back with a pint of cider for himself, and a third chair to join the other two. Producing a snapshot, he set it on his knee.

'Who he?' said Valentine. The face was puckish, with heavy lips, a man in his early thirties, with luxuriant hair in dark curls. But it was the eyes you'd remember, big and watery like a child's, but wary, as if he was always watchful.

'That's Marc Grieve – Chris Roundhay's lover. One of the seventy-four people we took off East Hills,' said Hadden. 'Died in 2001, RTA near Norwich.'

Shaw picked up the picture, studying the wide, curiously frank open face.

'So?' asked Valentine. 'We know Roundhay's DNA doesn't match. We know this kid's DNA doesn't match. What's your problem?'

'Once we had a blank on the mass screening I did a risk

assessment of the seventy-four suspects: was it possible we'd made a mistake?' said Hadden. He closed his eyes, deep in thought: 'Clearly we needed to focus on the five men who'd died since 1994 – including Grieve. In each case we took a sample from a member of the family. Grieve's case stands out because it was different in one significant way – he was *adopted*.'

Hadden sipped his cider. 'I've had a look at the file. Grieve was born shortly after his parents split up. His mother took in another man almost immediately – there was some domestic violence, social services were involved, and Grieve was taken into council care aged three months, and the boyfriend disappeared. The mother upped-sticks and went north – Newcastle. Died three years later from an overdose of methadone. The original father kept track of the boy. When Grieve was finally adopted he applied for leave to see his son, which he did, every other weekend for a few hours until he was eighteen. Over the years they kept in touch. It was from this man that we took the DNA sample which we then used as a proxy for Marc Grieve in the mass screening.'

Muzak blared from the fairground beyond the quay as a Ferris wheel began to rise into the air, the lights suddenly bright now the sun was setting. Out in the harbour navigation lights were beginning to appear.

'And you think the real father might be the boyfriend – the one who disappeared?' said Shaw. 'And that we got the wrong man, and that Grieve might be our match for Sample X?'

'Yup. Maybe. The error – if it is one – is down to me. I'm sorry.' Hadden's normal whisper cracked as he emphasized the apology.

'Where is this boyfriend?' asked Valentine.

'Social services never got his real name,' said Hadden. 'Once they involved the police he was never seen again. No, there's only one way we can be sure we've got Marc Grieve's DNA, Peter: one way we can rule him out as a suspect with confidence, and that's if we exhume his body. Twine's put a request into the magistrates for tonight – dusk, at Lynn Cemetery. As prosecuting officer . . .'

'I need to attend,' finished Shaw.

The evening he'd planned, with his family on the beach, seemed now like a scene from someone else's life. Instead of the open sands, a swim after sunset, he saw a narrow dark trench, the slit of the grave at his feet. He let his eyes drink in the evening light, as if he was trying to recharge a battery, because he thought he'd need the memory of the colours when darkness fell.

'But Grieve's dead, right?' asked Valentine. 'Even if he killed Shane White on East Hills he didn't kill Patch, Osbourne or Holtby? What am I missing here . . .'

Shaw stood, holding the metal chair perfectly balanced in one hand. 'Think about Chris Roundhay's version of events on East Hills. He said he spoke to Shane White, the lifeguard, then went back to Grieve. After that point the two of them – Roundhay and Grieve – were together until White's blood was washing in with the tide. If Grieve's a match for Sample X then Roundhay lied – again. So what really happened that he needed to mislead us? Maybe they both did it, maybe Roundhay held him down while Grieve put the knife in. If Grieve matches Sample X then Roundhay's in the frame. And unlike Grieve, Roundhay's alive.'

'But why bother? My money's still on Joe Osbourne,' said Valentine. 'Why don't we just wait for his DNA result? You said twelve to twenty-four. What's the problem?'

'The chief constable's press conference is the day after tomorrow,' said Shaw. 'Even if we get a usable sample off Grieve's bones tonight we'll be pushed to get a result in time. My money's still on Osbourne too, George. But if he comes back negative we need Grieve's result by Thursday. So Tom's right. We need to nail this. Once and for all.'

Hadden nodded into his cider.

Shaw thought of the first time they'd interviewed Roundhay at The Ark, on the day of the mass screening. He'd admitted telling lies in his original statement. Perhaps he'd simply replaced them with others.

'Let's pick Roundhay up, George. Get Paul to send a car round. He can join us at the cemetery. Let's ruin his day too.'

THIRTY-TWO

Lynn's municipal cemetery had been built by the Victorians outside the old line of the city walls, beyond the London Gate, on flat land running out through what had been a cordon of market gardens. At its heart stood a folly, a single church spire, the base open on all sides, so that anyone could walk in and look up into the echoing interior. Swallow nests dotted the stonework like mould, and a net stretched over the space held the desiccated corpses of fallen birds. Outside, the stonework was soot black, stained by a century of industrial pollution from the town's bottling works, jam factories and the sugar beet plant, all of which lay downwind towards the docks.

Shaw stood beneath the spire looking out across the gravestones feeling the space above him, the dead air trapped, seeming to press down. The view was no more uplifting: the Victorian's vision of a peaceful, civic last resting place for the town's dead had been ill-used by the twentieth century. The inner ring road ran along one side of the plot, the main road over the river down the other, so that now – at just past nine – lights moved everywhere and the swish of traffic was an eternal soundtrack.

A light cut into the darkness which cloaked the gravestones. A CSI van, a light flashing but silent, creeping through the gates and along one of the principal avenues of the necropolis, making its way towards a single lit electric lantern – the spot where Shaw had parked the Porsche beside Grieve's grave. When it stopped shadows moved, as if the ghosts of the dead had been called to a meeting.

It was time. Shaw walked towards the lights. Passing car headlamps flashed through the iron railings like a stroboscope; making the tumbled field of gravestones shimmer like the crowd at a pop concert. Shaw half expected to see hands raised aloft, clapping to an unheard beat. By the time he reached the CSI van the team had got a tent up over the grave. Justina Kazimierz stood in a forensic suit looking at the distant spire, black against the light-stained sky. She seemed to be whispering to herself, and Shaw wondered if she was praying. Tom Hadden stood by Shaw's Porsche, a file of papers spilt across the bonnet.

Doors creaked on a squad car and Valentine appeared with Chris Roundhay.

The thin fair hair was damp and untidy across the wide forehead. Shaw was struck again by the way the lantern jaw unbalanced the face, an unsettling contrast to the blue eyes.

'What is this?' said Roundhay, looking around. He looked tense, the shoulders bunched, but as each car's lights flickered by he could see that his skin was dry, his expression mildly inquisitive. 'What do I tell my wife?' demanded Roundhay. 'My family. I've left them all – we were having dinner, for Christ's sake.'

Shaw checked his watch, but his hand moved so slowly to turn the face that he managed to convey the truth – that the hour, for him, didn't matter. Which was, in a way, true; because when Shaw entered a graveyard he always felt the slackening of the leash of time. 'So you didn't attend your friend Marc Grieve's funeral?'

'No. Why . . .' Roundhay's eyes widened. 'Is he here – Marc?' He looked around at the gravestones and settled on the forensic tent, lit now from within. They could hear the sound of spades slicing into clay. Roundhay looked at his well-polished shoes.

'Mr Roundhay, did you speak to Marc in the years after East Hills? I'm talking since he married. See each other? Ever?' Shaw asked.

Roundhay's hands were hidden in a long coat, the night air ruffling his thin blond hair. 'He had another life. I left him to it.'

Hadden's head appeared in the tent doorway. 'Ten minutes, Peter.'

Shaw lifted apart the plastic leaves of the forensic tent and gestured for Roundhay to go first. He was aware he was being cruel, that he had no real right and certainly no good *reason* for exposing him to this. But he knew that Roundhay held many secrets, and that if he could just dislodge one, the rest might follow.

When they were all inside, Shaw read out the inscription on the stone, which had been hauled out of its position and set back.

The design was modern, ugly, asymmetrical and decorated with a bunch of craved grapes.

MARC JOHN GRIEVE
Born 8/8/76 Died 8/4/04

Three council workers were digging out the grave. The passing headlights on the ring road created a light show on the tent's side. Roundhay rearranged his feet as if he might fall over, but his face was still utterly expressionless, a passive mask. 'I didn't know he was here,' he said.

The labourers had already dug down three feet creating a dark slit. Valentine had been to exhumations before and was struck by the resemblance to a judicial hanging: the grave as the drop, the witnesses clustered, the air of almost electric anticipation and growing dread.

'I want to know what happened on East Hills that day,' said Shaw. 'And I don't want any lies. If you can't tell me the truth – and I mean right now – then we're going to dig up what's left of Marc's body and take a DNA sample from his bones. Because I think you've lied to us. I think it's Marc's skin on the towel we found on the beach at East Hills. I think you killed the lifeguard together because he'd taken pictures of the two of you, in the dunes, and he wanted money. I don't think you meant to do it. Or planned to do it. But I do want the truth.'

Roundhay rubbed his chest, where he'd built up the muscles, and Shaw guessed his heart was racing. Guilt or lost love? 'I'll say anything you want to stop this,' said Roundhay. 'But I've told the truth already.' He looked at Shaw, his eyes dead. 'What do you want me to say?'

It was an impressive performance, thought Shaw. He'd brought Roundhay here to put him under pressure, to drag him closer to an emotional edge. Instead, somehow, Roundhay had switched the pressure on to Shaw. 'Well?' asked Roundhay.

One of the men jumped into the grave to start digging from inside. Roundhay didn't flinch, but the colour had drained from his face.

Shaw had had enough. 'Get him out of here,' he said.

Valentine held the plastic tent flap open. Roundhay hesitated, as if it had become his duty to stand and watch his lover's bones revealed.

'Unless you wish to stay?' asked Shaw.

Roundhay fled. Shaw let the tension bleed out of his shoulders, into his back, down his legs, into the grave. Then the sound of a spade hitting wood made him jump. He went outside and watched the tail lights on the squad car carrying Roundhay recede through the dark, eventually joining the coursing flow of cars on the ring road.

A liar then, certainly. But a killer – not just of Shane White, but a multiple killer? The deaths of Marianne Osbourne, Arthur Patch and Paul Holtby were linked to East Hills – even if they couldn't, as yet, uncover the link. Was Roundhay capable of killing them all just to save his own skin? Shaw had met several murderers, shook their hands, given them tea to sip, listened to them talk, watched them cry. He didn't think there was a single, common telltale sign that someone was a killer. No cold eyes, no preternatural calm, no twitching facial muscle. But in each case he'd felt just like this: a *victim* himself, manipulated, controlled.

He felt empty, but most of all, hungry. Not just for food but for human company. He watched Valentine appear out of the dark. A bone saw buzzed from inside the tent.

'George. Let's get something to eat.'

THIRTY-THREE

'George, parmesan?' said Lena, passing the dish to Fran. They'd put Valentine at the head of the table so that he was looking out to sea towards the light that was still in the sky. It was the guest of honour's chair. The heavy heat of the long drought had returned after the storm so they'd all agreed to eat outside, the table set on the wooden stoop of the cafe. Shaw had hoped the deluge marked the beginning of autumn, his favourite season. But it seemed that the summer would cling on, weakened by a series of storms, each one only sapping a little heat from the landscape.

Somewhere out at sea, beyond the horizon, thunder and light-ning still crackled.

Valentine prodded at the shell-like pasta in its rich anchovy sauce. It was a small helping because he'd served himself from the large pottery bowl in which Lena had put out the meal. A bowl decorated with painted chillies which had made him wary. Fran stood at his elbow and shaved some cheese over his plate until he raised a hand.

They drank iced water poured from a jug and Valentine tried not to think how long it had been since he'd eaten a meal with another human being. He shared his chips with the gulls every night, although they always dropped the ones with curry sauce on. And in the canteen people would sit at the same table, but only if the place was packed, and even then you weren't sharing a meal, you were just sharing the table. His last meal with Julie had been fish and chips out of the paper. They'd sat on the front step and shared the chips, which meant he'd had to do without salt, and she'd had to do without vinegar, which was sweet, but annoying.

Shaw had invited Valentine home because his DS said he'd taken a room in Wells. And besides, he wanted company, and not just Lena and Fran: there was something about reversing the process of burial – hauling someone's bones into the light – which unsettled him. More practically, his DS must be hungry. Shaw rarely saw Valentine take solids, but he presumed he did eat. He imagined greasy breakfasts in one of Lynn's many cafes. The question *would he like to eat with them?*, was out of his mouth before he realized he'd crossed a line. They'd been partners for four years and this was the first time his father's one-time DI had come to the house. Now, looking down the table at Valentine's gaunt face, he knew he'd left the invitation too long.

The atmosphere was tense, not so much because of Valentine's unexpected presence, but because Shaw had shouted at his daughter; a very rare flash of visible temper. They'd been close to the house, walking in the exquisite light of dusk, when they'd seen her digging a hole out on the wet sand; just her head showed, and she was still shovelling gritty sand, which flew out in fan-shaped fusillades. Beside the hole the child's old dog barked.

They had house rules about holes in the sand. As a child Shaw had been on this beach, a mile south, near the pier, one late

summer's day. Two families had started digging pits in compÄti-
tion – a long, hot, afternoon of spadework, until they'd both got
down ten foot. Shaw, an only child, had watched in envy as the
two teams had revelled in the contest. Fathers, uncles, big brothers
stood back, shouting, drinking beer from cans, while the children
dug. That would have been fine. They could have posed for
pictures, then gone home. But the holes were only twenty foot
apart – why not dig a tunnel *between* them? Shaw had joined
the crowd on the edge of one pit, watching as a child's legs
disappeared into the horizontal shaft.

Then the tunnel had collapsed. He'd run for his father, who'd
been up in the dunes reading his paper in a deckchair. When they
got back men were in the two holes, trying to dig through with
their bare hands. When they got the child out they passed him
up and laid him out on towels. The gritty sand was pressed into
him: his eyes, his mouth, his ears, his hair. Then Shaw's mother
had led him away and his father, finding them later at a prear-
ranged spot up in town, had never told him if the child had lived,
which was stupid, because if he had survived he'd have said.
Shaw was pretty certain that was his first dead body. The eyes
had been closed so there was no clue there, but there had been
one hand, turned out, ugly, and one foot, turned in, uglier still.

So they had rules.

Shaw walked to the hole and shouted: the anger so sudden,
and mixed with so much fear and anxiety, that what he said was
just a burst of noise. Then he took her hand and hauled her up
so that she shouted, this time in pain.

'I was just finishing,' she said, looking up at him, scared, a
note of defiance in her voice for the first time. Now she was
looking at Valentine across the table as he ate his pasta. 'Did
you know granddad?' she asked. 'Granddad Jack?'

Valentine looked at her, sensing that Lena and Shaw were
waiting keenly for the answer.

'Yes, I did. He looked like you – a bit. Just round the eyes,
and the way you look out through your lashes.' He and Julie
hadn't had kids. It was wrong to say he didn't like them. It was
just that he didn't know them.

'Like Daddy?'

Valentine caught Shaw's eye and saw he was laughing. 'No. I
don't think so.' He coughed, trying to clear his voice of the effects

of thirty years of cigarettes and booze. 'He looks like your Grandma. He *sounds* like your Granddad. You know, sometimes, when I'm not looking and he says something, I think – for a second – that Jack's there.'

Valentine intercepted a look between Lena and Shaw. He'd never been good at interpreting such looks. They had a word for it now, probably an exam in it: *emotional intelligence*. This look between Shaw and his wife seemed to radiate reproach with disappointment. It was a wild guess but Valentine thought it meant one of two things: either that the next time Shaw brought someone home to dinner he should let her know in advance, or that they should have asked him to dinner before.

He wondered, for the first time, whether she'd told Shaw she'd been to Valentine's house to talk about his eye. He thought about Brendan O'Hare wrapped in his fluffy towels, seeking betrayal.

Fran announced ice cream, everyone else passed, and she went off to help herself from the Walls fridge. When she was out of earshot Shaw took Lena's hand. 'I'm sorry, I shouldn't have lost it.' He looked along the table at Valentine. 'Bit of a domestic.'

Lena shook her head and turned to Valentine. 'He beats her daily with a rock. Now. Coffee,' she said, getting up. Valentine didn't have the nerve to tell her he only drank tea. She was one scary woman. He checked his mobile – nothing. When he looked up he knew something had happened because Shaw had got up and was holding his head in both hands.

'Peter?' He wondered if Shaw's eye had lost vision, but when he saw his face the DI was laughing, an incredulous laugh.

'George,' he said. 'Thank God you came to dinner.' He felt behind him for his seat like an old man and fell back, his shoulders sagging. 'You're right about the voice. I heard it on my answer phone the other week and thought for a second it *was* Dad.'

He got up again, quickly, and took a bottle of iced white wine out of a bucket on the table. Shaw cracked the screw top, poured Valentine a large glass, and put a splash in his own.

'It's just a bit of what I inherited, isn't it? The vocal chords. The shade of hair. The stance. Not the temper – that's Mum's.'

Valentine nodded, trying to see where this was going.

'He wouldn't have been very proud of us,' said Shaw, sipping wine. 'We missed the obvious, George. Both of us. What did he always say? That the real challenge of a murder inquiry was holding on to common sense.'

Valentine let the wine touch his lips. He didn't really trust wine – too much alcohol in too small an amount of liquid. Shaw had slipped into lecture mode, and he knew better than to interrupt him now.

'What was this whole inquiry about?' asked Shaw, leaning forward. 'What was the key to it all? Why did we reopen East Hills in the first place?'

'New evidence,' said Valentine.

'What kind of new evidence?'

'DNA – genetics.'

'Exactly. The code which can lead us to a killer. Our problem is that we can't find a motive for the deaths of two of our victims: Arthur Patch and Paul Holtby. Let's turn this on its head. What would have happened if they *hadn't* died?'

Valentine caught the slight hint of the rhetorical question in Shaw's voice, so he didn't even shrug.

'If Arthur Patch was alive and well he'd have been at Wells' nick this Friday morning,' said Shaw. 'He'd have picked out young Garry Tyler – almost certainly. They'd have charged the kid, George. Then taken him down to St James' where the duty sergeant would have booked him in, got him a solicitor and then, standard routine, he'd have taken a swab and gathered a DNA sample.' Shaw's voice had gathered in strength as he spoke, and in volume.

Shaw came round the table, hands splayed on the wood, his face close to Valentine's. 'Next, Paul Holtby. If Holtby hadn't been murdered in the woods, George, what would have happened the next day? The demonstrators would have tried to break through the gates – they'd all have been arrested. My guess is they'd have bussed them down to St James' to process the lot. Teach 'em a lesson. Breach of the peace, maybe even some criminal damage. Both reportable offences. So, again, DNA samples all round, and straight on to the national database.

'It's the timing that's crucial. For the killer it couldn't be worse. Because at this point in the inquiry he knows – is absolutely certain – that we won't have found a DNA match from the mass screening. So what happens next; what *should* have happened next?'

'We'd have run the East Hills samples through the database looking for a close match – a family match,' said Valentine. 'Which we didn't do because O'Hare wanted to save £7,000 quid.'

'Right, but the killer doesn't know that. He presumes we will do the family match. He can't afford not to presume that. I think he killed again – twice – to make sure we didn't pick up that family link.'

Shaw drank the wine in his glass, held the cool liquid in his mouth, then let it trickle down his throat. He knew he was right because it was so simple. Sample X was the heart of the case. The killer had, at all costs, to stop the police finding a match. The mass screening was always going to draw a blank. But a family link was just as damning. The police would begin checking relatives: brothers, sisters, aunts, uncles, cousins – moving out through the family network until they got their man. The killer had to destroy any chance that would happen. And so he killed twice more.

Valentine leant forward and helped himself to another glass of the wine he didn't like. 'We've already got a suspect related to one of the wind farm demonstrators – Joe Osbourne,' he said. 'If anyone was going to end up in the cells – other than Holtby – it was Tilly Osbourne, his own daughter. It wouldn't have taken us long to find that link. And Joe's local – North Norfolk through-and-through. He could easily be related to this Tyler kid too.'

Shaw set the wine glass aside. 'Yeah. Maybe it is Joe. With a little help from his mate Tug Coyle, I think, running him out to East Hills for nothing then forgetting he was ever on board. Anyway, we'll know soon enough, George.'

Lena returned with the coffee and they sat watching the tide come in; the rows of white water just visible under a moonless sky.

Shaw's mobile buzzed, shuffling on the wooden table top. It was Paul Twine up at The Circle. They had a problem with Tug Coyle. He'd missed two appointments at St James' to give a new statement. So they'd sent a squad car round to check his address that evening – a flat in the Woodley estate. Neighbours said he hadn't been seen for a week. Much more worryingly he'd missed three shifts at the lifeboat station, having never missed one in the previous thirteen years. And his nets and pots were still strung out off the north point of East Hills.

Shaw tossed the mobile on to the table, then smiled at Valentine: the full hundred-watt surfer's smile. 'Coyle's done a runner.'

THIRTY-FOUR

Wednesday

Wells' lifeboat station was at the end of a straight mile of sea wall which led directly out to sea from the town quay. The beach stretched beyond, a vast yellow undulating plain, an early morning August crowd of several hundred reduced to isolated dots. Lifeboat crewman Tug Coyle was still missing. Peterborough CID had contacted his wife who said she had received her monthly support payment from Tug's solicitor, but there had been no call from her ex-husband, which was rare. The coming Thursday was his regular monthly date with his son. Usually he'd call to fix up time and place: often the town cinema, or the stock-car racing arena, or a fishing trip in summer. Coyle's car – a battered Vauxhall van – was not outside his flat or beside the lifeboat station.

Shaw put the Porsche in an empty slot marked for RNLI crewmen. As soon as he swung open the door he could smell the salt, hear the distinctive shouts of children playing out at the water's edge. The heat was already building, yesterday's thunderstorm a distant memory. The air over the modern corrugated iron roof of the lifeboat house buckled in the sun's rays, an anchored mirage. From the outside the building had all the charm of an MFI out-of-town showroom, painted in corporate shades of grey and orange. But inside the Aran-class boat gleamed. Half a dozen tourists were already up on the walkway which gave a view inside the boat's hi-tech cabin.

Valentine arrived and spread some A4 sheets on to the flat glass top of a display cabinet containing medals. Ignoring a sign he lit a Silk Cut. They'd talked this through the night before after coffee. If Shaw was right about the killer's motives then there

was a genetic link between the murderer and *both* the teenage
burglar and one of the thirty-seven demonstrators the inquiry
team had interviewed who would have been up at Docking Hill
on the day of the planned wind farm protest. The sure-fire way
to catch their killer was to put the thirty-eight DNA profiles on
the database and wait for the link to appear. But that would take
several days. And they didn't have several days. So they'd try to
do it on paper, by interview. They were dealing with close family
relationships: near family, so it wasn't an impossible task – it
just needed some painstaking work.

'So far?' asked Shaw.

'So far nothing,' said Valentine, sifting the papers. 'But Paul
seems to know what he's doing. The whole team's on it flat out.
He says it'll take twenty-four hours – maybe more. But we've
set up a fast track too, seeing if we can find a link between our
Garry Tyler – the burglar – and Joe Osbourne.'

He held up a head-and-shoulders print of a teenager: cropped
hair, belligerent stare. 'This is Tyler by the way, care of Wells'
nick. Jackie Lau's going out to see the kid's mother over lunch.
That's our best bet. Paul talked to Tilly Osbourne and she says
she can't recall any Tylers in the family, but hey, they're not that
kind of family and she's a teenager. Why would she care?'

They climbed a short spiral metal staircase into the mess room.
News of a crewman missing had brought several lifeboatmen
into the station. Shaw recognized most of the faces. No one had
seen Tug Coyle for forty-eight hours. He had been due on a
standard watch that morning at six but hadn't reported in, having
missed two shifts the day before, one the day before that. There'd
be a disciplinary hearing; if there wasn't a copper-plated excuse,
he might be thrown off the crew.

They asked to see Coyle's locker and one of the senior crew
opened it up: spare boots, gear for the lifeboat, roll-up tin,
torch, two heavy RNLI sweaters, two pairs of camouflage trousers, and a programme for the Norfolk Arena, featuring rally
cross and speedway. Valentine took the key, relocked the locker,
and asked them to leave it that way.

The deputy coxswain was a man called Petersen, Navy-clean,
with eyes that looked as if the sun had bleached the colour out
of them. He showed Shaw Coyle's rota: eight six-hour shifts a
week, plus any back-up shifts he could make. Available on call

24/7 except for an eight-hour gap on Thursday afternoons when he took his son out.

'Broken marriage,' said Petersen, shrugging.

When asked he said that Coyle was popular but not particularly sociable. They went back downstairs to the boathouse and Petersen nodded at the portrait on the wall of Tug Johns. 'You know he was his grandson? Difficult act to follow. Didn't help giving the kid the nickname, did it? Like he was supposed to be right there in the old man's footsteps. I knew Johns, and frankly I thought he was pretty unpleasant. Kind of skipper in the Navy you'd go a long way to avoid. Bit of a tyrant. You couldn't tell him anything. If you've done it, he's done it, only he's done it better. Coyle was better than that. But, you know, if we could see ourselves . . .'

The doors of the boathouse were open so they were looking down the ramp at The Cut, the tide flowing out and a yacht sliding past, East Hills on the horizon.

'There is one thing,' added Petersen. 'One of the crew comes from a family in the town that owns one of the huts – way out the end. Tug used to sleep over some nights rather than driving back to Lynn. Illegal, but like nobody's counting, and there's plenty that can't afford the local house prices anymore. Give me a sec, I'll get you the key.'

They stood together out on the sand, not far from a family encamped round a hole full of children. Both their mobiles buzzed with an identical incoming text. It was Paul Twine up at the incident room: CSI had phoned from The Ark, the lab result on Joe Osbourne's DNA had arrived. Negative – no match with Sample X. They'd sent a uniformed officer up to the hospital to give Osbourne the good news in person.

'Negative!' Valentine held his phone at arm's length and thought about lobbing it into the sea.

'How does that work?' He spat in the sand. 'Coyle, the ferryman, does a runner, but it's not Joe Osbourne out on East Hills. So who the fuck was out on the island?' He looked skywards and his neck cracked. 'Are we back to Grieve and Roundhay?' His voice had risen with frustration: 'And if we're back to them why the fuck has Coyle pissed off?'

Shaw just stood in the sand, rooted, feet in his own shadow, like he wasn't going anywhere.

THIRTY-FIVE

T o the east the long, graceful curve of the beach huts bled into a shimmering horizon of blue. Shaw and Valentine walked for half a mile but didn't seem to get any closer to the end. Most of the huts were open. The families in them fell into three groups. The Chelsea-on-Sea set: cooler boxes, literary novels and not too many kids. Then the families from the big camp site and holiday park beyond the pine woods who got a hut as part of their package deal: extended families, noisier, kids playing games, kettles whistling. And then just a few local families. They'd be wrapped up against the sun, dogs about, and perhaps some fishing gear set up to catch the tide as it came in.

Shaw had been walking while looking out to sea so that when the sudden clap of thunder came it was a shock. He spun round, to the land and trees, and saw the black edge of a storm cloud over the pines. As he tried to measure the speed of the cloud, lightning flashed: someone screamed in one of the nearby huts, and then the first fat raindrops fell. He looked back at Valentine, a hundred yards adrift, standing in his raincoat looking up at the charcoal-grey lid of cloud as it slid over the beach. The rain started to crater the sand.

Shaw broke into a jog. Halfway along the line of huts he got to one of the wooden stairways which led back over the dunes into the pinewoods. Beside the bottom step a standpipe, dripping into the sand. The next hut, No. 124, Shaw had once hired himself, a favourite spot for Lena and Fran. He stopped, recalling that it was about here on the beach that he usually lost his mobile signal. He checked: the usual six bars had been reduced to one, flickering. Within seconds the rain was an impenetrable screen, like a shower curtain, hiding the woods and then, by degrees, the sea. He waited for Valentine and then they trudged on, the beach crowds going in the opposite direction. No. 186 was indeed almost the last in the line, citrus lemon in colour, one of the older huts, so its stilts were shorter, the top step only just above the encroaching sand.

Over the door a brass nameplate read: North View.

Petersen, from the RNLI crew, hadn't given them a key in the end, but a piece of paper with a three-digit code to punch into a small box mounted on the hut. Inside was a key.

Valentine struggled briefly with a salt-rusted padlock, rain dripping from his nose. The first thing they saw when they got the door open was a sleeping bag on the floor. Military issue, good enough for Arctic camping, and set out neatly on a thermal mat. Shaw picked up a pair of discarded trousers – again, combat green.

'Likes his military kit,' said Shaw.

It was one of those moments when they were both thinking the same thing. Was Coyle the man Aidan Robinson had spotted on the edge of the woods above Marianne Osbourne's house in the days before she died? But they both knew that didn't work: Robinson and Coyle were family. If he could spot an army jumper and a military short back-and-sides, he could recognize his own cousin from a hundred yards.

'It's cheap. Army Surplus,' said Valentine. 'Doubt if it's a fashion statement.'

There was a locked shutter as well, so Shaw undid it, swinging it down to reveal a window which he unlatched, so that light flooded the interior. Looking seawards he could see a small fishing boat off the beach, a lone sailor bailing water in a kind of unhurried way. Inside the hut were two thermos flasks – again, heavy-duty issue. A cardboard box with Lipton's on the side contained apples, a sliced loaf, cheese and a bunch of salad onions. There was a newspaper – the *Daily Mail* – and a thriller, Clive Cussler, and a battery-powered camping lantern. The storm cloud was out to sea now, a few miles offshore, and the sun was coming back, brighter than before, but cooler.

'Coyle won't get far,' said Valentine. 'They never do unless they've got a fortune. Disappearing is an expensive business.'

But Shaw didn't think that was always true. This was a man who could survive on his own. A man who might turn out to be more like his granddad – Tug Johns – than anybody had ever thought.

Shaw leant out of the window and lifted the shutter, sliding in the locks, and was about to close the door when he glanced up above the lintel. There were two snapshots there, which he took down. One was black and white. Two kids in a boat, a man with white hair posed for the picture. 'Tug Johns and his grand-sons,' said Shaw. 'Maybe? It's certainly the grandfather . . .' He looked at the youngsters and was pretty sure the smaller one was Tug Coyle. You could see the man he was going to be – the crab-like carapace of shoulders and back, the short powerful build. It was harder to see Aidan Robinson in the other boy – the strange, steel-grey eyes were the same, but the face was much narrower, even feminine, with high cheekbones. Of the belligerent confidence, the stillness, there was no trace.

The other snap was in colour. A teenage boy, posing in front of a smashed-up stock car. Valentine retrieved the picture of Garry Tyler from his raincoat pocket. They had a match: hundred per cent, no doubt.

Valentine snapped the ID picture. 'Tyler. It'll be Tug's ex-wife's maiden name. It's the same kid. It's Coyle's son.'

THIRTY-SIX

They sat on the steps of North View together, looking out to sea, Valentine holding the picture of Garry Tyler. If Tug Coyle, the ferryman, was his father, then it suggested he was also their killer. But how could he be? He'd brought the *Arandora Star* into East Hills through seawater stained with the victim's blood. He couldn't have been in two places at once: on the beach with the murder weapon and in the boat, alone at the helm.

Shaw closed his eyes to rest the muscles, and it was then – robbed of the distraction of sight – that he heard the silence. The sounds of the beach had gone entirely, not just the gentle whisper of the holiday crowd but even the rustling of the pinewoods. He stood to see if a fresh storm cloud was edging over but instead found that about a hundred yards away, along the beach, an almost solid wall of mist was advancing east, drifting along the coast.

'Fret,' he said, using the local word.

They were common in summer, especially after storms, when icy rain fell on a warm sea. A fog bank, formed at the margin of sea and land, would condense in a few minutes then hug the coast. Soon they'd be within it and the thought made Shaw shiver because it would be cold in there, and damp, and the rest of the world would recede even further. If silence could have a physical form then this was it.

Shaw closed his eyes and waited for the moment. First he smelt the mist – that acrid, bitter edge to the salty air, and then he felt it, a bristling moisture on his skin. Opening his eyes he found he was enclosed in the whiteness: he could see Valentine and the hut, but nothing else. But almost immediately the fog parted to reveal a view of the sea: a wedge of blue, sun-splashed. There was a boat out there, the one he'd seen earlier, but the sailor on board was motionless now, his hand on a line. The boat, thought Shaw, was in exactly the same spot. 'That's it,' said Shaw. He stood, pointing out to sea. 'Coyle said he stood off East Hills that day for what – twenty minutes? Well, he wouldn't have let the boat drift – he'd have put down an anchor. Just like that guy. We thought someone might have swum off the boat, or out to the boat, but maybe it was just Coyle. He could have swum ashore, killed White in the water, *and swum back*. The boat would still be there. Then ten minutes later he brings the ferry in as the body of his victim drifts along the beach.'

'Motive?' asked Valentine, trying to light a Silk Cut with damp fingers.

'Maybe he'd been caught on film with Marianne Osbourne,' suggested Shaw. 'Or – this is better – she'd gone to him for help because White was blackmailing her? Don't forget he was Aidan's cousin – she must have known him. And he runs the ferry. So she asks for help and he makes a plan. They know White will be out there. He swims ashore like I said from the *Arandora Star* – a hundred yards, maybe less. White's not in the water, he's up in the dunes, lured there by Marianne. He kills White, with maybe Marianne a witness or accomplice. So it's his DNA on the towel. He's Sample X.

'Then we resurrect the case and send out letters telling everyone we're going to test all the men taken off East Hills that day. He knows we won't find a match. Does he think we'll work out it's him? Or does he think Marianne will buckle in the interview? She's rocky, unstable. She thinks she can't do it, so they talk at the house.

'The last time he visits – the day before the mass screening – he takes the cyanide pill with him. Where'd he get it? My guess is Tug Johns, his grandfather. Or at least it was in the old man's stuff – something left in the attic, or maybe one of the dugouts did survive. Old Tug was a shoe-in for one of these secret units. He's got all the skills plus leadership. So young Tug brings the pill. It's a gift for Marianne: a one-way ticket out of a life she can't face anymore. And he helps her take it. Maybe even makes her take it. Meanwhile there's a family crisis. His son is hauled in for the identity parade at Wells. Tug knows it's him. He knows we'll arrest the kid. The first thing we'll do is take a DNA swab for the database. And in one step that will take us to Tug Coyle. In this case the match is all we need, George. It's not like Tug Coyle can claim the forensic evidence is down to an accidental meeting on the beach. He was *never* on the beach – that's his story, has been his story for seventeen years. This would prove he lied, and the only verdict a jury would bring in would be guilty. So Arthur Patch has to die to keep young Garry Tyler out of trouble.' Shaw stood and walked forward in the wet sand, crunching razor shells on the high water mark.

'And Holtby?' asked Valentine.

'There's a DNA link, there has to be, we just need to find it.'

'There's a simpler answer,' said Valentine. He didn't really believe in conspiracy, grand theories of crime. He thought criminals were a lower order: not exactly stupid, just subnormal, without the wit to see the outcome of their own actions. So anything that smacked of accident, or cock-up, sounded right to him. 'It doesn't have to be DNA, Peter. What if Coyle got the pills from the dugout, and it is up in the pinewoods above The Circle? Maybe Holtby stumbled on something up there, something he couldn't ignore. It could have got him killed.'

Shaw looked out over the sands, noting how the rain had rubbed them clean of footprints, leaving just a stippled, virgin pattern. 'We need to up the search for Coyle,' he said. 'East of England constabularies, plus a radio and TV alert. And contact UK Border Agency, make sure they've got his details online in case he tries to catch a flight out, or skip on a ferry.

'Or a boat?' suggested Valentine. 'A small boat along the coast?'

Out at sea they heard a ship's foghorn through the mist,

answering the one on shore. It was three hundred miles to the nearest continental port. In a small boat Coyle had no chance. Which didn't mean he wouldn't try.

'He'd have to be desperate,' said Shaw.

They locked up and began to walk back, joining the crowd which was still trickling off the beach, children grumbling, parents hauling gear. Shaw had reached the hut he'd hired with the family, where the signal picked up, when his mobile vibrated in his pocket. It was a prompt call from his message box, so he retrieved the text. It was from the chief constable's secretary asking Shaw to call about the story which had appeared in that morning's edition of *The Daily Telegraph* concerning East Hills: did he know the source?

He was trying to think of a good answer when a single fresh text arrived from Twine. HUNSTANTON CLIFF CAR PARK. ASAP. INCIDENT.

THIRTY-SEVEN

T he coastal band of mist had thickened, the fret edging inland half a mile, the fog deepening from cotton-wool white to a darker hue – a hint of purple at its heart, and even a thread of amber seeping through from the hidden sun. The main car park at Hunstanton, a wide ten acre field on the cliff top, appeared almost empty as Shaw steered the Porsche through the entrance gate and let gravity trundle the car, in neutral, down the tilted grass. They passed a pair of VW camper vans in the gloom, then three sports cars with sailboards strapped to roof racks, then nothing – just damp grass. Shaw was always amazed at the speed with which a summer beach crowd could desert the seaside once the sun was gone. The pier back in town would be crowded, as would the pubs and chip shops. There'd be a queue for the cinema's matinee performance of the latest Narnia blockbuster. But up here, on the cliff top, you could throw a Frisbee and bet your mortgage it wouldn't hit a thing except wet grass.

'There,' said Valentine. A squad car was just visible in the grey mist, no light flashing. Shaw let the Porsche park itself, rolling to a halt, then dropped the window as the sturdy front-row-forward silhouette of DC Mark Birley appeared out of the fret. Birley was three years out of uniform, one of Shaw's team, still a fish out of water in the world of CID.

'Sir. It's Roundhay, sir. He's about fifty yards up the slope – near the top hedge. He's at the wheel of the car – a four-by-four. We had him under surveillance pending the DNA tests on Grieve's bones. Early shift yesterday saw him leaving for work in the family car and followed him in. Late shift took over at two. He got a cab home after a few drinks in town. Must have slipped out overnight on foot over the back fence. The wife called St James' at nine this morning and said he'd left a suicide note and that the car was missing.' Birley pointed a once broken finger into the mist: 'Just there – you can see the headlights.'

Shaw and Valentine peered into the gloom. You could see the lights, but the beam was faint, shifting, as a light breeze tumbled the skeins of mist.

Birley passed Shaw a mobile phone. 'He left this for you, sir, with the note. Specifically. He said he'd ring you on it at one thirty-five p.m. this afternoon, on the dot. You have one chance to answer.'

'What did the note say?' asked Shaw.

'Wife's with victim support – she's pretty much in pieces. She destroyed it. Fiona's with her, but all she'll say is it was private.'

They could hear it now, the low rumble of the four-by-four's engine.

Valentine leant over so he could see Birley's face. 'And we're sure he's not run the exhaust in? We're not sitting here while he fucking does it, are we?'

'Foot patrol said there was no sign of a pipe, tube, nothing. And the wife was sure he'd keep the promise – he'd call at one thirty-five p.m.'

Shaw checked his watch. 1.32 p.m. and pretty much, according to his watch, bang on high tide for Hunstanton. The mist seemed to swaddle all noise. There was a thin swish-swish from the coast road, and shreds of a metallic tune from the fun fair.

'Plan?' asked Shaw.

Birley nodded like he'd expected to be in charge. Valentine had noted this aspect of Shaw's command: that at any moment he could offer control to a subordinate. It worked well because everyone had to keep on their toes, be prepared to take responsibility. 'You take the call,' said Birley. 'Let him say what he wants to say. Then we rush him – I've got two squad cars here, other side of the hedge, half a dozen on foot up by the ticket machines. We've no idea what he's got in there but the favourite has to be pills.'

Pills. Shaw thought that if Roundhay was their killer after all then he might have a cyanide pill, in which case rushing the car was useless. But if they tried to get to him before the call he could crush a pill in a second. They didn't have a choice. He'd take the call. 'OK. Sounds good. We'll get a bit closer,' said Shaw, lowering the window, igniting the engine then inching uphill, trying to keep the dim headlights in view. They got within thirty yards. They could see the outline of the four-by-four's windscreen, lit by the vanity light within. Roundhay, his head back on the rest, both hands on the steering wheel.

'Well?' asked Valentine. 'What's this about?'

Shaw shrugged. 'One minute we'll know. Maybe it's confession time. Maybe he knows we'll get a match off his mates' bones. Maybe we're wrong about Coyle – what if he's done a runner for some reason we don't know, like debt? He's clearly short of a few bob. Who knows?'

Shaw peered through the fog. 'I don't like this, George. Not a bit.'

The phone rang and Shaw almost dropped it, catching it at the second attempt.

'Chris,' he said, trying to keep his voice level. 'Chris Roundhay?'

'You out there?' said Roundhay. Shaw thought the voice was a bad sign: cool, level and in control. He'd planned this, or something like it, and so far Shaw suspected everything had happened in the right order, at the right time.

'Here,' said Shaw, flashing the headlights.

'I'm impressed. I didn't think you'd find me in this fog. Don't get any closer.'

'OK. No problem. Whatever you want.'

'I needed you to know – for someone to know.' Shaw could see Roundhay's head working from side to side, as if trying to relieve stress in his neck. 'The week Marc died in the car, I saw him. He called, said he wanted to see me, so we met down at Wells on the long beach, on one of the dunes. His marriage hadn't worked out; he thought he'd made a mistake, denying things to himself, to me. We could meet, maybe. A day, a night, once a month – less if I wanted.'

Silence, but looking ahead into the mist they saw a slight movement and then the sound of the Nissan's engine died. 'I said I didn't want that. That I wouldn't see him again. That I had another life. He said he'd kill himself because he had nothing else to live for. I didn't believe him.' An edge of emotion at last, thought Shaw, Roundhay's voice catching on the last word.

'So he did. I'm sure of that. I don't think he planned it, but I can imagine his mind working like that. Just driving along and then the hopelessness of it taking him over, and then he'd just spin the driving wheel and know it was over. I wanted you to know . . .'

Shaw looked at his watch, part of his mind worrying away at the coincidence: that Roundhay wanted to talk at 1.35 p.m., exactly at high tide.

'As soon as I knew that he was dead I knew I'd made the wrong decision. That my life was hopeless too. But I buried that idea, like I've buried everything else. I carried on with my life. Now I can't. You'll know soon enough but it isn't his DNA on that towel. Or mine. I told you the truth about that . . . So it's over now.'

Shaw covered the phone. 'Tell 'em in the squad car, George. I hit the horn, they rush him.'

Valentine cracked open the door, slipped out, letting it just hang open. Shaw heard his slip-ons squeak as he walked away into the mist.

Shaw swished the droplets of fog off the windscreen. Peering into the mist he thought he saw the front passenger and driver's windows slide down. Through the half-open door Shaw felt what Roundhay, perhaps, had felt too – a light breeze, promising a return of the sun. 'Chris?'

'The truth – finally,' said Roundhay. 'I saw that woman – Osbourne – walking along the beach. And White followed her. But that was it. We made up, Marc and I – lay in the sun.' A two-second pause. 'We were happy, and that's the truth.'

The line went dead. Shaw's hand was poised over the horn, then he recognized a sound, a handbrake being released. He was out of the Porsche before the Nissan began to move. It inched forward at first, the headlamps appearing to widen like the eyes of a frightened cat. Roundhay let the car freefall, accelerating with the slope, quickly picking up speed, so that when Shaw got level the car had hit thirty-five mph, maybe forty mph.

Shaw ran, stumbling over the rutted field, trying to keep the rear lights of the Nissan in sight. He knew now why Roundhay had chosen high tide. The sea came up to the cliffs at high water, so there'd be nobody on the beach, or the rocks: no one *below*.

When the Nissan reached the edge the break lights didn't show and he'd hit fifty mph. There was a thud as the cliff edge caught the underside of the car, the front wheels dipping, so that the back flipped up in the air. Then three seconds of silence – stretched out, in which Shaw imagined the car turning in the grey misty air. There was no crash, just the thud of the roof hitting the water, a boom. When Shaw got to the edge it was still afloat, the tyres still turning, upside down, the water flooding in through the open windows. Then it sank, the lights still shining for a moment in the green dark water, before shorting out.

THIRTY-EIGHT

Shaw stood on the edge of the pine woods looking down on The Circle. Here, inland, there was no hint of the mist that had shrouded the coast. Lights shone from most of the houses, but the only noise came from the ruins of the Warrener's Lodge where the team was coordinating the hunt for Tug Coyle. Chris Roundhay's death and confession, which Shaw had no reason to disbelieve, and the DNA test on Joe Osbourne had removed two suspects from their list, which left Tug Coyle, and only Tug Coyle. Shaw's team was on site to coordinate the hunt. The UK Border Agency was now actively checking airport departures, and the Channel Tunnel. Interpol had been asked to alert Continental ports in France, Belgium, Germany and Denmark.

Shaw had left them all working and walked away to think, to

look down on the scene of Marianne Osbourne's death, the place
where for him this had all begun. In the sunflower field the
blooms were shut, waiting for dawn. In the half-light he saw
movement in the Osbournes' garden, the back gate opening, a
flash of white picket, then Valentine's gaunt figure, climbing the
hill as if it was the Via Dolorosa. The DS waved a brown envelope at Shaw when he finally got to the top of the slope. Pretending
to survey the view, he let his heartbeat recover, his eyes resting
on the floodlights spilling from the medieval, glassless, windows
of the Warrener's Lodge.

'Something,' he said, pulling a single sheet of A4 from the
envelope. 'I got Paul to trawl round the hospitals to see if there
were any admissions on the day of the East Hills murder which
looked like a knife wound, or any kind of violent wound. Not
all the records survive – nothing from Hunstanton, they all got
dumped when they closed the unit in 2000. What there was, we
checked, and got a blank. I said we'd call it a day. Luckily Paul's
got more patience. He ran a check on the *next* day too.'

He snapped his fingers, making the sheet of A4 crackle. Shaw
noted that Valentine had declined a clear opportunity to take the
credit for whatever breakthrough had occurred and instead had
cited DC Twine. It was a typically generous reference and gave
Shaw an insight into Valentine's popularity with his CID
colleagues. 'This is a one-page form detailing treatment given at
the Queen Vic's A&E on the day after East Hills,' said Valentine.
'At five that Sunday evening. The patient's name is Ruth Jennifer
Pritchard – aka Ruth Robinson, Marianne's sister. She arrived
with a heavily bandaged wound to her left hand, carefully
described in the notes as 'knife-like' – across the palm, cutting
down to the bone with a sharp, clean edge. She was seen by a
doctor then stitched up by a nurse, sent home with a reference
on to her GP. The doctor who examined her was called Sylhet.
'I'll read you the doctor's note,' added Valentine, squinting at
the squiggle. 'Patient insists – that's in italics, *insists* – that the
wound is result of accident. No other obvious injuries. Not
distressed. Cheerful, matter-of-fact. Student at home for summer
with family. Low risk. Self-harm?? That's with two question
marks.'

Shaw pinched the bridge of his nose. This case had a strange
quality. The way forward seemed to be continuously cloaked.

They had been unable since the mass screening results to adequately explain how their missing *male* killer had left East Hills. Now they had a *female* suspect who might have been on the island that day. And how did any of that fit in with the runaway Tug Coyle? The inquiry had not been assisted by the fact that virtually none of their key witnesses seemed to understand the concept of the absolute truth.

Shaw's patience snapped: a nanosecond of electricity which allowed him to make a decision without thought. 'Let's talk to her – now. I don't care if it's a bad time.' He set off downhill, Valentine in his wake.

They found the Robinsons still in their back garden at a picnic table. They'd lit half a dozen tea lights. Despite the two extended benches attached to the table they sat together, looking up at the woods. The chickens clucked amiably on the far side of the wire. As Aidan recognized the detectives his arm encircled his wife's wide shoulders. Shaw felt again an almost tangible darkness in their relationship, as if they pooled their stillness in something less inert, something denser – not two people at all, just one couple.

'I'm sorry,' said Shaw. 'I know this is a bad time. It's late. How's Joe?'

'Tilly's up there now. They think he's developed pneumonia. He's very ill – we'll go later.'

Their eyes met then looked away, but they didn't break their embrace.

'It was the questions – the stress,' said Aidan. 'You comfortable with that?'

'I'm sorry, I'd like to talk to Ruth alone,' said Shaw, ignoring the question.

Ruth soothed Aidan's arm, brushing the dark hair downwards towards the hand.

'That's not going to happen,' said Aidan, and Shaw saw, even in the half-light, the blood colouring his cheeks. Shaw thought about calling his bluff – he had enough to get Ruth down to St James', into a cell. But for now they'd play it his way. He took a seat, blocking their view of the woods. 'You should know that the mass screening of the East Hills suspects – the men – produced no results. No match at all.'

They both watched him.

'We've had to conclude, reluctantly, that the killer somehow left the island,' said Shaw. 'He probably swam ashore. Or tried to. Our question is, why did he leave the island in the first place?'

From the incident room at the Warrener's Lodge they heard laughter, quickly stilled. Shaw could feel the tension in the air; the question seemed to have baffled the Robinsons. Aidan worked one of his massive hands into the suntanned muscles of his neck. 'Because he didn't want to get caught?' He tried a laugh and Ruth smiled, but he knew he'd hit the wrong note because he rushed to fill the silence that followed: 'Why wouldn't he swim for it? Makes sense. Surprised you didn't think of it back then.'

'Well, for the record,' said Shaw, 'we – the police, that is – didn't think of it in 1994 because seventy-five people went out to East Hills and seventy-four came back, plus Shane White's corpse. So if the killer swam for it, how did he get on the island? You see, it's trickier than it looks.'

Aidan licked his lips and Shaw thought his head – big-boned and broad – looked precarious despite the thick, muscled neck.

'We think he swam because he fought with White, perhaps for the knife, and in the process he picked up an injury – something which showed, something which would have prompted questions – questions he didn't want to answer. So a wound – on the face, perhaps, or the hand.' Shaw held his hand out and Valentine gave him the A4 medical form. 'You – Ruth,' he said, locking eyes. 'You went up to A&E the day after East Hills to have a wound on your hand stitched. A knife wound.'

He'd tried to catch her off guard and succeeded, because she was still gaping at him as he leant over the table and flipped over her left hand – across the palm was a thin white line of scar tissue.

'She's always had that,' said Aidan quickly, squaring his shoulders.

'No she hasn't,' said Shaw. 'She's had it since the day she was seen by . . .' He reread the A4 sheet. 'Dr Sylhet. His notes make it pretty clear that in his judgement the wound was caused by a knife. Whose knife, Ruth?'

'Look – what is this?' asked Aidan.

'Well, Ruth? It's a good question. *What is this?*' asked Shaw. Neither of the Robinsons seemed ready to speak. 'Shall I tell you what this is?'

Ruth raised a hand to stop him. 'No. I'll tell you. I went swimming that afternoon, the Sunday. We always did – the family. Dad and Mum, Marianne and I. But she was in shock over what happened the day before at East Hills, so she stayed with them on the beach and I went in alone, at Brancaster. There's a wreck out by the point. There was a swell, a rip tide that I didn't judge right. I just wanted to rest, climb out of the water, and I put out a hand and it just got ripped by the metal. It was Dad said I had to go get it stitched – I wasn't bothered. The salt cleaned it up.'

Shaw still held her fingertips. 'The scar's straight. Dead straight. Dead clean.'

She wouldn't meet his eyes. 'I was lucky,' she said, drawing her hand back.

'Yeah, yeah, course. I remember,' said Aidan. 'After East Hills, I had to drive you up to the Lido for work after you got it stitched.'

'Now I'll tell you what actually happened,' said Shaw, ignoring Aidan. 'I think you, Ruth, went out that day on the boat with Marianne to East Hills. You were friends with Tug because he was Aidan's cousin, so it's my guess you never had to pay for a ticket. Unlike Marianne. She'd come to you for help, hadn't she, because she was being blackmailed by Shane White. She always came to you for help and it was your job – your role, really – to be there for her. You followed Marianne into the dunes and confronted White. Threatened him – but you weren't alone. You needed support. Aidan couldn't help – not with his leg injury. So you asked Tug, asked him to be there, to add muscle – a hint of real threat.

'So he anchored the boat and swam ashore. But it went wrong and Shane ended up dead. Who killed him? My guess is Tug. But I think you both tried. Then he swam back, but your problem was the wound you'd picked up in the fight. Then you realized there wasn't a ticket, so you *could* disappear. The boat was full of trippers – no one had recognized you. So you swam back. And Tug kept the secret. With Marianne.'

'What does Tug say?' asked Aidan, a smile disfiguring the thin lips.

Night had fallen and a bat fluttered over them like a dying neon light, attracted by the candles.

'Tug's missing – has been for forty-eight hours, as you may know, Mr Robinson. After all, he is family.'

Shaw held on to that thought: *family*. 'You and Tug shared a grandfather, of course. Who lived here for the last years of his life. Where's his stuff? Any wartime memorabilia?'

Aidan squared his jaw. 'What's he got to do with this?'

Shaw looked back at the house. 'Big attic? We'll start there, shall we?' Perhaps, thought Shaw, Coyle hadn't found the dugout in the woods to get his supply of cyanide pills. Perhaps Aidan helped him. Shaw thought that might be Aidan Robinson's role in all this – the key accomplice.

'Just routine,' added Shaw, knowing just how menacing that phrase could be to the guilty.

'Meanwhile we'll be tracking down Tug Coyle. We'll find him. Then we'll match his DNA to Sample X – and that, for you two, is when the fun begins. That's when you both find the answer to the really important question: which is thicker – blood or water?'

THIRTY-NINE

Thursday

A helicopter whoop-whooped over the woods above Creake, the pilot briefly holding his position, so that the aircraft hung against the blue sky like a hawk. Beneath it trailed the thermal-imaging camera, like a miniature torpedo. Shaw could see it through the branches of the cedar tree which grew from the ruins of the Warrener's Lodge. The outdoor incident room was busy, all the phone lines in use as the search for Tug Coyle was stepped up. They'd got one bit of news: Interpol had some sightings from two Belgium ports – a single mariner, a small yacht. They'd asked the local police to check it out. Excitement was like lightning in the air, waiting to crackle. With the chief constable's press conference timed for four that afternoon they all knew that with one more push, and one more stroke of luck, they could get their man. Shaw was even more convinced in the brash sunlight of day that

that man was Tug Coyle, with Ruth Robinson a willing accomplice.

But even if they caught Coyle that didn't mean they had a case. They needed the evidence to make sure the murder charges stuck in court. A decent defence lawyer would attack the DNA evidence, try and insinuate that the police had contaminated the sample, either by accident or design. A guilty verdict required a direct forensic link between the killer and the cyanide pills. The search of the Robinsons' attic had drawn a blank. Their best chance still lay out in the woods. Or, more accurately, *beneath* the woods.

A uniformed constable appeared at the door of the ruin. 'Sir. DC Twine would like a word – he's up on the edge of the field, beyond the sunflowers. He said it was urgent.'

As they climbed the slope the helicopter swung overhead, a single Day-Glo arm signalling from the open door. Twine was kneeling on the grass, unpacking a ground-floor plan of what looked like an ambitious garden shed. A single room, an ante-chamber; but then Shaw saw the narrow almost vertical staircase entrance, and a long tunnel leading away.

'We got this from the MoD, it's a generic plan of the style of one of the hundreds of these dugouts built along the South coast in 1939, but they said it would be close to anything put in by sappers here.' Twine, usually a picture of controlled efficiency, was struggling to keep excitement out of his voice.

'This is what we're looking for underground,' he said, switching his eyes to Valentine's face, then back to Shaw. 'It's effectively a miniature Nissan hut. So heavy-duty corrugated steel, a curved roof, sunk under the earth. Entry's through this hatch, which is double-locked in iron, then down about fifteen feet in a series of high steps which are concrete. The emergency exit tunnel is also held in place beneath a curved roof. Steel again.'

'And they've found it?' asked Shaw.

'Maybe.' Twine had a plastic see-through overlay with the outline of the dugout superimposed in white: box-like, with the escape tunnel as a kind of tail. 'This is exactly to scale,' he said, putting it to one side.

Then he spilt out a set of aerial pictures. 'They took these on the first run after dawn. This is what we're interested in,' he said, stabbing one of the images with his Mont Blanc, edging the

see-through outline into place on top of it with his other hand.
Nestling beneath the tree canopies there *was* something where
Twine was pointing – a blurred yellow, just shading to orange.
The shape had no hard edges, no real architectural form, but it
did have a single trailing tail. The match with the overlay was
close – not perfect, but close.

'I've just sent a team up with a map,' said Twine. 'And I've
asked for dogs.'

On cue they heard barking from down on The Circle and the
squad appeared, three handlers, three dogs, cutting straight across
the open meadow, through the sunflowers and into the woods, the
Alsatians straining ahead. They set off in pursuit, catching the dogs
up when they reached the open space with the lightning tree.
Unleashed, the dogs plunged on, heading downhill towards the
stone folly set above the Old Hall estate. The trees began to thin
out – no longer pine, but the original oak and birch. Ahead they
could hear barking and somewhere unseen the insistent buzz of
police radios. Finally they entered a clearing – gorse and bramble
cut back so that the dogs could sniff the earth. Three uniformed
officers in fluorescent bibs were already digging. One offered Shaw
an Ordnance Survey map on which Twine had marked the spot
with a red cross. Shaw noted that it was less than 300 yards from
the glade where they'd found Holtby's burnt corpse.

'Looks like it's been years,' said Valentine, craning his neck
to see into the hole they'd dug. The earth was compacted, hard,
with a yellow-clay layer, undisturbed. The air of palpable excitement was dissolving fast. This didn't look like their killer's lair.
It looked like an archaeological dig. The dogs, ears down, circled
aimlessly.

'The trapdoor entrance should be just below the surface, but
they're down two feet already,' said Twine. He looked at Shaw,
avoiding the moon-eye. 'Could be it was just filled in after the
war . . .'

Shaw walked off into the trees, checking his mobile, trying
to hide his disappointment behind pointless action. The UK
Border Agency had sent him a text confirming that the Irish
Garda had added Tug Coyle to the list of individuals who should
be stopped at airports and ports. He rang the chief constable's
secretary and left a message for O'Hare. He'd email a brief for
the presser as arranged but they were making rapid progress in

the inquiry. He planned to use the press conference to help launch a nationwide public appeal for information in their efforts to track down a prime suspect. The secretary asked him to wait and relayed the message into a meeting. She had a message for Shaw when she got back: the chief constable would take the press conference.

Texting DC Campbell in the incident room he asked her to put together a rough press release on the hunt for Tug Coyle and arrange for a decent picture of him from the RNLI records to be sent to St James' for the attention of the press office. Then he rang the force's chief press officer, an ex-Fleet Street tabloid crime correspondent who'd come to Lynn to prepare for retirement, and filled her in on developments.

Then a single, jarring sound made Shaw's heart skip a beat – the clash of metal on metal. He ran back to the dig. The trapdoor they'd uncovered was iron, badly corroded, set in a flaking concrete frame.

'These doors were all counter-weighted,' said Twine. 'There'd be a wire along the ground to a tree, or a wood pile, or something they could find easily – then just a handle, camouflaged. Idea was if they were being followed they couldn't afford to be discovered struggling with the trapdoor – it had to be up, down, and no sign, in seconds.'

They looked at the rusted trapdoor in the pit. 'That was seventy years ago,' said Valentine. They put a pickaxe through the eggshell thin iron and the door lifted, the hinges turning to dust. The hole beneath was deep, apparently featureless, a concrete coffin on its end. Shaw caught the scent of the trapped air escaping. It smelt like history – decades of damp and dark. The brief flare of hope, already fading, guttered out.

'OK,' said Shaw, taking a torch from Twine. 'Follow me down, Paul. We might as well check this out.'

'I was going to call St James' – get an engineer out, check it's safe?' offered Twine.

'Right,' said Shaw. That was sensible. But despite the clear evidence the dugout had been unused for more than half a century Shaw felt impatient. Why wait? They needed to get this over and put all their resources into finding Coyle.

'It probably collapsed long ago,' said Shaw. 'I'll check it out; you stay here.'

With a hand on either side Shaw lowered his six-foot frame into the hole then, as his toes sought the floor he let himself drop, his blood freezing for just one heartbeat while he was in mid-air. The impact of his fall raised dust. The downward stairwell led out of the vertical shaft and was narrow, so he turned side on, and edged towards the first step. He approached each following a routine he'd developed shortly after losing the sight in his left eye. Without 3D vision steps could be lethal, especially as often the banister post in domestic stairs was not on the bottom step, but the penultimate step. So he put his foot on each edge and let the toes rock over it, before stepping down to the next.

He heard Twine drop in the well behind him. The dust flowed down the steps, heavier than air, settling round Shaw's boots where he could see some amber earwigs manically trying to find cover. The smell was extraordinary, a kind of visceral rot, a fundamental decay. Lifeless but for the scurrying insects. Eight spiral steps down brought Shaw to an iron door, locked with a padlock and chain, corroded so badly they'd become one piece of metal.

Shaw asked for lock-cutters and the request went back up the line. The lock-cutters came back within thirty seconds with Twine. Shaw felt the sweat the DC had left on the cold metal. He clamped the mechanical jaws on either side of the U on the padlock. When the steel gave the door fell away from him, the old hinges shattering, so that he found himself just staring into the black outline of the entrance, peering into a profound darkness.

And then he knew. Because there was nothing stale about the air which brushed his face. His heightened sense of smell unpacked the traces threaded together: paraffin, certainly; then stale bread and, most pungent of all, ground coffee.

Until now the light from above had been enough, filtering down the stairwell. But here they were beyond the final turn in the staircase so that only the faintest trace of illumination spilt beyond the threshold. Shaw flicked on the torch, covering his eyes for a second against the glare. The beam was narrow and clogged with the dust billowing into the room.

As the air cleared he noticed three things: the floor was concrete but freshly swept; one of the iron bunks set against one corrugated wall had a pillow; and on the single narrow metal seat against the far wall sat Tug Coyle, tied into the chair by a rope across his chest, his head tipped back to reveal the fleshy throat. Shaw knew he was dead because of the ugly angle at which one of his feet touched the floor, turned violently on to its outer edge, sole inwards, the other straight out, extended to the extreme limit, so that he could see the pale lifeless skin of the leg. The percussion of the falling door still echoed in the small space and Coyle's head fell forward, his teeth clashing. as if biting at the air.

FORTY

The dogs found the other – emergency – exit to the dugout before Shaw had time to trace the long, tail-like tunnel to meet them. About thirty yards long, it was reinforced, like the main shelter itself, with a double layer of corrugated iron. The final door was vertical, not a trapdoor, but let into the side of a small clay cliff, obscured by brambles and hawthorn, the lock well-oiled and new.

Justina Kazimierz, the pathologist, appeared out of the woods in a white, ghostly, SOC suit, clutching the black forensic bag. She led the way back in, pausing only for a second on the threshold, followed by Shaw and Valentine. In the end chamber Tug Coyle still sat roped into the seat in which he'd died.

Shaw, standing back as she began her initial examination of the victim, thought how bizarre it was that an inquiry that had begun with a distant view of a field of sunflowers should lead here, to a lightless subterranean tomb, a lifeless vault.

'So much for our prime suspect,' said Valentine, putting an unlit Silk Cut between his teeth. He'd already sent a PC back to the incident room with orders for Twine to wind up the nation-wide search for Tug Coyle.

Tom Hadden had lit the room with two halogen lamps, their beams turned to the metal walls. The effect of the illumination was to make the space smaller, and the thought of six men living here, beneath the earth, for up to two weeks, while the invading German army moved inland, made Shaw's skin creep. Hadden worked in one corner, bent over a set of ammunition boxes. He straightened, a hand at his back, a face mask pulled up and set on his forehead where the once-ginger hair had thinned. 'I think this stuff's alright,' he said, one hand on a box. 'But I've asked someone from Sheringham to come up. Clearly, until then, there's a danger. But I reckon it's minimal. In the meantime, softly softly,' he added, lifting the wooden lid on one of the boxes: 'Bullets – .38s. One of the others is grenades, pretty much rusted into the box. And this . . .' He lifted out a kind of metal tripod. 'Stand for a Thompson sub-machine gun. State of the art – if Winston Churchill's prime minister.'

He'd set other items on the iron mesh of the top bunk – the one without a mattress or blanket, just the single pillow. Shaw recognized a Primus stove, a Tilley Lamp, a pair of entrenching tools.

Hadden tapped a metal box on the floor with the cap of his boot. 'Chemical toilet,' he said. 'Not been used – not for fifty years anyway. But these are more interesting . . .'

In one corner, set on end, were two large animal traps.

'I'll get these back to the lab,' said Hadden, touching the metal rim of one of the traps. 'They're a match to the one that brought down Holtby, but we should be able to get closer than that. I reckon they're identical. And they're post-war. No more than ten years old. Less.'

'Shaw.' Dr Kazimierz's voice was slightly furred, indistinct, and when they all turned they could see why. She was behind the dead man, kneeling, cutting away the shoe on the hidden, left, foot.

Shaw squatted down. The pathologist applied a swab to the heel of the foot and showed him the blood.

'He's been dragged in, on his back, heels kicking.' Standing, she came round to the front of the chair and set her head, motionless, about six inches from Coyle's face. She sniffed theatrically. Shaw got in close too.

'Almonds again?' he asked.

She took the dead man's head and gently lifted it from its position of rest. 'Rigor's gone,' she said. 'So he's been dead twelve hours, maybe a little less.' Taking his chin in one hand and clasping his upper jaw with the other, she went to open the mouth. Valentine looked quickly away but heard the plastic click of the joint.

Coyle's teeth were milk-like and even. Wedged between two at the back on the right was the wreckage of a terracotta pill.

'Our fourth victim,' said Shaw, rocking back on his heels. He thought through each one, in the order in which they'd been found: Marianne Osbourne in her deathbed, Arthur Patch, dying in a half-second flash of exploding gas; Jeff Holtby, clawing at the broken bones in his leg, amongst the shadows of the wood. And now 'Tug' Coyle, the East Hills' boatman.

'But why?' he asked Valentine. 'Why did he have to die, and why hide his body here?'

Valentine was in no position for logical reasoning. He didn't like death, not up close like this, and he didn't like enclosed spaces, so he wasn't having a great day. Plus they'd just lost their prime suspect less than five hours before a press conference in which they'd planned to announce his name, starting a national media frenzy which might have just saved their careers. More importantly, *his* career. Now all they were left with was Ruth Robinson's mysterious knife wound – hardly the foundations of a successful multiple murder inquiry – and Sample X, which might be many things but certainly didn't belong to a woman.

Hadden set up a tripod camera to record the documents still pinned to a wooden board by the bunk beds. 'You can have these after I've got a picture,' he said. 'They're original – they may not survive being taken down.'

The halogen light was turned to illuminate them. There was a single A4 sheet with a railway timetable on it. The line terminus was listed as Hunstanton which dated it as pre-1962 and Beeching's Axe. There were also two large-scale plans – one of the dugout, showing exact dimensions, and the relative position of the gun emplacement on the edge of the wood. The other showed a smaller facility, a single room, with one entry/exit. It was shown relative to an inked-in octagonal structure.

'That's a pillbox,' said Shaw, getting closer. 'That eight-sided shape . . .'

'There's one about 200 yards further down the hill, on the edge of the trees,' said Hadden.

'But what's this?' added Shaw, putting his finger on the one-roomed structure.

'Paul's briefing mentioned something . . .' said Hadden.

Valentine chipped in: 'Yeah. Sometimes there'd be a second dugout nearby, like a safety option. Makes sense. Main unit would come in here. But one person would go to this smaller one – like a lookout. They were usually on the edge of open ground. So it was that person's job to judge when the unit should emerge. The beauty of it was, if they got seen or captured, they'd lead the Germans back to this smaller one, not the main base. I'll get a search under way.'

Shaw was going to leave then, because the metal walls were pressing in, making him feel giddy. But he took one more look round the room, trying to imprint the scene on his memory, noting that one touch of comfort – the single pillow. He slipped on a forensic glove and lifted the pillow's edge. There was a snapshot underneath, face down.

'Tom,' he said.

Hadden broke off his work with the tripod and came over, using a metal pair of callipers to flip the picture over. It was Tilly Osbourne, a recent snap, taken in her garden, the bungalow behind. She was at the heart of this, thought Shaw, and therein lay the real mystery, because on that summer's afternoon in 1994 when Shane White had died on East Hills she hadn't even been born. He thought how often a trauma within a family – Marianne's experience that day on East Hills – seemed to echo in the next generation. What was Tilly's secret? Did she even know she had one?

'Bag it,' he said.

Once outside Shaw walked away from the spot, downhill, the trees thinning slightly, so that some sunshine cut down, like searchlights. He felt his limbs were heavy, each leg a weight to lift, and he was depressed by the knowledge that the killer had taken another victim. He felt a sense of imminent failure; knowing, at some subconscious level, that the answer to the mystery of the East Hills killer was before them now but they were too close to see it. 'Wood for the trees,' he said.

Behind him he heard a twig snap and Valentine joined him. They were in an open glade with a view down into the valley, the sea glimpsed between the hills, still scarfed in mist, the church tower at Morston just showing like a rock.

Valentine was on his mobile, trying to get through to the incident room. 'What we going to say at the presser? We won't have an official ID on Coyle before then – we could play dumb, stick with him as prime suspect. What you reckon?'

Shaw didn't answer. He was perfectly still, looking seawards. The fog was drifting, buckling, as it slipped past the single medieval tower of the distant church, like a slow motion replay of a wave crashing against a lighthouse.

'Peter?' asked Valentine, sensing the moment.

It was the mist on the coast that brought back the memory. Shaw would have been six – maybe seven. The last day of the summer holidays and his school uniform laid out on his bed. His father had come home early from St James' and announced they were off to the beach. Shaw had felt contempt then for his father, who'd worked throughout the summer and had chosen this day for the beach – a fret, thick and cold, lay along the north Norfolk coast and had done for two days, bringing with it the smells of winter: damp pine needles under the trees and the salty tang of cooler water. But his father had just smiled, bundling beach things into a hamper, then dragging them all down to Wells quay in the car. The ferry out to East Hills had been cancelled that day. But there was a boat waiting for them, the engine running. Shaw had recognized the man at the tiller as one of his father's shadowy band of 'contacts' – most of them criminals who swapped snippets of information for being left alone. This one was called Joyce, he remembered, and only had teeth on the left side of his mouth – and then only in the top of his jaw. He slapped young Shaw on the shoulder, pressing the muscle, as if assessing a calf at market.

The boat was called *Myriam*; Shaw remembered that detail too. Sitting in the damp boat, watching the cool grey water slip past, a little of his father's obvious excitement had been contagious. Shaw had stared into the mist, wondering what would happen next. As they slipped past the lifeboat station the foghorn had sounded, making his mother jump, so perhaps she too had sensed that this was special. A day they'd recall a lifetime later.

Fifty yards further on and the world changed: they were free, wonderfully released from the grey gloom of the fret, and instead swamped by sunshine. The fret was only a hundred yards wide, beyond the beach the sun shone unfettered. The seascape seemed bathed in all the extra light the landscape had lost. Shaw remembered the sensational switch of colours, from sepia to blue and green, and then, half a mile ahead of them, the mustard-yellow sands of East Hills topped with its ridge of pine trees. And not a single human being in sight.

It had been his first trip to the island of East Hills. He'd been allowed to explore after they'd eaten a picnic. And running along the island's single path, which clung to the ridge, he'd got to the northern point and made his great discovery. Nestling amongst the stone pines, almost lost in the encroaching sands, had stood the pillbox. Looking inside he'd let his eyes adapt to the dark so that he could see the remains of an old fire, a few bottles and some litter. He'd looked out through the gun slit to sea and felt the beginnings of a thousand daydreams, in which this secret place would provide the stage and the backdrop. But what he'd never imagined was that the place may have had a past of its own. That close to the pillbox the *Stay Behind Army* might have dug one of its secret dugouts. That it might still be there. And that it might be the answer to everything.

FORTY-ONE

nside the sea fog the light levels were astonishingly low, as if dusk had fallen and night was gathering. And the temperature was cool, autumnal, with even a hint of ice. Valentine sat in the RNLI inshore boat with his back to the prow, watching the shadowy outline of the quayside at Wells recede behind Shaw's shoulders. The DI had declined to explain the rationale behind their being in a boat heading for East Hills, and Valentine's pride prevented him asking the same question twice. The *Arandora Star*, the East Hills ferry, lay moored, all trips cancelled for the day. Beside them sat Ruth Robinson. She hadn't said a word since they'd left The Circle. They'd found her alone, two coffee cups untouched on the table, her hand held in a fist. When Shaw had asked she'd unflexed the fingers and they'd seen what she held: a single cyanide pill.

'He said I should take it,' she'd said, sitting at the table, her voice dull with shock. 'That it was for the best because he wouldn't be coming back. He said you'd never find his body. Why was that important?' She'd looked at Shaw, appearing to search his face for the answer. 'He said that he'd done it all for me. *All?* I don't dare think what he meant.' She'd covered her mouth with both hands. 'I won't dare.' She'd shaken her head, struggling to understand. 'We said goodbye,' she'd added, pushing the pill away. 'I couldn't take it.' Shaw had noticed the patina of tiny cracks in the seventy-year-old rubber casing of the pill. 'I said I'd be here for Tilly, now Marianne's gone, and I will be. I told Aidan that and it seemed to suck the life out of him. I've never seen him so . . .' She'd searched for the word, her eyes filling with water. '*Crushed.*' She'd brushed the tears from her eyes roughly with the back of her hand. 'I can't understand what's happened to us; what's happening to me.'

Since then, silence. But she hadn't complained, following them to the Porsche and then sitting quietly as Shaw drove down to Wells. No questions, which told Shaw he was right. Using the hands-free he arranged for the RNLI's inshore boat to be at the quay. And he'd summoned back-up – the police launch from Lynn, but they'd be an hour. The coastal forecast he'd picked up from Petersen on duty watch at the lifeboat house. The fret was thickening and ran out for nearly a mile, nearly to East Hills, but not quite.

When he said the words 'East Hills' on the mobile he looked in the rear-view mirror and watched her close her eyes. At the lifeboathouse they said that 'Tug' Coyle's boat had gone from its buoy in the channel. Petersen had heard an engine chugging past about two hours ago, just seen, off the point. 'A small fishing boat, but not Coyle at the helm,' he said.

'We know,' said Shaw, seeing again the body strapped to its chair, the heels bloody. Shaw looked ahead into the mist. On the port side he could see the first of the buoys leading out of the harbour: green, the size of a small car, rusted. He steered the boat a few degrees to starboard and let the engine pick up a few revs. A pain cut across his blind eye but it bled away as soon as he closed it, and he was relieved to feel that his heartbeat remained stable.

The second green buoy came into sight just as he lost contact with the grey outline of the pinewoods on shore. Now there was nothing but the buoy itself in the circular, colourless world which surrounded the boat. He cut the engine and started using the single paddle, switching from port to starboard expertly, guiding the boat ahead. The only chance he had, thought Shaw, was to approach the island silently. Visibility was about thirty yards but it seemed to lessen unpredictably, the mist suddenly closing around them. It was like a pulse – the mist thickening, then thinning, as if the fret was breathing.

The foghorn boomed.

Valentine had rooted out a flask in her kitchen before they left and made tea – dark, steeped with tannin. He poured some into the cap and offered it to her. When she took it her hand was steady, but she didn't raise it to her lips, she just cradled it for warmth.

The foghorn boomed again and this time it seemed to release something within her, as if a lock had been picked. She looked about her for the first time and saw nothing but the circular grey horizon. 'He never did tell me everything,' she said, her voice a whisper, as if she were holding a conversation in her own head. 'But I trusted him.' She hauled in some air. 'The night of the East Hills killing, the day of the *murder*,' she added, as if it was an accusation, 'I couldn't find Aidan. He wasn't up at the house, at The Circle. His Mum said Tug Coyle had phoned from a call box, and they were going out night fishing, and that Aidan was in town getting bait. That she wasn't to worry. I was hurt. They did go fishing, the two of them, but I was only back for the summer and it was Saturday night, so it felt like he didn't care. It was Mum who told me about East Hills because it was on the radio. She'd had a call from Lynn to say Marianne would be dropped home after she'd given a statement; they were all giving statements, so there was nothing to worry about. So we waited. She was in bits, really, hysterical, when the police dropped her at our house. Dad gave her a drink and I got her to bed. It was late – after eleven – and there was another call. It was Tug again – he didn't say where he was, just that I was to meet Aidan the next evening at dusk on Holkham Beach. There was no need to worry or mention the call to anyone else, Tug said, but I should bring the first aid kit from the Lido.'

She'd been staring into the mist but now she glanced back to Shaw. 'I did a course when I got the job – the summer before Durham. So Aidan knew I could do stitches.'

Ahead Shaw caught sight of the pines on East Hills, then lost them again in the fold of the mist.

'Tug brought him ashore – they were in his fishing boat, not the ferry. Aidan looked dreadful – dirty, like he hadn't slept. And pale – almost bloodless. We went into the woods and he took

his shirt off and there was this knife wound – a few inches, clean
but deep, and there'd been lots of blood. I said I wouldn't do
anything unless he told me what had happened. He said he
couldn't tell me.'

Valentine lit a match and the sound made her jump. Shaw
noticed that the flame burnt upright, unmoved by the slightest
wind. If he examined the silence he could just hear the whisper
of the sea falling on unseen sands.

'I put in the butterfly stitches, cleaned him up. Then I asked
again. Told him I had a right to know. That did it – he just
snapped. I didn't expect it to happen – I thought I knew him so
well. Looking back it was the pressure, the fear. But at the time
it was so frightening. He had a knife in his belt – a knife I didn't
recognize – and he drew it and cut the air between us, back and
forth, twice. His eyes . . .' She had a look of horror on her face,
as if she could see him there.

'It was supposed to be a warning. But when I looked down
my hand was half red below a razor-sharp wound, the blood
dripping into the pine needles.' She looked at her hands. 'And
when he looked down there was a spray of blood on his legs and
feet.' She peered into the mist: 'I couldn't stitch the wound with
one hand. So he drove me to A&E.' She dipped her hand in the
sea, then lifted it out, letting droplets fall into the perfectly calm,
oily, water. 'Years later, he'd often take my hand and say sorry
again. He said he was sorry that day too. When I came out of
A&E he was there in the car. That was when he told me why
he'd gone out to East Hills. The lifeguard, White, had taken
pictures of Marianne with men and he was after money. Marianne
had come to Aidan for a loan – £50.' She laughed at the amount.
'Of course, that would have just been the start of it. He'd have
been back. Aidan gave her the money. He said he didn't want to
worry me about it, which I understood.' She nodded to herself.
'But I was hurt Marianne hadn't come to me first. She was going
to give White the cash that Saturday out on East Hills. Aidan's
always been very protective of Marianne, like a big brother. He
wasn't worried about the money but he thought White would
want something else in payment – sex. So Aidan went out on
the boat that day to have it out with him, to try and end it.

'When Marianne walked off into the dunes he followed. White
was waiting for her, but when Aidan arrived he was angry that

she wasn't alone. Aidan told White it was over – that he wanted
the negatives and then he didn't want to hear from him again.
White just laughed in his face, pulled the knife.

'Aidan didn't plan to hurt him, let alone kill him. That's what
he always said and I believe him. There's a cold streak in Aidan
– I know that. Something died inside him when he had that
accident. He lost a life then – a life he'd imagined was his to
live. But he's not a calculating man. Never that.

'He said there was a lot of blood – that they'd both been
wounded. The only thing he really remembered was the slipperi-
ness of that boy's skin, covered in blood. It had never bothered
him until then, the sight of blood. But after that it was like a
phobia. That's why he always wrung the chickens by the neck.'

She looked over the grey water where a seal had broken the
surface and was poised, scanning them.

They heard the dull percussion of a diesel turbine and the
silhouette of a trawler slid by, fifty yards off the port side. The
base note of vibration made a small bone buzz in Valentine's ear.
Another fishing boat went past, this time unseen, but the wake
reached them and rocked them, the noise of oily water slapping
unnaturally loud.

'It wasn't the truth, was it? Not all the truth?' she asked. 'Since
Marianne died he hasn't talked to me. Nothing. He won't touch
me.' She looked from Valentine to Shaw, her face suddenly wet
with tears. 'I can feel the lies. I can imagine what it is – that he
was in those pictures with Marianne. I'm not stupid. I heard the
rumours when I came back from Durham: that she'd gone after
what was mine. But I could live with it; I've always lived with
it. What really frightened me, what's frightening me now, is that
there's another lie worse than that lie. That there's something
else he didn't tell me.'

She cupped her face, an almost theatrical gesture, as if she'd
run out of ways to react to what was happening to her life. 'I
think he was there when Marianne died . . .' She covered her
mouth as if retrieving the words. 'So I can see that might be the
truth, but somehow even that doesn't seem *enough*.' She used
the back of her hand to wipe her face, first left then right, then
left again. 'What I don't understand is that he said he did it all
for me.'

FORTY-TWO

S haw had the sequence of the buoys leading out of Wells Harbour by rote. He'd been the pilot of the inshore RNLI hovercraft for nearly four years and he'd memorized most of the navigation along this stretch of the coast, from Lynn to Cromer. He knew that after the third green buoy on the port side he needed to look to starboard for the first red buoy, beyond which he should turn south-east to pick up the deep rip-tide channel which slipped past East Hills. So something had to be wrong because he was staring into the white mist, scanning a featureless seascape, when he saw two red buoys. Then three. Then none.

The blood drained to his heart so he blinked, trying to encourage the eye to water, his hands tightening on the paddle, which was poised in mid-air. He closed his eyes, the darkness full of strange cluster-bombs of blue light, then opened them to discover he had complete double-vision – everything in twos, one image slightly to the side of the other, slightly elevated. Nausea swept through him like a poison. The sharpness, the clarity, had gone, so that he was seeing a world with blurred edges, two worlds shadowing each other.

Valentine was looking at him. 'Peter?' he said. Ruth Robinson just looked into the mist, her head awkwardly forward, tensed to hear, to catch the first whisper of waves falling on the island beach.

'You navigate, I'll paddle,' said Shaw, his voice strained, his eyes closed. Reason told him that if he robbed his brain of the evidence his eye was failing then it would stop flooding his bloodstream with adrenaline. Sweat, beaded on his forehead, fell into his blind eye. He put the paddle down then held his hands together, the fingers braided. Valentine was shocked by the thought that he might have done that to stop them shaking.

'Peter?'

'I'm OK,' he said. 'Just do what I say.' He picked up the paddle and dipped the blade expertly into the water, the sound

as delicate as a trout taking the bait. He could do it blindfold,
so he kept his eyes closed, feeling the boat slip forward in
response to each stroke. 'Over your right shoulder there should
be a red buoy,' he said.

'Not a thing,' said Valentine.

'Right. We've drifted a bit. It's OK. Look around.' Shaw's
voice was light now, controlled, and it made him feel better to
hear it.

Valentine turned and the shift of weight rocked the boat.

Shaw kept his voice matter-of-fact. 'Just move your head.'

Valentine tried that but the vertebra in his neck cracked as he
swung his bony, axe-like, skull from left and right. 'There, I see
it,' he said. 'It's to our right – three o'clock.'

'Take us past it – leave it on our right. Then look out for
another, ahead, and do the same with that.'

Shaw felt the change approaching before his skin felt the sun.
The temperature rose, the damp, almost sulphurous smell of the
mist dissolved, but most of all the acoustic world came back in
sharp definition, as if the 'treble' had suddenly been switched
up on a gigantic sound system. A gull shrieked, the branches on
the stone pines whispered, and he opened his eyes to see East
Hills bathed in sunshine, the image pin-sharp.

Then his mobile beeped. It was a text from Twine. He didn't
want to strain the eye by reading it so he handed the phone to
Valentine. 'It's Joe Osbourne,' he said. 'He died an hour ago.
Tilly was there.'

FORTY-THREE

Shaw stood on the sand, looking along the deserted beach towards the far point of East Hills. The pain in his blind eye was still there but blunted, distant. His vision had stabilized but the images were oddly vivid, as if his good eye was suddenly connected to a high-voltage cable. And his other senses, hearing and smell, were jangling, picking up too much information: he seemed to be able to track each gliding gull, catch the scent of every scrap of seaweed, every gull-pecked crab. From the trees on the crest of East Hills he caught the sharp scent of pinesap and the creaking of a crow's wings as it clattered out of the high branches.

The sunlight seemed to flatten the island, driving away any shadows, while the mist lay behind them, obscuring the distant shore. Shaw knew that with the turn of the tide the mist would roll slowly out to sea, foot by foot, and would envelop them within the hour. Ruth Robinson sat in the boat, her hands seemingly too heavy to lift, her body rocked by the gentle nudging of the gunwale against the rubber buffers of the little pier.

'If he wants you, will you come?' Shaw asked her.

'You won't find him,' she said. 'I want to go back. Tilly needs me.'

It had been her first thought, on hearing of Joe Osbourne's death, that Tilly would be alone. But Shaw couldn't go back. 'When the launch gets here, go back with them. And George, follow me up.' He kept his voice low, and as flat as the sea. 'Head for the pillbox. Until then, let's keep it quiet.' From his pocket Shaw retrieved a copy of the plan they'd found in the dugout of the small underground shelter, set relative to a six-sided building. 'I think there's one of these dugouts up by the pillbox,' said Shaw. 'That's where he's gone.'

'You could leave him,' said Ruth Robinson. 'Let him do it. He's got a pill left. Would that be a crime?'

It was an odd use of the word and it made Shaw pause. 'Then we'd never know,' said Shaw, feeling a wave of sympathy for this woman, trapped between two futures, both desperately dark. To let her husband die and to die herself, one day, in ignorance of what he'd done, what he'd hidden from her. Or to let him live, give him the chance of life, and then live with the consequences of that – to know the truth, to know why all those people had to die. In a way it was she who was in hell, a hell of his making.

He walked up the beach towards the ridge, checking his path against the plan. The pillbox was north, near the point, the secret dugout just off the path, between twenty and twenty-five feet short of the concrete octagonal perimeter wall. Within a minute he was close, walking through the dappled shadows of the pines, until the brutal concrete structure came into view. He stopped, looked back and saw the mist was closer, on the island already, amongst the trees, the whiteness tinged purple like a garlic clove. The air was hot and dry. The wind the slightest of zephyrs, which he could only feel if he stood still, judging which side of his face was the coolest.

In the stillness Shaw walked the path by placing each heel down, then the toes. He checked his mobile – there were no signal bars but he killed it anyway, waiting for the screen to blank out. As he took each step he thought about what might be beneath – the single room, a storm lantern, perhaps, and Robinson. Alive still?

The pillbox was thirty feet away when he dropped to his knees, feeling the sand at the side of the path with his hands, spreading it in fan-like patterns to either side. Fifteen feet from the pillbox he stopped, about to stand, about to retreat to search again, when his left hand connected with gritty sand – gritty and *immovable*, like sandpaper. The sand covered a trapdoor, wooden with an iron trim, and at its centre he found an iron handle.

The mist arrived, seeping through the trees, the temperature dropping instantly, the sunlight gone. In these few seconds Aidan Robinson could end it all, biting down on the lethal capsule. Shaw felt a growing dread that he was, perhaps, already too late, a fear that he'd find Robinson's corpse, rigor creeping over him like the sea fret over East Hills.

He stood, feet together, astride the trapdoor, took the iron handle in both hands, bent his knees and leant back, letting the trapdoor balance his weight; then he pulled, flipping the heavy iron cover up on well-oiled hinges. The hole gaped, mist falling into it like dry ice. He dropped down, landed in sand, then turned quickly to face into a single room lit by a candle-stub, the light of which caught the ribs of corrugated iron in the roof. It was as if Shaw had been swallowed and was in the stomach of some metallic whale. The candle guttered with the impact of his fall.

Aidan Robinson sat in the only chair on the far side of a table, the edge of which pressed into his body. His arms hung by his side so that Shaw couldn't see his hands. His face was glistening with sweat, the whites of his eyes catching the light. Under stress time slows down, and so for a second, or less, Shaw thought Robinson was dead because there was something frozen about his shoulders and neck, as if he'd been nailed to the rigid back of the chair. Then the large, broad skull rocked left and right, the eyes moving in and out of the light, from silver to black and back again.

There were no other chairs, just a rusted bed. What he noticed immediately was the tremendous thud of the falling waves out on the sandbanks at sea, even on this calmest of days. In a storm the noise would be overwhelming, sublime – an operatic back-drop. Each percussion made Shaw's ears pop with the change in pressure.

Shaw could smell fear. Trapped fear. 'Aidan,' he said. The sand of the floor seemed to suck all the energy and edge from his voice, as if he was in an acoustic booth.

'That night. While they searched the island above.' Shaw manufactured a laugh. 'You were down here. Tug came for you next day in his boat. This had been your secret – the grandsons' secret, Tug Johns' secret. He was in the unit up at Creak, wasn't he? But being on the crew at the lifeboat he had a brilliant idea – why not a dugout here, too? The ultimate lookout, watching over the harbour.'

Shaw thought about sitting on the bed but there seemed to be a spell on the room, on Robinson, and he didn't want to break it. 'You didn't plan the murder did you? Either of you.'

Aidan Robinson shook his head, and for a moment Shaw thought he wouldn't speak at all and that was because he had the sixth capsule ready, lodged between his back teeth, perhaps, or in one of the unseen hands? Yes, in a hand, hidden.

'He pulled the knife,' said Robinson. His voice, low, monotonal, was flattened further in this box, sunk deep in the sand. There was

something in the way he spoke that suggested this man wasn't
contemplating death but that he had moved beyond it. The table
held a tin cup, turned upside down, and a knife: mock antler handle,
nine-inch blade, the metal oiled, but with traces and spots of dust,
and stained slightly, possibly by rust.

'The pictures were of you – you and Marianne,' said Shaw.
'Ruth's here now, down on the beach. She's guessed that. But
she knows there's more.' Shaw judged the knowing inflexion of
the sentence perfectly.

Robinson's muscles went into spasm, so that a fleeting expression of pure surprise seemed to cross that normally placid, fleshy,
face. But the eyes were still dead and Shaw had a sudden insight
into this man's life – the years of humiliating work in the battery
sheds of the poultry farm, the stench of the caged birds, the bloodless cull.

The foghorn sounded, making Shaw's eyes flicker towards the
pale square of light above the doorway through which the mist
was tumbling. Shaw told himself he didn't have long: that this
man was strong enough to break, and that he'd kill himself and
anyone who tried to stop him. 'Why did Marianne have to die?'
asked Shaw, finally, judging it the one question that might unlock
the motives behind Robinson's crimes.

Robinson's face seemed to freeze, as if his skin had tightened.
Shaw watched his tongue licking his lower lip. His shoulders
dipped forward. For the first time Shaw picked up a scent in the
room: subtle and exotic, so that the closest Shaw could get to
describing it was liquid iron.

The question seemed to be provoking a crisis in Robinson, so
Shaw moved on: 'I understand why the old man had to die.'

Robinson's eyes locked on his.

'Tug Coyle's son was the burglar who knocked down Arthur
Patch. You were close friends, cousins, so he'd have mentioned
the ID parade. The youngster would have been picked out, then
we'd have taken his DNA and put it on the database. And you
thought we'd run a check – for family – after we got a clean
sweep on the mass screening. There'd have been a match of sorts
between Sample X and young Coyle, and so we'd have started
looking at the family. Eventually we'd have got to you. But first
we'd have got to Tug. He was prepared to lie for you back in
'ninety-four, but he wasn't going to go on doing that, was he?

And he cracked in the end, which is why he's sitting in the dugout up in the pinewoods. Somewhere else that Granddad showed you, of course.'

Robinson didn't seem to react. He was quite clearly in a separate world. and Shaw had the strong feeling that he was waiting for something to happen there. Flexing his jaw, the joint cracked and Shaw saw it then – the terracotta pill, lodged in the back of Robinson's mouth. So what was in the hidden hands?

'But Holtby's death is the key to this,' said Shaw. 'Or rather, the motive for his death is the key.'

He reached into his wallet and took out the snapshot of Tilly he'd found beneath the pillow in the dugout and put it on the table – face up, turned to Robinson, whose eyes fixed on it with a look of terror.

'You'll know where I found this, of course. Perfectly natural – a doting uncle, a favourite niece. But it made me remember another picture. Tug's been sleeping rough in one of the beach huts along towards Holkham. He had some snap shots pinned up over the door. There was one with two kids, ten-year-olds or close, with an elderly man. I guess that was granddad, Tug Johns, and his two grandsons. Aidan and Tug Junior. You were very different then, Aidan – thin, gawky. But it was the face that reminded me . . .'

He touched the picture of Tilly with the tip of a finger. 'We've just checked with the chicken farm,' said Shaw. 'They tell us you've been off work for several days – since the day Marianne died, in fact. So, you've been up in the woods, in your secret place. Did you sleep? It's on odd image to keep with you. Your niece. But she's not your niece, is she?'

Robinson tilted his head back into shadow, then forward a second later, but even in that brief time there had been a trans-formation. The muscle structure had collapsed, the eyes welling over, the lips wet. And his body seemed to have given up its fight as well, the shoulders slumped, the torso twisted slightly to one side, but still the hands held out of sight.

'You're her father.'

Robinson sobbed, his chest heaving, saliva spilling from his gaping mouth.

'Holtby died to stop the demo up at the wind farm. Tilly was determined to get arrested – all of them were. And we'd

have taken DNA and we'd have got our familial match with
Sample X, eventually, once we'd discovered her father wasn't
Joe Osbourne.'

'I gave him money to go away, just walk away and forget
about the wind farm,' said Robinson, not bothering to deny it,
the sentence erratic and breathless. 'A grand in twenty-pound
notes. He threw them at me.'

'That's the problem with some people – they just won't be
bribed,' Shaw said, undeflected. 'But that wasn't why he died,
was it? It wasn't to save *your* neck at all. It was to make sure
Ruth never knew you'd had the child. Because while you were
fascinated by Marianne, you only ever loved Ruth.

'Does she think it's your fault there are no children? It must
have seemed like a kind lie. They can be the worse. She couldn't
get pregnant and that was the tragedy of her life. And it was the
tragedy of yours that Marianne could. And that's why you wanted
to die here, where you thought we couldn't find your body, so
we'd never be able to prove it. Prove that you were Tilly's father.'

Robinson was shivering, so that when he went to nod it turned
into a jerk of the jaw to the side.

'How long did it last – your affair with Marianne?'

'She said she needed me.' He looked up at the curved metal
roof, gathering himself, edging back from the emotional brink. 'She
wouldn't let me go. It was never blackmail, I can't claim that.'

'But how long? Years? And then when we reopened East Hills
you called in to make sure she still had her story straight. But
she wouldn't lie again so you helped her take the poison. Did
she change her mind, Aidan? Did she want to live at the last
moment? Her jaw was broken. Is that what the kiss was for – to
say sorry, sorry that for you she was better dead than alive?'

He'd shot the question and Robinson shook his head before
he could stop himself. Then he squeezed his eyes shut and Shaw
was shocked by the tears that fell, soaking the round, plump,
face. 'I didn't kill White – Marianne did. That's what haunted
her. That was our secret.'

'Why would I believe *that*?' asked Shaw, tired now of the
self-pitying tone and reminded of the lies this man had told
already. The *military* man above The Circle. That was clever. A
half-truth, because it had been him, steeped in everything his
grandfather had taught him.

The fog horn again, but oddly distant, as if the mist was thickening. 'She did kill him,' said Robinson. 'I tried to beat him up – the muscles were all for show. The kid was a coward. But it was tough because the foot drags and he was quick and he had the knife. He cut me – once, across the stomach. In the end I got him down in the sand, told him he wasn't to speak to Marianne again, ever. I'd been round his flat; I had the pictures and the negs. Marianne was just there, watching.'

The candle-stub was beginning to gutter so that the room was filling with shifting shadows. The blade of the knife hardly shone at all now.

'I hit him then – knuckles in his eye socket. I heard the bone crunch. I'd knocked the knife out of his hand but I didn't see Marianne pick it up. I was wounded, standing there, the blood just oozing out of my side. I knelt down and when I looked up she'd done it. In a second. A single wound, slashed sideways, and her face empty of everything. And his face – white, and gone – already gone, so that his eyes were dead. I tried to stop the blood with my hands.'

Robinson looked at Shaw, his eyes catching the light, as if the scene was playing out between them on an invisible screen.

'We dragged him down to the sea – the beach is steep there. I couldn't go back on the boat, the wound was bad, but it wouldn't kill me, I knew that. Then I told her about this place – that I'd stay, that there was a medical kit here so I could put on a bandage, keep the wound clean. She had to go. I told her to go straight in the sea and wash her costume because it was stained too. Then she should bury it deep. And I gave her my towel to bury because it was soaked in the blood I cleaned off my hands. When she could she was to tell Tug what had happened and get him to come back when the island was safe. He knew where to find me.'

Shaw listened to the silence and was convinced that there was a noise embedded in it – a very light noise, as if invisible feathers were falling on the tabletop between them.

'And you came back to die,' said Shaw. 'But you're still alive.'

Robinson leant forward until his head almost touched the table. When he straightened up the cyanide capsule was there, between his lips. It glistened, obscenely, like something visceral, something, Shaw felt, *internal.* Then he spat it out. 'I knew I couldn't do it. I'd seen the others . . .' He said it with absolute conviction, as matter-of-fact as reciting his own name. 'But I won't leave here alive.'

Shaw tried to judge how quickly he could get to the knife.

'Marianne couldn't do it either. She begged me to help, so I did,' said Robinson. 'I left the curtains open so she'd always see the flowers. And then the kiss.'

'I can't pretend you won't get life,' said Shaw. 'But think about Tilly, Aidan. Your daughter. She's lost her mother. Today, Aidan, she lost the man she thought was her father. Joe's dead.'

Aidan's eyes widened. 'I don't . . .'

'Stress, shock, the asthma. I think he just gave up. Tilly was with him. But she's alone. And you're going to leave her now?'

'She's got Ruth,' said Robinson.

He saw it then as clearly as Aidan Robinson had seen it. The future: Ruth with the daughter she'd always wanted, Tilly untainted by the knowledge that she was Aidan's child. An impossible future, but the only hope this man could imagine, gone now.

Very slowly Shaw let his hand move towards the knife. Robinson didn't move, or even follow the movement with his eyes. He retained the rigid pose he'd kept, as if trying to sit to attention. 'You can bring them together,' said Shaw, trying to make himself believe it. 'That's what you should do with the time you've got left.' Shaw took the knife from the tabletop and held it in both hands, like a ceremonial dagger. 'We should go to them,' he said.

But there was something wrong because as Shaw turned the blade in his hands he saw that it left a bloodstain on his fingers.

'Too late,' said Robinson, lifting both arms and putting his hands, palm up, on the tabletop. Both wrists were cut to the bone.

FORTY-FOUR

Shaw left the Porsche on a double-yellow line outside St James' and ran up the semicircular steps to the front doors of police headquarters, Valentine, wheezing, just behind. The sergeant on the main reception desk was one of Shaw's father's old colleagues: Sgt Timber Woods. He'd taken retirement ten years earlier, it being plain that he couldn't catch a cold without uniformed assistance, and was eking out a decade until his sixty-fifth birthday working in the Records Office downstairs and taking shifts on the front desk. As one of the senior DI's had said at Timber's retirement party, he might not live longer, but it was certainly going to feel that way.

'Bloody hell, Peter.' Woods looked up at the hall clock – a Victorian original, big enough for a mainline railway station platform. It was 3.14 p.m. Not only was Shaw late for the press conference, he'd also failed to file the chief constable a summary brief of developments, leaving him to face the great unwashed of Fleet Street alone and unprepared.

'Presser started on time,' added Woods. 'O'Hare's had all units out for you. He's ballistic. If you haven't got a good excuse I'd make one up,' said Woods, clearly energized by the misfortunes of others.

Shaw's mobile had contained so many messages when he'd turned it back on he hadn't bothered to read any of them. He headed for the lifts, knowing Valentine might not make the stairs to the seventh floor. There was piped-in music in the lift: Stravinsky's *Rite of Spring*. 'You got him?' asked Shaw, his heart pounding smoothly, his blood making an oily churning noise in his eardrums.

Valentine was bent double, but he held out his mobile. 'Yup.'

Once they'd got Aidan Robinson into the RNLI launch Shaw had asked Valentine to wait for his phone signal to return on the trip back, then try and get through to Lionel Smyth, reporter at large for *The Daily Telegraph*. They needed to plant a question with him to ask at the East Hills press conference. Several questions – a series, interlinked. Valentine had got Smyth first ring; he was with the rest of the press at St James', grazing on sausage rolls, waiting for the briefing to start. Valentine got him to find a quiet corner out in the corridor and carefully marked his card: three questions. The last one was the best one. In its own way, a *killer* question.

As they came out of the lift Shaw got a text from DC Campbell at A&E at the Queen Vic. ROBINSON STABLE. ROTA 24/7.

Campbell would stay with Robinson, then they'd run shifts until they got him charged and to court. One of the medics who helped load Robinson, lifeless, on to the force helicopter on the beach at Wells had told Shaw the cuts at the wrist were deep but had missed both the brachial arteries, so there was hope, because while he'd bled for a long time into the sandy floor, he'd bled slowly. That had been the liquid, iron, smell: dripping blood.

The Norfolk Suite was decked out in oak panels and fitted with a conference table at the front, microphones, full multimedia, including a whiteboard and acoustic ceiling. It was where O'Hare held his senior management meetings and was one of half a dozen rooms in Peter Shaw's life he hated with a passion equal to the love he felt for being outside, on the beach. It was packed – maybe fifty reporters, with a TV camera and radio at the back. A table of coffee cups and biscuits. Wine bottles ready for the post-conference drinks.

As Shaw burst through the doors O'Hare was on his feet. The chief constable's voice was barely more civilized than a snarl. 'So that completes our summary of the mass screening. I was hoping . . .' He caught sight of Shaw, then Valentine.

'Ah. DI Shaw. Sergeant. Please . . .' He held a hand out, indicating the empty seats at the front, facing the press. Shaw walked down the middle of the room between the rows, Valentine took cover along the wall, but they met at the front. The force's press officer was nominally the chair, seated in the middle of the row facing the reporters. She was sporting a weary smile. Valentine sat on the desk edge despite a glare from the chief constable.

'Great,' said O'Hare. 'Good of you to make it, Peter.'

There was nervous laughter from the press. Shaw noted Smyth, from *The Daily Telegraph*, in the front row. The nervous woman from the *Guardian* was in the second row, notebook poised.

O'Hare couldn't stop his body language betraying him. His shoulders had relaxed and the forward, aggressive, angle of his head and neck had returned to upright. He'd been facing an uphill struggle to convince Fleet Street's best the North Norfolk Constabulary was only just a step behind the East Hills killer. Now that job was Shaw's.

'So. If I can introduce DI Peter Shaw,' said the chief constable, 'investigating officer in the reopened East Hills inquiry. Peter, perhaps you could get us all up to speed and then . . .'

'Sir,' said Shaw, holding up a hand, cutting him dead.

O'Hare went to speak but Shaw didn't give way. The chief constable's surprise at being overrun while he was speaking was palpable. In the stress of the moment his tic returned, the quick sideways jerk of the jaw.

The room was silent but for the hum of the air conditioning.

'We have today made an arrest in connection with the East Hills murder of 1994,' said Shaw. He had the confidence to pause, readjusting the microphone, letting the silence lengthen and not rushing to fill it.

'Charges are imminent,' added Shaw, 'and therefore reporting restrictions will come into place very shortly. However, I'm happy to indicate that we are no longer looking for anyone else in respect of the killing of Shane White on August 26, 1994 at East Hills, Wells-next-the-Sea.'

Everyone started talking, most to each other, a few stabbing numbers into their mobile phones. Mid-afternoon was a crucial time for the TV networks and evening papers, so most would have to alert news desks that a big story was coming. The PR woman tried vainly to regain order. Shaw stood, rapping the table, his eyes on Smyth, his sight back to pin-sharp. 'Some details . . .' he said, confidence and adrenaline giving his voice that serrated edge. The TV lights, which had been off, thudded on with a muffled explosion of electricity. 'I am able to give you *some* details.'

Gradually the hubbub subsided. Shaw looked at his audience. Valentine looked at O'Hare, whose body was absolutely still, no – rigid.

'We shall name the man arrested in due course. I should add that we expect to lay before the same defendant several further charges of murder. The victims in these cases will also be named shortly – all these offences stem, in part, from the East Hills killing.'

He looked at the press officer and smiled. She smiled back, but then caught sight of O'Hare's face, which shone with a kind of feral intensity, as if he'd been deprived of some obscene pleasure. The sight, perhaps, of Shaw being torn apart by the baying hounds of Fleet Street.

There was a stunned silence in the room, then a barrage of questions. Shaw chose the woman from the *Guardian*. 'Can you talk us through the motives in these killings and how they're linked to East Hills?'

Shaw stood. 'Delighted. We believe Shane White died, as we always suspected he had, as a result of his activities as a black-mailer. He tried to extort money from a young woman who he had caught on camera with her boyfriend. We believe this young woman and her boyfriend killed White – probably without premeditation. Probably together. The girl was still on the island when the police arrived. The boyfriend hid on the island because he'd been wounded in a struggle with White. Just how he managed to avoid the search of East Hills, which was extensive, is some-thing we'll be able to share with you once the case has moved to court. But I can say now that I don't think any blame can be attributed to those who conducted the search, or indeed the initial inquiry.'

Shaw poured himself a glass of water, his hand unnaturally steady. 'Our reopening of the East Hills inquiry sparked a series of killings – as I said, all designed to protect the identity of the boyfriend. The first victim was the girlfriend. The killer doubted she would be able to face cross-examination, and she was in a fragile mental state. Her lies had saved him once, but he doubted she would be able to lie again. We believe he assisted her in taking her own life and that he provided her with the means to take her life – a cyanide capsule. He had six of these capsules. Again, the source of the capsules is something we will reveal in court once we have secured the neces-sary forensic evidence. Three other victims followed. All died from ingesting cyanide capsules, all of them administered by the killer against the victims' wishes. Two of these victims – an elderly man from the village of Creake, near Wells, and a young man from Morston, just along the coast, died to make sure we couldn't trace the killer using the DNA from the towel. He feared we would track him down – not through a direct DNA match, which as you've heard drew a blank, but through a partial family connection which would have been revealed by a so-called *familial* search of the DNA database. That's a search in which we look for close matches, not direct matches. It's a one-off, special search. The final victim – a middle-aged man related to the killer – died because he was, like the girlfriend, not prepared to go on shielding the identity of the killer. That will be the basis of our case. I'm confident a court will find the evidence overwhelming. Charges are imminent.'

Someone at the back whistled and there was a scattering of applause. The woman from the *Guardian* hadn't lowered her hand. 'So we're saying that while the mass screening failed because there is no *direct* match with the DNA on the towel, it prompted the killer to kill again, because a check would have led the police back to him through an *indirect* family link?'

Shaw let the full surfer's smile light up. 'Exactly. Beautifully put.'

Valentine was watching Smyth of *The Daily Telegraph*. He didn't raise his hand, but held a gold propelling pencil vertically.

'Yes?' said Shaw, nodding. There was so much talk still going on in the room that the press officer had to call for silence again. At the back the door swung open and another TV crew piled in. Shaw pointed at Smyth. 'Your question?'

'Remind me,' said Smyth. 'I don't understand. What's a familial check? Why's that different from the mass screening?' Valentine breathed a little easier, confident now that Smyth would ask the questions as he'd been given them.

'Well. We started by trying to match Sample X – that's the DNA recovered from the towel found at East Hills – with any of the eight million profiles on the national DNA database. We drew a blank. Then we took samples from the men on East Hills and tried to match them with Sample X. We drew a blank. That was the mass screening. Then it's standard practice to run the sample through the national database looking for partial, or close, matches. If we get such a match then it usually means we've found someone closely related to the person we're after. So we can often trace them from that point. It's a long shot, clearly. But standard practice.'

'And that's what the killer was afraid of?' asked Smyth.

'Right,' said Shaw, letting his eyes shift to the next reporter with his hand up.

But Smyth, Shaw knew, hadn't finished. 'And that was done when? This familial search?' he asked, reading the question as he'd written it down in his notebook. Tension was building in the room. Two or three reporters were shouting questions now and two TV presenters were getting miked-up.

Smyth's question appeared to have shocked Shaw. He looked at Valentine and shrugged, then along the desk to O'Hare. The chief constable was still staring at the back of the room. But now he slipped off the edge of the conference table and stood. Shaw had a sudden insight into O'Hare's psychology and sensed that he was able to think better on his feet, like a street fighter. It almost made him feel sorry for him.

The room, sensing the moment, fell silent. 'In this case,' said Shaw carefully, 'it was decided to dispense with the familial check due to financial pressures on the budget. But of course our killer didn't know that. So he acted as if the check was going to take place. The chief constable has, I think, already briefed you on the current budget situation.'

But Smyth had one more question. 'But if this familial check had been made, just to be clear, it would not have led to our killer because he'd killed again, several times, to make sure the DNA trail wouldn't lead to him. Right?'

'Well, that's a theoretical question,' said Shaw.

'You're right,' said O'Hare, unable to resist self-justification. But he'd said it too quickly, and even his cauterized emotional intelligence suggested he'd been led into a trap.

'Except . . .' said Shaw. He had a briefcase with him and he opened it, papers spilling out. Valentine walked over with a further wodge of files. It was a little bit of theatre they thought might indicate they hadn't come prepared for this very moment.

Smyth, in the front row, was smiling now, nodding gently. 'Any time,' he said, getting a laugh.

'Here,' said Shaw. He offered the slender file to O'Hare but the chief constable cut the offer dead with his hand. 'What the killer didn't know,' said Shaw, 'and what is going to become obvious if this case moves to court, is that a close family member – his daughter, in fact – *was* already on the database, but he had no idea. She was arrested last year by the Metropolitan Police

during a street demonstration. It's just that she kept that a secret.'
Shaw shuffled some papers, but he didn't waste any time, because
he wanted O'Hare back in the firing line as quickly as possible.
'It was an anti-war demo and she was arrested, processed, but
released without charge from Paddington Green police station
along with several hundred others. But we did take a DNA sample,
as is our right under the law, although that may all change next
year with the new legislation currently going through parliament.
She was seventeen at that time and didn't inform her parents,
which was also her right. So a familial check would have taken
us straight to the killer – just about, once we'd sorted out a few
complications.' Shaw let the silence stretch. 'That would have
been on Sunday,' he added, letting the last word almost trail
away.

Smyth asked the final question. The killer question. 'How
many people have died since then?'

Shaw sniffed, shrugged. 'Three.'

He leant back; the TV cameras switched to O'Hare. The
questions began.

O'Hare fought a valiant rearguard action but, on the third time
of asking, was forced to confirm that a familial search would
have cost less than £7,000. And it had been his decision, and his
alone, to ditch the familial check. He didn't say that Shaw had
formally requested such a search but he knew Shaw, or Valentine,
would leak that detail to Smyth after the presser was finished.
The chief constable tried to bring Shaw back into the discussion,
reminding the press that they had a suspect in the cells. But
they'd got all they'd get on that story – Shaw had made that
clear. So they returned, relentlessly, to the fact that the chief
constable's cost-cutting campaign had resulted in the deaths of
three innocent people. Given that reporting restrictions were about
to come crashing down on their murder suspect *that* was going
to be the story.

Valentine had his mobile out, texting. He'd got Jan Clay's
number the last time they'd spoken and he thought he'd meet
her, if she had the time, for a drink on the quayside at Wells.
The whole of St James' was a non-smoking building, and especially the Norfolk Suite, but he lit up anyway, and no one seemed
to mind.

Shaw closed his eyes; aware of being outside himself, locking in. Only one question remained to answer. At the moment of Marianne Osbourne's death did she change her mind, did she reach out for that startling yellow and black image, the field of sunflower heads. Did she want to live? Shaw suspected she'd asked her lover, the father of her child, to make sure that this *was* the end – to press down with all his force, violently, so that she would have no choice but to accept death. Only Marianne knew the truth. Shaw would let the question die with her, so that he wouldn't be tempted to take it home for Lena.

He'd had his phone on silent for the press conference. There was a picture text from his wife. It showed the sea from the stoop: the mist had risen, so this might be the last warm evening of the summer. An entire Indian summer, perhaps, compressed into one sunset. In press conferences he always took his watch off, laying it face down on the desk: so he could see it was 4.08 p.m. High tide was at 6.06 p.m. He'd be in the sea by then. Lying on his back, floating in the warm water, trying to memorize the precise shade of the colour blue that filled his entire vision.